A STONE'S THROW

ALSO BY JAMES W. ZISKIN

A STONE'S THROW

An Ellie Stone Mystery

JAMES W. ZISKIN

SEVENTH STREET BOOKS®
AN IMPRINT OF PROMETHEUS BOOKS
59 JOHN GLENN DRIVE • AMHERST, NY 14228
www.seventhstreetbooks.com

Published 2018 by Seventh Street Books®, an imprint of Prometheus Books

Cover design by Jacqueline Nasso Cooke
Cover image © Getty Images
Cover design © Prometheus Books

This is a work of fiction. Characters, organizations, products, locales, and events portrayed in this novel either are products of the author's imagination or are used fictitiously.

Inquiries should be addressed to
Seventh Street Books
59 John Glenn Drive
Amherst, New York 14228
VOICE: 716–691–0133
FAX: 716–691–0137
WWW.SEVENTHSTREETBOOKS.COM

22 21 20 19 18   5 4 3 2 1

Library of Congress Cataloging-in-Publication Data

Names: Ziskin, James W., 1960- author.
Title: A stone's throw : an Ellie Stone mystery / James W. Ziskin.
Description: Amherst, NY : Seventh Street Books, 2018. | Series: Ellie Stone
   mysteries
Identifiers: LCCN 2018001272 (print) | LCCN 2018003470 (ebook) |
   ISBN 9781633884205 (ebook) | ISBN 9781633884199 (softcover)
Subjects: LCSH: Reporters and reporting—Fiction. | Women journalists—Fiction. |
   Murder—Investigation—Fiction. | BISAC: FICTION / Mystery & Detective
   / Women Sleuths. | FICTION / Mystery & Detective / Historical. | GSAFD:
   Mystery fiction.
Classification: LCC PS3626.I83 (ebook) | LCC PS3626.I83 S77 2018 (print) |
   DDC 813/.6—dc23
LC record available at https://lccn.loc.gov/2018001272

Printed in the United States of America

To Robert, a plunger who lived big and died young.

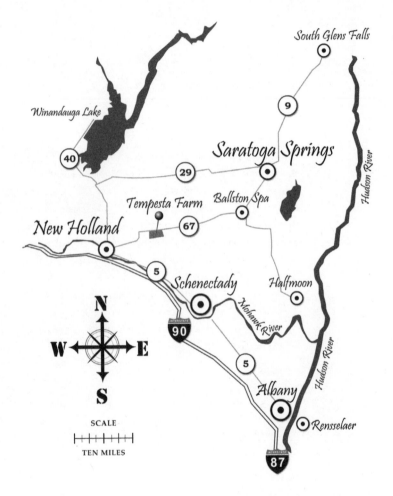

By its very definition, a second chance requires a first failure. A mistake of youth, perhaps. A regretted lapse of judgment, or even an outright, calculated, felonious act. And everything in between. To be sure, the shades along the continuum grow darker moving from left to right, but where is the tipping point? When is the precise moment when we know, without doubt or debate, that an invisible line has been crossed? The distance between right and wrong has no frets—only invisible gradations that modulate the pitch until we realize that it's something more than off. More than simply sharp or flat. That's the point where gray turns to black.

CHAPTER ONE

SATURDAY, AUGUST 11, 1962

The flames leapt into the last of the night's darkness, casting their dancing orange light against the weathered planks of the nearby outbuildings. The fire had engulfed the entire structure—a horse barn—swallowing it whole, from its timber walls to its pitched roof and wrought-iron weathervane at the top.

I watched from a safe distance, shielding my face from the heat with my hands. Deep inside the blaze, boards and beams whistled and popped, crackling as they withered and wasted under the assault of the fire. And when the last three walls collapsed upon themselves, the roof fell and sent a great cartwheeling ball of pyrotechnics skyward, spitting sparks and setting alight the cool August night, just as if day had broken. Then, flattened and starved of its fuel, the fire exhausted itself within minutes. Soon, it could manage little more than a hissing black smoke. All went dark again.

Tempesta, the derelict Sanford Shaw stud farm, consisted of forty structures—barns, stables, outbuildings, and feed sheds—spread over eight hundred acres of rolling meadow adjacent to a wooded grove off Route 67. Bordered by the highway on one side and a stream several hundred yards to the southeast on the other, the farm butted up against the Montgomery County line from the Saratoga side. As such, Tempesta Farm fell under the jurisdiction of the Saratoga County sheriff. Which was why the tall, heavyset figure lumbering toward me came as a surprise. My old pal, Montgomery County sheriff Frank Olney.

"You're up early on a Saturday," he said.

"Maybe I didn't go home last night."

Frank said nothing. And he didn't smile either. He didn't approve of such behavior or, for that matter, jokes about it. His rectitude was one of the traits I liked most about him. And least. Unlike the men who think a ribald story or a pat on the behind is just a little harmless fun—and their birthright as males of the species—Frank Olney always walked right and true on the side of decency. Sure, he was short-tempered, wound as tight as a spring, and partial to short ties and uniforms a size too small, but no honest person ever questioned his integrity. He shot as straight as a die. And that was what I found tiresome about him. He sometimes made me feel like a wretch on the downtown express to hell. But I loved him for never making me feel like prey or a chippy unable to resist his overweight, middle-aged charms. I ran into enough of those types at the newspaper.

"What brings you here?" I asked. "Isn't this Sheriff Pryor's territory?"

"I was in the neighborhood," he said. "I'm ready to help out if he needs a hand."

"How do you think this happened?"

He stared at the smoldering pile of cinders before us, his lips twisted into a reflective pout. "No electrical storms last night, so that's not what caused this."

The distant wail of an approaching siren interrupted Frank's musings. He wiped his sweating face with his cap. It was a chilly, wet morning, but the barn continued to pump heat.

"That'll be the Volunteer Fire Department," he said. "Just in time to save the foundation."

"So if it wasn't lightning, what do you think? Arson? An accident?"

"Kids most likely."

"Any chance there were horses in there?" I asked.

"No. This place has been empty for years. Since the war. The Shaws got out of breeding and racing before they moved the carpet mills south."

New Holland had been orphaned by the Shaw Knitting Mills after World War II, ending nearly a century of carpet manufacturing along the Mohawk River. The most powerful industrialist in nineteenth-century New Holland, Sanford Shaw had built the stud farm on Route 67 on the advice of his physician, who prescribed a relaxing pastime to reduce the "nervous tension in consequence of the rigors of the manufacturing business." This according to his biography, *Carpeting the Eastern Seaboard: The Life and Legacy of Sanford J. Shaw*. While Tempesta may have begun as a pleasant distraction for a captain of industry, it soon blossomed into an important breeding stable of Thoroughbreds, especially once his elder son, Joshua, took an interest in horse racing around the turn of the century.

The son and heir's passion kept the farm going even when New York State outlawed gambling and effectively killed Thoroughbred racing for three years in the 1910s. When Sanford Shaw wanted to send his best horses to France, Joshua prevailed upon him to keep Tempesta running. His vision was rewarded when, in 1913, a favorable court ruling restored betting—partially at least—in New York. But it wasn't until the old man died in 1925 that Joshua threw himself—and most of the family's fortune—into breeding champions in earnest. Tempesta horses won derbies and stakes races from Kentucky to England to France, and in nearby Saratoga Springs, while Joshua Shaw lived the life of a globetrotter and bon vivant.

Then came the Depression, which hit the mills hard, followed by the war. Horse breeding took a backseat to patriotic duty. Following a polo injury, Joshua was replaced at the helm of the Shaw Knitting Mills by his younger brother Nathan shortly after the attack on Pearl Harbor in 1941. Tempesta Farm was abandoned and the horses sold off. The grass grew, consuming the three-quarter-mile training track, jumping course, and nearly everything else on the property. The forty barns and other buildings, including the caretaker's house and dormitories, were left to molder a stone's throw from the August excitement of Saratoga. Forsaken and all but forgotten, Tempesta now seemed a world away from its former glory.

"So what are you doing out here at this hour anyway?" asked Frank. "Don't tell me Charlie Reese sent you for this."

"Couldn't sleep. I heard about the fire on the police scanner and called him. Woke up his wife again. I think she hates me. Charlie thought it was probably nothing, but I wanted to have a look-see to be sure."

Frank threw a doubtful eye in my direction. "These abandoned barns burn down every so often. Not going to be one of your bigger scoops."

At length, the fire truck arrived. The ace driving the thing attempted to maneuver close to the smoldering remains and, after a couple of aborted three-point turns in the grass, declared defeat, pulled the brake, and told his mates to make do.

Having drawn about twenty yards of hose from the truck, two volunteer firemen took turns dribbling a weak stream of water over the embers. They swamped what was left of the fire in less than an hour, all the while yawning, scratching their behinds, and even smoking a couple of cigarettes. I chronicled the touch-and-go battle with a roll of Tri-X film and a dozen flashbulbs.

I wanted to get some daylight shots, but it was just five twenty, and the sun wouldn't rise above the trees to the east until nearly six thirty. Frank offered to stand me to breakfast until then. Fifteen minutes later, we were seated across from each other at the Ballston Diner in the sleepy hamlet of Charlton, about halfway between Galway and Scotia.

I caught Frank eyeing the waitress. She was across the room, back to us, taking down the orders of four locals who were fueling up before a day of fishing. A curvy creature with bottle-blonde hair and thick red lipstick, she was about forty or forty-five. What Marilyn Monroe might have looked like in ten years, if she hadn't died just a week earlier. Sad story, I thought, as I watched the waitress flirt with the men. She held them in her thrall, as if charming snakes, with a simpering smile and heaving bosom. Then, with a bounce and a flourish, she dotted the last *i* and crossed the last *t* in her pad and sashayed to the kitchen. The boys clearly liked her going as much as coming, if gazing at a swinging backside meant what it used to. Frank was enjoying the view as much as the anglers. I cleared my throat.

"The coffee's good here," he said, suddenly aware of his own distraction. "I stop in from time to time."

"And that pretty waitress wouldn't have anything to do with it?" I asked, ribbing him.

He blushed and said he didn't go in for that kind of shenanigans.

Somewhere during the past five years in New Holland, I'd learned that Frank Olney was a widower. But I didn't know the whole story. And while he was my favorite cop—one I considered a friend—I couldn't bring myself to ask him about it now. We didn't share intimacies. I dropped the teasing when I noticed his discomfort. Perhaps he was lost in a memory of his late wife. Or maybe he was lonely and thinking he'd actually like to go in for some of those shenanigans with the pretty waitress. Poor Frank. This was one of those moments when I wished he would loosen the cork a bit.

She appeared above us. "Hiya, Frank. Who's your date?"

Now his ears burned beet red. "Aw, Billie, it's not like that. This is Ellie. A newspaper reporter. Friend of mine."

"I haven't seen a lot of reporters who look like you," she said. Probably a compliment. Maybe not. "What'll you have?"

I ordered an English muffin, dark, and coffee, black. Frank asked for his usual.

"What have you been up to lately?" he asked me once Billie had bounced off with our order. "You haven't been around much."

"Things have been quiet."

"You don't come visit an old friend?"

"You sound like a Jewish grandmother," I said. Frank didn't quite know how to take that. I gave him a break and changed the subject. "You said there've been other fires at Tempesta. Isn't there a caretaker or a guard on the property?"

"There was a fellow named Chuck Lenoir. Lucky Chuck, they called him. He used to watch over things after everyone left. He was loyal to the Shaws. And them to him. Especially the judge's father, Nathan. He might still be around."

"Lucky, eh? Was that because he knew his horseflesh?"

"The name was . . . ironical. That's the word. The only luck Chuck ever had was not dying when that horse kicked him in the head." Frank chuckled. Then, perhaps thinking better of it, he coughed and added that Chuck was never quite the same after the injury.

"Actually, he suffered some brain damage. Went blind in one eye, limped, and slurred his words."

"When did all this happen?"

"A long time ago. Mid-thirties, I'd say."

"Anyone else I might contact about the property?"

Frank squinted at the ceiling. "There's Issur Jacobs from the New Holland Savings Bank. He tied up some of the loose ends when the Shaw Knitting Mills moved south. Might still have some crumbs to take care of. He's pushing eighty but never misses a day at the bank."

My coffee arrived, and I took a sip. "Probably no reason to talk to either of them."

Frank dropped me back at the Tempesta stud farm where I'd left my car. His deputy, Stan Pulaski, had shown up and, hands on hips, was surveying the scene. It must have been a slow day on the Montgomery side of the county line. A couple of Saratoga County cruisers were parked on the grass, and two deputies had taken charge of the scene.

"Stan'll take care of you if you need anything," said Frank as I climbed out of the car.

The day was overcast and cool for August. Barely sixty degrees. I felt clammy from the soot and the light rain, and my clothes reeked of smoke. It was barely quarter past seven, but I already wanted a second bath. The firemen had finished their task and long since decamped. Stan made small talk as I shot another roll of film in the daylight.

"You think they'll let me take some photos inside?" I asked him.

"Inside where? There's no more barn."

The two Saratoga deputies leaned against the fender of a county car, puffing on cigarettes. I approached to ask if they minded if I took a few pictures inside what used to be the barn.

"Have yourself a ball," said one of them.

"Do you think it's safe?" I asked Stan. "Walking on the ashes, I mean."

He took a couple of steps closer to the remains and offered that, though wet, it appeared cool enough. Over the past four years, I'd ruined many pairs of heels slogging through mud and water in pursuit of news stories that didn't pan out. I'd finally learned my lesson. Now I traveled prepared with a pair of old canvas tennis shoes in the trunk of my car for just such occasions.

I learned later on that the destroyed building was one of the foaling barns. What remained of it now was swamped by large pools of sooty water. No hotspots anywhere, but the footing remained uneven and slippery. I picked my way through the mess, stepping over partially consumed planks of wood, as well as muddy embers and ash. Already soaked and black, my sneakers would have to go. Stan wandered around in his boots, lucky dog, without a worry in the world, until he took a careless step, slipped on a wet timber, and landed on his rear end in the slop.

"Careful, or you'll fall."

Stan picked himself up and scraped the muck off the seat of his pants with both hands. He called out thanks without irony. He tended to take things literally.

"Have you got everything you need yet?" he asked, now wondering how to rid his hands of the mud.

"Not quite," I said, staring at a length of charred fabric at my feet. It looked like silk. Black-and-orange diamonds on white, and soaking wet. I squatted to investigate, tucking my skirt between my thighs and calves to keep it from touching the mud. I tugged at the cloth, which was caught beneath what was left of a long, wooden beam.

"What's that?" asked Stan, arriving at my side.

I pulled harder on the silk, and the blackened beam rose and tumbled off to one side. I loosed a scream and dropped the fabric. Stan recoiled, tripped over his own feet, and landed in the slop again.

CHAPTER TWO

"What the hell?" said Sheriff Henry Pryor, who'd finally arrived at the scene with the county coroner on his heels. Standing there in baggy street clothes, hands resting on his wide hips, he glared at the mess. Judging by the creases in his furrowed brow, I estimated he'd spent about forty-five years on this earth perfecting his ill temper.

"It's a body, Sheriff," said one of his deputies. The one named Bell. "Two, actually."

He hadn't cared a whit about the fire until Stan and I stumbled over the bodies. Well, Stan did most of the stumbling. . . . Now the deputy was most officious and acting as if he'd discovered King Tut's tomb.

"What were they doing in there?" asked Pryor.

Deputy Bell shrugged and pointed at me. "I don't know. She found them."

The sheriff nodded. "Yeah, Frank Olney radioed me that you were here. So what possessed you to go rummaging through the debris?"

"Just being thorough."

"You didn't take any pictures of the bodies, I hope."

Wide-eyed, I shook my head, convincing myself it wasn't a lie if I didn't actually pronounce the words. I had, in fact, fired off a few frames of the charred corpses.

Pryor scowled at his men. "My boys shouldn't have let you in there. It's dangerous and a crime scene besides."

The two deputies swallowed their medicine without protest.

"Who do you think they might be?" I asked the sheriff, who deferred to the coroner.

Herb Edelman, a rotund man in his fifties with a bald pate, was hovering over the remains on bended knee.

"One's clearly a woman," he said without looking up at me. "The other appears to be an adolescent male. I'll know better after the postmortems later today. But this isn't any great mystery. Smoke inhalation. Asphyxiation. Seems a shame to cut them open to prove it."

At least he was keeping an open mind.

"May I call you later for the results?" I asked.

He turned and squinted up at me, still on his hands and knees in the muck. "No later than seven. I watch *Perry Mason* at seven thirty."

"I met William Hopper, you know," I blurted out before I could stop myself. Edelman appeared unimpressed. Too bad. My brief encounter with television's Paul Drake had been the only bright spot during my trip to Los Angeles earlier in the year, and it still gave me thrills. I kind of had a thing for Paul Drake, even more so after he'd called me beautiful and winked at me. "Any chance that's an adult male?" I asked, steering myself back to the subject at hand.

With all the grace of a punch-drunk prizefighter stumbling to his feet on the count of nine, the coroner pushed himself up off the muddy ground with both arms and a couple of grunts. Vertical once more, he coughed himself red in the face. After several restorative breaths, he wiped his hands on a cloth, which he tossed aside like a soiled tissue. Someone else would clean it up. Or maybe not. In no hurry to answer my question, he retrieved an Old Gold from a crumpled package in the breast pocket of his jacket, flicked his lighter, and puffed smoke into the air.

"Maybe a jockey?" I prompted, tired of waiting for him to get around to a reply.

"It's possible," he said. "Autopsy will tell."

"An autopsy can tell if he was a jockey?" I asked, doing my best Judy Holliday impression. Either he had no sense of humor or I wasn't funny.

"What about the caretaker?" Stan asked the sheriff. "You don't suppose that's Chuck Lenoir. He's a pretty small guy."

Pryor considered the shorter of the two bodies. "Lucky Chuck? Is he still around? He'd be pretty old by now. Why the Shaws kept him on, I can't understand. Seemed pretty useless to me."

"And the woman?" I asked. "Anything that might help with an identification?"

"No pocketbook that I can see," said the coroner, puffing away on his cigarette. No wonder standing up winded him as if he'd just run a four-minute mile backward. "Burned beyond recognition. Everything except for some red hair, an earring in the left earlobe, and a bit of fur. Looks like fox. My wife has one just like it."

"It won't be easy putting a name on her," said Pryor. "Unless someone's reported her missing. I'll ask around in Saratoga, Schenectady, and New Holland."

"We might get lucky and find a fingerprint," added Edelman.

"What about the fabric around the male's neck?" I asked. "Almost looks like racing silks."

The sheriff grunted.

"Could be a lady's scarf," offered the coroner.

I doubted that. Orange-and-black diamonds weren't exactly the latest Paris fashion.

I asked the sheriff if the firemen had given any opinions on the cause of the fire. He shook his head. "Those boys are lucky if they know which is the business end of the hose. I'll get the Saratoga fire chief out here later today to have a look."

I thanked him and the coroner for the information and headed back to my car. I had film to develop and a story to write; my friend Fadge was taking me to the races at one.

I managed to drop off my two rolls of Tri-X at the paper, pound out an economical story on the dead bodies discovered in the barn, and phone my editor, Charlie Reese, all before eleven. He asked me what my plan of action was.

"I'll check with Sheriff Pryor later. He's going to have the fire chief inspect the scene for signs of arson. And he might have some information on any missing persons who fit the descriptions."

"What are the descriptions of the victims?"

"Pittsburgh rare."

Silence from Charlie's end. I knew he didn't approve of such dark humor.

"Sorry," I said. "The coroner is doing the postmortems today. I'll talk to him before *Perry Mason* airs. And I'd like to locate Lucky Chuck Lenoir. He's the caretaker of Tempesta."

"What else?"

"It's a long shot, but there's Issur Jacobs at the New Holland Savings Bank. He handled affairs for Shaw Knitting Mills after they moved away. That can wait till Monday morning."

"Anything I can do to lend a hand?"

There was a burr under my saddle. Charlie sensed it.

"What is it?" he asked. "What's wrong?"

"Judge Shaw," I said. "I'm assuming he's still the legal owner of the property."

Charlie drew a breath. "Yes, I see."

I was well acquainted with Judge Harrison Shaw. His daughter, Jordan, had been murdered in a local motel nearly two years earlier, and I met with the judge many times while working on the story. He'd asked me to help find his daughter's murderer, and I complied. And succeeded. But the memory was a painful one for me. In the end, once the case had been solved, he'd refused my awkward offer of friendship and commiseration; my own father had been murdered the year before. The rejection had left me feeling gutted, humiliated, and angry.

Charlie hemmed. While not the most constant pillar of support, he was, nevertheless, usually in my corner. But now he was offering precious little in the way of help. I'd have to screw up my nerve and face the judge on my own.

"Keep Georgie Porgie out of my hair, will you?" I said, opening an escape hatch for Charlie that he didn't really deserve.

"I'll try. But you know Artie Short."

George Walsh, Georgie Porgie to those in on the joke—which meant everyone at the paper except George—was the rotten-egg smell that hung in the air at the *New Holland Republic*. When not sharpening his pencils— the only skill remotely related to writing in his arsenal—George strutted around the place like the cock of the walk. Son-in-law of the publisher, Artie Short, he enjoyed, as such, the unearned and undeserved rank of golden boy, in spite of his struggles with spelling, typing, and making sense of the funny pages. His spectacular gaffes and embarrassing flubs were legendary at the paper, viz. his opinion piece on the Godless Cuban Revolution and "Fido Castrel." As an homage to his witlessness, I'd thumbtacked that masterpiece of finger painting to the board at my desk right after it appeared, and it was still hanging there, yellowing like a stain, fully three and a half years later. His occasional sports stories, which read like last century's mawkish leftovers warmed up with impenetrable analogies and incongruous, facile clichés, prompted either head-scratching or laughter, depending on the generosity of the reader.

I was excited about my first trip to the Saratoga racetrack. My only previous experience with a horse race had come years earlier, shortly after the war, when my father took me with him to Italy for an entire summer. I was ten. After two weeks of museums, libraries, and symposia, he promised me a treat. The Palio. A horse race, he said. Oh, God, I thought, longing for the seasickness of our ocean crossing instead. But the trip to Siena turned out to be one of the highlights of my summer. We enjoyed ringside seats from the windows of an apartment above the Piazza del Campo. A professor friend of my father's had invited us to watch the pageantry. Ten horses and riders, who were called *fantini*, decked out in livery from the different *contrade*, or districts, of Siena, started the race. But only seven horses and six riders finished the three laps of the piazza that day, with the others either falling on the sharp turns of the dirt-covered oval or running out of the requisite energy and inclination to see the endeavor through to its conclusion. The winning horse, Piero—I wrote it in my diary—galloped to the finish ahead of Oca and claimed victory for the *Giraffa contrada*. A commotion broke out when some disappointed partisans roughed up their *fantino* for failing to uphold the honor of their colors. I loved the pomp and drama. Well, not the beating of the jockey—but my father shielded my eyes and guided me away from the window before I saw too much blood.

"Do you know anything about the Tempesta stud farm?" I asked Fadge over a cup of coffee at Fiorello's, the ice-cream shop across from my apartment on Lincoln Avenue.

The big guy—six-two and tipping the scales at more than three hundred pounds—held the undisputed title of My Dearest Friend in the World. A boon companion for sharing late-night pizzas and off-color jokes, he was, I knew, also more than a little sweet on me. But at that moment, he was seated on a stool at the counter brooding over the *Daily Racing Form* in preparation for our day in Saratoga and indifferent to, if not unaware of, my presence.

Fadge was, in fact, an inveterate horseman. A gambler. Shameless "plunger," in his words. He liked to bet, and the larger the wager the more interesting the outcome. His business took a backseat to the betting all year round, but especially when the Saratoga Thoroughbred season rolled around in August. If he couldn't locate a relief soda jerk to man the shop during the meet, he would simply lock the front door, wedge his considerable self behind the wheel of his car, and hurtle off toward the track with little regard for posted speed limits or slow-moving vehicles in his path.

Absorbed in his study of the *Racing Form*, he hadn't heard a word I'd said, so I repeated my question about the stud farm. Still nothing. To test his hearing, I slipped off the stool at the counter and approached the cash register behind the nearby candy case. I pushed down hard on the stiff No Sale button, and the cash drawer popped open, producing a bright *ching* as it did. Fadge remained oblivious. I could have emptied the till and tapped-danced my way out the door, and he wouldn't have been any the wiser. I closed the drawer and rejoined him on a stool at the counter instead.

"Ron," I said more insistently. Only his older customers ever called him by his given name. Eyes bulging from a thyroid condition, he regarded me as if I'd roused him from an erotic dream with a bucket of cold water. "What do you know about the Shaw Tempesta Farm out on Route Sixty-Seven?"

"What? Tempesta Farm? What did I miss?"

"There was a fire out there this morning before dawn," I said. "An old foaling barn burned to the ground."

He shrugged at me. "So? That's nothing new. The place is abandoned."

"Why did they close it down anyway? I know they moved the carpet mills south, but Saratoga is still there. Why shutter the farm?"

"The Shaws kind of lost interest in horse breeding after the fire that killed twelve horses."

"How awful. What happened?"

"It was before the war. Thirty-seven or -eight, I think. A fire broke out in the stables, and twelve of the Shaws' finest Thoroughbreds died."

"How did I miss that in Sanford Shaw's biography?"

"The Shaws didn't talk about it. The biographer must have got the message."

"That's so sad."

Fadge nodded. Although his interest in horseflesh was, in the main, a sporting one, he nevertheless had a soft spot for the beasts. At least for the ones that won money for him.

"The place went into decline," he said, returning to his *Racing Form*. "It's been derelict now for at least fifteen years. So the fires usually have one of two explanations: bored kids with matches or Jewish lightning."

"No, Fadge. This is different. Two people were killed."

"Two people? Who?"

"Wait a minute. Did you just say 'Jewish lightning'?"

He blanched and rubbed a hand over his face. "Sorry. It's an expression. Besides, you're always making fat jokes at my expense."

I knew he hadn't meant anything by it. And, yes, I was guilty of making the occasional remark about his weight, but that didn't mean I liked what he'd said. I poked him in the ribs. Hard. He rubbed his side but didn't dare protest.

"Sorry, El," he repeated. "Tell you what. Go draw yourself a Coke on the house while I finish up here."

"A Coke? For the 'Jewish lightning' crack? No thanks. And you can finish your handicapping in the car. I'll drive."

The bells above the door jingled, interrupting our quarrel, and a short, rotund woman in her late fifties waddled in carrying a small dog in her arms.

"Mrs. Pindaro," said Fadge. "Thank you for helping me out."

She smiled and placed the dog—a pug named Leon—down on one of the stools at the counter. "Happy to do it, Ronnie. You know I used to help out your father years ago. I think I remember the ropes. Though the prices have certainly gone up." Her left nostril flared as she aimed a reproachful eye at him.

I fancied Fadge was reconsidering his choice of pinch hitter. He hated customers who groused about prices.

"I hope you don't mind that I brought little Leon along," she said. "I can't leave him alone too long. He has to do his business, big and small, whether I'm home or not."

"No problem, Mrs. Pindaro," said Fadge. I was sure he didn't like the idea, but with the races beckoning and no one else to mind the store in his absence, what choice did he have? "I'm sure things will be quiet today," he continued, lying to the poor lady. A Saturday afternoon in August promised to be anything but slow.

Little Leon sat beside me on the next stool, huffing his dog breath on my arm. I tried to give him a pat on the head, but he must have thought I had food in my hand and wouldn't have any of the petting. I settled in and ignored him, and he returned the favor.

Fadge noticed the time, jumped off the stool he'd been holding down, and untied his fudge-splattered apron. "Damn, we're gonna be late for the first race. Let's go, El."

He opened the cash register, scooped a wad of bills from the till, and grabbed his *Racing Form*. Then he was out the door like an eager three-year-old colt bolting from the starting gate. I trotted along behind.

❧

It may have looked like the runner-up in a demolition derby, but, aside from backfiring regularly, Fadge's Nash Ambassador ran well enough. The driver's side door had been dented shut three years earlier, and, as a result, whosoever was piloting the jalopy had to climb in from the passenger side. That Saturday afternoon, the honor fell to me. I took the wheel, shifted into first, and roared off down Lincoln Avenue, giving Fadge thirty precious minutes to finish his brilliant plan to beat the odds and walk away from the track with a fortune in his pockets. He sat beside me among the discarded wrappers, newspapers, and empty soda bottles, scribbling notes into the margins of his *Racing Form*. He wouldn't even let me put on the radio. Claimed it distracted him.

Windows open a crack for some fresh, cool air, the Ambassador cruised along Route 67 as if she'd just rolled off the showroom floor. We were approaching Tempesta Farm. I nudged Fadge, interrupting his handicapping, and indicated the scene of the fire with a tilt of my head. He folded his paper and gazed out the window. About 150 yards from the highway's shoulder, beyond the warped and weather-beaten rail at the top of the training track's homestretch, the ground was blackened and scarred and bare. The smell of charcoaled wood still hung in the air. Fadge watched the pile of cinders slide by.

Sheriff Pryor's squad car, five state police cruisers, and seven other county vehicles had blocked off the drive, directly in front of twelve stone monuments guarding the entrance. A Saratoga Springs Fire Department station wagon sat parked at the side of the highway. I took my eyes off the road to glance at the scene. At least thirty men were fanning out over the grounds, ten or fifteen feet apart, heads bowed as if searching for something. I turned my attention back to my driving.

"You weren't kidding about the barn," said Fadge.

"What are those stone pillars for?" I asked.

"Sanford Shaw put them up. A tribute to his favorite horses."

"They look like tombstones."

Fadge shrugged. "A lot of people assume they're markers for the twelve Thoroughbreds that died in the fire. But those monuments were there long before then."

The farm disappeared in the rearview mirror.

"So tell me what happened," said Fadge. "Two people were killed?"

"A woman and a boy. No idea who they were, but the sheriff's looking into missing persons."

"A woman and a boy," said Fadge as if repeating a riddle.

"Actually, I think the boy might have been a man. A jockey."

"How come?"

"The body had some racing silk wrapped around its neck. Maybe part of a jockey's flak jacket. Black-and-orange diamonds, like a jack-o'-lantern. Does that mean anything to you?"

"Not Tempesta's colors," he said. "Theirs were purple and gold. Back when they were racing. And black and orange isn't the most common combination."

"So you don't know of any farm that uses that design?"

"Actually, I do. Goddamn Harlequin Stables," he said with a raw annoyance that betrayed a recent wound. "I lost out on a huge payoff yesterday thanks to one of their horses, Wham's Dram. Closed like a ton of bricks and blew up my parlay. I would've won nineteen hundred bucks if not for that SOB."

I nearly drove off the highway. "Nineteen hundred dollars?"

"Eighteen hundred sixty and change."

I was struck dumb.

"What part don't you understand?" he asked, at his most condescending.

I barely resisted the urge to lecture him on his betting habits and asked instead what kind of name was Wham's Dram.

"Never mind the horse's name. That's not the point."

"But you pronounce it funny. *Waahm's Draahm.*"

"That's how you say it. But forget about the damn horse's name."

"Okay, then what do you mean Wham's Dram ruined your parlay?"

"I was on a hot streak yesterday. Won the sixth, seventh, and eighth. So I let everything ride on Fagin the Wolf in the ninth. I've had my eye on him since he ran second in May at Aqueduct. He was nine to one at post time yesterday."

"Seems rather reckless," I observed. "You should have been more provident and saved some of your winnings."

"Fortune favors the bold. Anyway, Wham's Dram was the heavy favorite," he continued. "And, on a hunch, I dropped twenty bucks to place on Old Dan, another horse I figured was due for a good outing."

"*Old Dan?*" I asked, taking my eyes off the road long enough to gape at Fadge's two heads. "Wasn't there a nag named 'Off to the Glue Factory' you might have bet on instead?"

"Fifteen to one, El," said Fadge, enunciating each syllable as if to prove his point. "Look, it's easy," he continued, ignoring what must have been my stunned expression. "You do your homework, you're patient, and you take calculated risks. I was a neck away from nineteen hundred bucks."

"But for Wham's Dram."

"Exactly."

"And where did Old Dan finish?"

Fadge's cheeks flushed red. "Out of the money," he said barely audible over the hum of the tires on the road. "Last."

I shook my head. "You said Wham's Dram was the favorite. Why should you bet so much against him?"

"Because I study form and jockeys and trainers. I got a couple of clockers who hang out at the Oklahoma. They give me tips on how the workouts are going."

"What's a clocker, and what's the Oklahoma?"

Fadge explained that clockers were the men who hung around the Oklahoma training track adjacent to the racecourse, timing the horses and gauging form with a stopwatch and a clipboard.

"Anyway," he said, returning to the rationale for his wager. "Wham's Dram wears blinders because he's bothered by other horses running alongside him. That's why his trainer usually runs him along the rail. At least that way he's got nobody to his left, only to his right."

"I'm confused."

"Pay attention, El. I figured the jockey—goddamn Johnny Dornan— would run him along the rail and maybe get boxed in by the other horses.

It was a big field. Plus Wham's Dram ran last week with a different rider, and he was carrying some extra weight. I thought he was ripe for a disappointing outing. And I'd been watching my two horses for months. I thought they could outrun the rest of that field. But that damn Johnny Dornan took Wham's Dram wide and caught Fagin at the wire."

Fadge certainly seemed to know his stuff. But then again, he'd lost a bundle. I asked if he knew of any other stables who might use the same racing colors.

"The colors, yes. But the *ensemble*," he said with a flourish, "no. The combination of colors, design pattern, sleeves, and cap has to be unique. Orange and black may not be the most common scheme, but I'm sure there are a few stables between here and Kentucky with those colors."

"But they wouldn't have diamonds?"

He shook his head, and we fell quiet for about a half mile as he dived back into his *Racing Form*.

"So do the cops think it was an accident or something else?" he asked finally, folding the paper once again.

"Sheriff Pryor has to figure out who those two people are first. Then the fire chief will advise if it looks like arson."

Fadge seemed distracted. His concentration broken, he forgot about his *Racing Form* and stared out the window at the gray clouds instead. I took advantage of his availability to ask about the history of Tempesta. He knew Lucky Chuck Lenoir. Well, in fact. He said he'd been working as watchman as recently as two winters before.

"How tall is he?" I asked.

"Little guy. Five-five or -six. A sneaky little jerk, too." (Fadge used a different word.) "My dad threw him out of the store for stealing cigarettes about thirty years ago. Then I had pity on him and let him back in. Caught him stuffing two packs of Pall Malls down his pants and threw him out again." He paused to reflect. "Under the circumstances, I let him keep the cigarettes."

℘

For five dollars, we parked on some man's lawn on Union Avenue, close to the racecourse's front gate. I pointed out to Fadge that if we'd been willing to walk a little farther, he'd have had more money to bet on the horses.

"My time is better spent at the track studying form than strolling through Saratoga," he said as I set the parking brake. I rolled my eyes. "Besides, it's starting to rain again."

"Oh, no. Does this mean they'll cancel the races?"

The derisive look Fadge gave me said enough. We climbed out of the car and made our way to the gate, sheltering under the same umbrella.

Fadge insisted I show my press card at the entrance, and the bored lady waved me past without charge. For twenty-five cents, I picked up a program to keep as a souvenir. I asked him which horse he was betting on as his turn came at the window.

"Watch and learn," he mumbled out of the side of his mouth. "And no lectures or you're walking home."

"Hey, Ronnie," said the cashier from behind the bars of one of the two-dollar betting windows. "Ready for a big day?"

Fadge blushed, for my benefit, I believe. I wondered what the odds were that a random cashier, fifty-seven—as the number over his window identified him—would know him by name. Fadge managed to shrug off his embarrassment and placed his wagers, calling out number combinations and bet types.

"Forty bucks," said number fifty-seven.

"Thanks, Bob."

Fadge had bet forty dollars in a few seconds. I gulped. Shuffling through his betting slips, he asked me if I wanted to place a wager. I was positively green and begged off.

"What did you bet on anyway?" I asked.

He explained his strategy. Five two-dollar wagers on a horse named Sunstruck to win the first race, and six each to place and show on another named Will Dance, a long shot he thought might surprise. Then he "wheeled" (whatever that meant) Sunstruck along with three horses in the second race for another eighteen bucks of daily double bets.

"Come on," he said. "Give it a try. I won't make fun."

I agreed but only on the condition that he back away and not listen as I wagered my meager all. Remembering Fadge's horse from the first race, I screwed up my nerve, stepped up to window number fifty-seven, and asked

Bob for two dollars to show on number two. Sunstruck. He nearly swallowed his cigarette.

"Two dollars to *show* on Sunstruck?" he repeated. I nodded. "You're a regular bridge jumper," he said and handed me the ticket.

What a bridge jumper was I had no idea. Rather than appear uninitiated, I pretended to be in the know and nodded coolly. I resolved to ask Fadge later what it meant.

Beaming with pride at having made my first-ever pari-mutuel bet, I found Fadge under the eaves of the betting shed, leaning against a post. He asked what I'd decided on, but I told him he'd have to wait for the result of the race.

"It's not like a wish," he said. "You can tell people what you bet."

We headed toward the grandstand, passing the paddock on the way. There, horses were being paraded around an enclosure for the bettors to examine before each race. Owners, trainers, and jockeys mingled with the public while the mounts were saddled and inspected. As it was raining, the crowd was thin, with most spectators opting for the shelter of the grandstand and clubhouse.

We found a spot under an awning to watch the race. Even with the intermittent rain, I felt the excitement of the moment. The horses were magnificent, and the pageantry elegantly festive. The clubhouse brimmed with nineteenth-century charm, in spite of the cigar-chomping men in sweaty shirts and rumpled hats nearby on the grandstand side. I found the experience electric, made even more so by the secret knowledge that I had two big ones riding on some wonder horse named Sunstruck wearing the number two on his saddle cloth. And, shortly after 2:00 p.m.—a good omen, I thought—a bell rang, and the starting gate bolted open. My horse took a short while to get his head into the race, but by the quarter pole, he'd taken the lead. And to my utter disbelief, he held on the rest of the way to win by almost a length.

I threw my arms around Fadge, nearly strangling him. He strained to read the tote board to calculate odds or his winnings or who knows what, before flicking me to one side like a piece of lint. For a few heady moments, I understood how gambling might become an addiction. Winning was a thrill. Finally, once the result was posted as "official," Fadge emerged from his trance, turned to me, and asked which horse I'd bet on.

"Sunstruck," I announced, barely able to contain my joy.

"Great," he said. "How much did you bet?"

I told him just two dollars, but he congratulated me all the same. "Nothing wrong with a two-dollar bet. I took it easy, too."

Recalling his admonition against giving him lectures, I said nothing. Forty dollars hardly qualified as taking it easy in my book.

"Not bad for your first time," he continued. "Beginner's luck. And Sunstruck to win pays"—he glanced back at the tote board in the infield—"six dollars and ten cents. That includes your original two bucks. But still, you won four dollars and ten cents."

"But I didn't play him to win. I bet on him to show. How much do I win?"

Fadge shook his head as if he'd been slapped silly. "To show? But he was the heavy favorite."

"I won, didn't I? Now how much?"

He looked to the tote board again. "Congratulations," he said at length. "You won your two dollars back. Plus thirty cents."

"Oh."

"A regular bridge jumper."

CHAPTER THREE

In the end, the thrill of watching Sunstruck thunder across the finish line failed to hook me on gambling. The emotion expended and anxiety experienced, stacked up against the return on investment—thirty cents—didn't appeal to me. After only one race, I knew that I lacked the heart of a plunger.

Fadge, on the other hand, was too engrossed in his own wagers to notice me. This was work for him, after all. He won the daily double, a two-seven combination, worth $38.90. But that, he informed me as he collected his winnings, was the payoff for a two-dollar bet. He'd wagered ten. That came to nearly two hundred dollars. Plus, he'd placed ten dollars on Sunstruck to win, which paid him another $30.50, so after two races, the smug son of a so-and-so was stuffing two hundred twenty some dollars into his pocket.

"You're good luck to me," he said. "Dinner's on me tonight."

This was too rich for my blood. I lacked the nerve to risk so much on an animal I couldn't reason with. While Fadge finalized his strategy for the third race, I studied my thin little program. Disappointed by my paltry winnings, I was now more interested in the names of the horses. I amused myself with King Toots, Organ Grinder, Lincoln Center, and Dauntless Dick, though the mirth was short-lived. But then the name of one of the jockeys, J. Dornan, caught my eye. That was the rider who'd ruined Fadge's big play the day before. I searched the program and found his name listed in four of the day's starts, including the first and second races. I elbowed Fadge and asked him if he'd noticed Johnny Dornan aboard any of the horses. After the second request, he acknowledged me and said no.

I asked a couple of the less-harmless-looking men lurking nearby if they knew, but they were more interested in asking for my phone number than sharing any information. Then another man tapped me on the shoulder and pointed to the air. The PA system was echoing through the park, announcing that jockey J. Dornan had been scratched from the day's races. All of them. When Fadge scurried off to place his bets, I grabbed his

Racing Form and searched for any news of the jockey. Maybe he was ill or had been arrested. Who knew? I was hoping for something, anything that might explain his absence. Anything but a fire on a derelict stud farm off a backroad highway in Saratoga County. There was nothing.

It was raining steadily, and my escort was otherwise occupied, so I sat on a bench inside the grandstand. I picked up a discarded copy of the Albany paper, and, curious, I glanced at the previous day's race results. The last race had indeed been won by Wham's Dram, with Johnny Dornan aboard. There was no information in the paper about the jockey's colors, but a photograph showed the smiling rider in diamond silks atop Wham's Dram in the winner's circle. Could have been orange and black. I had no reason to doubt Fadge's expertise when it came to the attire of jockeys. And I had to admit that pattern looked quite similar to the piece of fabric I'd found in the ashes at Tempesta Farm. Impossible to say for sure in black and white, but the likelihood of Johnny Dornan climbing up into the saddle ever again was growing dimmer by the minute.

The rain let up enough that I could enjoy the parade at the paddock with my camera at the ready. I stood on the other side of the rail fence, mere feet away from the horses. Led by grooms around the enclosed circle, the animals passed, steaming in the cool, wet air, and I snapped photos of each. Leisurely, with graceful—almost indolent—strides, the Thoroughbreds sauntered through the mud as a few devotees studied them alongside me. I overheard some conversations and comments, men in drenched sport coats or leisurewear discussing quality and quantity of sweat—who could distinguish sweat from rain?—and temperament as they related to readiness to run. The serious horsemen, however, the ones who projected competence and knowledge, said little or nothing. They simply watched with a steady gaze. Some were well-dressed cosmopolitan types, while others looked like professional gamblers, humble but on top of their game. The rest, the hobbyists, pretenders, and admirers, made glib observations about form, breeding, and personality, as if they had the dope directly from the horses' mouths.

A couple of ladies in fancy hats to my right admired the beauty of a roan's coat until the poor horse—being a horse after all—answered nature's call not ten feet in front of them. They waved their gloved hands in front of their pinched noses and beat a hasty retreat to the clubhouse. Two heavyset men chewing soaking wet cigars pronounced the excretion a sure indication that the horse would fly to victory as a result of his lessened weight. They used a word I don't favor. Armed with this valuable new intelligence, they sprinted off to the betting window to wager their all on the regular roan. None of the pros seemed excited by what they must have seen thousands of times.

A magnificent, shimmering black beast rounded the turn and edged close to the fence rails where I was leaning with my camera. He threw back his head and snorted. The bit clattered against his teeth, and then he nickered in my general direction. Fixing me with his right eye, the horse made it clear that he was aware of my attentions. More than a hint of self-consciousness. Animals sometimes exhibit shyness, after all. I clicked two frames of his glorious face, and he perked up, as if he knew what a camera was for. Or that he was a handsome boy.

"He says hi, miss," said the young groom escorting him.

I smiled. "Hello to him. What's his name?"

"This here's Purgatorio."

The horse passed and continued on his leisurely round. Then I noticed his racing colors. Black-and-orange diamonds.

"Excuse me," I asked, chasing after the groom. "Is he from Harlequin Stables?"

The groom whispered that he wasn't supposed to talk to anyone while walking the horses. "I shouldn't have said nothing at all before."

"Can't you nod yes or no?"

"Look at your program," he said out of the side of his mouth.

I shrugged and checked the race card. Purgatorio was indeed an issue of Harlequin Stables.

"You couldn't have just said yes?" I called to the groom.

He made a great show of acknowledging three men about twenty yards ahead to my right. One was a jockey in black-and-orange-diamond livery. The other two were dressed in street clothes. The man in charge— the one on the receiving end of the others' deference—was a drooping, gray man in an ill-fitting suit. And though he was heavyset, it appeared he'd recently lost some weight; at least that was the impression given by his luffing trousers, belted high on his belly, and the billowing jacket draped

over his narrow shoulders. He looked to be about sixty-five or seventy.
The third man in the parley, about twenty years younger than the boss,
was dressed modestly in off-the-rack slacks, a light jacket, and a well-worn
cap. He stood a step or two back from the jockey and the man in charge
without saying a word.

The boss barely acknowledged the groom, and then only with a vague
nod. He turned his attention instead to the horse. With intense focus, he
examined Purgatorio as a physician might a patient. Or perhaps an artist
sizing up a would-be model. The horse and groom passed, and, for a long
moment, I watched the three men. The jockey noticed me and alerted the
man in charge by motioning in my direction. They turned, regarded me
briefly, then took a few steps away from the paddock and my scrutiny.

I rewound my film and loaded a new roll.

"That's the owner," came a voice over my shoulder. Fadge. "His name's
Louis Fleischman. And the jockey is Nick Blakely. Not a rider I'd pick for
any horse of mine."

"What if your regular jockey were AWOL?" I asked.

Fadge nodded. "Johnny Dornan."

"Scratched from every race today. Who's the other guy?"

"Don't know."

"The trainer?"

"I doubt it. He's not paying attention to the horse."

"Excuse me, Mr. Fleischman," I called out to the one Fadge had identified as the owner. "May I ask you a question?"

He seemed annoyed by the interruption but was decent enough to ask
what I wanted.

"I'm with the press," I said, approaching and showing my card. Fadge
followed a discreet distance behind. "Eleonora Stone from the *New
Holland Republic*."

He peered at my credential from several feet away, then threw a silent
glance to his companions. "What can I do for you?"

"You're Louis Fleischman, aren't you? The owner of Harlequin
Stables?"

He peered at Fadge standing behind me, surely wondering why I
needed a three-hundred-pound bodyguard.

"Yeah, I'm Lou Fleischman. What's your interest in Harlequin?"

"Actually, it's about Johnny Dornan."

Again the men exchanged looks.

"Can you tell me where he is? Why he was scratched from every race on today's card?"

His expression darkened. He said the jockey was sick.

"So he'll be back tomorrow?" I asked.

Fadge leaned in and whispered in my ear that there were no races on Sunday.

"I mean Monday," I corrected.

"I sure hope so."

"Can you tell me where he's staying here in Saratoga?"

"Why the interest in Johnny Dornan?" he asked, all the while eyeing Fadge.

"A piece of your stable's racing silks was found this morning on Tempesta Farm."

"Tempesta? I thought they shut down years ago."

"They did. It's abandoned. And now they're down one barn, too. It burned to the ground before dawn. Took two bodies with it, and one of them was wearing Harlequin livery. Do you have any comment?"

He stared at me for a long moment, his expression difficult to read. "I don't know anything about that," he said. "Look, miss. I've got a horse in the next race and don't have time for some girl reporter."

Fadge pushed past me. "Hey, pal, talk nice to the lady, or I'll give you a lesson in manners."

Fleischman backed away. The third man stepped forward. I knew Fadge to be a sweetheart but also a hothead with a short fuse. He was double extra-large, quite strong, and ferociously protective of me. A quick assessment of the comparative ages and health of the men convinced me that my hero would have little trouble pounding Louis Fleischman, the jockey, and even the third man into a flattened blob of Play-Doh.

I grazed Fadge's arm with my fingers, stopping him in his tracks. Over time, we'd come to share an unspoken communication, he and I. An intuitive understanding of what the other wanted with nothing more than the subtlest of nods, blinks, or pursed lips to go by. He turned to me and, without a word, knew I was signaling that I was up to the challenge. There were times when I welcomed his brutish strength, but, in general, I preferred to fight my own battles. At least until fists flew.

"I didn't mean anything by it, young man," said Fleischman. "Apologies to the lady."

Fadge stared him down for a couple of beats before nodding his approval. He stepped aside, and I reemerged from his imposing penumbra into the light of the sun. I exaggerate, of course; the day was quite gray after all. But if Fleischman thought I'd let go of the bone, he was mistaken. I repeated my request for a comment about the Harlequin racing silks found around the neck of a dead man.

Fleischman ran a hand through his thin, gray hair. Then he forced a weak smile at me. "Sorry, miss. I've got some business to attend to. But why don't you have a chat with Carl, here?" He indicated the man in the cap. The one who hadn't said a word. "Carl, how's about you take the young lady to the bar in the clubhouse? Put everything on my tab."

Carl remained rooted to his spot.

I glanced at Fadge, my eyes soliciting a thumbs-up or thumbs-down from him.

"He seems harmless. I'll catch up with you later."

A drink sounded pretty good to me. "Hello, Carl," I said. "My name is Ellie."

⁂

Carl Boehringer flashed a pass at the clubhouse gate and escorted me inside. Without speaking a word to me, he found a table in the Jim Dandy Bar, a short distance from the box seating and betting windows of the first level. It was 3:25 p.m. The fourth race was set to start in five minutes, so we had the place mostly to ourselves. As we took our seats, the public address system crackled to life and announced an update.

"In the fourth race, number four Purgatorio is a late scratch. Number four Purgatorio has been scratched from the fourth race."

"What's that about?" I asked Carl.

He shrugged with all the vigor of a slug.

"Purgatorio looked in rare form to me," I said, offering my expert opinion.

"He's jumpy. A nervous type."

I studied him. A man of average height with a long face. His eyes drooped a little in the corners, giving him an air of sadness. Or perhaps fatigue. He wasn't a chatterbox; that much was evident from our short acquaintance. I decided to try to draw him out—keep my mouth shut a few beats longer than socially acceptable in polite conversation—to see if he'd volunteer anything.

"As horses go, he's a sweet guy," said Carl at length.

"Beautiful animal, too. Maybe I'll bet on him next time he runs."

He mugged an indifferent pout. "So long as you don't mind losing your money."

"How's that?"

"Purgatorio's handsome, all right. But he runs like he could take it or leave it."

I stared at him some more, inviting him to explain.

"*Doesn't respond well to competition*," he said, as if quoting someone. "Lou must've changed his mind about running him today."

"But he seemed all set to go. Why scratch him at the last second? Let him get some exercise, if nothing else."

Carl probably thought I was an idiot, at least as far as horseflesh was concerned. "For one thing, you don't want a horse to hurt himself. Do you know how many horses break down every year and have to be destroyed?"

"No. How many?"

Carl didn't have the exact number and, in fact, seemed irritated by my question.

"Lou said I should get you something to drink. What'll you have, miss?"

I moistened my lips with the tip of my tongue. Yes, I wanted a drink.

"Ellie," I prompted. "Gin and tonic, please."

He made his way over to the bar, uninhabited save for one bartender examining his manicure with little interest in anything or anyone else in the place. I watched Carl from my seat and scolded myself for pretending I knew the first thing about horses. In my experience, I had better success interviewing subjects when they didn't take me for a lightweight. Or a scatterbrained woman. I reminded myself that the idea was to keep Carl, not me, on his heels.

"So tell me about Johnny Dornan," I said once he'd returned and shoved a glass in front of me. He'd brought nothing for himself.

"Johnny's a good jockey." Carl rubbed his ear and didn't exactly look me in the eye. I sensed he was one of those men who disliked having to converse with women. Or maybe he was shy. He seemed eager to push off. "Lou even lets him ride for other owners now, provided there's no conflict with Harlequin. Since Johnny's under contract, Lou takes a small portion of his fees, of course."

"How long has Johnny been with Harlequin?"

"Since a year ago last spring. Had a good meet last year. Even better this year."

"Only two years riding? Where was he before that?"

"Must've been riding the leaky-roof circuit. We don't talk much."

"But how did he come to ride for Mr. Fleischman?"

"Lou discovered him down at Aqueduct a year ago last March. Gave him a golden opportunity he probably didn't deserve."

"Was Johnny not grateful?"

"I suppose he was. But he always brags that his wins are his thanks to Lou." He paused to reflect on something. "I'll tell you one thing. Lou was cheesed off this morning when Johnny didn't show. Like he didn't appreciate Johnny disappearing after all he done for him."

"I thought Lou said he was sick."

"Might be. No idea, miss."

"Ellie," I repeated.

I bought fifteen or so seconds extracting a cigarette and lighting it. Then I took a slow sip of my drink.

"How was Johnny last night after his big win?" I asked.

"Having a good time. Lou took us to dinner, and Johnny had a girl. Maybe he's with her now. Or maybe he's sick."

"Do you remember her name?"

"Micheline."

"Micheline?"

"From Montreal. Speaks French."

"Pretty girl?"

"A real looker. And tall. A couple of hands taller than Johnny." He chuckled to himself. "Little prick." Carl mumbled an apology. "But he always manages to find pretty girls, no matter how tall."

"Do you know where he's been staying here in Saratoga?"

"Same place as me. Mrs. Russell's Boarding House in Ballston Spa. Lou gives us an allowance of ten bucks a night for room and board. We can stay wherever we want. And we can pocket whatever's left over. Russell's ain't bad for the price."

"But you didn't see Johnny this morning?"

Carl shook his head deliberately.

"So you two are friendly?" I asked, well aware that he seemed to dislike the jockey. "Staying in the same place and all?"

"I wouldn't say that. Lou says I got to drive Johnny around. Keep an eye on him. Make sure he shows up on time."

Carl had failed in his mission that day.

"And did Johnny go back to the boarding house with you last night after dinner?"

"He did. Snuck Micheline inside. The girl wasn't too happy about creeping in like she wasn't good enough to walk through the front door. But she went along for the ride anyway."

"The ride?"

He stared at me for a long moment, exhaled a pained sigh through his nose, then offered another limp "Sorry, miss" for his off-color language.

"Ellie."

"Mrs. Russell doesn't like that kind of stuff at her place," he continued. "She's strict about fraternizing, as she calls it. She'd throw Johnny out if she knew he was entertaining girls in his room."

"So Johnny went to his room with this Micheline, and that's the last you saw of him?"

"That's right. I heard him plenty, though. Both of them." Again he apologized, but his grin told me he wasn't all that sorry.

"Doesn't sound as though he was sick. What time was that?"

"About ten. I took a pill and went to sleep. We had to be up early today. Like any day in August except Sunday."

"What's Johnny Dornan like?"

"He's arrogant. He's unpleasant. And a little mean. Likes to make other people feel small. Maybe because he's such a midget."

"He's not popular with the other riders?"

"Least of all with the other jockeys. Johnny's got a reputation for jostling and crowding other horses. Grabbing other riders' crops, saddlecloths, and reins. Pushing off, that kind of thing. Whatever might give him an advantage. He's sly, though. Rarely gets caught by the stewards. But the other riders know what he's up to, and they don't like him."

"Anyone else who might hate him? Maybe want to do him some harm?"

"Wait a minute," said Carl. "Are you suggesting this fire was no accident?"

"Not sure yet. But I like to consider all angles."

Carl seemed to be debating his answer. At length, he said that he'd never seen anything to support the rumors, but he'd heard them all the same.

"What rumors?"

"That he used to be in bed with gamblers. And not your amateurs like you see here at Saratoga. Guys who take betting serious. So serious they like to improve the odds before they risk their money on an animal that don't speak English."

"Mobsters?"

"Don't quote me on it. I'm only telling you what I heard around the stables."

"And you're saying that the rumors are that he used to do this? In other words not anymore?"

"I haven't heard about anything recent."

"Does Mr. Fleischman know this?"

"I can't speak for Lou. You'll have to ask him yourself."

I made a mental note to do exactly that at the earliest opportunity. "Does Mr. Fleischman stay at Mrs. Russell's too?"

"No. Just me and Johnny. In the seven years I've been working for Lou, he's always stayed over at Grossman's Victoria on Broadway with his wife, Rose. They keep kosher. Me? I like my ham and lobster. Especially when someone else is paying." Carl paused to reconsider. "Actually, Lou likes his ham and lobster, too. He only keeps kosher when Rose is around."

"And what do you do for Lou, anyway?"

"I don't think talking about me was part of the deal. Lou said to buy you a drink and answer your questions about Johnny."

I wandered around under a light rain, trying to find Fadge, eventually spotting him at a ten-dollar betting window a few minutes before the sixth race began. He was perspiring, his face flush, and he was displaying all the pique of a rhinoceros that's just been darted in the rump by a tranquilizer gun. Not the moment to approach the beast. I opted instead for another drink by myself in the Jim Dandy Bar. That was when Lou Fleischman sidled up to my table.

"Join you?" he asked.

"It's a free country."

He took the seat opposite me, exhaled a long breath, and wiped his face with a handkerchief. After a few restorative gasps, he craned his neck to find a waiter. "Where's your big friend gotten to?"

I shrugged, quite bored at that point with my first day at the races. If it hadn't been for my special moment with Purgatorio and the intriguing disappearance of Johnny Dornan, I might have nodded off in a corner somewhere.

"Sorry about earlier, young lady," he began. "You caught me at a bad moment."

"Nothing a drink won't put right."

He smiled. A mushy, unsavory smile. The kind that scares children. "Sure thing." He turned to find a waiter.

"Carl had to go order at the bar."

With a show of great exertion, Fleischman pushed himself out of his chair and headed to the bar, limping slightly as he went. A couple of minutes later, he waddled back into view and slipped a drink in front of me. He retook his seat and considered me for a moment before raising his glass of beer to his lips for a long gulp. Emitting a throaty effluence that bordered on a belch, but didn't quite qualify, he proceeded to nod in admiration of the beverage in his glass.

"That's good," he declared. "Schaefer's."

I ignored his observation. His breath had already told the tale.

"Cheers, by the way." I raised my glass and took a sip, barely wetting my upper lip.

"Tell me about the fire," he said, either unaware of or indifferent to my sarcasm. "They really found two bodies inside?"

"Burned beyond recognition."

"But not so the racing silks?"

"Not quite," I said. "Just enough orange-and-black checks to wrap around one of the necks. The male."

Fleischman groaned and took another swig of beer.

"The coroner identified one of the bodies as that of a woman. No age or name yet."

"And the other was Johnny?"

"Could be. At first they thought it was a boy. Or maybe a short man. No taller than five-four or -five."

"Jesus. I was with him yesterday. Had dinner with him last night after he won the ninth race."

"Wham's Dram?" I asked, trying to show off a bit. "Johnny Dornan ran him wide and caught Fagin the Wolf at the wire."

"That's right. A fine bit of riding."

"Wham's Dram is bothered by other horses in his sights and wears blinders. Isn't that why he likes the rail?" I was rather enjoying this.

"You're pretty well informed," he said, tipping his glass in my direction before draining what was left in it. "What's your name again?"

"Ellie. Ellie Stone."

"Jewish girl?"

I nodded.

"Stone. Did your family come from Germany?"

"Yes. About eighty years ago. My grandparents were from Bonn."

"I was born in Hamburg. Came over as a boy. Call me Lou."

He lifted his empty glass to me and, finding no Schaefer's at the bottom, frowned and asked me if Carl had taken care of all my questions.

"Most of them. I was hoping you'd answer the ones he couldn't. Or wouldn't."

"If I'm able."

"What exactly does Carl do for you?"

Lou was taken aback. "I thought you were interested in Johnny Dornan, not Carl. Or me."

"It's just that Carl wouldn't say. I didn't think it would be such a big secret."

"He does a little of this and a little of that. He's like my right hand."

He couldn't have known, but dodging my questions only made me more curious. My compulsion for tying up loose ends and squaring corners made it difficult for me to abandon unfinished crossword puzzles or let go of unanswered questions. I was itching to get to the bottom of what Carl Boehringer did for Lou Fleischman, but this wasn't the moment to indulge my obsession.

I asked about Johnny Dornan instead. If he knew about the gambling rumors Carl had mentioned. Lou dismissed the talk as gossip and jealousy.

"Do you think I'd let him ride for me if he was crooked?"

I moved on. "How was he at dinner last night?"

"In high spirits. He won two races yesterday."

"Was he drinking? To celebrate?"

"Not Johnny. He has to watch his weight. He allows himself one small glass of wine with his meal—and I mean small. With Johnny, there's no need to hover over him. He's a pro. And serious about maintaining his weight. Not like some jockeys who can't control themselves. They gorge themselves then stick a couple of fingers down their throats afterward."

"What about you? Do you eat and drink in front of your jockeys?"

"Sure," he said with a grin, patting his belly. "I'm not the one riding the horse."

"Even last night?"

"Normally, I would have stayed in on a Friday. The Sabbath, you know. But last night was a special occasion. Two winners yesterday, so I enjoyed a nice bottle of wine to celebrate. I gave Johnny a bantam portion."

"Was there anyone else with you?"

"Rose didn't come. It was me and Carl and Johnny. And his date, Micheline."

"Tell me about her."

Lou gazed into his empty glass, then looked again in vain for a waiter. "He likes the ladies, Johnny does. Problem is they don't always like him."

"Why's that?"

He smirked at me. "A guy can have all the charm in the world, but if he's pint-sized . . . Well, the ladies naturally shy away."

"Does Johnny have all the charm in the world?"

"Hardly. Johnny is what fancy people call an 'acquired taste.' His personality is not why I keep him around."

"Unlikeable?"

"I wouldn't argue with that."

"What about Micheline? Did she enjoy Johnny's company?"

He twitched, his face betraying discomfort. "You understand, young lady, some girls will compromise on height if there's another incentive."

I sipped my drink. "I see."

He shook his head. "No. Johnny didn't pay her nothing. I did." He glanced around yet again for a waiter. "Jesus, what do I got to do to get a drink in here?"

"About Micheline?" I prompted.

"I thought Johnny deserved some pleasant company after his ride yesterday."

"Where might I find her?"

Lou Fleischman mulled it over for a long moment. "You don't think she was the girl in the barn, do you?"

CHAPTER FOUR

"How much did you win?" I asked Fadge as we filed out the front gate.

"You're looking at it the wrong way," he said. "It's not about one day. I've got a plan for the entire meet. The whole year, really."

"Don't tell me you lost. How is that possible? You were up more than two hundred dollars after the first two races."

"I told you no lectures. I'll win in the end. I take a scientific approach to racing. Not like the rest of these slobs."

"Scientific?"

"Yeah. I've got years' worth of charts and ledgers tracking horses and jockeys and trainers. And I've devised situational strategies for betting."

"Okay, I'll bite. What are a couple of the situations?"

"Everything from rain to rider. I consider how far the horse has traveled to get here, and how long since his last race. Then there's starting-gate position and time of day. I even look at the outside temperature. And some stallions react differently when racing next to a filly. Why do you think I've kept every edition of the *Racing Form* for the past fifteen years? I never throw them out in case I need to do a little research."

I thought it would take an IBM 1401 mainframe computer to make sense of his situational strategies.

"I've seen your filing system," I said. "A dozen eight-foot-tall stacks of old newspapers on your back porch. You're like the third Collyer brother."

"I have to keep the papers on the porch. The pantry's filled with my record collection. And I know where everything is."

"Within ten feet, perhaps," I said as we reached Fadge's car. "But putting your grubby little hands on what you need is the challenging part."

"My hands aren't little."

"Anyway, for all your scientific approach and research, you lost. At least I came away on the plus side today."

"You won thirty cents on the first race, and the program cost you a quarter. Congratulations. You won a nickel."

"That's still better than you did."

If Fadge thought his bad luck had run its course, he was mistaken. Instead of heading straight back to New Holland, I insisted we take a detour.

⁂

Thanks to Carl Boehringer, I knew that Johnny Dornan was staying at a boarding house on McLean Street in nearby Ballston Spa. A sprawling gray clapboard affair with a wooden staircase running up the side for the convenience of the roomers, Mrs. Russell's covered much of an entire city block. Not a fancy place, it could have used a couple of coats of new paint and some landscaping. The jungle of grass in front of the house had long since claimed the uneven, crumbling sidewalk in the name of Spain. A sign on the porch advertised the August rate for singles at eight dollars per night, board included.

Fadge set the brake and huffed a theatrical sigh of impatience, intended to communicate his displeasure at having to endure this errand, especially on the heels of his disappointing day at the races. I patted him on the hand and promised I would be quick.

"Wait for me," he said. "You might need my help."

"Because Mrs. Russell is so dangerous?"

If not dangerous, the proprietress was, nevertheless, a tough old bird. We found her in the parlor just to the right of the front hall. She sat perched on the flattened folds of a worn armchair, transfixed by the wrestling on a television whose picture fluttered rhythmically from bottom to top. Hair in curlers, she was puffing on a cigarette and munching on saltines slathered in margarine. She washed down her meal with what was either gin or vodka. As we moved closer, the smell told the tale. Gin.

"Excuse me, are you Mrs. Russell?" I asked from behind her.

She threw up a hand, a cigarette pinched between her thumb and forefinger, to silence me. I glanced at Fadge, who seemed to be calculating in his head how long this torture was going to last.

"That's it, that's it," she said, encouraging the warping image on the screen before her. "Pin him, pin him, you son of a . . . !"

Fadge rolled his eyes and took a step into the room, perhaps with the idea of imposing on Mrs. Russell to tear herself away from the TV and speak to us.

"Whoa!" she shouted, then turned to locate Fadge. "That's perfect. Don't move a muscle, big boy. You fixed the vertical hold."

Indeed, the television picture had stopped its jittering and was now clear and stable. Mrs. Russell whooped and hollered as the match concluded—right on schedule before the half hour—with the referee on all fours pounding his palm thrice on the canvas. Scrambling to his feet, he raised the right hand of the one who looked to me like a garbageman in baggy underwear, and proclaimed him the winner.

Our hostess pushed herself out of her chair, brushed the cracker crumbs off her lap onto the floor, and turned to face us. She was a giraffe of a woman, at least six feet tall. Somewhere between fifty and eighty years old, impossible to tell for sure. Olive Oyl's uglier sister, Fadge later described her.

"I'm gonna have to hire you to stand there, big fella," she said to Fadge. "Best reception I've ever had."

On cue, perhaps out of self-consciousness, he shifted his weight from one leg to the other, and the television's picture went back to its gyrations. Mrs. Russell shrugged an "oh well" and, cheeks hollowing, took a final pull on her cigarette before stubbing it out in the heaping ashtray—still smoldering from her last smoke—next to her chair.

"What do you two lovebirds want?" she asked. "A room?"

Fadge chirped yes before I could respond.

"Actually, no," I said, elbowing him in the ribs.

Mrs. Russell sized us up and granted that it was probably better that way. "Not sure if I could feed this one on eight bucks a night." She indicated Fadge with a jab of her thumb.

I snorted. Fadge didn't find her remark funny, if his bulging eyes and grinding teeth were any indication.

"My name is Eleonora Stone, Ellie Stone. I'm a reporter for the *New Holland Republic*."

"Congratulations. Now what do you want?"

"I'm making inquiries into the whereabouts of Johnny Dornan. He's been staying here, I believe."

"Yeah, he's one of my roomers. Sullen little so-and-so, but he gives me good racing tips now and then. I won eleven bucks last week."

I wondered if that might mean he was still in cahoots with gamblers. Or was he simply passing on his own insider observations?

"Have you seen him today?"

She shook her head. "It's a big place. And he's got the staircase outside if he don't want to come in this way."

"There was a fire last night," I said. "This morning, really. About fifteen miles from here, on Sixty-Seven near the Montgomery County line."

"What's that got to do with Johnny?"

I exchanged a glance with Fadge. He blinked, tacitly ceding me the privilege of breaking the news.

"Two people died in the fire. And a length of racing silk was found in the rubble. The colors and pattern matched Harlequin Stables' livery. Johnny rides for Harlequin." I paused for effect before adding that Johnny hadn't shown up that day at the track.

Mrs. Russell stared at me for a full ten seconds, then turned to consider the human antenna for five more. She wiped her lips with her long, dry fingers.

"Are you saying Johnny perished in the fire?" she asked finally.

"We don't know. That's why we're making inquiries."

The old lady staggered backward in a melodramatic manner, bumped into the armchair, and steadied herself against it. "I can't believe it. Johnny's one of my boys." This was a change of tone from her earlier "sullen little so-and-so" remark, but I let it pass. "We're like a family here. I even looked the other way when he snuck girls into the house."

"Can you tell us when you last saw him?" I asked as gently as I knew how, given her newfound affection for the jockey.

She frowned and waggled her head, as if shaking off a right cross to the chin. "Must have been yesterday morning early. He was on his way over to the track as always. With Mr. Boehringer."

"Yes, I've met him. Tell me, does Johnny Dornan have a car?"

"Not that I know. Mr. Boehringer drives him where he needs to go."

"Might we have a look in his room?" I asked.

Mrs. Russell snapped back to life. Aiming a sharp glare at me, she said nothing at first. Then she seemed to be considering it.

"We won't touch anything," said Fadge, beating me to the punch.

"And we might find something that helps locate him," I said. "Maybe it wasn't Johnny in the fire."

"All right," she said. Finding her land legs again, she pushed away from the armchair. "And if we find his wallet, he's a week behind on his rent. I'm sure you won't object if I settle his bill."

Mrs. Russell led the way down a long corridor on the third floor. Jangling a large iron ring of keys, she shuffled along in house slippers. About halfway down the dim hallway, I noticed a ridge in the carpet ahead. Fearing a fall, I reached for her elbow to catch her should she trip. But she cleared the hazard like a hurdler, stepping over it without looking, as if she'd been avoiding it for decades.

Johnny Dornan's room was the last one on the right, next to the door that gave access to the outside staircase. After an exhaustive search for the correct key, a process involving visual inspection but no actual insertion into the lock, Mrs. Russell shook her head and announced that she had the wrong key ring.

"Gotta go get the other one," she said.

"What if we try the latch?" asked Fadge, reaching for the brass knob. The door swung open with a creak.

The landlady seemed spooked, as if there might be someone inside, so Fadge went in first. The room was empty, at least of marauders or burglars. Johnny Dornan's place was simple, laid out in a crooked rectangle, with an unmade metal-frame bed near the window. There was a water pitcher on the nightstand, braided rug next to the bed, and faded wallpaper above the wainscoting. A simple light in a glass shade hung from the painted wood-paneled ceiling, and the sheer curtains on the windows were surely an afterthought, not a functional or aesthetic choice. They weren't substantial enough to shut out the sun or the attentions of someone determined to peep inside. And they were ugly to boot. I noticed a couple of dark prints on the walls, depicting street scenes of some bygone era, but nothing else to brighten the décor.

Johnny had left the room uncluttered if rumpled. It appeared he'd brought little with him for his month-long stay in Saratoga. A suitcase in the corner, a leather satchel hanging on the room's only chair, and a shaving kit, hair oil, and a toothbrush on an old, chipped washstand in front of a mirror. The bath and toilet were down the hall. Everything pointed to an itinerant, Spartan existence. That made sense to me; he was a jockey, after all, presumably traveling from track to track, barn to barn, following the horses wherever they were running next.

Mrs. Russell checked the drawers of the dresser, I can only assume, on a quest for Johnny Dornan's wallet. But from what I could see, all she found was some shirts, underwear, and slacks. Her sour face confirmed my suspicions; she'd struck out, not pay dirt. So much for the past-due rent.

"Doesn't look like he lit out," said Fadge, nudging a copy of the *Saratogian* on the nightstand with a flick of his forefinger. It was opened to the sports section and the race chart. "I'd say he intended to come back."

"A fat lot of good that does me," said Mrs. Russell. "That little jerk still owes me a week's rent. Well, you two will have to cover it."

"Why would we pay his bill?" I asked, not particularly surprised that Johnny was once again a "little jerk" in her eyes. "We've never even met the man."

"And his riding cost me a fortune yesterday," added Fadge.

"All right, then, out," she said. "You have no business here if you're not going to honor his debts. Let's go, big fella."

With no option, we obeyed. Ever the gentleman, Fadge held out a hand, yielding the right of way to me and our hostess. We all tramped out into the hall, and Mrs. Russell shut the door.

"Let yourselves out that way," she said, indicating the exit to the external staircase.

"That wasn't much help," I said as we climbed into Fadge's car. This time he went first, of course, since the driver's door was dented shut.

He started the engine and threw the car into gear.

"Here," he said, producing the newspaper he'd noticed in Dornan's room and tossing it to me. "He wrote something I couldn't quite make out from a distance."

"You swiped his newspaper?" I asked.

"Yeah, the old bag called me 'big fella' one too many times."

Fadge stopped to phone Mrs. Pindaro from a booth in Ballston Spa. He described her as apoplectic when he returned to the car.

"I had to bite the bullet," he explained. "Jeff Zeitner's been bugging me for over a year to give him a job. I just called him and told him to get down to the store to relieve Mrs. Pindaro."

"What happened? I thought she was an old hand at this."

"She's having a breakdown. Probably because someone ordered a black-and-white milkshake, and she's against integration."

"Wait a minute," I said as he pulled away from the curb. "Isn't Jeff Zeitner that fourteen-year-old kid who's always hanging around the store? Zeke? The one you're always yelling at? Is that even legal?"

"Sure. In India. And I like the kid. I yell at him because I like him."

"You're entrusting your business to a fourteen-year-old kid?"

"Better Zeke than Mrs. Pindaro. At least the place will be there when I get back."

I shook my head again, wondering why he even cared.

Johnny Dornan had tried his hand at the newspaper's crossword puzzle but hadn't gotten very far. And what he'd managed was a mess. I was tempted to scratch out his answers and correct the thing, but I resisted. He'd also written notes in the margins to handicap the horses he'd faced Friday.

"Strong finisher," he'd scrawled next to one. "Rabbit," next to another. He offered an unflattering description of one of the other jockeys in the form of a vulgar slur, and I noted the name, Quesada. All this seemed like preparation for his job. Odious but nothing unusual.

"Find anything?" asked Fadge as he sped west on Route 67.

"Why do you suppose there was no Friday paper in his room?" I asked.

"That's not Friday's?"

"No, Thursday's. It looks as though Dornan was in the habit of sizing up the competition the night before he rode. So why didn't he do the same for today's races?"

"Because he didn't race today."

"But would he have known that before he died in a broken-down foaling barn on Tempesta Farm?"

Fadge shrugged. "Maybe he intended to, but someone invited him to a barbecue."

I frowned my disapproval at him, but he was watching the road.

"Anything else in the paper?" he asked. "Where's *Lolita* playing? We should go see that."

"Pig," I said, flipping to the next page in the paper. "There's a corner ripped out in the market ads. And he wrote something there. Only a couple of letters are left."

"What's it say?"

I squinted at the chicken scratch. "Not sure. But wait a minute. You're not going to believe this. You know how in the movies, the detective rubs a pencil over the top sheet of paper in a pad, and it reveals what was written on the previous page?"

"Yeah. It's ridiculous."

"Don't be so quick to judge. The ink on the backside of this page transferred what he wrote to the page beneath it. Like carbon paper."

Fadge took his eyes off the road a moment to throw a skeptical glance my way. "I don't believe it. What's it say?"

"The first two letters might be R-O. Then the rest of it is on the page underneath. I can't decipher with you bouncing all over the road. Pull over a minute, will you?"

"You'll have plenty of time to read it when we get back to the store," he said. "And if I find that little Leon did his business on the floor, I'm gonna dropkick him over the telephone poles across the street."

"I'll never forgive you if you do," I said and returned to the problem at hand: the handwriting next to the A&P advert, below the double-stamps Wednesday box. I puzzled over the challenge as I might a particularly difficult crossword clue. It was written in a childish hand and was muddled by the newspaper text underneath. I was going to be sick if I continued trying to read in a moving car. Especially one piloted by Fadge, who drove as if you scored points for each pothole and bump you hit.

"Forget about the dog. Your boy, Zeke, is in charge now. Pull over to the shoulder for a minute, will you?"

With the car stopped, I concentrated on the scrawl.

"So?" he asked. "What's it say?"

"It looks like . . . 'ROBINSON S FRIDAY MIDNIGHT.'"

"Who the hell's Robinson?"

"I don't know. It could be a meeting. Johnny had dinner with Lou Fleischman on Friday night. Do you suppose he met someone else afterward? Someone named Robinson?"

"Arson," said Sheriff Pryor over the phone.

"You're sure?" I asked with a gulp.

"As sure as the fire chief. He found three points of origin for the fire inside the barn. That's pretty much impossible to happen by accident. Someone wanted it to burn and burn fast."

"Anything else to indicate arson?" I asked, searching for confirmation as I'd been trained to do.

"Windows all smashed to let in more air. Every one of them. At least the ones low enough to reach on foot. The higher windows were cracked and smoked. Some were broken but in a different way from the lower windows. It was arson all right."

"But if it was arson, that means those two people were murdered."

"No doubt about it."

CHAPTER FIVE

According to the sheriff, the coroner was surprised to find that the male victim had a small-caliber bullet—.22 or .25—lodged in his skull, right between the eyes.

"Dead before the fire began," said Pryor. "The woman, on the other hand, was strangled to death. No smoke in either of their lungs."

"Where does that leave us?" I asked.

"Us?"

That had been foolish of me. The sheriff surely didn't consider me part of his investigation. And I doubted he understood the simple rhetorical device I'd employed when asking what would come next. I tried a different tack.

"Was there evidence of activity elsewhere on the farm?"

"None. We walked over the eight hundred acres. Pretty forsaken out there."

"Have you established the victims' identities?"

"Not yet. We're still checking with local authorities for missing persons."

"And Louis Fleischman? Have you spoken to him?" I asked, thinking he might be grateful for the tip. He wasn't.

"Who's that?"

"He owns Harlequin Stables."

"This was *Tempesta* Farm, miss," he said with all the condescension he could muster.

"Yes, I noticed the sign out front. But Harlequin Stables' livery matches the bit of racing silk tied around the man's neck." I waited a few beats, allowing the drama to ripen, and, with it, a healthy dose of my own disdain. "And one of their jockeys has been missing since Friday night. A man by the name of Johnny Dornan."

"Anything else for *our* investigation?" he asked, outdoing his previous personal best for rudeness. Still, I fancied I could hear him scribbling the name into a pad frantically as he spoke.

I almost didn't tell him, but in the end I thought he should know. "Do you know anyone named Robinson?"

"No. Why?"

"Johnny Dornan's landlady showed me his room. I saw a note there that suggested a midnight meeting with someone named Robinson S."

Pryor wasn't interested. He told me it sounded like a dead end. "Lots of people named Robinson. Could've been anyone."

"But don't you want to check into it?"

"I think I can take it from here," he said. "But, uh, tell me. Where was this Johnny Dornan fellow staying?"

⁂

Fadge's promise to stand me to dinner had evaporated along with his winnings, so I had to make do by myself. For an hors d'oeuvre, I scrounged some gin-soaked olives that I kept in the icebox, washed them down with a glass of whiskey—not a combination made in heaven—then dined on deviled ham straight from the can. I peeled and quartered an apple for dessert. Frank Olney was next on my list. I phoned him as I sat down with paper and pencil and my second drink.

"What's the update?" he asked.

I relayed the details of my conversation with the Saratoga County sheriff, and Frank listened patiently.

"I spoke to him, too," he said once I'd finished. "He didn't share everything with you."

"He's holding out on me? Why?"

"He's friendly with the Saratoga paper. Always hunting for votes, and you're in the wrong county."

"Is he up for reelection this year?"

"Not till sixty-four. But he's always running."

Given his winning personality, Pryor needed the head start.

"So what didn't he tell me?"

"Don't cite me as your source, or he'll never tell me anything else."

"Scout's honor."

"He said they turned up an empty pint bottle not far from the bodies. Near where one of the walls used to be."

"What kind of pint bottle?" I asked, suspecting the answer. "Milk?"

"Brandy. Blackberry. But remember this is off the record."

"Don't worry. I'll say that I saw the bottle myself when I was on the scene."

"That'll work. He also said there was the remains of a campfire. Same area of the building."

"A hobo's hotel."

"Looks that way."

I remembered having seen other outbuildings at Tempesta, including a dormitory formerly used by grooms, farmhands, and assorted workers. And a large caretaker's house about four hundred yards from the foaling barn, on the far side of the training track. Why wouldn't the hobos have set up housekeeping there? Surely it would have been more comfortable than a musty barn. Or was it the killer or killers who'd been camping out there? I asked Frank what he thought.

"Your guess is as good as mine, at least until someone identifies the bodies."

"Have you ever heard of anyone named Robinson? Robinson S. something. Maybe a gambler? Or someone in the horse-racing industry?"

"I'm sure I know someone named Robinson. Nobody comes to mind off the top of my head, though. Why do you ask? Who's Robinson?"

"I had the opportunity to poke around inside Johnny Dornan's room at the boarding house where he's staying. He'd scribbled an appointment for midnight Friday on his newspaper. It seems he was meeting someone named Robinson. Robinson S."

"Can't help you on that," he said. "I trust you informed Sheriff Pryor about the name."

"Of course. But he wasn't interested. Told me he'd run his own investigation without my help."

Frank was quiet, surely trying to gauge the veracity of my statement. At least that was how it felt to me. Sometimes he was strictly by the book. Other times, he'd bend a rule—or some criminal's arm till it broke—if that got him what he wanted. I changed the subject and asked if he'd had any reports of missing persons.

"None in Montgomery County."

"What about Lucky Chuck Lenoir? Is he around?"

"Yeah. In Greenwood Cemetery. I made some inquiries. He died peacefully in his sleep last Christmas."

"So he's not our charred corpse."

"Maybe he was a little lucky after all."

CHAPTER SIX

SUNDAY, AUGUST 12, 1962

Lou Fleischman had given me a phone number for Micheline, the treat he'd arranged for Johnny Dornan on Friday night. He didn't know her last name. It was a Schenectady exchange, and nobody answered when I dialed. Either Micheline was in a church pew early that Sunday morning or she was still out from the night before. I wasn't ready to commit to a third, more sinister possibility. To wit, her lying on a slab in the morgue, burned beyond recognition except for a patch of red hair and an earring.

No, I didn't want to get ahead of myself. There was no proof that the hired girl from Montreal was dead or, for that matter, that Johnny Dornan was the short male found in the ashes. If forced to wager, I'd have put my money on them, of course, but I needed something concrete before I could put it in any story of mine. The next edition of the *Republic* wouldn't be out till Monday afternoon, which meant I had about twelve hours to come up with more than a roll of Tri-X film of two volunteer firemen swamping a razed barn with a hose.

At a little past ten, I joined Fadge across the street for a coffee and a hard roll. Deep in study of the *Daily Racing Form* again, he ignored me. I read the papers in my usual booth at the rear of the shop. The Soviets had launched two different cosmonauts into space twenty-four hours apart, and they were at that very moment orbiting Earth in something resembling a couple of dented Volkswagens. Putting aside my worries that we would never catch the Russians in the space race, I set about plotting my day. First up I intended to locate Micheline. I rose, made my way over to the phone booth, and dialed the number Fleischman had provided. Still no answer. I got an operator on the line and asked for the address and the subscriber's name: Burgh, Jas. on Steuben Street in downtown Schenectady. Micheline was from Montreal, so I'd expected a French name. Maybe Burgh was her husband or a boyfriend. More likely, he was her, ahem, business manager.

I returned to my table to review my notes. Since Sheriff Pryor was dispensing information with an eyedropper, I needed to do some of the legwork for myself. Next on my list was to confirm the identities of the two bodies inside the barn. And while the police in the neighboring localities had received no missing person reports, it seemed obvious that the dead woman—like Johnny Dornan—had failed to return to her room Friday night. That is if she weren't a local with her own place. Still, I figured a roundup of the motels and hotels in the area might provide a lead on her identity. I had a list of the more reputable boarding houses and hotels from a Saratoga Springs Chamber of Commerce brochure. That would keep me busy for a while. Finally, I had to be home before six to write up my story for Monday's edition and drop it off with the typesetter downtown at the office.

"Why are you poring over the *Racing Form*?" I called across the room to Fadge. "Aren't you working today?"

He lifted his head and regarded me as if I'd just walked through the door. "I'm handicapping tomorrow's races."

"You should put the same effort and attention into running your business."

He went back to his *Racing Form*. "This is my business."

And I returned to my notes. After a while, Fadge appeared above me with a glass of Coke. He shoved it under my nose.

"Buy something or get out."

"Thanks but no thanks," I said. "I was just leaving. Got a full plate today."

"Maybe we can meet up later and grab a bite to eat?"

"You still owe me dinner from yesterday. Remember? You promised before your picks went south."

He frowned. "That's right. You were the big winner. Maybe you should pick up the tab."

The house on Steuben near Emmett Street was a simple brick apartment building, with six units on three floors. Burgh occupied 3A, according to the mailbox in the entrance. I let myself in and climbed the stairs.

"Yeah?" asked the man who answered the door. About forty or forty-five, he was dressed in shirtsleeves and a pair of brown slacks held up by suspenders. He wore a fancy watch and a large ring of some kind. His after-shave screamed Aqua Velva, or a reasonable facsimile, and he'd slapped on plenty of it. From beneath two bushy black eyebrows, he glared at me with a suspicion bordering on menace.

"Mr. Burgh?" I asked, questioning the wisdom of visiting the place without my muscle. He didn't answer, but I concluded I'd reached my party. "I'm trying to find Micheline."

"Who are you?" His voice was reedy and coarse.

"My name is Ellie." I didn't want to say anything more, at least not until I had to.

"She ain't here," he said after considering me for a moment in the dim light of the landing. "In fact, she don't live here. Who gave you this address anyway?"

I gulped. "Bell Telephone."

"How's that?"

"Lou Fleischman gave me your number. I got the address from Information."

He chuckled. "I thought you were selling something."

"Avon calling."

He ignored my crack. "Lou gave you my number? What business does a girl like you got with Micheline?"

"I understand that Mr. Fleischman engaged her services Friday night for one of his jockeys. A man named Johnny Dornan."

"Maybe. What of it?"

"Johnny Dornan is missing. So I thought I'd try to track down Micheline to see if she knows where he might be."

"Friday night? That's barely thirty-six hours ago," he said. "Don't you think he might just be on a bender somewhere? Or maybe him and Micheline hit it off better than expected and are holed up somewheres."

"That's possible, of course. But my urgency is prompted by a fire that killed two people in the early hours of yesterday morning. A man and a woman."

"No kidding? Where?"

"At Tempesta Farm in Saratoga County."

Burgh chewed on that for a moment. "Are you a friend of Dornan's?"

"Never met him."

"No chance it was an accident?"

"Sheriff says murder. Bullet between the eyes."

He drew a fatalistic sigh. "Probably deserved what he got."

The man in the doorway—I still had no verbal confirmation of his identity—stared me down, seemingly trying to figure out what my game was. I was sure he didn't think I was a cop or some kind of investigator.

"I haven't talked to Micheline since Friday when we set things up. She's not one of my regulars. She only works when she needs extra money and likes the guy. Kind of picky in that way."

"Does she have a . . . a day job?"

"How would I know? All I see is a pretty young brunette with a shapely caboose, if you'll excuse the palindrome."

What the actual word he'd been aiming for might have been, I couldn't say. But I had little interest in dissecting his malapropism. "If you don't mind, may I ask what you do, Mr. . . . Burgh, is it?"

"Jimmy Burgh," he said. "And I'm kind of private about my business. You can always ask around, of course. People know me."

"I see. Could you at least tell me Micheline's last name? Maybe her address?"

Burgh smiled at me, revealing a gold incisor on the upper-right side. It wasn't a friendly expression. He came across as nicer when he scowled. "How about you give me your full name and tell me what you do before we go any further? Tit for tat." He glanced at my chest, and I surely blushed.

I would have preferred to remain just Ellie, but I didn't exactly have a choice. I told him.

He nodded. "Which paper do you work for?"

"The *New Holland Republic*," I croaked.

He seemed relieved. I felt embarrassed and insulted for my paper.

"Her name is Charbonneau," he said, and then he spelled it. "Lives in Rensselaer."

"A phone number?" I may have been pushing it.

"You never heard of a phone book?" he asked.

"Thank you, Mr. Burgh. I'll look it up myself, shall I?"

He nodded his approval. I turned to slip back down the stairs.

"Miss Stone," he called, and I stopped. "You're not going to mention my name in your newspaper. You got that?"

"Who's Jimmy Burgh?" I asked Frank Olney. I was seated in a phone booth outside a furniture shop on Central Avenue.

"Who?"

"Jimmy Burgh. I met him in Schenectady a little while ago. Some kind of small-time hoodlum. He provided the girl for Johnny Dornan on Friday night. A pretty young thing named Micheline Charbonneau."

"I can check with Schenectady police," said Frank. "Did he tell you anything useful?"

"Besides a threat not to mention him in my article? No."

"Ellie, are you taking care not to go sniffing around where you shouldn't?" He sounded alarmed. "You don't know who these people are."

"I'm a big girl, Sheriff."

Frank wasn't satisfied. "Where are you?"

"In a phone booth halfway between Schenectady and Albany."

He wanted the number so he could call me back after he'd spoken to the Schenectady police. I appreciated the worry but insisted I could take care of myself. As I waited, I found "Charbonneau, M." in the Albany phone book at an address on Second Avenue in Rensselaer. I wanted to try the number right away but had to cool my heels until Frank called back. A few minutes later, the phone finally rang.

"How do you get yourself mixed up in these things?" he asked without preamble. "This Jimmy Burgh is a real bad character. Gambling, prostitution, fencing goods, running numbers. A real prince. Steer clear of him, Ellie."

I told him I would try, leaving out that Jimmy Burgh already knew my name and where I worked.

"What trouble are you off to find next?"

"*Cherchez la femme.* Micheline Charbonneau. I've got her address. Got to run."

"Be careful."

There was no answer when I dialed Micheline's place, so I decided to chance a visit. Across the river from downtown Albany, the squat, two-story red-brick building sat on the corner of Second Avenue and Walker

Street. Rensselaer. Four apartments, two on each floor. I climbed the stoop and tried the front door. It was open. Inside the poorly lit lobby, I located the names Stevens, Charbonneau, and Schuyler on one of the mailboxes. Apartment 1A.

I rapped on the door and waited for someone to answer. It was nearly two o'clock. I needed to speed things up if I wanted to finish my story in time to catch Harry, the typesetter, before he put Monday's paper to bed. I knocked again, and this time I heard a shuffling behind the door.

The door cracked open, and a young woman peered out at me. She'd been sleeping on her hair. Blonde hair. Her eyes were ringed with black mascara from the night before, and she'd neglected to wipe off her lipstick.

"What is it?" she asked.

"I'm a friend of Micheline's," I lied.

She rubbed her right eye with the heel of her palm and yawned, big and wide. "She's not in."

"Darn. I was hoping to catch her."

The young woman let the door open fully. "How do you know Miche anyway?" She pronounced it *Meesh*.

"She lent me some money," I said, sidestepping her question. "I wanted to return it. My name is Ellie."

I extended a hand. She wiped hers on the robe she was wearing and placed it in mine. Dead fish handshake.

"I'm Joyce Stevens. Come on in. I think we have some iced tea if you're thirsty."

She led the way into the parlor. I could see the kitchen off to the right and a couple of bedrooms down a darkened hallway.

"No church today?" I asked once we'd reached the kitchen.

"Oh, no. I couldn't show my face in church after last night." She giggled, then, perhaps remembering that she didn't know me, put on a serious face. "I mean I'm not very religious."

She reached into the fridge and pulled out a pitcher. I watched her knit her brow and wrinkle her nose as she poured the tea into a glass. Measuring the proper amount was tasking all her faculties.

"Sorry for my appearance," she said as she handed me the tea.

She pushed her hair out of her face, and I saw that she was quite pretty, if you didn't mind bloodshot eyes and day-old makeup. I figured she was twenty-two or twenty-three.

"I met a couple of ROTC fellows from the university last night. Young, but a lot of fun."

"No Micheline?"

"She's in Canada visiting her mother. How do you know Miche, anyway?"

"From work."

"At the Safeway?"

"That's right," I said. "I'm a cashier."

She considered me for a long moment. "Miche never mentioned anyone named Ellie. You don't look like you work at the Safeway."

"Neither does Micheline," I said, bluffing my way.

"Yeah. You're right about that."

"How long has she been away?"

"Since Friday. She's always taking off to visit her mother. A real momma's girl, our Miche."

Micheline was someone else's girl, I thought. And she certainly hadn't been in Canada Friday evening. Either Joyce Stevens was unaware of her friend's night job or she was lying to cover for her. I wasn't convinced she was smart enough to tell a convincing lie.

"Have you known Micheline long?"

"A little more than a year. We were waiting tables at a diner near GE. For a while we got good tips from the guys from the plant. They'd come in just to talk to us."

"So why'd you leave?" I asked.

"The men were all trying to make time with us. We wouldn't have minded if they were single. Or rich." She giggled again. "Then some of them got a little too familiar. All hands. We complained to the owner, and he fired us. My cousin Brenda said she had a couple of free rooms, so we moved down here with her."

"Too bad about the job."

She said it didn't matter. "There's more than one way for a girl to get by."

A second young woman appeared in the kitchen doorway. Fully dressed and presentable at two on a Sunday afternoon, she was a big girl. A pretty brunette in the way Roller Derby queens are pretty. She eyed me with suspicion.

Joyce introduced her as Brenda Schuyler, the third roommate.

"You're a friend of Miche's?" she asked me.

Joyce volunteered that I worked at the Safeway as a cashier. Brenda scowled at her.

"And you believed her?"

"Why shouldn't I?"

Brenda stared daggers at me as she answered her naïve friend. "Because she's got a nice big car outside. And she's a little too smooth around the edges to work at the Safeway, don't you think?"

Joyce didn't know what to say. I wanted to protest her characterization of my car but resisted the urge. Brenda couldn't have known it had once been driven into the lake and had never been quite the same since.

"She can't be a cop," said Brenda. "But don't say another word about Miche or yourself. I don't trust her."

I decided to come clean. "I'm not a cashier at the Safeway. I'm a newspaper reporter from New Holland."

Brenda turned to Joyce and fired a wicked glare at her. "You see why you shouldn't blab to strangers?"

Then she ordered me to leave.

"But wait," said Joyce. "If she's a newspaper reporter, shouldn't we find out what she wants with Miche before we throw her out?"

I explained about the Saturday morning fire at Tempesta and that two bodies had been found in the rubble. Both women appeared spooked. Joyce asked if Micheline was one of the victims.

"I believe it was someone else," I said. "But I can't be sure yet."

"It wasn't Miche," said Brenda. "She's in Canada."

"But there is the possibility it was your friend," I continued, ignoring her pronouncement. "That's why I need your help. When did you last see her?"

"Don't answer her."

Joyce wilted under Brenda's stare. I begged them to tell me where I might find Micheline, but they stuck to the story that she was in Montreal visiting her mother.

"She spent Friday night with a man named Johnny Dornan," I said. "He's a jockey over at Saratoga. And he's the man who was found dead in the barn."

Joyce looked to Brenda, appealing to her for permission to speak openly with me. But Brenda held fast, insisting that Micheline had taken a Greyhound bus to Montreal Saturday morning. Ten minutes later, I'd still made no progress against their intransigence, and Brenda showed me the door with all the civility of a Roller Derby jammer.

CHAPTER SEVEN

I found a secluded phone booth where I could make my calls in peace. There was no time to drive to Saratoga to interview the innkeepers in person, so I filled my purse with change acquired at a nearby Laundromat and started going down the list provided by the chamber of commerce.

As Saratoga hadn't yet entered the world of direct distance dialing, I had to call the operator to connect me to my parties. After more than an hour of slipping nickels and dimes down the slot and asking for one hotel, motor inn, and boarding house after another, I'd gotten nowhere. No guests had disappeared without settling the bill, no one was missing, and several desk clerks I spoke to expressed doubts about the propriety of my inquiries. The man at the Gideon Putnam, in particular, seemed insulted by the suggestion that any of his guests would "skip out" without paying.

Finally, after moving on to the Yellow Pages, I hit upon a possible lead. The Friar Tuck Motel on Route 50 confirmed that a guest—a woman—had not returned to the establishment since leaving in a sedan late Friday night.

"Must've been after eleven," said the woman who'd identified herself as Margaret. "But if she thinks she can run off without paying, she's mistaken. I've got her stuff locked up where she can't get it."

"Anything worth coming back for?" I asked.

After some coaxing, Margaret admitted there was little of value beyond a dented cigarette lighter, a half-drunk fifth of cheap rye, and a suitcase of clothes. It took little effort to convince her to share everything she knew. Perhaps, like Mrs. Russell, Margaret thought I might help her collect from the deadbeat guest.

"She checked into a single room three days ago under the name of Mrs. Everett Coleman of Manitoba, Canada," she recited as if reading from the register. "Of course I discovered later she was stashing a fellow in the room with her."

"He was staying there, too?"

"One night at least. The bed was all mussed on both sides."

"His name wasn't Robinson, by any chance."

"Don't know what his name was. He didn't register."

"Can you describe what they looked like?"

"She was average. Mid to late thirties, I'd say. Best days behind her, but not bad."

"What color was her hair?"

"She was wearing a rain hat when she checked in, but I saw her the next night getting into her car. All dolled up in a fur. Fox, I'd say. Looked to be a brunette. Maybe a redhead. Not a carrottop. More auburn."

"And the man who shared her room? Did you get a look at him?"

"Just a glance Friday night when they were leaving."

"You didn't see his face?"

"No, he was wearing a cap or a hat of some kind. But I can tell you he was a shrimp."

"A shrimp? Like how tall?" I didn't want to influence her with leading questions.

"Put it this way," she said. "Give him a red coat and paint his face black, and he could stand out front as a hitching post."

I felt uncomfortable with her attempt at humor. Was she simply describing a jockey-sized man or adding a ham-fisted bit of racism to her joke? Either way, I needed more information. She'd mentioned a car.

"I assume you record the license plate numbers of your guests."

"Of course we do," she said and put down the phone. There was a sound of shuffling papers—most certainly the register—for several seconds before she came back on the line. "She was driving an older model Chrysler. Black. License B-Y-W-sixty-six."

"B-Y-W-six-six," I repeated, noting the number in my pad. "And that's a Manitoba plate?"

"Nope. Good old New York State."

Margaret's bigotry notwithstanding, I felt encouraged by the information I'd gathered. "Maybe a redhead" and "a shrimp" fit the descriptions of the burned bodies as well as anyone could have hoped. Nevertheless, the characterization of the woman as being in her thirties with her best days behind her troubled me somewhat. That didn't exactly match Jimmy Burgh's "palindrome" of Micheline as a pretty young brunette with a shapely caboose. But for all I knew, Micheline had disguised herself for the consumption of the nosy motel clerk. If she'd wanted to hide her true identity, a wig, a frumpy outfit, and some strategically applied makeup might have done the trick.

I wondered about the timeline. Would she have had time to give Johnny Dornan "a ride" in his room at the boarding house, then drive with him to the Friar Tuck for a costume change? All within an hour and a half? Was I trying too hard to put Micheline in the burned-down barn? Would a dead Micheline make my story any easier to report? I asked myself why I cared either way if it was Micheline or not. I certainly took no pleasure in the thought of her murdered, then incinerated, in the foaling barn at Tempesta Farm. But if she hadn't perished there, some other poor woman had. One way or another, two people were dead. Which brought my thoughts back to the shrimp. Margaret's description pointed to Johnny Dornan as the man in the barn, especially when you took the racing silks into account. Which meant I'd been off base thinking this Coleman woman had been staying with the mysterious Mr. Robinson at the Friar Tuck Motel.

But the Coleman name itself bothered me. Wouldn't it have been convenient if the woman had registered under the name "Mrs. John Dornan"? Instead, I had a mystery that stretched halfway across the continent to Manitoba, Canada. And where in Manitoba?

I slouched against the wall of the phone booth pondering these questions, wondering how to proceed. I could try Bell Canada Information, of course, searching the larger cities first. But Manitoba was a huge, rural province that stretched from the US border in the south to the Northwest Territories and Hudson Bay to the north. Who knew if they even had telephones outside of Winnipeg?

Digging into my purse, I counted the change I had left. About three dollars' worth. Drawing a sigh, I picked up the receiver and dialed 0.

"Manitoba Information, please."

"Mani-what?" came the operator's voice.

"Manitoba, Canada."

As polite and helpful as the Bell Telephone Canada operator was, she could locate no Everett Coleman in Winnipeg. Or in Brandon, Steinbach, or Thompson for that matter. Flin Flon—yes, that's a town in Manitoba— also came up snake eyes. There were plenty of Colemans, all right, but none who answered to the name Everett. I tried a couple of subscribers anyway—those with the initial E—until I ran out of change. None knew anything about Everett Coleman or his redheaded bride.

I considered other options. In the morning, I would ask Norma Geary, my industrious gal Friday, to search the morgue—that was what we called the archives at the paper—for any stories on Everett Coleman. I doubted that would lead to anything, but I had to cover the bases. I also wanted her to check all the nearby phone directories for Robinsons. Individuals and businesses. The lone initial *S* bothered me, of course. If it stood for Robinson's last name, there was no chance of finding who it was. Maybe Johnny Dornan had left off part of the name. Or maybe it hadn't trans- ferred through the paper. No, that wasn't it. The appointment day of Friday followed the initial too closely. Not enough space for any missing letters. I made a mental note to examine again the newspaper Fadge had swiped from Johnny Dornan's room. In the meantime, I still had a trick up my sleeve, even if I was loath to pull it. I knew a fellow at the Department of Motor Vehicles who could look up the license registration for me. But there might be a price to pay for the information. Benny Arnold would surely take the opportunity to extract a date in exchange for his help. Dreading the consequences of such a transaction, I half-heartedly flipped through the phone directory in the booth. What if Mrs. Coleman lived in Schenectady County? It was possible, after all. Her car was registered in New York State.

I couldn't find her in the Schenectady book, but, lo and behold, there was a "Coleman, E." in Halfmoon in the Saratoga County directory. I dialed the number without enough change, unsure of what I would do if someone answered. No one did. The number had been disconnected.

CHAPTER EIGHT

"A bout time you showed up," I said, leaving the kitchen door open for Fadge.

I lived on the second floor of a duplex, above my intrusive and judgmental landlady, Mrs. Giannetti.

"I've got a business to run," he said, dumping an unwieldy paper bag and a pizza on the table, dropping the copy of the *Racing Form* he'd pinned under his arm in the process.

"There's your business," I said, motioning to the paper.

"Hey, I didn't come over here to take grief from you. I came over to get you drunk and have my way with you."

"Give me that pizza. I'm already two drinks ahead of you."

Lounging on my sofa in the parlor, me with my glass of Scotch and Fadge with his quart of beer, I asked him what he'd brought along this night.

"Something I picked up at the Blue Note in Albany last Thursday," he said, reaching into the paper bag. "Nina Simone. *Forbidden Fruit*. How about you?"

In recent months the two of us had begun our own ad hoc music appreciation society. Each of us would bring a new record to our Sunday night pizza party in my apartment after he closed up the store.

"One from my father's collection," I said, producing an LP I'd stashed next to the leg of the sofa. "Villa-Lobos's *Bachianas Brasileiras*. You're going to love this."

Fadge frowned. "That's what you said last week about Janaslov."

"Janáček," I corrected. "Don't worry. You'll like this better. I promise. It's Brazilian."

"What news of Johnny Dornan?" Fadge asked me as we listened to Nina Simone and sipped/gulped our beverages.

"Nothing much so far. I tracked down his date to an apartment in Rensselaer. A professional girl named Micheline, hired by Lou Fleischman as a treat for Johnny. Dropped my story and film off at the paper a couple of hours ago."

"You spoke to his date?"

"No. To her roommates. They insist she's in Montreal."

"And you think she's on a slab in the morgue."

"Could be. But then I spoke to someone at the Friar Tuck Motel on Route Fifty in Saratoga. Do you know the place?"

He coughed up a laugh. "What a dump. A good place to crash with a two a.m. beauty queen you picked up in a saloon."

I fired my most judgmental glare at him, and he quickly changed his tune.

"Not that I would know, of course," he said, sitting up straight and offering to refill my glass.

"Apparently someone fitting the description of the dead woman from Tempesta was staying at the Friar Tuck," I explained as Fadge handed me my drink.

"How can you be sure? You said she was burned to a crisp."

"Except for three things. A bit of red hair survived, an earring, and a scrap of burned fox stole."

"Anything else?"

"A shrimp."

Fadge took a swig of beer and popped the last crust of pizza into his mouth. "Shrimp like the cocktail?"

"Like a jockey. The man she was staying with at the Friar Tuck was a shrimp."

"Sounds like a good bet to me."

"The description of the redhead at the motel sounded a little older than Micheline. Of course she might have been trying to disguise herself."

"You should find out who the lady at the motel is instead of trying to make her fit your solution."

Fadge was right. It was too easy. If I could shoehorn Micheline into the barn with Johnny Dornan, my story would be halfway done. But I knew deep down that it was laziness on my part. The pieces didn't fit together. More likely than not, it was someone else.

"I'm going to drive out to Halfmoon tomorrow and try to get to the bottom of this," I said with a sigh. "There's a man living there with the name the desk clerk provided. It's probably a dead end, but I have to be sure."

"Anything else to go on?"

"A license plate. The car the woman was driving. But that means talking to Benny Arnold. And you know I don't want to do that."

"Leave him to me," said Fadge. "He owes me a favor."

MONDAY, AUGUST 13, 1962

I bolted from the gate Monday morning, grabbing a quick coffee and a hard roll at Fiorello's before heading down to the New Holland Savings Bank. I hadn't set foot in the place since an unsatisfactory tryst with a teller two years earlier had left me with little choice but to transfer my passbook account to another bank. Maybe my erstwhile quick-draw Lothario was on vacation, I told myself. Or perhaps he'd be too busy with the early-morning crowds to notice me. As things turned out, I ran smack into him on the marble steps leading up to the polished brass-and-glass entrance. He pretended not to know me, which suited me fine.

Issur Jacobs was high in the saddle at 9:00 a.m. A clerk announced me to the venerable man, and in short order I was seated before him in his office.

"What's this about Tempesta Farm?" he asked, polishing his pince-nez.

"There was a fire in the early hours of Saturday morning," I said. "Two people died in one of the old foaling barns."

"My God. How terrible."

"You didn't hear about it? No one phoned to let you know?"

"Why should anyone let me know? I no longer have any dealings with the Shaws. We tied up the last of their business four years ago. Now their lawyers handle everything to do with their assets here in New Holland."

I sized up the man sitting behind the leviathan desk that dwarfed him. He was impeccably groomed, small, and bald with fine features. I figured he went for a haircut and shave once a week, and had his nails clipped and buffed at least as often. He sat bolt upright in his leather chair, looking like a captain of industry from the last century. His bow tie was perfectly straight and dimpled at the knot, his vest tight, and his shirtsleeves pressed and starched. Indeed, the only concession he appeared to make to comfort and the summer heat was that he'd doffed his pinstriped jacket and draped it over a hanger behind his desk.

"Then you're not familiar with who's running the farm?"

"No one that I'm aware of. There's nothing left up there except the old barns and the caretaker's house. What you should do, young lady, is speak to Judge Shaw. He was the executor of his father's estate. He'll be able to point you in the right direction."

I must have looked doubtful, since he softened.

"I've seen your articles in the paper, Miss Stone," he said. "Including two years ago when poor Jordan Shaw was murdered. Is that why you're reluctant to speak to the judge?"

"Of course not," I said, in a pathetic attempt at bravado. "I met Judge Shaw several times during the investigation. And his wife, too."

"Yes, Audrey Shaw." He nodded but offered nothing else to illuminate his thoughts on her.

He didn't really need to. I knew Audrey Shaw and her cold enmity toward me all too well. She had wielded her maternal grief like a dagger to slice out my heart as I struggled to come to grips with my own father's murder a year before her daughter's.

"Then there's nothing I can do to help you," he said.

I stared at him, wishing so much that he could offer something more. Something to obviate the need to meet or speak with Judge Shaw or his cruel wife.

"You seem like a nice girl," he said. I had my doubts. "A nice Jewish girl. Why don't you come to services next Friday?"

"I beg your pardon."

"Services. At the temple on Mohawk Place. Friday. We've a fine rabbi and a new cantor. The community is starved for new faces. And there are a couple of nice young boys I could introduce you to. From good families."

"Oh, Mr. Jacobs, I don't think so."

"You've been away too long from your faith. Your people, young lady. Come back."

"Thank you for your time, Mr. Jacobs," I said, averting my eyes from his persistent stare. "I've got to be going now."

⁊⊙

As Vinnie Donati gassed up my Dodge Lancer at Ornuti's Garage, I phoned Norma Geary at the paper from the booth inside. She answered her line on the first ring and greeted me with congratulations for my story, which was set to appear in the afternoon edition. I asked her to try to dig up some information on Johnny Dornan. Where was he from? Where did he learn to ride horses? Anything she might find would be helpful.

"And can you search the local phone books for him and a man or a business named Robinson S.? That might be an initial. Or maybe nothing. I don't know."

"Will do," she said. "What else?"

"I'm also trying to find the name Everett Coleman, but not in the phone directory. I've already got that. I'm wondering if there's a newspaper article. An arrest, a wedding, anything."

"I'm on it, Miss Stone." Norma liked to call me that despite my many attempts to convince her that I preferred Ellie. I'd finally given up and accepted it as a charming quirk of our relationship.

Back outside at the pump, Vinnie asked me if I'd heard about the fire out at Tempesta Farm. I said maybe.

"Five people and ten horses died," he announced.

I forked over three dollars for the gas. "Don't believe everything you hear, Vinnie."

There was a stop downtown I should have made on my way out of town, but I couldn't quite bring myself to pay a visit to Judge Shaw's office on Main Street. Sure, I told myself, I'd call him later. Maybe that same day. But my trip to Halfmoon was more important. In truth, I doubted I'd find anything of value on my fishing expedition. The phone had been disconnected, after all. Mr. and Mrs. E. Coleman had surely long since departed or simply perished in the fire on Tempesta Farm. Still, the prospect of driving fifty minutes to the far end of Saratoga County appealed to me more than climbing a flight of stairs to Judge Harrison Shaw's chambers, located a couple of blocks from the *New Holland Republic*'s offices on Main Street.

It was past ten thirty when I pulled into the dirt-and-grass driveway. If forced to guess, I'd say no vehicle had used it in at least five years. The old clapboard farmhouse, long since stripped of its protective paint, was mostly gray with liver spots and warping weather panels. It was listing visibly to port, and I feared a stiff breeze might well knock it over. The deck of the front porch had collapsed on one side, and the torn screen door in the entrance hung half open by the rusty bottom hinge, the only one of three still dispatching its duties. The yard was overgrown in places and hard, bare dirt in others. An old garage, doors thrown open wide, was crammed with junk, and the carcass of an old pickup at least thirty years old languished shipwrecked in a sea of tall grass beyond the end of the drive.

I climbed out of my Dodge and approached the pile of lumber with care. I even left the driver's door open in case I needed to make a quick escape from what looked like an amusement park haunted house. This was the address I'd found in the phone booth directory the day before, the one listed as "Coleman, E." I climbed the steps gingerly, fearing a fall through the rotting boards, but they bore my weight, such as it was, and saw me safely to the door. I rapped three times on the dusty glass behind the screen and waited. A second attempt roused something inside.

"If you're here for the meter, it's broke," came a man's voice from some-where inside.

I explained that I was not there to read the meter.

"I said it's broke, and I'm not paying for no electricity."

"I'm not from Niagara Mohawk," I called out as a man in his late fifties or early sixties appeared in the doorway. His face was long and haggard, with a week's growth of black-and-gray whiskers sprouting from his chin. He was wearing a long undershirt and, so it appeared, nothing else. I wanted to avert my frightened gaze, but the shotgun he was pointing at my chest held my attention.

"You're not from the electric company," he said as if to accuse. All of his upper incisors were missing, and canines, too. The rest of his teeth didn't appear to be long for this world either.

"I've been trying to tell you that," I said.

He lowered the gun. Now it was pointing at my knees. "Then who are you?"

I gave him an abbreviated explanation. He didn't strike me as the patient type, and until he put the weapon away, I wasn't resting easy.

"Do you know a man named Everett Coleman?" I asked.

"Are you funning me?"

"No, I'm looking for Mr. and Mrs. Everett Coleman."

"What for?"

There was no way to sugarcoat this. I drew a deep breath and explained. "Because I think they died in a fire Saturday morning."

More confused than ever, the old man gaped at me. He let the muzzle of his shotgun drop until it was pointing at his own feet. I was safe for the present.

"Everett Coleman, you say?"

I nodded.

"I'm Everett Coleman. And my wife's been dead for eight years. No great loss there. She run off with a trucker and left me with the girl."

"Do you own a black Chrysler by any chance?"

He scoffed. "A Chrysler? I don't own nothing, can't you see? Nothing except for this shack of a house." He made a limp gesture with his left hand, as if to showcase the property.

"Have you ever been to Manitoba?"

"What business would I have in Africa?"

Of all the false leads I'd ever chased, this might have been the oddest. As I was searching for the words to excuse myself without scaring him into hoisting his shotgun again, I decided to cover the last base and ask one more question.

"You mentioned a girl. What girl?"

"I'm gonna put some pants on," he said. "Then you can come inside, and we'll talk."

"Actually, I prefer to wait outside."

He tilted his head and aimed a crazy eye at me. I thought for a moment that he was going to squeeze the trigger a mite too hard, discharge his weapon, and blow off a couple of his toes.

"I'm sorry," I said. "Of course I'll come in."

Clothes make the man. Everett Coleman slipped into an old pair of trousers and donned a short-sleeve shirt for receiving hours. He offered me some water in a grimy glass, which I sedulously avoided. We sat opposite each other in the parlor, him on the worn sofa, me on a wooden chair. I asked if he minded if I smoked. His eyes grew to twice their size, so I held out the package to him. He leaned forward on the couch and, ogling the cigarettes with avidity, rubbed his fingers together as a greedy child might while trying to decide which chocolate to choose from a sampler.

"Take the whole pack," I said at length. "I've got another in my purse."

I didn't need to repeat the offer. In short order, he'd lit a cigarette and leaned back on the sofa to take a deep drag. Then another.

"The wife left me when I was serving in the navy overseas," he said without preamble. Smoke oozed from his nostrils. "I was wounded at Guadalcanal. Shrapnel from a shell in my hip. Can't walk straight no more, at least not without a lot of pain."

"I'm sorry."

"Won the Purple Heart. But Betty, she didn't care. Didn't even bother to send a Dear John letter. All I got was a wire from my sister saying that no-good tramp of a wife of mine dropped off my girl and run away with a long-haul trucker named Len. Some shirker with a 4-F classification."

"How terrible. How old was your daughter?"

"Sixteen at the time. She was born in twenty-six."

"It must have been hard on a young girl, losing her mother like that."

"Well, they were cut from the same cloth, mother and daughter. So no great loss, like I said."

"What's your daughter's name?"

He squeezed the cigarette between his lips and sucked the life out of it. "Vivian. After my sainted mother." He frowned and stared at the smoldering end of his smoke. "She didn't do honor to the name."

Everett Coleman told the sad tale of an undisciplined, wayward daughter. A wild child through her early teens, and a lying, smoking, drinking, car-stealing dropout by the age of sixteen. At seventeen, she married a boy five years her senior and moved away.

"Good riddance to bad garbage," he said.

He gave me her married name—McLaglen—and said the last time he'd heard from her was in October of 1943, when she dropped by with her baby-faced husband, Ernie, to ask for money. He didn't give her any.

"I was flat on my back, just back from the convalescent hospital downstate. Recuperating from my wounds. I didn't have enough money for myself, so I wasn't about to fork anything over to her and that good-for-nothing husband of hers."

Ernie McLaglen died in Korea seven years later, according to Coleman. He'd seen a notice in the paper. But that day in 1943 was the last time he'd seen his daughter. Vivian hadn't even shown up when his "no-good tramp of an ex-wife, Betty," died from cirrhosis of the liver in 1954. Betty had come back to die in South Glens Falls, where she'd come from, after years of jumping from one loser's bed to another's.

I asked Everett Coleman if he had a photograph of his daughter. Finally, after nearly twenty minutes and three cigarettes, the penny dropped, and he asked me what my business was anyway.

"As I mentioned before, there was a fire Saturday morning. On a horse farm over by the Montgomery County line. A man and a woman were killed."

He nodded slowly, his tired lips sagging a bit into something almost resembling a frown. "And you think it was Vivian?"

"It's a possibility."

"Well, it don't make no difference to me. Not now. She's been dead to me for years."

"Would you have a photograph of her?" I repeated.

CHAPTER NINE

Everett Coleman didn't know anyone named Robinson, but at least I had a couple of names to go after. Vivian Coleman and Vivian McLaglen. How Manitoba figured in the story, I had no idea. It might well have been a random choice on Vivian's part. I would worry about that later.

I phoned Sheriff Pryor from a gas station on Route 9, hoping he'd be interested in trading information now that I had something to offer in return. A deputy informed me the sheriff was out and took my contact information with an unconvincing promise that he'd call me back.

Knowing I could always count on my pal Frank Olney to help, I dialed the operator and asked for the Montgomery County sheriff. Within thirty seconds, he was on the line. I explained the situation, that I was in possession of two new names to track down, and the Saratoga sheriff's office wasn't available to help. He said he could check with the state police in Albany to see if they had any information on Vivian McLaglen or Vivian Coleman.

"I'll stop by to see you later," I said, ready to hang up.

"I've got a court appointment. I'll find you this evening. Fiorello's at six?"

"I'll buy you a cherry Coke."

❧

I spent a few hours at the paper, making calls and writing copy for Tuesday's edition. Between meetings with Charlie Reese and dodging the publisher, Artie Short, I managed to reach Sheriff Pryor by phone. Since I didn't want to give away any of my information for nothing, I had to play it cool, testing the waters as it were. In no time, however, Pryor made it clear that he wasn't interested in anything I might have stumbled across.

"I think I can run this investigation better if I keep the press out of my hair," he said after I'd cast my lure.

"But are there any developments?" I asked. "Has anyone been reported missing in Saratoga?"

"No one yet." I could tell he was itching to hang up.

"Do you have plans to make any statements to the press about the case?"

"Not at this time."

"Will you put out an alert to the local papers before you do?"

"I'll let you know," he said, and ended the call.

Norma Geary appeared at my side, holding a few folders to her chest. She reached around my right shoulder and placed one of them on the desk before me.

"What's this?" I asked.

"Photograph of Johnny Dornan."

I opened the folder and examined the picture, a tight, five-and-a-half-by-eight-inch shot of a young man's face. He was beaming from beneath a racing helmet, and I was sure it had been taken in the winner's circle and that Johnny was still perched on the saddle of his mount. His jaw was strong, chin cleanly shaven, teeth straight and white, and his fair eyes twinkled against his tanned skin. I couldn't tell the color in the black-and-white photo. Studying the young jockey with care, though, I fancied I saw a fierce competitive streak in him, bubbling up from deep inside.

"Kind of handsome, wouldn't you say?" I asked Norma.

"Not bad. Funny, he doesn't look short enough to be a jockey."

"I should hope not. All you can see is his head." I slipped the photo into my purse. "What else do you have for me?"

"A list of Robinsons in the Albany-Schenectady-Troy area," she said, placing another folder before me. "And Saratoga County, too. Plenty of names to go through."

"What about Everett Coleman? Nothing in the papers?"

"Not yet. It's like searching for a needle in a haystack. But I'll keep trying."

"Anything else?"

"There's this," she said, producing a third folder from her collection. "Vivian McLaglen's wedding announcement."

I gave a start. "From nineteen forty-three?"

"No," she said, flipping open the file and pointing to the notice in question in a yellowing newspaper clipping. "This is from fifty-one."

"That's odd," I said. "Her father didn't mention that she'd remarried. Of course they aren't close, but still."

The article appeared to be one of a thousand social announcements from any small-town newspaper anywhere in the country. There was the grainy photograph of the bride sitting in a plain dress with a bouquet in her lap. No gown, no pomp. Pretty much what you'd expect for a second wedding, especially for a war widow. She was quite pretty despite the lack of zeal in her expression. I calculated in my head. She was still shy of her twenty-fifth birthday on what was her second wedding day. Nothing extraordinary there. But then I noticed the folio at the top of the page.

"This is from the *Republic*," I said. "'Dateline Rensselaer, NY.' And it's not the social page. This is a wire story on page three."

"That's not all, Miss Stone. Did you notice the headline?"

I hadn't. And when I did I was even more confused.

"But this says she married someone named Tommy McLaglen. That can't be."

I read further. And I realized why the wire service had picked up the story. Vivian McLaglen had married her own brother-in-law. What on the surface appeared to be a heartwarming human-interest story was really a not-so-subtle lampoon of the inbred hillbillies who kept things in the family: "War Widow Finds Love Close to Home," was the subhead. I found it mean-spirited and humorous at the same time.

"How on earth did you find this?" I asked Norma.

"A gal has to have some secrets," she said, and I stared at her. "Okay, I confess that I was getting nowhere until I asked Mr. Reese how I might find a name from an old news story. He said to ask Mr. Rayburn."

"Rayburn the Linotype operator?"

"The very same. He remembered this story, and I dug it out of an old box in the basement. Remarkable memory he has."

Barney Rayburn was a little gray man who wandered around the plant wearing oversized eyeglasses that resembled welding goggles. They were constantly slipping down his nose, which only drew attention to the perpetual expression of befuddlement on his face. For the first year I was at the paper, I thought he was trying to remember whether he'd left his car's headlights on. So to produce a name from a ten-year-old wire story about a quasi-incestuous wedding in Rensselaer qualified as remarkable indeed.

"So what does it mean?" asked Norma.

"The fact that she married her brother-in-law? I have no idea."

⁂

Fadge was tying on a freshly laundered apron when I strolled in at quarter to six. He was wearing that half-frightened, half-gleeful look I'd seen on his face before. As if perhaps he'd just caught the mayor stealing cigarettes, had thrown him into the gutter by the seat of his pants, and couldn't wait to tell someone. The place was deserted.

"What's wrong with you?" I asked.

He motioned for me to follow him to the back room. There among the cases of soda and ice-cream freezers, he wiped his perspired face with the skirt of his new apron.

"What is it?" I repeated.

"El, you can't tell anyone."

"Tell them what?"

"I just got back from the races."

"The races? Who was minding the store?"

"No one. I closed up today. But that's not the point. Listen to me."

"Fadge, you're going to go broke if you close in August. Come January you'll be bellyaching that no one's buying ice cream."

He was nearly shaking now, glancing through the open door to the empty store outside. "El, will you shut up and listen? I closed the store and went to the track."

"And?"

"And?" He licked his lips. "I won three thousand dollars."

I stumbled back against the ice-cream freezer. "You won how much?"

"I was on fire. Couldn't miss. Everything I picked came in."

"But three thousand dollars?"

He shushed me and threw another glance outside. Still no one there.

"I was so hot that I started cashing in my tickets at different windows so no one would know how much I was winning. And I left after the seventh to avoid suspicion."

"You won three grand in seven races?"

He gulped and nodded. "It was unreal. I started with the daily double. It paid two hundred and twenty-two bucks. And I had it three times. I was up more than six fifty before I knew it. The long shots were coming up winners today. And I've been playing Johnny Sellers since the start of the meet. He's the jockey leading the way for the racing title this year, and he didn't let me down today."

I still couldn't quite believe it. Three thousand dollars in four hours. It didn't seem possible.

"What are you going to do with the money?" I asked, breathless.

His eyes twitched back and forth a couple of times, then focused somewhere in the distance. "I'm going to reinvest it," he said at length.

"In the store?"

"Hell, no. The meet's barely started. With this bankroll, I've got a chance to make a big score."

"You can't be serious. You'll lose it. Spend it on something. Enjoy it. You'll never have another windfall like this again."

The bell above the door out front jingled, and Fadge jumped.

"Jesus. It's Frank Olney," he said. "Do you suppose he heard about the money?"

"Relax. You didn't do anything illegal. Besides, he's here to meet me."

I warned Fadge that we weren't through discussing his dangerous gambling habit, then went out to meet Frank. For our comfort, he indicated the booth that butted up against the post office cage opposite the soda fountain. Fiorello's housed a small annex of the city post office. Fadge was authorized to sell stamps, make out money orders, and weigh packages like a normal postal employee. I'd never understood why he would want the extra hassle, but he maintained that it brought in business.

Yeah, for the post office, I'd thought.

The bench creaked under Frank's considerable weight as we sat down. For his part, Fadge ducked into the post office cage and stashed his winnings in the United States government safe. I could hear him spinning the dial and twisting the latch. I wondered how many federal statutes he was breaking by doing so. And with a law enforcement officer not five feet away.

"Any luck on Vivian Coleman?" I asked Frank, putting Fadge's felonies to one side.

"Quite a bit, actually," he said, tenting his fingers on the table between us. "She's got an arrest record as long as your arm. Dating back to her teens. Car theft, writing rubber checks, and wire fraud."

"Oh, my," I said, thinking her father may have had a point about how rotten she was after all.

"And there was a morals charge in Albany back in fifty-two. Busted in a man's hotel room."

"Did any of it stick?"

"The morals charge did. She did five months in county jail."

"Sounds like trouble."

Frank nodded. "And you think she might be the lady in the barn?"

"It seems more and more likely. I've seen a couple of photographs of her when she was younger. Hard to tell hair color in black-and-white, but she could have been a redhead." I drew a sigh. "Her father told me she was always dyeing her hair a different color, so who knows?"

"Are you two going to order anything?" That was Fadge, who'd appeared above us.

"I'm trying to watch my weight, Ron," said the sheriff, who wasn't there to patronize the store.

Fadge stared at him. "We've got No-Cal Soda."

"Isn't that for housewives on a diet?" asked Frank.

"Works for sheriffs, too."

Looking horribly embarrassed, Frank nodded and said sure. I ordered a Coke.

"Did you tell Sheriff Pryor your suspicions about the two women?" he asked once Fadge had shuffled back to the counter. "Might help him narrow down the options on an ID."

"He's not playing nice, so I didn't tell him. I thought maybe you could let him know and get him to tell you something more."

"Okay. I'll say I got an anonymous tip."

"Thanks."

"What about the man inside the barn? You still think it's that jockey?"

"Yes, I'm sure. The woman who checked into the Friar Tuck Motel over in Saratoga was with a man who answers Johnny Dornan's description."

"What exactly was the description?"

"A shrimp. The clerk said she was with a very short fellow in a cap of some kind. That's all she saw."

Frank frowned. "Sounds about right. So what's your next step?"

"Actually," I said as Fadge arrived with a Coke for me and a bottle of

No-Cal ginger ale for Frank, "I was waiting for Ron, here, to tell me how his conversation with Benny Arnold from the DMV went today."

I patted the bench next to me, signaling for my big friend to join us. He glanced back at the door, and, finding no one clamoring for a sundae, he slipped in next to me. *Slipped* may be overstating the case. I wondered silently which of the two men weighed more, Fadge or Frank. They called to mind a wrestling tag team. The only thing missing was the tights.

"What are you smiling about?" asked Fadge, glaring in my direction. I wiped the grin off my lips and prompted him again about Benny.

"I talked to him this morning. Before I left for the track."

"Did he have a name and address for the car?"

"He said he'd drop by here after work to let me know what he found."

That was my signal to hightail it out of there. I didn't want to be cornered by him again. But, as luck would have it, Benny was just climbing the stoop. Fadge squeezed out of the booth when he heard the bell above the door.

"How are you doing, Benny?" he asked.

Hoping to remain hidden in the booth, I tried to shrink into the wall. Frank caught on and maintained silence over his bottle of No-Cal, but I feared Fadge would like nothing better than to make a little sport of my discomfort.

After ten minutes of small talk at the counter, Fadge finally asked Benny if he'd followed up on his query of that morning. The DMV clerk said something I couldn't make out from my hiding spot, but Fadge seemed to appreciate his answer.

"This is great," he said. "Thanks."

"Say, Ron. What do you want with this information anyway?" asked Benny.

Fadge didn't miss a beat. He explained that the car in question had backed into his outside the track. The woman driver never even turned around. She roared off but not before Fadge had memorized the plate number.

"I can see why you're sore about it," said Benny. "Your Nash is a wreck."

Fadge said nothing, but I knew he was stewing. Despite the car's dents and backfiring, he was attached to his Ambassador as only a torturer could love his victim. You always hurt the one you love.

Benny excused himself, saying he had to get home to watch *To Tell the*

Truth and *Pete and Gladys* with his mother before turning in. I mouthed, "*Pete and Gladys?*" to Frank across the table, but all he had to offer in return was an indifferent shrug.

"*Pete and Gladys* finishes at eight," I whispered. "His mother puts him to bed at eight."

But just when I thought I'd escaped an awkward meeting with the DMV clerk, that fat rat Fadge stabbed me in the back.

"Hey, Benny, do me a favor, will you?" he asked from his position behind the counter. "Before you go, would you mind handing me that glass I left in the booth over there?"

I was trapped. The interview that ensued was painful enough. But watching Fadge make faces at me from behind Benny was more than a girl should have to endure. I silently vowed revenge on my so-called friend as Benny asked me—again—why I wouldn't go on a date with him.

"Am I too unattractive?"

"No, not because of that, Benny," I said, realizing it had come out all wrong. "It's just, well, you're not Jewish."

"Actually, I am."

Damn. That had backfired.

"Reform?" I asked tentatively.

"No. Conservative."

"Reform," I said with woe, pointing a finger at myself.

CHAPTER TEN

I reclined on the sofa, drink sweating on the end table, and the hi-fi playing Bruch's *Scottish Fantasy*, which somehow reminded me of the rolling hills of Tempesta Farm, especially in the cool August we'd been experiencing. But, in the end, I knew it was a delusion. A will-o'-the-wisp. This wasn't Scotland, even if the town of Scotia was barely eight miles from the spot where two people had perished in a barn fire only two days before. Nevertheless, the music provided a suitable score for the whiskey I was enjoying. I sketched out my plans for the next morning, starting with a visit to the address Benny Arnold had given to Fadge. The one associated with Vivian Coleman's license plate. Race Avenue in South Glens Falls. That would be a long drive, even farther than the trip I'd made to Half-moon that morning. I unfolded a map and spread it out on the low table before the sofa to plan my itinerary. Not only would Route 9 take me to South Glens Falls, but it also passed through Saratoga Springs. To kill two birds, I decided that I could stop to pay an early visit to Sheriff Pryor on the way.

I was restless. I wanted to sleep, but my constitution didn't allow for bedtime so soon after the closing credits of *Pete and Gladys*. And I was hungry. At half past ten, I feasted on a banquet of cocktail weenies and kosher pickles from the icebox. Meat and vegetables, I reasoned. There was nothing worth watching on television, so, to clear my head, I tore through the day's crossword puzzle in a matter of minutes. That finished, I pored over the list of Robinsons from the local phone books that Norma had prepared for me. It was a daunting task. More than a hundred. I decided to concentrate on the Saratoga County Robinsons. There were twenty-nine private subscribers and five businesses. I ruled out the women, not sure I was doing the right thing. But I thought men tended to refer to women by their given, not family names. That reduced my number to seventeen men named Robinson in Saratoga County. My head was spinning, and I resolved to ask Norma to phone each of them in the morning. There was one place, Robinson's High Life Tavern, that I wanted to see for myself.

Next I set my mind to thinking about Vivian McLaglen and her two husbands. Maybe she'd loved them both. Maybe she'd only loved one. But of all the men in the world whom she might have married, she'd chosen two brothers. That intrigued me.

∂〇

TUESDAY, AUGUST 14, 1962

I rose early, dressed, and skipped down the stairs to my car. Normally, I would have stopped by Fiorello's to say good morning to my pal, but it was six thirty, and he was still snoring like a tractor in his bed. Instead I stopped for a roll and a cup of coffee at Dean's a few blocks away. If Fadge had ever found out, he'd have killed me. He had a funny way of demanding customer loyalty even when his store was closed.

It was a few minutes past seven when the deputy at the desk of the Saratoga sheriff's office told me that Pryor was busy and couldn't see me. I left my phone number again without much hope of a return call. On my way out of town, I drove down Union Avenue heading for Route 9. I turned onto East Avenue and noticed the Oklahoma Training Track on my right, directly across Union Avenue from the main racecourse. Thinking I might squeeze in a few minutes to take some photographs of the horses running through their morning paces, I pulled over and climbed out of my car. Admission was free, after all, and South Glens Falls wasn't going anywhere.

There was a modest grandstand on one side and some racing fans milling about alongside the track admiring the Thoroughbreds. A man was selling newspapers and the *Racing Form* at the entrance. I picked up a copy of the *Saratogian* and handed him a dime. He dished out three cents' change without even looking up at me. I wandered over to the track and leaned against the rail to check the headlines.

Riots in Berlin on the anniversary of the Red wall, two Soviets orbiting Earth, and the continuing saga of accused spy Dr. Robert Soblen. But I wasn't interested in international news that morning. I turned to the local stories and found a short mention of the Tempesta fire on page three. There was no byline. I knew Sheriff Pryor had spoken to the *Saratogian*.

What I couldn't understand was why the paper wasn't screaming bloody murder. The single-paragraph story only went as far as labeling the fire that had claimed two lives as "suspicious."

The smell of freshly tilled dirt, made more pungent by the hints of horse sweat and manure hanging in the air, left little doubt that I was at a racetrack. A thundering of hooves rounded the home turn and grew louder as it approached, shaking the ground beneath my feet. Then three or four Thoroughbreds roared past, and the tremor moved on like a wave, receding into the distance. Squinting into the weak sun and reveling in the cool breeze, I watched them disappear into a slow mist rising from the turf of the infield to the east.

Having retrieved my Leica from my purse, I loaded some Kodachrome and began shooting the scene. Horses under riders off in the distance, galloping then cantering then walking through their workouts, their powerful lungs puffing billows of steam through their nostrils. Then there were the men with binoculars pacing along the rail, stopwatches pressed into the palms of their hands. I snapped a few frames of one of them, a well-dressed gentleman who was all business, as he scribbled—I can only presume—the dates, time of day, furlongs, and splits for the horses he was tracking. Fadge had taught me the word "split."

I shot a few more photos of the sun warming the grandstand and was about to screw on a longer lens when a voice from behind me on the track warned me to watch out.

I turned, ducked, and pushed back from the rail, coming face-to-face with a great black horse frisking to a stop a few feet away from me. Knees folded high against his midsection, a jockey leaned forward in the saddle atop the animal. I recognized the colors first—black-and-orange diamonds—then the beautiful beast, his smooth coat ashimmer, steaming perspiration. Purgatorio. He studied me with one eye, much as he had a couple of days before, but this time he might have been wondering why I wasn't snapping pictures of him, handsome boy that he was. He bobbed his head twice, jerking at his reins and clacking the bit in his mouth. Then he settled down and stepped sideways, inching closer to the rail.

"Whoa, boy," said the jockey. "Don't be afraid, miss. Tory won't hurt you."

The horse lowered his head and issued a soft blow from his nostrils. Then he nickered and leaned over the rail. I reached up and asked the jockey if it was safe to pet him. The horse, not the jockey. He smiled and said sure. Purgatorio twitched when I touched his nose, pulling back.

"Doesn't he like me?" I asked.

"Give him a chance," said the jockey. "He's skittish by nature. Doesn't warm to just anyone. But he likes you, or he would've taken a bite out of your hand."

I stood back to give him some space as I admired him. "You call him Tory?"

"Purgatorio's a mouthful."

In his place, I probably would have ended up calling him Purgie. Tory seemed more dignified.

"He's such a beautiful fellow," I said. "Did he have a good workout this morning?"

"Not bad. He runs with a lot of joy out here on the practice track. Loves to stretch his legs, provided there are no other horses too close."

I sensed Purgatorio knew we were talking about him. He watched me with interest, and his ears swiveled like a cat's each time the jockey mentioned his name.

"Will he be racing anytime soon?"

The jockey thumped the horse affectionately on the neck a couple of times, producing a series of resounding whacks, as if beating a kettledrum with a mallet. That seemed to soothe the animal.

"We'll see, won't we, boy?" he said to Purgatorio, but actually addressing me.

"Is it true that he's spooked by other horses?"

"Not so much afraid. He just doesn't like them. But he does get spooked by the starting gate. Sometimes he'll kick and buck and won't go in. Depends on the day."

"If he doesn't like horses, who does he like?"

"The grooms. Some of his riders, too. And you."

The horse took a confident step in my direction, and I held out an open hand to show my good intentions. He snuffed my palm, then nudged it with his muzzle.

"You'd better give him a treat when you hold your hand out like that, or else . . ."

"He'll take a bite out of it?"

"That's right."

"I've got some Life Savers in my purse."

"No. That's not on his diet. Bring him some Cheerios next time you come. He'll love you for it."

I introduced myself, and the jockey did the same. Mike.

"May I take a picture of him?" I asked, lifting my camera for inspection.

"Sure."

I aimed my Leica at Tory, and he snapped to attention, tossing his head back as if to flip the forelock out of his eyes. "Do you work for Mr. Fleischman?"

"Yeah," said Mike as I focused and clicked off a few shots. "I work for his trainer, Hal Brown."

"Are you going to race today?"

He blushed. "No. I'm only an apprentice. A morning rider. Maybe in a couple of years I'll get my chance. Maybe not; I'm a little tall."

"How little?"

"Five-six and a half. Mr. Brown says maybe I could ride jumpers."

"Jumpers?"

"Steeplechase horses. They carry more weight than the flat racers. That means jockeys can be a little taller. And heavier."

Unsure of how I might lighten his load, I commiserated to the extent I could. Then I offered to take a couple of photos of him and the horse.

Mike beamed and struck what looked like a practiced pose atop the horse. One that perhaps he hoped to use in a couple of years under a blanket of flowers in the winner's circle. I got five good frames of the two of them, and I wondered which liked the camera more, the horse or the rider.

"I'll bring you prints in a day or two. Will I find you here?"

"I'm here most every day. Except Sundays."

I turned my attention back to Purgatorio and patted him tentatively on the muzzle. This time he submitted.

"He's very sweet. You said he likes his riders. What about Johnny Dornan? Did he ever ride him?"

"Once," said Mike. "But Tory, here, didn't like Johnny, did you, boy?" He thumped him again on the neck. "I don't like the SOB either, if that counts for anything."

"Funny, he seems perfectly nice in his photograph."

"I guess you can fool the camera after all."

"Do you know if Mr. Robinson liked Johnny?" I asked, trying a new tack for this particular question. Spring it on him casually.

"Who's Mr. Robinson?"

⁂

"Beautiful horse," came a voice to my left as I watched Tory trot off toward the barn with Mike aboard.

I glanced back to find a man in his late twenties or early thirties, dressed in a well-tailored, checked sport coat and tan slacks. He had the *Racing Form* tucked under his right arm and wore a pair of field glasses around his neck. I thought he cut a tall and slim figure as he gazed off into the distance, ostensibly admiring Purgatorio recede from view.

"He is," I said, turning to face him properly. "Purgatorio. Harlequin Stables."

"Not a great runner," observed my companion. Now he was jotting a note into his *Racing Form*, showing little interest in me.

"He doesn't like other horses running alongside him. And is spooked by the starting gate." Why did I insist on pretending to be an expert on racing?

He lifted his head and looked me in the eye. "That would explain why he doesn't win."

"Blinders might help."

"Not that boy. He's a beauty, for sure. But better suited as a photo model. I saw how he mugged for your camera."

"You were watching me?" I asked.

He smiled. "Not exactly."

"Are you one of those clockers?"

"You know about clockers?"

"A little."

"Well, I'm not a clocker. I was watching the ponies the way I do every morning in August. Then you walked into the picture and brightened the view."

I stared at him for a long moment. "You're awfully fresh."

"So I've been told. Usually with a slap in the face. Since you haven't gone to that extreme, I'm hoping I'm on solid footing."

"The jury's still out. Now if you'll excuse me."

"Then I'll say good day, miss."

I nodded and strode off toward the exit, enjoining myself not to turn back for a look. But at the gate I couldn't resist a peek. He was there where I'd left him, now leaning against the rail, watching me still. I surely blushed and scolded myself with a not-so-silent oath.

Robinson's High Life Tavern was a Colored bar on Congress Street in Saratoga. The place was empty and dark on a Tuesday morning, but outside on the stoop, a stocky man of about forty was hosing off the steps. I called to him from over his shoulder. He turned and removed his right thumb from the hose's nozzle, and the jet of water slackened into a weak dribble.

"I'm trying to locate a man named Johnny Dornan," I said.

"Johnny Dornan? The jockey?"

"You know him?"

"Not personally. But do you think a man gets to my age without having some bad habits?" He squeezed the end of the hose again and returned to the task at hand. "I've been playing the horses since I was ten years old, young lady. Book bets, too." He glanced back at me. "That's not for public consumption, you understand."

"I'm not a cop."

"Didn't think you were. But what do you want with Johnny Dornan anyway?"

"He's disappeared. I'm a reporter trying to locate him."

"Well, he doesn't hang out in my tavern, I can tell you that. Skinny little white boys are pretty scarce around here. What made you think he had business in this part of town?"

"He had a meeting at midnight last Friday with someone named Robinson. Or maybe a place called Robinson's."

"My name's Robinson, all right. Horace Robinson, proprietor." He threw his left thumb over his shoulder to indicate the bar behind him. "But I never met your jockey. Don't believe I ever bet on him either."

So much for the High Life Tavern. And Horace Robinson, proprietor, too.

"But I know some folks who've met him." He tucked in his chin and bowed his head to fix me with a knowing stare.

"Bookies like yourself, perhaps?" I asked.

He chuckled. "You're a funny one, you know that? You come here all young and innocent, like a lost schoolgirl. Then you start asking about bookies."

"You haven't answered my question, Mr. Robinson."

"I'm not going down that road, miss. I'm only saying that your boy Johnny Dornan had some shady connections. And word is he can be bought."

"And you couldn't steer your way clear to give me a name?"

"The name I'm thinking of wouldn't like it. No, miss, not at all."

"Thank you for your time, Mr. Robinson."

He regarded me with just the hint of a curious grin on his lips. He cocked his head, wished me luck, and returned to his hosing.

"We open at noon," he said, his back to me. "Good drinks and hot food. But not too many white folks."

I pulled into a crumbling vacant lot on Race Avenue between First and Second Streets and parked in front of a two-story building. A sign announced Lou's Bar. At the top of a rickety flight of external stairs, there appeared to be a small apartment on the second floor. Across the empty lot, a tire shop, cordoned off by a chain-link fence, presented lopsided towers of worn-out tires, rusting rims, and grimy tools in every imaginable shape and size. Not too far off was the Patrician Paper factory, which surely employed half the town.

The mailbox at the base of the stairs bore no name, just the street number. I was about to climb up to the second story to knock when a man stepped out of the dark bar. About fifty, dressed in a flannel shirt with the sleeves cut off, he looked me over for a few seconds before asking what I wanted.

"I'm trying to reach the people who live upstairs," I said.

"There's no one up there."

"No Mr. and Mrs. Coleman?"

"Who?"

"Coleman," I repeated.

"No. There was a couple about a year ago." He stroked his chin and searched his memory. "Now what was their name?"

"Was it McLaglen, by any chance?"

"That was it. They only stayed a couple of weeks; then they lit out."

"They didn't sign a lease?"

He shook his head. "Who would sign a lease for this dump? They were weekly. Paid twice; then they were gone."

I glanced up at the second floor. He had a point. The windows were greasy, mullions chipped, their paint gone. And the door had that friendless, abandoned-by-time air, like a rotted tree trunk. There were no signs of life above Lou's Bar. The Colemans/McLaglens must have used the place only long enough to register the car.

I stopped for coffee and a sandwich near Wilton on Route 9, then called Norma from a phone booth to ask her to look into the rest of the Robinsons in the area.

"Sorry to dump such a dreary job on you," I said.

"Not at all, Miss Stone. It sounds exciting. Tracking down the person who might have been the last one to see Johnny Dornan alive."

"More likely a dead end."

"I'll say I'm calling from a radio contest and ask them if they follow horse racing and can name the last Triple Crown winner. If they have no idea, they can't possibly know Johnny Dornan."

She was a clever one, our Norma Geary. Stuck in a low-paying job because she was too old, invisible, and—let's face it—because she was a she in the first place. And yet she could outthink an anvil like George Walsh any day of the week.

Putting that to one side, I asked her to patch me over to Charlie Reese. I needed to check in. He told me Artie Short wanted to know what I was up to.

"Don't worry," he said. "I covered for you."

"Oh, no. What did you sign me up for?"

"Since I know you're up to your skirts on this Tempesta story, I told him I'd assigned you to cover a garden party in Saratoga today. Some of the fancy set are raising money for charity. It's perfect for you."

"What?"

"Take it easy," he said. "You can write that piece in your sleep. And I made some calls. You'll have to interview the head lady tomorrow or the day after. That'll free you up to do some digging in Saratoga. And it'll keep Artie out of our hair."

I drew a sigh. "Where is it and when?"

I knew where to find Fadge. He was hunched over his program, calling out two-dollar wagers at betting window fifty-seven. Out of respect—and horror at the sum of his bets—I waited till he'd finished and caught his breath. He was counting his change and checking his slips when I tapped him on the shoulder.

"What are you doing here?" he asked.

"Is that how your mother taught you to greet a friend?"

"You surprised me, is all."

I told him I'd been in the neighborhood after wasting the morning in South Glens Falls.

"No luck with the sheriff either?"

"None. But I spent a half hour over at the training track talking to a horse."

"Anyone I should bet on?"

"No. He's spooked by the starting gate. And besides, he's not running today."

We made our way over to the clubhouse, and Fadge showed a pass. Since I was with the press, the nice man at the gate let me in as well.

"You don't usually pay for the clubhouse," I said. "Moving up in the world?"

"I get better access to the owners and trainers in here. I sidle up to the ones I recognize and pretend to read the *Racing Form*."

"And that works? You eavesdrop?"

"That's the idea."

I suggested we try it. We identified a couple of swells in linen suits chatting outside the Jim Dandy Bar on the first level, and agreed they were good candidates.

"I think that's Carl Hanford," whispered Fadge.

"Who?"

"The famous trainer. Pay attention, El."

We edged close to the two men. Fadge opened his paper, and I pretended to admire the flowers in the pot by the bar door.

"The thing is, folks don't realize how bad he's hurting," said the man Fadge had identified as Carl Hanford. "He hides it well. But his knees are in bad shape."

Fadge threw me a wink.

"I'm sorry to hear that, Joe," said the other man. "Arthritis is a terrible curse. Please give my best wishes to your dad. I hope he's back on his feet again real soon."

I resisted the temptation to laugh. Fadge slunk off to watch the first race.

"May I get you a drink?"

A waiter. How lovely. Seated in the Jim Dandy Bar, I glanced up to place an order and did a double take.

"You?" I asked.

"Who else would I be?"

It was the fresh young man I'd spoken to that morning at the training track. He repeated his offer of a drink.

"You realize I mistook you for the waiter."

"I'm at your service."

"Gin and tonic would be nice."

My new friend nodded brightly and—I'm fairly certain—clicked his heels. Then he set off to the bar to fulfill his errand.

"There you go, miss," he said a few moments later, placing my G and T on the table before me. He held a drink of his own in his other hand. A highball glass, sweating from the ice inside.

"So, you're not actually a waiter," I said as he took a seat opposite me.

"Afraid not." He smiled a toothy grin. The dimples, one in each check and a third on his chin, seemed to wink at me. "Mind if I join you?"

I returned his smile without the dimples.

"Freddie," he said, extending a hand across the table. His grip was cold from holding the drink.

"Just plain Freddie?"

He blushed, artless and charming. Only a shade or two. Not a full-blown sunburn. "Frederick Whitcomb." He withdrew his hand. "Freddie to my friends."

"That's an odd name."

"Girls named Eleonora shouldn't throw stones."

"How do you know my name?"

"Your press card," he said, pointing to my purse where I'd clipped it earlier.

I slid the pass back inside my bag, as if covering my nudity.

"Actually, to be perfectly honest, I still beat you," he continued. "My full name is Frederick Carsten Whitcomb the third."

"I'll make a deal with you. Call me Ellie, and I'll call you Freddie. The third."

"Deal."

Viewed properly from the front, Frederick Carsten Whitcomb III was no Greek statue, but he had charm to spare. Well mannered and well groomed, he called to mind a young Lord Peter Wimsey, only without the monocle. His tanned skin and fit physique gave him an athletic air, like a tennis player or a golfer. I was glad of his company, for the moment. At least until my four o'clock appointment in the penalty box: the garden party fundraiser.

"You know I've never waited tables," he confessed.

"Too bad. I like a man in uniform. If you're not a waiter, what is it you do?"

"I help my father with the family business. Manufacturing and some tobacco farms."

"That's it?"

"I dabble in the stock market." He reconsidered. "I mostly just watch the share prices go up. Not much dabbling required, really."

That explained it. Idle rich.

He crossed his right leg over his left and leaned in to consider me from close up. Squinting as he scanned my face, he informed me that I hadn't mentioned my age.

"And I'm not going to," I said.

"I have the right to know. I don't want to end up in jail on a morals charge with a precocious high schooler."

"What makes you think you're getting anywhere near a chance to rate a morals charge with me?"

Okay, the repartee was fun, but I couldn't keep up the gymnastics much longer. It was exhausting. I smiled and asked if he was from Saratoga.

"Washington. Northern Virginia, actually. But I make the pilgrimage to Saratoga every August."

"So you like to play the horses?"

"You could say that." He lit a cigarette, which he held out for me. I begged off. Charming though Freddie Whitcomb may have been, I was not yet ready to share saliva with him. He continued unfazed and adopted the smoke for himself. "But I come more for the horses themselves. And the social scene. What about you, *Eleonora*?"

He was trying to restart the flirting. "We had an agreement about names. I'm a reporter for a local daily not far from here."

"I knew that already. Press pass. Strange, though, I had you pegged for a New York girl. NYU. Or Boston? Maybe Brandeis?"

My smile dimmed. I'd heard that song before. Were NYU and Brandeis code? A not-so-subtle attempt to establish if I was Jewish? Freddie continued on, though, chatting about something called Travers Day, which was coming up on Saturday, and I scolded myself for being too sensitive. I primed my smile again and interrupted his musings on an upcoming soirée at the casino in Congress Park.

"Barnard," I said.

He was confused. "No. My name is Frederick. Freddie, remember?"

"I studied at Barnard. History and journalism."

The penny dropped. "Then I was right. You are a New York girl. I studied linguistics at Pennsylvania. Let's see if I can guess your address from your accent." He rubbed his chin and squinted at me. "I'm getting a hint of Park Avenue. No, Madison and Eightieth," he said deadpan. "Or maybe Hell's Kitchen. West . . . Fifty-Fourth Street? Staten Island? Flushing?"

"Lower Fifth Avenue," I said with a chuckle. "Off Washington Square."

"Washington Square? Are you an heiress, Miss Stone?"

Poor Freddie. He couldn't have known that he'd stirred up a hornets' nest of emotions in me. No, I wasn't exactly an heiress, but my late parents had left me quite comfortable. I didn't have to work if I didn't want to, but of course I loved my job. Parts of it, at least. Not the garden parties and social page froth, but a double murder on a ghostly stud farm, yes.

"Did I say something wrong?" he asked. My expression had surely betrayed my troubled memories of family. I waved off his concerns as breezily as I could manage. Then he invited me to dinner.

"I was thinking that a couple of swells like us shouldn't waste our time with the hoi polloi. Besides, we gotta eat."

There he was, the linguist, bending language and accent with his agile tongue, as if his high station afforded him such privilege. As if he knew the simple folks who actually spoke that way would indulge him for his charm.

"I can't," I said. "Not tonight."

Freddie coughed, took a sip from his highball glass and a drag on his cigarette.

"But I'll check my agenda for Friday. If the offer's still good."

"Make it Saturday. I'll take you to a fancy gala at the Canfield Casino after the Travers Stakes."

CHAPTER ELEVEN

The Saratoga Springs Friends of the Library Society gathered at the Gideon Putnam Hotel at 4:00 p.m. Tuesday to raise funds and awareness for underprivileged minority education. I appeared a few minutes late and seriously underdressed. The fifty or so ladies in attendance were decked out in floral dresses, pearls, sunglasses, and the occasional hat with ruffled bow. I was wearing a plaid skirt and white blouse. The nice woman who checked me in withheld her judgment, though, and pointed the way to the garden where the festivities were getting under way. I took a seat in a folding wooden chair on the lawn, near the back of the congregation. A woman in a violet dress and matching jacket—the society's president as I later learned for my story—was delivering a welcome to members and friends. Then she introduced the event's guest of honor, the fundraising drive chairwoman, Mrs. Georgina Carsten Whitcomb. I choked.

Mrs. Whitcomb addressed the gathering in a warm, engaging voice. I wouldn't have been able to guess the exact provenance of her honey-flavored Southern accent, of course, had I not already met her son. Northern Virginia. She expounded on the need for those of means to help those without. Especially children. And that went double for Colored children whose circumstances were exacerbated by poverty, broken homes, and genetics. I caught myself wondering why her white-woman's-burden rhetoric hadn't sent me running for the exit. Despite myself, I had to admit that the sweetness with which she'd delivered the speech somehow tempted me to grant her some leeway. Or was I failing to condemn her because I'd allowed myself to be charmed by her son? Of course I found everything she'd said abhorrent and insulting, especially to Colored children and their parents.

I put those thoughts to one side for the moment and scribbled notes into my pad. Then, sensing she was wrapping up her case for philanthropy, I unsnapped my Leica and shot a couple of frames of her at the dais. Once the assembled erupted into thunderous applause—no more than the gentle pat-pat-pat of gloved hands, really—I rose and swung around to the front for some photos of the attendees. Ten minutes later, I had a couple of rolls of Tri-X to document the historic step forward in education and race relations.

I waited patiently as several ladies heaped their praise upon her as if with a shovel, and then I approached her for a photograph for the paper.

"I don't believe we've met," she said. "I'm Georgina Whitcomb."

"Very pleased to meet you," I said. "I know who you are. My editor sent me to interview you. My name is Eleonora Stone from the *New Holland Republic*." There was an awkward pause as she undoubtedly searched her memory for that reference. "It's a local newspaper about twenty-five miles from here," I added, hoping to resolve the confusion.

Why had I introduced myself as "Eleonora"? For one thing, I hated that name. And for another, did I think it made me sound better born? What was wrong with my birth anyway? Ladies like Georgina Carsten Whitcomb didn't usually put me off my game, but I was on her turf. A Jewess from Manhattan among the Mayflower set. And I was underdressed.

"Lovely to meet you, Eleonora," she said, beaming with kindly eyes. "What a beautiful name. Yes, I was told you'd be joining us today."

She posed in a confident, practiced way for several photographs, producing one winning smile after another. I sensed there wasn't a throwaway frame in the bunch. She'd done this kind of thing before.

"If you have some time now, we could get the interview out of the way today," I said once I'd finished. "Then I won't need to bother you again."

"My dear Eleonora, you are a lamb. But I'm afraid these ladies have me tied up as tight as a drum today. Might we try tomorrow? You can reach me here at the hotel."

Rats. "Of course," I said.

"Then I'll expect you for tea at four."

She grasped the tips of my fingers with her gloved hand and squeezed ever so gently. Then she shimmered off, surrounded by the society's president and two other ladies with lavender-colored hair.

I rewound my film and drew a sigh of relief. The speechifying hadn't been so bad, and I had no intentions of sticking around for the cucumber sandwiches. But then I noticed a woman staring at me from five feet away.

"Good afternoon, Miss Stone," she said.

I was startled. The queer grin and penetrating, unblinking eyes unset-

tled me, even more so because I recognized her all too well. It was Audrey
Shaw, wife of Judge Harrison Shaw, and mother of the murdered Jordan.

"I didn't expect to see you here," she said.

And I never would have wanted to cross her shadow at such an event.
Or any other, for that matter. She made my skin crawl.

"Mrs. Shaw. How lovely to see you again."

She regarded me for a long moment, her head tilted a touch to the
right. She forgot herself for an instant, her eyes betraying the unspoken
animosity she bore me. Then, presently, the façade went back up.

"I'd like a drink," she said in a conspiratorial stage whisper. "And I'm
sure you'd prefer something stronger than tea after that performance. Let's
talk inside."

I followed her—reluctantly—into the hotel bar. Audrey Shaw was
an alcoholic, that much I knew from experience. She and I had shared
a bottle of the judge's finest Scotch one chilly afternoon in December
nearly two years earlier. On that occasion, she'd taken a particularly
savage joy in twisting the dagger of my father's murder into my heart. It
made her feel better about her own loss, I figured. But I still hated her
for it.

As she led us to an out-of-the-way table, I scolded myself for having
avoided my necessary interview with her husband about the murders
on Tempesta Farm. Not that such a meeting with Judge Shaw would
have spared me from this calvary, but at least I would have felt like less a
coward. Now, at a table in the elegant Gideon Putnam Hotel, I sat face-
to-face with Audrey Shaw. She was exquisite in a pencil skirt and mother-
of-pearl blouse, that is if you didn't mind the perfectly horrid pink toque
and its faux-silk flowers perched on her head like a bathing cap. Her nails
drummed on the tabletop as I scanned the room, desperate for a waiter. A
busboy would have sufficed. She smiled at me.

"What brings you to this garden party?" she asked at length. "Are you
interested in helping little Colored children?"

How was I supposed to answer that without sounding wretched? I
ignored the second half of her question and told her I was there in my
capacity as a reporter.

She chuckled in a most condescending manner. "Really? This is going
into the *Republic*? Does anyone in New Holland care about educating
Negro children?" She paused for maximum effect.

"I care," I said, though I doubted she'd been expecting an answer to her gem of cynicism. "It's a good cause."

"Perhaps you'll donate five dollars to soothe your conscience."

I stared daggers at her.

"Please, Miss Stone. I'm only having some fun with you. The judge and I are donating two hundred dollars today, so I believe I have the right to kibitz, as your people would say."

"You wanted to speak with me?" I said, no longer trying to conceal my pique.

"Is it wrong to want to catch up with an old friend?"

"We're not friends, Mrs. Shaw."

She pursed her lips and signaled to a waiter, who arrived at a trot. "Two whiskeys, please," she said. Then to me, "You still enjoy your Scotch, don't you, Miss Stone?"

"I do."

The waiter withdrew.

"I'm sorry," she said. "I don't mean to make you uncomfortable. We have a history, you and I."

"Why did you want to talk to me?" I asked again.

"The truth? I was bored. I thought we might have a chat. Maybe start over."

"You want to be my friend? That's not necessary."

"I went through hell two years ago, as I'm sure you can imagine. I was hard on you."

"I'm a big girl. No apologies necessary. But I would like to ask you something."

"About Jordan? About your father?"

"No," I said. "About Tempesta Farm."

"Tempesta? What about it?"

"You know there was a fire out there early Saturday morning. Two people died."

She nodded.

"I was wondering if your husband still owns the property."

Audrey Shaw shifted in her seat, clearly uncomfortable with the direction our conversation was taking. The waiter returned with our drinks just in time to give her a few seconds to regroup, and she blinked the briefest smile at him as thanks. She retrieved a cigarette from her purse and lit it.

"I assume the family trust owns it. It's not as if Harrison spends his weekends out there shoeing horses and mucking out stables."

"Did the Saratoga sheriff contact him about the fire?"

She took a long sip of her drink, professed her ignorance on the subject, and suggested I ask her husband. We sat in silence for a long moment. I was glad for the respite. For once I was dictating terms with Audrey Shaw. At length, however, she softened, perhaps as the whiskey worked its magic.

"Do you remember that afternoon we spent together?" she asked. "You impressed me, did you know that?"

"As a matter of fact, I understood exactly the opposite. I thought you despised me."

"For what you wrote about Jordan? No, I know you only reported your story as you saw fit. It was what the great unwashed masses wanted."

"I was very forthcoming with your husband about what I was going to write."

"Enough, Miss Stone. That's all in the past. You and I have suffered terrible tragedies."

A few sips later, we'd achieved little to solidify a friendship, understanding, or even a truce. All I knew was that I disliked that woman, all the while pitying her and wishing I could decipher her intentions. I sensed she was trying to establish some connection with me, though I couldn't quite figure what she wanted. She certainly didn't consider me a surrogate daughter, which I didn't want to be anyway. She'd made that clear to me two years before when she told me I couldn't hold a candle to her Jordan. But now, in a relaxed state, she loosened up and even touched my hand.

"I can tell you loads about these ladies for your article," she said with a wicked smile. "Most of them are from Kentucky or Virginia. Do you really think they care two whits about Negro children? Or anything beyond their own comfort and public image? Plus I know who's sleeping with whom."

"Perhaps they're no different from us."

"From me. Not you, Eleonora."

I started at having heard her use my given name.

"Ellie," she corrected herself. "Let's have another drink, and I'll tell you a story about Tempesta Farm."

The light stretched across the lawn outside, its temperature cooling with the sinking sun, and Audrey Shaw told me of her first visit to New Holland.

She was barely twenty, recently engaged to Harrison, the future Judge Shaw. Their families knew each other, but not well, so naturally his parents wanted to spend some time with her before the wedding. Audrey Jeffers hailed from Baltimore, where her father had served on the state racing commission. He'd known Harrison's uncle, Joshua, the famous horseman, and greatly respected his grandfather, Sanford Shaw, the man who'd built Tempesta Farm. Audrey confessed that her parents' only hesitation at the prospective match was Harrison's uncle Joshua, whose reputation as a playboy was known up and down the Eastern Seaboard and as far afield as Europe.

"To tell you the truth," said Audrey Shaw, sipping her drink, "Uncle Joshua was the most interesting Shaw of them all, and I include my husband in that beauty pageant."

The chaperoned visit in late August and early September of 1937 went off well, despite concerns over Uncle Joshua's profligacies, and both families were amenable to the match.

Audrey Shaw corrected herself. "Actually, my visit *was* going well until the fire destroyed the Race Barn and took twelve of the Shaws' finest Thoroughbreds with it."

"You were there?" I asked.

"The August meet had just wrapped up, and I stayed on a little longer to be with Harrison."

"How did it happen?"

She shrugged. "They never established for certain how the fire got started, though there were rumors a stableboy was to blame. Or maybe it was one of the farmhands. I don't recall. But Harrison once told me that the fire was an accident. No one could have done that on purpose."

She continued her tale. Audrey Jeffers had spent her days at the track, or riding at Tempesta, and split her evenings between soirées in Saratoga and quiet dinners at the Shaw family mansion on Market Hill. The fire erupted in the Race Barn after midnight on September 3, 1937. Nathan Shaw was roused from his sleep by his brother, Joshua, and together with Harrison they raced out to the farm in the dead of the night to take stock of the situation. By the time they'd arrived, the barn was gone, and so were twelve cherished horses.

"I was packed off back to Baltimore the next day while they dealt with the aftermath," said Audrey Shaw. "Shall we have another?" She signaled to the waiter.

In for a penny . . . I nodded. "What happened next?"

"My father wasn't sure the wedding would come off after the tragedy. As if perhaps the Shaws would associate the fire with my presence. But soon enough we discovered I was expecting, so not only was the wedding on but rushed forward."

So much for the chaperoned visit. I must have looked shocked because she explained further.

"I miscarried, so the wedding was moved back to June of the next year as originally planned." She offered a sad smile. "It was the event of the season."

Back at the office, I dropped off my film at the lab then tapped out the skeleton of my garden party story. I still needed to interview the guest of honor, who was the chairwoman of the charity drive. Unlike Audrey Shaw, I believed subscribers would be interested in reading about Saratoga high society. The Spa City occupied a special place in the hearts of New Holland citizens. Each August, the racing season, and the glamour it epitomized, provided an escape for readers: the fancy garden party would break the routine of their humdrum lives. So even if Audrey Shaw was right that few would care about lending a helping hand to minority children, they would still enjoy the photos and stories of the rich and glamorous. My article, however, promised, at best, to be a two-paragraph snoozer. Fifty rich ladies decked out in their finery doing their part to help the underprivileged, each trying to out-donate the last, but within reason, mind you. I imagined they'd met beforehand to establish a pecking order of generosity and how much each would give. A bit of charitable collusion. Okay, some of Audrey Shaw's cynicism may have rubbed off on me.

I stashed my notes in my desk, leaned back, and rocked in my chair. The locked filing cabinet against the wall caught my eye. It was past six, and almost everyone had punched out for the day. But I'd noticed George Walsh skulking around about twenty minutes before. Unsure if he was still polluting the sector, I surveyed the newsroom, then peeked down the hall. No weasels in sight, so I returned to my desk and retrieved a key from my purse. Rummaging through the cabinet, I located the file I needed, rolled the drawer closed, and locked it up again. Georgie Porgie had stolen one too many of my stories, and I'd learned my lesson the hard way. I now kept all my notes and contacts locked up tight. Well, not the garden party story; George was welcome to that one if he wanted it. But the folder I held in my sweaty little hands was different. I ran my fingers over the name tag I'd pasted to the top—*Jordan Shaw Murder*.

I stashed the folder in my purse, slipped the cover over my typewriter, and headed home. I needed privacy and a stiff drink for the phone call I was about to make.

CHAPTER TWELVE

I dialed Judge Shaw's home number at half past eight, hoping he and his wife had finished their dinner. Perhaps she'd gone straight to bed after the garden party. I never found out; the judge himself answered the phone on the third ring. I lost my nerve and hung up.

I debated whether to run across the street for a chat with Fadge, but I was tired and ready to turn in. I decided one short drink wouldn't hurt, so I made a withdrawal from the freezer, nearly ripping the skin off the palm of my hand on the metal handle of the ice tray. I poured myself an inviting two fingers; then the downstairs doorbell rang. I glanced at the clock above the stove—a few minutes past ten. A little early for Fadge to be closing the store. I climbed down the back stairs to open up. It wasn't my dear pal standing on the stoop.

"Surprise," said Freddie Whitcomb, who seemed—rightly so—a little embarrassed.

"Hi," I stammered. "This is a surprise. How did you find me?"

"You're in the book."

I wasn't sure how to react. On the one hand, it was mildly flattering that this attractive man had taken great pains to seek me out. Well, perhaps flipping through a telephone directory didn't qualify as *great pains*, but he had driven all the way over from Saratoga. On the other hand, I wondered if I should be alarmed that he had done all that solely on the basis of our brief acquaintance. Should I slam the door, lock it, and call the police? Or invite him up to share my drink?

"Look, I know this might make you feel uncomfortable," he said. "But I assure you I'm only here because you were irresistible at the track. And I promise I'm harmless."

I softened a bit. Maybe a lot. "If you're harmless, why on earth would I dream of letting you in?"

I allowed Freddie Whitcomb to join me upstairs for a couple of drinks. We chatted in my parlor, me with my Dewar's, him with some brandy I'd been saving.

"Lovely place you have," he announced, raising his snifter, which I took as an indication of his seal of approval.

"It's all right. Although I do have to be mindful of my landlady downstairs. You, too, by the way. She's a light sleeper and hears every footstep."

"I'll tread as lightly as a sprite," he said, then took a big gulp of his brandy.

"So what brought you here tonight?" I asked. "I thought we had an arrangement for Saturday at the casino in Saratoga."

"We did. And we do. But I must say, Ellie, that your charms should not be dispensed without a license. You're intoxicating."

I snorted a laugh. "And you're a shameless flatterer. You wanted a drink and didn't know where to find one."

He threw his most seductive smile my way and said he knew very well where to find a drink, but he wanted one served by me. I liked that. Two points for Freddie.

"I have a secret," I said, tipping my glass in his direction.

"I've got loads of secrets."

"But this one involves your mother."

Freddie feigned shock. "Not Mother. Oh, dear."

"I'm meeting her tomorrow at the Gideon Putnam in Saratoga. For a story I'm writing for the paper."

"Well, whatever you do, don't mention my name."

"Thanks for the tip. I wasn't planning on it."

"She doesn't approve of me, I'm afraid."

I glanced at my watch. It was approaching eleven. I rose and switched off the light in my bedroom. Then the light in the kitchen.

"It's getting dark in here," he said.

I didn't explain to him, but in case Fadge had it in his head to drop by unexpectedly after work for a visit, I wanted there to be no doubt that I was in bed.

"Would you like to go out and grab a bite to eat?" he asked. "I saw a little ice-cream shop across the street."

"I'm not hungry. And I've got some peanut butter and Spam if you'd like something."

Freddie's appetites, however, were running in other directions that night.

WEDNESDAY, AUGUST 15, 1962

Freddie rose before dawn, dressed, and apologized for having to run out on me.

"It's okay," I said. "I've got to go to work."

He winced an apology at me. "So sorry I kept you up last night."

"No, you're not."

He kissed me. Nothing too romantic; we hardly knew each other, after all. Sweet and friendly, it was better than a handshake. He asked if I was free that evening, but I had to beg off. Then he buttoned his collar and was off down the stairs. I followed him in my robe to wave good-bye and—damn it—ran straight into my landlady, Mrs. Giannetti, on the front porch. It wasn't yet six. What was she doing up at that hour? She watched Freddie jump into his car—a red MGA roadster—before turning to stare me down with a reproachful arch of the eyebrows. She held her tongue that day, but I was confident she was only biding her time; I'd get an earful at some point, calculated to deliver the maximum sting. I dragged myself back upstairs to get ready for the day.

The Montgomery County Jail was located in the administrative building north of town on Route 22. The sheriff's office was on the ground floor, the cells in the basement, and the courtroom on the second floor. I'd had occasion to visit often over the past four years while covering everything from family court hearings to murder investigations. And, of course, to visit my pal Frank Olney and his deputies. I was on friendly terms with all of them. It pays to play nice with cops when you're covering local news, but I also liked the guys. And they were always protective of me. Deputy Brunello once referred to me as "the sweetheart of Sigma Chi," and the nickname stuck. I don't believe any of them had ever been on a college campus, let alone pledged a fraternity, but they all knew the song. More or less. And, bless their hearts, they even sang me part of the refrain from time to time.

"And the moonlight beams on the girl of my dreams
She's the Sweetheart of Sigma Chi."

In fairness, I believe that was the only part they knew, but I was touched and flattered by their affections all the same.

"Good morning, Ellie," said Pat Halvey from behind his typewriter. "Haven't seen you in a while."

"I've been busy. How've you been, Pat?"

"Bowling regularly. Not much else."

Pat wasn't the world's greatest conversationalist. But he was a pretty good bowler.

"Is Frank in?" I asked.

He buzzed the sheriff, and in short order I was seated across from Frank Olney, who told Pat to bring me a cup of freshly perked coffee and a Danish.

"I've got some news for you," said the sheriff, swiveling in his chair. "Spoke to Pryor last night and told him about the anonymous tip. I also mentioned that I'd come across the name Robinson and a possible meeting with Dornan on Friday night. He lapped it up. Said it might be the big break he was waiting for."

"He didn't seem to care when I told him about Robinson."

"He was real thankful and called me back this morning. Found the husband."

"Tommy McLaglen?"

"That's right. How'd you know his name?"

"My assistant dug up Vivian McLaglen's wedding announcement."

Frank nodded and pushed a sheet of paper across the desk to me. He'd scratched McLaglen's name and address on it. "He's been living in Albany for the past six years."

"Thanks. Anything else?"

"His arrest record might tell you something. Burglary, gambling, and simple assault."

"Sounds like my kind of guy."

Frank pursed his lips. He didn't approve.

"What's he look like?" I asked to give him a break.

"I don't have a picture, but his file says he's medium height and weight. Dark hair and eyes. Swarthy complexion."

"Did Pryor tell you how tall exactly?"

Frank lifted the corner of a paper on his desk and glanced sideways at it. "Five-nine. Were you thinking he might've been the guy in the barn?"

"No, I'm sure it was Johnny Dornan. Now I'd like to find out why. What was a successful jockey in the middle of a good meet doing with a woman of Vivian Coleman's pedigree?"

"She'd been mixed up plenty with gamblers. Maybe your Johnny Dornan was crooked."

"Maybe." I grabbed the paper with the name and address and folded it into my purse. "You think there's any chance I might find McLaglen at home on a Wednesday morning in August?"

"Probably not. But according to his parole officer, he works at Union Station in Albany, waxing floors and emptying trash."

"Thanks again, Frank. I owe you breakfast at the Ballston Diner."

He blushed crimson. "Aw, come on, Ellie. That ain't right."

Information had no number for Tommy, Tom, or Thomas McLaglen in Albany. I was loath to waste another long car drive on the off chance of finding a half-wit or hoodlum lazing about home in an undershirt and no pants. But armed with the knowledge that he worked at Union Station, I thought the odds were good that I could track him down. Plus, I had some other work in that part of town I could squeeze in if all else failed. For some time, Charlie Reese had been on my back to document the neighborhoods surrounding the capital buildings in the South End of Albany. They were all scheduled to be razed to make way for Rockefeller's new complex of government buildings. That was as good an excuse as any, so I phoned Charlie and told him of my plans.

"What about your society-page piece?" he asked.

"All but done. Just missing a face-to-face with the chairwoman of the fund drive. I'm meeting her at four this afternoon in Saratoga."

"Good. And there's a story I need you to file on the Little Titans football physicals."

"What?"

"You know, football season's starting in a few weeks."

"Why isn't Ralphie Fisher covering it? It's sports, after all."

"He's out of town, and Gabe Morrissey's been out since his hernia operation."

I cursed all of them, including Gabe's abdominal protrusions, and not entirely under my breath. "So I have to go write a story on twelve-year-olds dropping their drawers and coughing for Dr. Geraldo?"

"You don't have to go inside," said Charlie as if agreeing to a concession. "And of course no pictures of that. Maybe a couple shots of the boys waiting with their dads outside. Some upbeat quotes about how excited they are about the upcoming season. You can knock it out in ten minutes."

"When and where?"

Union Station was a grand edifice. Built around the turn of the century, it reigned over much of Broadway near the river. That part of the city had fallen into decay and retained little of its former glory. Governor Rockefeller had ambitious plans for downtown Albany, however, as evidenced by the roaring demolition going on several blocks to the west of the station.

At a few minutes past ten, I entered the majestic Beaux Arts building from Maiden Lane and peeled my eyes for sweepers. Finding none on the job, I checked with the stationmaster. He asked me what I wanted with Tommy. I lied that I was his niece, and he pointed to a door marked "Maintenance" halfway down the platform.

"Keep it short," he offered as parting advice. "He's got work to do."

The door indicated by the stationmaster was wide open. Seated cross-legged on the floor, a man in his thirties was sweating like a yak as he monkeyed with the innards of an overturned marble-buffing machine. I cleared my throat to get his attention.

"Inside the terminal," he said. "Past the newsstand, to the left of the phone booths."

"I beg your pardon?"

"The ladies," he said, dragging the greasy back of his hand across his brow.

I'm sure I blushed. "Oh, no. I'm not ... Actually, I was looking for Tommy McLaglen. Would he be you?"

"Yeah. I be he." He chuckled. "Who be you?"

I introduced myself and said I was there to inquire about his wife, Vivian. The smiling face collapsed. He pushed himself off the floor and wiped his hands on a rag. The muscles of his forearms tensed and twisted under his skin as he did. I thought he was ruggedly handsome in a broken-nose, take-me-now-on-the-floor-of-the-stable kind of way. Lady Chatterley's type, not mine.

"What's this about exactly?"

"I'm investigating a fire that burned down a barn on an abandoned farm in Saratoga County."

"What's that got to do with Viv?"

I gulped. This was her husband after all. Breaking the news of my suspicions wasn't going to be easy.

"I'd like to speak to your wife about the fire," I said, playing for time.

I needn't have worried. Tommy McLaglen tossed the rag on the workbench behind him and sneered. "I don't know where she is. I've only seen her once in the past eight years."

"Eight years? But you're still married."

He stared at me for a moment. "Yeah. So how's she mixed up in this fire business? Did she set it?"

My words caught in my throat despite myself. "Oh, Mr. McLaglen. She didn't set the fire. I believe she died in it."

I might just as well have kicked him in the gut. He bent over, held a hand over his midsection, and wobbled into a seat on a stool next to the workbench.

"Are you saying she's dead?" he asked once he'd composed himself.

I weighed my words before pronouncing them. "There's been no identification yet."

He drew a long sigh, rubbed the bridge of his nose, then straightened his spine. He stared at me for a full ten seconds before speaking.

"I'm sure she deserved what she got," he said before producing a handkerchief where he buried his face to weep.

Tommy McLaglen unburdened himself. He told me how his brother had married the young Vivian Coleman during the war when she was still in bobby socks and barrettes. He'd loved her even then. Even when his older brother brought her home to two parents who couldn't have been more disappointed if she'd arrived cash on delivery. Tommy was sixteen and didn't know what to make of the beauty his brother had bagged. And she had little idea of the effect her charms exerted on him. Or perhaps she realized all too well. The silent, meaningful glances at the dinner table, the encounters in the corridor, brushing past one another as they headed to and from the shared bathroom. There was always a little extra friction in Vivian's grazes, a lingering of her fingertips on his shoulder or hand. Something more than a sister-in-law should ever need to share with her husband's younger brother.

"They moved out after a year and a half," he said, head hanging low, elbows resting on his knees. "I didn't see her for another year, except for at Easter and Pop's birthday. That's when it happened."

"You slept with her? Your brother's wife?"

He offered a sheepish shrug. "We started meeting up after Pop's birthday party. At run-down hotels, in my car, at the movies. Anywhere we could be alone for a few minutes."

My mouth had gone dry. I said nothing, willing him to continue.

"We were in love. She hated Ernie. My brother. We talked about running off together, but neither of us had any money. Then my mother nearly caught us one day. She was supposed to be working, but she forgot her gloves. She cleaned houses in Delmar."

"Did she guess what was going on?" I asked.

"I think so. She never said anything to me, but I got the cold shoulder for a couple of weeks. And she never left me alone with Viv again."

"So things cooled off?"

"I joined the navy and served two years at sea. When I came back, Ernie got called up for Korea. He moved Viv out to California where he did his boot camp. Then he shipped out. He was killed in action three months later."

"And you two decided to get married after that?"

"We waited six months. Had to make it respectable."

They'd failed, at least in my opinion. I can't imagine what his family thought.

"If you don't mind my asking, what happened?" I asked. "With your marriage, I mean."

Tommy grabbed the greasy rag again and wiped his eyes and face. Then he fixed me with his stare.

"Did you say you were a reporter?"

"Yes."

"Why am I telling you all this?"

"Because you want to know what happened to Vivian," I said, figuring that an assertive answer was my best bet.

He seemed skeptical, but the urge to share his story was too strong. He cast his gaze to the tiled floor and continued.

"She didn't love me. At least not for long. That wasn't her way. She was always looking to trade up for something better. Like she was standing on your back and lifting her head a little higher to see something else above the clouds. Then she wanted that. Nothing was ever good enough. She frittered away every dime I managed to scrounge on clothes and hair and shoes. Always saving up Green Stamps for some new outfit or cosmetics. Never on anything for me." He was vexed, and not with me. "Nothing was ever enough for that girl. Suppers out, dancing, drinking. She didn't get it that I had to be rested for work."

"I'm sorry."

"And she never had enough of telling me I was no good. Loved making me feel small. Even when she was arrested for solicitation. One year after we were married. Can you beat that?"

I clasped my hands behind my back and buttoned my lip. Our conversation had jumped the rails and fast. I wanted to get him back to answering questions, not pouring out his heart. I asked him if Vivian had pierced ears.

"Pierced ears? Yeah, sure. Her and a friend did it to each other one night with a sewing needle. But that was a long time ago. Why do you ask?"

"The woman in the barn," I said simply.

He glanced away. "I see."

"There was a second body. A man. Looks like it was a jockey named Johnny Dornan. Does that name mean anything to you?"

He shook his head. "I don't play the horses. As a matter of fact, I quit gambling altogether. Didn't have the stomach or the pocketbook for it."

"What about Robinson? Know anyone by that name?"

"Jackie Robinson. Brooks Robinson. Frank Robinson."

"Baseball fan, are you?"

He shrugged.

"Sorry. Not them," I said. "So how did it end between you and Vivian?"

"She was always hatching some new scheme to make money. I went along with a lot of her ideas, and got myself into all kinds of trouble. A swindle, a little robbery, maybe flexing some muscle for a guy who could help us later on. She had all the bases covered. And it was always me doing the dirty work. I got picked up a couple of times and even spent a couple of months in jail. All for some job she thought would set us up for keeps."

"Was it while you were away that she left?"

"No. She didn't leave me. She got sent away."

"Then it was you who broke it off?"

He hesitated a brief moment before he answered. And then he sneered bitterly. "My mother put an end to it. She came to our place the day before Viv got out of jail and threw out all of her stuff. Right out the window into the alley. Then a friend of Pop's came to change the locks on the door, all before Viv got out."

"What happened after that? Do you have any idea what she's been up to for the past eight years?"

"Not since she left. When she figured out her key didn't work, she took up with some guy and ran off to Virginia or Maryland; I don't recall exactly. Somewhere with a gambler by the name of Ledoux. I heard he played the horses and was bad news. But I figured Viv probably stuck with him just long enough to get out of town."

"And you never saw her again after that?"

"Just once for about five minutes. She came to see me about three years ago. Maybe she was going through a rough spell, but that fresh face and gorgeous figure were gone."

"What did she want?"

"Said she was in trouble, could I help her out of a jam? I didn't wait to find out what it was. I threw her out."

"Good for you."

"Sometimes I think I could kill her. Strangle her," he said as a matter of fact. "For all the pain she put me through. So many times I wanted to cry. Like a baby, you know." He wiped his eyes with the back of his hand.

"But when she used to say my name all sweet-like, I turned to putty in her hands."

"Sounds like you had it bad."

"Things are good now," he said. "I found a group that helps me. I'm off the sauce, out of trouble, quit gambling, and I'm making a life for myself."

"Does that mean you've forgiven Vivian?"

He rubbed the oily rag on his hands again, as if to wash them of her memory. "I'll never forgive her."

CHAPTER THIRTEEN

The South End of Albany had received its death sentence and was awaiting the bulldozers and wrecking balls to carry out the execution. Forty city blocks, nearly one hundred acres of urban habitat, were to be razed to make way for the South Mall project in the next three years. Some of the working-class row houses had already been pulled down, and this was only the beginning for the area Rocky had dubbed "a slum."

I wound a roll of Kodachrome into my Leica and wandered through the streets for the next two hours, snapping photographs of the barber shops, tailors' windows, pawnbroker emporia, shoe repairs, groceries, and pizzerias. I wasn't exactly Cartier-Bresson, but I thought a series of storefronts and their signs made for an interesting thematic strain to follow. It would have been rude to take pictures of people, so I contented myself with the dark-brick tenements and swinging signs hanging above the doomed businesses.

By the time I'd finished off five rolls of film, I felt a sadness for the place. Still bustling and alive, the South End seemed determined to live its last months with as much normalcy as its residents could muster. I stashed my camera and sat down in Mirabile's Restaurant on Daniel Street near Public Market Square. The lunchtime crowd was in full force, and I wondered where these people would go for their spaghetti and meatballs once the block was demolished. I ordered some ravioli and Chianti to toast a farewell.

⁂

I almost missed my appointment with the Little Titans, but I managed to snap a few frames of Tri-X of a young boy and his father. Both were wearing purple jerseys. The father's was faded, its white numbers cracking and peeling, the result of harsh detergent, passing years, and an ever-expanding belly that tested the limits of the fabric's elasticity. But it made for a good father-son photo.

I stopped at the office and rapped out a one-paragraph masterpiece on the football physicals. Then I labeled my film for the lab and wrote the caption, "Titans, Big and Small, Ready for Season." Feeling satisfied, I made for the exit, but Norma intercepted me on the way.

"I've gone through the list of Robinsons once," she said. "I managed to reach forty-two of them. I won't bore you with the details, but no luck so far. The others didn't answer, so I'll have to try again later."

I asked myself how I might manage without her. She'd dialed about a hundred numbers and tricked forty-two of them into answering a phony question about horse racing. The answer, by the way, was Citation. The last horse to win the Triple Crown. God, if I spent any more time with Fadge, I was going to end up like one of those track rats.

"There was one interesting call I should mention," she said, interrupting my musings. "A man at Robinson's High Life Tavern in Saratoga."

"Oh, my. I forgot to tell you I'd already spoken to him."

"He remembered you. Didn't know your name, though. Now I suppose he thinks you're with WPTR."

"Did he answer your question?"

She nodded. "And then some. He sounded a little suspicious that two ladies were asking him about Johnny Dornan in as many days."

"Any new information?"

"Just that he expected me to mail him the prize for knowing the answer."

"Well, is he getting it?"

"He caught me off guard. I said of course we'd be sending a ten-dollar gift certificate for dance lessons at Arthur Murray's."

I laughed. "Okay. Can you make the arrangements? I'll get Charlie to sign off on the expense and deliver the certificate myself."

Mrs. Whitcomb was waiting for me on the patio at four o'clock sharp. She greeted me warmly, again with the kindly smile, and invited me to have a seat. A waiter glided up to our table and poured me some tea from the silver service. It was dangerously close to 5:00 p.m., and I would have preferred something stronger. I reminded myself that I needed my wits about me if I was to make a good impression on her. But in the next instant, I was asking myself why I needed to make an impression on her, good or otherwise. Sure, I had spent the night with her athletic son, and had a big date with him for the gala fundraiser on Saturday. But so what? Was I expecting the wedding of the season—one to rival Audrey and Harrison Shaw's—to come out of it? There was no reason to expect that Georgina Whitcomb would ever know about my hours of passion in her darling Freddie's arms.

"Are you all right, Miss Stone?" she asked, rousing me from my internal debate. "You seem distracted."

"Please pardon my rudeness," I said. "I was trying to remember the questions I'd prepared for you."

"Never mind those, Eleonora. I may call you that, I hope. Lately I find myself wanting to call all young people by their given names. It's a privilege that comes with age."

"By all means. Or you can call me Ellie, if you prefer, Mrs. Whitcomb."

Yes, I realized that the privilege was a one-way street. She could call me by name all she wanted, as she might a dog. But I was sticking to formality in return.

"Let's have a nice visit and a little nourishment. I'm sure our conversation will give you all you need for your article."

A second waiter rolled up with a cart overflowing with sandwiches, scones, preserves, and clotted cream. I deferred to my hostess, who indicated her selections with her index finger. I wasn't hungry but chose a square of lemon cake to be polite.

The small talk that ensued was entertaining enough. Mrs. Whitcomb had wit and charm to burn, but I remained on edge. I tried to ingratiate myself to her by stating my intention to donate twenty-five dollars to the fundraiser. What was I thinking? She smiled but said nothing. At length she noticed a young couple a few tables away suffering through an awkward date and regaled me with a story from her youth.

"I came out in twenty-two, Ellie. And the very next summer my mother wanted to make a match for me. She had someone all picked out. His name was Jonathan. I wasn't about to be trundled off at seventeen to marry some tongue-tied boy from Hotchkiss. I wanted to go to college and see a little of the world, too. What girl doesn't want that?"

"Indeed," I said and immediately wondered who I had become. *Indeed?*

"The boy in question was the friend of a friend of my brother's. I managed to get word to him, and what do you know but he had no interest in me either. He had a girl he wanted to marry. So we hatched a plot. We would agree to our parents' request and meet for tea, much as those two over there are doing."

"Did you end up marrying him?" I asked.

"Patience, my dear Ellie, patience. Together, Jonathan and I both agreed to nix the match on the grounds that we hadn't hit it off. It was a perfect plan. He'd be free to marry his girl, and I'd spend four years at Trinity College before settling down with a good man." She stopped herself to make a correction with a small chuckle. "I still think of it as Trinity College, even though they renamed it Duke my sophomore year."

"What about Jonathan?" I asked.

"As they say, the best laid plans of mice and men . . . We stuck to our script. All was going according to plan until Jonathan's parents worked him over. After a weekend of high pressure, he lost his resolve and said he'd marry me after all."

"Oh, my. What did you do? Marry him?"

"Not by a long shot. I disappeared for a week, stayed with a cousin in Philadelphia, and lay low."

"But how did you manage to avoid the marriage?"

Georgina Whitcomb rocked back in her seat and allowed herself a smile of satisfaction. "Well, Ellie, I had one trick left in my bag. I knew the name of Jonathan's beloved. She was a girl from a good family. Not at the top of the social register, perhaps, but good Methodist stock. I arranged a meeting with her and me and Jonathan at a fish-and-chips house in Cape May. It was all very cloak and dagger. But as soon as they saw each other, the deal was done. They sealed their union over fried fish and potatoes and tartare sauce. I was off the hook."

"I can't exactly quote you on that for my story," I said.

"Of course not, Ellie. Jonathan and Anna are still fast friends of mine. Let's say instead that I fervently wish all children, regardless of race or creed, to enjoy the same opportunity to succeed in life. And the first step on that journey is a good education."

Before heading back to New Holland, I paid a visit to Grossman's Victoria on Broadway. It was nearly six, and I figured as likely as not that Lou Fleischman would be in, perhaps getting ready for dinner. As a matter of fact, he was sinking into an armchair on the front porch, nose buried in the newspaper.

I interrupted his reading. He recognized me as the Jewish girl reporter, but he couldn't quite put a name to my face. We'd only met once, after all. Once I'd prompted him, he warmed and promised he wouldn't forget it again. I asked if he had some time to chat, and he invited me to join him for his evening stroll around nearby Congress Park.

"I was hoping to speak to you some more about Johnny Dornan," I said as we headed up Circular Street at a snail's pace. Lou Fleischman was no Thoroughbred and complained of hip and foot pain as we walked.

"You're not the only one wanting to know about Johnny. I've been dodging a reporter from the *Saratogian* all week. And the Albany papers have been calling, too."

"I have an idea to get everyone off your back."

"How will you accomplish that?"

"I'll ask you a few questions, you'll answer them, and then I'll quote you in my newspaper."

Lou stopped in his tracks, right there on the sidewalk of Circular Street, huffed a couple of breaths, and told me I had to be kidding.

"Not at all. Come, let's keep walking, and I'll explain."

He seemed unconvinced, but probably figured I could do him no harm if he refused to answer. We turned into the park on a footpath and strolled along in silence until we reached the World War Memorial Pavilion. He finally asked what questions I wanted him to answer.

"First," I said, "I'd like to know if you've been contacted by the sheriff's office about the fire."

"Why would they want to talk to me?"

"Those were your racing silks they found, weren't they?"

He nodded. "Yes. And I suppose I can answer your question. The sheriff came to see me on Saturday afternoon, but since it was the Sabbath, the hotel manager convinced him to come back on Sunday."

"Wait a minute," I interrupted. "I saw you last Saturday. You weren't keeping Shabbos. You were at the racetrack."

Lou blushed. "Okay, I confess. I'm not the most observant Jew. I like bacon and shrimp and working seven days a week. It's a sore point with my wife, Rose."

"I'm not judging you. So what did the sheriff ask you?"

Lou chewed on that one for a while, undoubtedly debating whether he should answer. In the end he did.

"He came back Sunday and wanted to know if Johnny Dornan was missing. What could I do? I told him the truth."

"And did he ask you about anyone else by name?"

"He might have."

"Did he ask if you knew a woman named Vivian Coleman?"

"No."

I sensed a caginess in his answer. "Okay, Lou. Did he ask you if you knew a woman named Vivian McLaglen?"

"No, he didn't."

Damn it. Was Lou holding out on me? There was still the same guarded tone in his answer, so I went over my questions again in my head, repeating them in hopes of finding the technicality he was hiding behind to avoid telling me the truth.

"So no one named Vivian," I said. "On Sunday. Did Sheriff Pryor perhaps mention someone named Vivian to you another day?"

"As a matter of fact, yes, he did bring up that name. On Tuesday. Both names, now that you mention it."

"You're a tough witness, Lou."

"And you're a damn good inquisitor."

"So the sheriff came back to ask you more questions on Tuesday." It was a statement on my part, not a question. Frank Olney must have done exactly as he'd promised and shared the names with Pryor.

"Can I assume that Micheline wasn't the woman in the barn?" he asked.

"I can't be sure. What did the sheriff tell you about her?"

"Nothing. And I didn't mention her name, either. Information is a valuable thing, Ellie. I learned a long time ago not to give it away for free."

"I have another question for you," I said. "I'd like to know if Johnny Dornan had any enemies."

"What makes you ask that?"

"The sheriff says this is a case of murder. The man who died in that barn was shot between the eyes before it burned down. And you told me yourself that Johnny wasn't the most likeable fellow in the stable."

He toed a small twig on the cinder path with his worn shoe, then kicked it—after a fashion—into the grass. "You're pretty well informed about what happened on that farm."

"I was there, remember? Saw the bodies. I was the one who discovered them."

Lou shuffled off down the path, and I followed.

"That's the Canfield Casino," he said, stopping in front of a handsome Renaissance Revival brick building in the middle of the park.

"I know. I'm attending a charity gala there Saturday night."

He chuckled. "Like I said, you're well informed about everything. From Wham's Dram and the fire at Tempesta to this."

"Does Johnny Dornan have any enemies that you know of?" I repeated. "Maybe Robinson."

"Robinson who?"

"A name I came across. Never mind. So were there people who hated him?"

"Who doesn't have enemies? Johnny wasn't any different. He had a knack for rubbing people the wrong way. But someone who'd want to kill him? I'm not so sure."

"What kind of people did he rub the wrong way?"

"Other jockeys."

"Anyone else?"

"You're not tricking me into answering that."

"Gamblers?"

He stared me down for a moment then continued on his path past the casino. I followed a few paces behind. We arrived in a garden at the far side of the park and stopped in front of a rectangular pool where two opposing Triton statues were spouting water at each other through conch shells.

We watched and listened to the splashing without a word. It was a beautiful evening, cool with a few clouds high in the sky. I allowed myself a moment to admire the weather and the park. Lou Fleischman could wait. The less I said, the more he wanted to speak. Then he turned to me, pointing to the Tritons. His eyes seemed to challenge me to answer a question.

"Spit and Spat," I said, and he shook his head in mock defeat. I came clean and indicated a plaque a few feet away. "The names are written over there."

A pair of ducks waddled into the vicinity, hopped onto the low fountain wall, and splashed into the pool.

"I like Peking duck," said Lou apropos of the birds. "My rabbi says I can eat duck, you know."

"I'm still not judging you."

"Do you like duck?"

"I like *ducks*. Plural. I wouldn't want to eat these cute little fellows."

He stared at the birds that were quite tame and bold around humans. "I can't talk about gamblers, you know. Don't ask me to. I can't."

"Then tell me about Purgatorio."

"Purgatorio? My horse? What about him?"

"I met him. Twice. He's a beautiful animal."

"And hopeless as a racehorse. He couldn't outrun me with a head start. His trainer thinks it's all in his head."

"Is that Hal Brown?"

Lou was finished admiring the ducks and the spitting Tritons. He started back in the direction we'd come along the cinder pathway. He glanced my way as we walked. "How do you know these things? Like the name of my trainer?"

I smiled to myself. Yes, I was showing off a bit and enjoying it.

"Hal thinks he can teach the horse to win," he said, not waiting for an answer. "Me, I'm not so sure."

"What happens to a racehorse when his career is over?"

"It's not all beer and skittles, I can tell you that. Retired horses are expensive to feed and care for. They can live into their twenties. That might mean ten, fifteen, twenty years of board and veterinary services."

"That doesn't answer my question," I said.

"It's not nice to think about, but if a Thoroughbred isn't worth breeding, you sell him off for whatever you can get. Problem is the only people who want to buy useless racehorses are little girls with rich fathers who spoil them."

"And what happens if you can't find a buyer?"

Lou stopped again and drew a couple of breaths. I compelled him to look me in the eye. He scratched his cheek and made a face, as if I was putting him out.

"Some might be abandoned somewhere. On public lands. Or put down or slaughtered for meat to sell abroad. Most breeders love their horses, but it's a business. If an animal doesn't have what it takes, you've got to make tough decisions."

I must have looked aghast because Lou tried to soften the message with a joke. He said Purgatorio was still a long way from the glue factory.

"Not funny."

"Sorry about that. But don't worry your pretty little head, Ellie. I've got too much invested in him to write him off so fast."

"Where did you get Purgatorio? Was he foaled at Harlequin, or did you buy him?"

"Bought him in a two-year-old claiming race. Cost me eight grand. Not one of my better purchases. At least not yet. He's got great bloodlines. Just can't race."

We resumed our stroll, cinders crackling beneath our feet as we walked in contemplation of the fate awaiting slow-footed Thoroughbreds. I wondered to myself what kind of people besides rich little girls bought "used" racehorses. The kind who had them slaughtered for meat when the poor beasts were done entertaining us for sport?

Shaking thoughts of Purgatorio from my mind, I willed myself to return to the topic at hand. I was there to get information and permission from Lou Fleischman to go to press with a bombshell that might make a name for me and sell some newspapers at the same time.

"You've told me about my friend Tory," I said. "But what about Johnny Dornan? Where did he come from?"

"What do you mean, where did he come from? Like his hometown?"

"Not exactly. He was unknown two years ago. Then suddenly last summer he's a twenty-seven-year-old rookie jockey riding winners in Saratoga. Where did he come from? Hannibal, MO?"

"No. I found him at Aqueduct," said Lou. Apparently he hadn't seen *Damn Yankees*. He stopped to light a cigarette. "You want one?"

"I don't like to smoke while I'm walking. Makes me lightheaded."

"You don't mind if I . . . ?"

"Not at all. But you seem a little short of breath, Lou. Are you sure you want that?"

"You have no idea how much. Rose tries to get me to quit. My doctor, too. But a man's got to have some vices, after all. I don't chase women; I don't drink to excess. What else do I have?"

"Peking duck?"

He took a puff and smiled.

"Bacon and assorted other *treif*," I added. "When your rabbi and Rose aren't around."

"You won't rat on me, will you?"

I patted his arm and said his secrets were safe.

"So was Johnny riding at Aqueduct when you discovered him?"

"A couple of small-time owners were giving him some mounts. Not very good horses. He couldn't win on those nags, but he came cheap at the time so they used him."

"Then why did you hire him?"

"Like I said, he came cheap. And I needed a new morning rider for workouts. So I gave him a job. Then one of my regular boys broke his collarbone falling off a horse, and Johnny got his big chance."

"How'd he do?"

Lou took a deep drag on his cigarette, then held it at arm's length to admire it. "You know, I don't think I could ever give up smoking. Rose says it isn't kosher, but I don't buy that. My pop smoked. My uncles, too. Now my doctor says it's no good. Maybe so. But it's too late for me. Maybe if I were a younger man." After one last puff, he tossed the cigarette onto the ground and resumed his walk. "Johnny did great. That rotten little *kelev she-beklovim* was a damn good rider."

We exited the park back onto Circular Street, and soon we were standing before his hotel. He said he had to get back to Rose for supper.

"I enjoyed our walk, Ellie."

"Me too, Lou. So may I quote you that Johnny Dornan is missing and the sheriff has spoken to you about the racing silks? And Vivian McLaglen?"

He thought it over for a moment, drew another sigh, and nodded. "But you don't say anything about gamblers. I didn't mention gamblers."

I watched him shuffle onto the porch of Grossman's and disappear inside. As he did, I asked myself if he was the type of breeder who could make tough decisions about has-been horses. And I wondered if Purgatorio was insured. Lou Fleischman had spent eight thousand dollars on him, after all. What if that beautiful animal was worth more dead than alive?

"How did you do today?" I asked Fadge as I swiveled on a stool at the counter.

"Not bad," he said. "Came out fifteen dollars ahead."

"Fifteen? How are you going to survive on fifteen dollars a day? You spend five bucks just to park your car on some guy's lawn."

"Hey, I made three grand day before yesterday. Not every day is going to be like that. Like I told you, I'm in this for the long haul."

"Unlike this place. Who was minding the store today?"

"Zeke."

"Again?"

Fadge shrugged. "My uncle Sal was here with him."

I shook my head in woe.

"El, Uncle Sal was working here with my dad before you were born. Before I was born."

I said nothing in reply. If Fadge wanted to confide his business to a kid and his uncle who—sweet though he was—counted Methuselah as his younger brother, who was I to complain?

I sat in my usual booth in the back and, longhand, wrote out my article that would name jockey Johnny Dornan as the presumed male victim. While Sheriff Pryor steadfastly refused to share any information with me, I had a person of interest—to wit, Louis Fleischman—who was on record that the sheriff had approached him to inquire into Johnny Dornan's whereabouts.

Norma Geary had pulled some good photographs of Johnny Dornan from the wire services, and I had pictures of everything else: Harlequin Stables' livery, the racetrack, and, of course, the burning barn.

I was on a roll, so I went to work on finishing my fundraiser story. The recap of the Friends of the Library Society garden party was already done. All that remained was to distill the notes of my interview with Mrs. Georgina Whitcomb down to something manageable, and work the quotes into the narrative of my story. It was hardly the best piece I'd ever written, but I managed to shoehorn some of Georgina Whitcomb's warmth and charm into it. I liked the old bird, and not because she was Freddie's mother. In fact, I felt proud of my little society-page bit of fluff, so I treated myself to a nickel's worth of music from the jukebox. I scanned the catalogue before finally settling on "Rockin' Good Way," a sexy little duet between Dinah Washington and Brook Benton. I glanced over to the counter where Fadge was packing a quart of butter pecan ice cream for Mr. McAndrews who lived next door to the store. The big fellow was struggling to chisel the rock-hard ice cream out of the tub for a man whose guts he hated. And I admired him in that moment. Admired him for his hard work and his taste in music. I was sure no other jukebox in the city had such great selections.

I grabbed a bottle of Coke from the cooler and retook my seat in the booth. Reading through some notes on Johnny Dornan, I became aware of a shadow hovering nearby. I glanced up expecting to find Fadge eclipsing the sun, but it wasn't him at all. It was a young woman. I didn't recognize the blonde beauty standing there until she spoke.

"I need to speak to you, Ellie," she said as the song came to an end. "About Miche."

It was Joyce Stevens.

CHAPTER FOURTEEN

"**B**renda doesn't know I'm here," she said in a low voice.

Fadge appeared above us. Clearly impressed by the attractiveness of my companion, he turned on the charm as if opening a fire hydrant and asked Joyce what she would have. She said she didn't want anything. Normally Fadge would have thrown her out. He had no tolerance for stragglers who bought nothing. But as strict as he was about his buy-something-or-get-out policy, he was also a man and a fool when it came to pretty girls. He flashed his sweetest smile and withdrew.

"I'm worried about Miche," said Joyce.

"I thought she was in Montreal."

"That's what Brenda says, but I'm not so sure. She had a boyfriend a while back who was very controlling. She broke it off with him, but he kept coming around. So we came up with a standard lie that she was visiting her mother in Canada."

"When did you see her last?" I asked. "The truth this time."

"Last Friday afternoon."

"Had she packed a bag for a trip?"

"No. She was getting all dolled up for her date."

"Her date with Johnny Dornan," I said to clarify.

She averted her eyes, glancing at her hands. "Yes."

"Did she know Johnny already, or was he just another appointment set up by Jimmy Burgh?"

"Yeah, she knew Johnny. But only through Jimmy. She thought he was fun. She met him last year when he was racing at Saratoga. And this year she saw him once before last Friday."

"What about you? Did you ever meet him?"

"Once. He was okay. A little full of himself and too short for my tastes. But he had cash and was willing to spend it on Miche."

"Did he ever tell you where he was from? Or how he got into racing?"

"No, but Miche once said he was a fellow Canadian."

That was news to me. I made a mental note to check into the Manitoba angle again, this time asking for Johnny Dornan's name.

"Did she say where they were going Friday night?" I asked.

"Just that it was another *date* with him. I knew what that meant." She paused, possibly going over some tragic scenario in her head. "Do you think it was Miche in that barn?" she asked at length.

"The sheriff's still not sure. And I think it's someone else altogether. Where might Micheline have gone?"

"That's just it, Ellie," she said, her eyes pleading with me for help. "I don't know. I've asked at the Safeway, her old boyfriend, even Jimmy. No one knows where she is."

"How well do you know Jimmy Burgh?" I asked as Fadge materialized again, this time bearing a small hot-fudge sundae.

"For the pretty young lady," he said to Joyce. "On the house."

I gave him my most disapproving shake of the head. Where was my ice-cream sundae? "Pathetic," I mouthed to him. He harrumphed and delivered the treat to Joyce, who smiled appreciatively at the big lug.

"Forget about Jimmy for a moment," I said, once her knight in spattered apron had pushed off. "Tell me about Robinson."

Her face twisted like a screw. "Who's Robinson?"

"You don't know anyone by that name? Maybe an acquaintance of Micheline's?"

Joyce insisted she didn't. "Sounds like a Colored name. I don't know any Negroes."

I almost asked her if that was by choice or happenstance, but I didn't have the time or patience to explore Joyce Stevens's prejudice. Instead I asked if Micheline had a car.

She shook her head. "Brenda has an old DeSoto if we absolutely need a car. I borrowed it to come here tonight. But Miche and I take the bus mostly. Or cabs, if someone else is paying."

"Someone like Jimmy Burgh?"

She averted her eyes again. "Yeah."

"So here's my question to you. If Micheline isn't the woman in the barn—and I'm almost certain that she isn't—how is she getting around without Brenda's DeSoto?"

I called my editor from the phone at the back of the store and filled him in on my Johnny Dornan story. He approved it and said he'd arrange things with Composition at the paper.

"I want this on the front page," he said. "Upper-right-hand corner."

"What about the cosmonauts?"

"We'll find room for the Red space monkeys somewhere else."

I agreed to meet Fadge at Scafitti's restaurant on East Main Street after he closed the store. In the meantime, I rushed to the office and handed in my stories and photos to old Mr. Rayburn, the Linotype operator.

"Is Mr. Reese okay with these?" he asked, peering through his horn-rimmed glasses.

He still wasn't used to the girl reporter. Probably thought I was the worst thing since lady drivers. Or women voters.

"I spoke to Mr. Reese twenty minutes ago, and he approved them both. In fact, Composition is redoing the first page for the fire story."

"I haven't heard anything about that."

Just then the aptly named Norm Belcher from Composition rolled into the room like a freight car. "Hiya, Ellie baby," he said, his voice rattling with characteristic mucus somewhere deep beneath one of his several chins. He'd recently taken to making suggestive comments about my posterior whenever his boss wasn't around.

"Where have you been hiding that sweet little derrière of yours? I haven't seen anything that round since the last full moon."

He cackled and slapped Mr. Rayburn on the back, presumably to invite him to share in the laugh, but instead knocking the glasses clean off the old man's head and into the guts of the Linotype machine. It took Belcher three minutes on his hands and knees to extricate the spectacles. I took advantage of his disadvantage to snap a couple of photos of his sofa-sized rear end on full display. I intended to make several prints and post them around the office in the morning.

"Charlie wants us to redo the front page," Belcher said sheepishly to Rayburn as he handed him back his spectacles. Then he scurried off without another word to me.

Old Mr. Rayburn rubbed his eyeglasses with a handkerchief and shook his head. "That man is an ass."

Over drinks and a pizza at Scafitti's, Fadge asked me about my attractive friend.

"Where've you been hiding her?"

"Park your tongue, you pig," I said. "She's a roommate of the girl who spent the night with Johnny Dornan before he burned to a crisp."

"I won't hold that against her. She's a pretty one."

"And you could surely have her. For the right price. And I'm not talking hot-fudge sundaes."

"Are you jealous?"

"Well, your crack about 'the pretty young lady' didn't include me. . . . If you think you can get me into bed, by all means go ahead and fatten me up with ice cream. But Joyce Stevens is going to cost you. I'm sure you could secure her services with a portion of your winnings from the other day."

Fadge gaped at me with his bulging eyes. "What are you saying?"

"She's available at popular prices through Jimmy Burgh."

"Who's Jimmy Burgh?"

"Someone I met in Schenectady the other day. An *impresario* of sorts. A manager. I could put you in touch with him."

"Are you saying he's a pimp? And that girl you were talking to in the booth tonight is a prostitute?"

I touched my nose with my right forefinger and pointed to Fadge with my left.

He shoved half a slice of pizza into his mouth and chewed on my words for a moment. "That pretty girl tonight was a . . ."

"Precisely."

He shook his head in dismay, as if he'd been swindled. I gave him no shrift, however, scolding him for his shameless flirting with a pretty face.

"Since when do you hand out samples to random squatters? I've never seen it."

"It's called marketing, El. If you knew the first thing about business, you'd understand that you have to spend to attract customers."

"Spare me," I said. "She lives forty miles from New Holland. She's never coming back here. You were trying to impress her to see where it might get you."

He seemed to be over her already. "Can't blame a guy for trying."

We enjoyed our pizza, and the conversation turned back to Johnny Dornan. Fadge wondered why there was no talk of the jockey in the papers.

"Everyone's being careful," I said. "But have a look at the *Republic* tomorrow."

"You're naming Dornan?"

I nodded as I chewed. After a swallow and a gulp of beer, I explained that I'd had a long chat with Lou Fleischman.

"He gave me permission to quote him on the sheriff's questions. It seems Pryor was very curious about Johnny Dornan's whereabouts in reference to the Tempesta fire."

"That should make for quite the feather in your cap, El," said Fadge. "Congratulations." He raised his glass to me. "So what's next?"

"Where to begin? I've got to find out where this Johnny Dornan came from. Joyce told me tonight that he was Canadian. And the motel clerk at the Friar Tuck said Vivian McLaglen claimed to be from Manitoba."

Fadge continued to chew his pizza.

"What about you?" I asked. "You're an expert horseman. What do you know about Johnny Dornan?"

"Not much beyond how he ruined my parlay last Friday."

"Do you remember seeing him at the track last year?"

"Yeah, he was a newcomer. I knew the name. He won a few races. I seem to recall one of my clockers saying he was kind of shifty. Some story from years ago, but he couldn't tell me more."

We contemplated that dead end for a few beats, and then Fadge asked what else I had.

"I still need to talk to Judge Shaw. The whole thing happened on his property, after all. And then there's the car."

"What car?"

"Vivian Coleman's. Or Vivian McLaglen's, whatever her name is."

"Why do you need to find her car?"

"According to Mrs. Russell, Johnny didn't have a car of his own. So someone must have picked him up Friday night after he retired to his room with Micheline. I think it might have been Vivian McLaglen. And I think they went to meet someone named Robinson."

Fadge nodded. "Makes sense."

"So if Vivian and Johnny were tooling around in her Chrysler Friday evening, what happened to it? Did they drive it to Tempesta to meet their murderer? Or did their murderer take them there in another car? Either way, I want to know where it is now and who left it there."

"Can Frank Olney help you on that? Any abandoned cars towed away?"

"Maybe. But what if the killer wanted to dispose of the car instead of leaving it on the side of the road? Or what if he's still driving around in it?"

"All good possibilities," he said. "It's not going to be easy. Kind of like finding a needle in a haystack."

I finished my slice of pizza. Fadge had polished off the rest. He sat back and picked his teeth, a practice I believed should be carried out in private. But propriety had never been the big guy's long suit.

"Ready to go home?" he asked.

"Not quite yet. I want to make a stop first."

"Where? It's after midnight."

"Let's take a little drive out to Tempesta Farm."

CHAPTER FIFTEEN

The radio announced the temperature was fifty degrees, downright cold for August. Fadge and I peered through the windshield at the twelve monuments guarding the entrance of Tempesta Farm.

"Good morning, it's one a.m.," a man's voice crackled over the airwaves. *"Crowds cheered in Moscow as the so-called twin cosmonauts Andrian Niko-layev and Pavel Popovich made separate landings on the steppes of Kazakh-stan Wednesday, capping a dramatic . . ."*

Fadge switched off the radio.

"How can those cosmonauts be twins?" he asked. "They don't even have the same last name."

I rolled my eyes at his joke. He was a confirmed newshawk who could tell you at all times what in the world was happening and where. I attributed his near-savant knowledge to the countless hours spent reading newspapers as he waited for business to walk through his ice-cream shop's front door. Especially during the winter months.

"Do you really want to go tramping through the wet grass in the middle of the night?" he asked.

"If those twins can circle the planet for four days, we can brave the elements for twenty minutes. I want to have a look around. The caretaker's house and the dormitories are over there."

"Over where? I can't see a thing."

"Don't be a coward. There's a full moon. Besides, I know where to go. I've been here before, remember?"

"And you're not afraid of getting arrested for trespassing?"

"No."

"Or murdered in a burning barn?"

"A little," I said. "But that's why I brought you along for protection. Come on. Let's go."

We climbed out of my Dodge, and, armed with a flashlight in one hand and my purse and Leica slung over my shoulder, I led the way onto the property. A cool breeze blew through my hair and ruffled the panels of my skirt. I buttoned my jacket. Fadge was wearing a dark wool sweater that made him look like a bear walking upright. We reached the site of the burned-down barn, which was still cordoned off by several sawhorses and a handwritten sign that read, "Crime Scene. Keep Out."

"Are we going in there?" asked Fadge.

"No, I've already been through the barn. Let's have a look over there," I said, indicating a structure on the front stretch of the oval training track about a hundred yards off.

As we approached, we could make out a shadowy, wooden building, leaning slightly to one side, capped by a turret of sorts and a pitched roof. There was a large open porch, fenced in by a railing. Some of its posts were rotting in place, while others had simply dropped out of line and lay dead on the deck like fallen teeth. The wind whistled through the large windows, whose glass panes, mullions, and transoms had long since been smashed by vandals. The silhouette gave the impression of a skeleton, the mortal remains of a great beast that had expired eons before but still sat stubbornly in place to remind all that once it had lived.

"Kind of spooky," I said, my teeth chattering in the cool air.

"This is the judge's stand," said Fadge as we came to a stop before it. "They used to hold a race day for the mill workers and farmers. Back around the turn of the century. Matinée Races, free to all. Everyone came out with the family to see the horses. There was cotton candy, popcorn, and peanuts. And five or six races. This judge's stand is where Sanford Shaw himself watched over the proceedings and awarded the winning jockeys."

"It looks as if it's about to fall down."

"It's condemned," he said, pointing to a weathered sign plastered on the door.

"Let's move on. There's that long oval building over there. What's that?"

"The indoor track. For winter training. And that must be the dormitory next to it."

Two hundred yards west of the judge's stand and the finish line of the main course, the indoor training track stretched 150 yards or so on the straightaways. The walls of the low-slung building were buckling under the weight of the roof. And like the other outbuildings on the property, its faded gray boards, punished by weather and years of neglect, were a pale reflection of their former glory.

We slipped into the dormitory through a door that had fallen off its rusted hinges. The smell told us right off that animals had appropriated the living quarters once reserved for stableboys, farmhands, and blacksmiths. A mustiness mixed with odors of wet hay, excrement, and putrefaction of flesh. Some unfortunate beast had died inside the building, and not too long ago, either. A surfeit of skunks had set up housekeeping somewhere in what had used to be the kitchen. We couldn't see them but knew they'd been there.

"You don't suppose that's a dead human decaying in here, do you?" I asked, holding my nose.

"No. I think that's what's stinking up the place," he said, pointing to a large festering mass about thirty feet across the room. I aimed my flashlight at it, but even so we couldn't tell for sure if it was a deer, a bear, or a buffalo. Two things were certain, though. One, whatever it was, it was dead. And two, we weren't going any closer to investigate.

"Oh, God," I said. "Let's get out of here before I'm sick."

I hightailed it for the door, stepping out into the fresh air. After a moment, I wondered what had become of Fadge. I peered back through the door in time to see him puking up his pizza almost as quickly as he'd ingested it an hour earlier.

"Are you okay?" I asked once he'd staggered from the vomitorium.

"I'm fine. Just a little upchuck."

"More like Niagara Falls. Here. Have a stick of gum," I said, producing a package of Beech-Nut Peppermint from my purse.

We continued farther west, past the 350-foot-long Yearling Barn—there was a blistered painted sign over the door identifying it—and a couple of triangular grain storage huts, before finally arriving at the caretaker's house. It looked like any other large farmhouse. White clapboard, two stories and an attic, three chimneys, and a wraparound porch. The residence was in better condition than the rest of the farm buildings, probably because it was the last to be retired from service. Lucky Chuck Lenoir had been in residence as recently as the previous year. Still, the house had seen better days, and they were pretty far in the rearview mirror.

We stepped up onto the porch and approached the door. "It's padlocked," said Fadge, rattling the knob with his meaty right hand.

"All the windows seem to be intact. And shuttered. Although the wood does appear to be rotted in places."

"Are you suggesting we bust in?"

I drew a deep breath as I gazed up at the house. Everything was dark. It felt lonesome and lonely, abandoned. In a few years, this place would be as battered as the other buildings on the property. Wood needs paint or stain. Without protection, rain, ice, and sun will lay waste to it in a trice. Too bad, I thought. Such a magnificent farm had gone to seed in little more than twenty years.

"Let's go," I said. "There's nothing to see here in the dark anyway."

We tramped off back toward my car some quarter mile away.

"You want to get something to eat?" asked Fadge. "Whitey's is still open."

"You want to eat again? You inhaled a pizza an hour and a half ago."

"Yeah, and heaved it all back out fifteen minutes ago."

I glanced at my watch as we reached my car. It was ten past two. I told Fadge that I couldn't stomach the idea of a trilby sandwich and fries and gravy at Whitey's.

"It's like everything in life, El," he said, popping open the passenger door and climbing in. "If you want to be good at something, you've got to work at it, even when the mood doesn't strike you."

I sat down beside him in the driver's seat. "Are you saying I need to train to be an eating machine like you?"

"Precisely."

I noticed the glove compartment was open. "Close that for me, will you?" I asked, and he obliged. "Wait. Open it and see if anything's missing."

"There's nothing in here but your press pass, registration, and a couple of rolls of film. Is that everything?"

I pursed my lips and shifted into drive. "Yes. Still, it's strange."

We drove off down Route 67 toward New Holland. The road was empty at that hour.

"Mind if I put on the radio?" Fadge asked.

"Wait a minute. How do you suppose the glove compartment came to be hanging open like that?"

Fadge said he didn't know. Maybe it had fallen open when we left the car to explore the farm.

I glanced at the box in front of Fadge, then back to the road. "It's never done that before. Jiggle it a little to see if it opens."

Fadge gave it a try, but the latch held fast.

"I know what you're thinking," he said. "You're thinking someone opened it."

"I should have locked the car."

"This is New Holland. No one locks their doors."

"Don't you remember two years ago? That juvenile delinquent Joey Figlio stole my car twice because I didn't lock the doors."

"Maybe it was him."

"Not funny."

"Don't be paranoid. I must have knocked it open when I got out of the car."

I drove on in silence, hardly buoyed by Fadge's reassurances. I resolved to go back to the farm in the light of day and have a serious look around. And this time, I would lock my doors.

CHAPTER SIXTEEN

THURSDAY, AUGUST 16, 1962

With barely three hours' sleep, I opted for an early start after my late-night adventure. I phoned Norma Geary at home to see if she'd made any progress on the Robinson list. No bites, and she only had nine names left. Same on her Johnny Dornan search. Nothing yet, she said, but she was running through old wire-service stories searching for Johnny Dornan's name in the racing results. I asked her to call Bell Canada to see if there were any John Dornans in Manitoba. That would keep her busy for a while.

I drove past Tempesta a little after seven, visor flipped down to block the low sun to the east. But even if the dark had been chased away by the morning light, I wasn't yet ready to explore the ghostly stud farm on my own. First I wanted to have a look at the cars parked at a dozen or so motels in Saratoga County before they'd all been packed off for the racecourse later in the morning or early afternoon.

My list of motels included the Adirondack, Gateway, and Grand Union. And Scherer's, Top Hill, and Turf and Spa. Then there was Design's, Lewiston Motor Courts, Circular, and Tom's Lodge. And that was a partial list. I hadn't even included the hotels and boarding houses. There were too many to cover alone in one morning. But in the end, I managed to visit twenty-two motels and motor lodges in the general vicinity of the racetrack. I was looking for a black Chrysler with the license plate BYW 66. Vivian McLaglen's car. It was a futile game of bingo. I even stopped at the Friar Tuck and introduced myself to Margaret, the helpful busybody who'd provided me with the make and model of Vivian's car in the first place. She told me the car hadn't returned since the previous Friday night when she'd last seen it.

"And I'm out the eighteen dollars she owes me," she said.

"Do you still have her belongings?" I asked.

"Yes, but not much there."

"Would you let me have a look?"

She pinched her face and shook her head. "No. I'm not giving away nothing for free."

I sighed. "Can I buy it?"

Margaret sold me Vivian McLaglen's things for twenty dollars. That was what the missing woman owed on her room at the motel plus a little extra to cover the "irregularity" of the transaction. I confess that I really hadn't wanted to part with any money, let alone so much, for an unknown quantity. But, in the end, my curiosity won out. It was like a wager, I told myself. Fadge plunked hundreds of dollars on unreliable horses, expecting a return on his investment. And one couldn't reason with horses. So why shouldn't I risk a small sum—okay, not so small—on Vivian McLaglen?

I lugged two suitcases and a couple of bags of miscellany from the Friar Tuck registration office to my car and drove off west on Route 50. A few miles down the road, I pulled over at a gas station. The attendant filled my tank with high test and checked my oil. I rummaged through the trove I'd bought from Margaret. As she'd described several days earlier, there were clothes—nothing unusual there—except that there was only two or three days' worth of things to wear. I wondered where the rest of her clothing might be.

I found some other items among her belongings as well. A couple of newspapers, cosmetics, and an almost empty pint of blackberry brandy. Really cheap stuff, I thought, recalling that a pint of the same swill was found in the rubble of the Tempesta barn. Then I asked myself if there was such a thing as *fine* blackberry brandy. Crumpled at the bottom of one of the paper bags were a sales slip and some Green Stamps. There was no business name or address on the sales slip, but the total suggested a liquor store and maybe a couple of pints of cheap hooch. Folded into one of the girdles inside a suitcase was an old laundry ticket. I turned it over and over, searching for a clue to its provenance. But there was nothing beyond Lee's Fancy Chinese Laundry with a Second Street address. That could have been anywhere from New York to Honolulu. Or even Manitoba. I checked the laundry marks in her garments, but those were secret codes that surely only spoke to Mr. Lee himself. The rest of Vivian's effects provided little help in determining where she'd gone. I had my theories, of course. But all of them ended with her dead in a burned-down barn.

Daylight provided a reasonable sense of well-being. Of course, there may have been all manner of marauders haunting the property, but I felt safer knowing the sun was in the saddle. I parked my car in much the same spot as I had the night before, but this time I locked the doors before setting out on my mission. It was a warm day, with temperatures in the eighties. I tramped off toward the caretaker's house, camera at the ready, hoping at the same time to find something and nothing.

Tempesta wasn't quite so spooky by day. The rolling pastures and weathered outbuildings gave the impression of an Andrew Wyeth painting, and I found myself humming the *Pastoral Symphony* to steel my nerve. Still, I couldn't shake the awareness that someone had pried open my glove compartment the last time I'd visited the farm. I wondered if that had been the act of an opportunistic thief, a murderer, or, as Fadge had maintained, the result of some inadvertent action on his part. It was too late to back out now. The caretaker's house loomed ahead.

I reached the place and circled it, sizing it up, scanning all sides from roof to foundation, in search of anything I might have missed in the dark. It was a white clapboard house, as I'd noted the night before, crowned by a mansard roof of gray shingles. I figured it had been built seventy or eighty years earlier. It was unlikely that anyone had been inside since Lucky Chuck had died the previous Christmas, and I wanted to prove that to myself. For my own sense of well-being and security. I knew I'd have to break in, but I wasn't sure which door to test. Something in the rear, of course, in case someone happened to be driving by on the highway and spied me smashing a window.

First, I tried the back door. It was locked, though I was sure the old wood would not hold up in the face of a couple of swift kicks—even from a smallish woman such as myself. But I didn't want to leave a mess or reduce the door to splinters. I tried the eight windows in the back of the house, then the six on the eastern side, but none budged. I was about to check the windows facing the highway when I noticed a pair of storm-cellar doors on the western side of the house. An ancient padlock was threaded through the staple of a hasp, but its shackle had rusted through. It was open.

I grabbed the iron handle and pulled up on the heavy wooden door. It took all my strength to budge the thing, but in the end it yawned open, unleashing the cold, musty smell of decades of darkness and damp and fungus and even machine oil. I peered into the hole, asking myself if I really wanted to enter the house through the gates of hell. The answer was no, but I did it anyway. Cupping my skirt to the back of my knees, I stepped into the doorway and climbed down the steep stairs.

Except for the light streaming in from the storm doors, the cellar was pitch black, and I'd neglected to bring my flashlight. I retrieved my cigarette lighter, sparked it to life, and tried to remember the last time I'd filled it with fluid. I'd have hated for it to run out of gas before I'd reached daylight. One tentative step after another, I waded deeper into the darkness with only the faint glow thrown by my lighter to guide me. The basement was filled to the rafters with busted furniture; shelves, barrels, and boxes spilling their tools and farming equipment into an obstacle course on the floor. My path was hazardous, nails and screws scattered everywhere. I felt my way with one hand while holding my torch with the other. The detritus formed a sort of maze with corridors and walls of varying heights and widths. I could see no more than a few feet ahead of me, and my efforts to locate a staircase had so far proved fruitless. I bumped up against the old iron furnace, cold and oily and unyielding.

I changed course and walked straight into a cobweb, which caused me to shriek and drop the lighter. It took me the better part of a minute to brush the dusty web off my face and out of my hair, and still I couldn't say if a spider might have crawled down my neck. My wayward lighter managed to evade my sweeping hands for another minute and a half as I crawled around on the filthy floor searching for it. Finally upright again with a weak light to show the way, I pushed on deeper into the cellar.

Another cobweb grazed my cheek, or so I thought. After jumping out of the way, I realized it was only a string attached to a bare light bulb above my head. I gave it a yank, certain it would be dead. It was. Surely the electricity had been disconnected when Lucky Chuck Lenoir died the previous Christmas. My lighter, growing ever hotter in my hand, would have to do until I located the stairs and the sunlight above.

The air was close and moist, cool, and malodorous. Cellars usually are. But as unpleasant as the dank smell was, the darkness somehow added fuel to it. A scurrying along the floor to my right told me I was not alone. I wanted out of there. I quickened my pace despite the risks of a fall, and finally a crack of light appeared overhead, sneaking through the wooden planks and around what had to be a doorframe. I'd found the stairs. Now, if only the door was unlocked, I'd be spared a return journey through the dark, past the rats—or whatever I'd heard—and the cobweb jungle.

I climbed twelve groaning steps, grateful that they withstood my weight despite their age and state of disrepair. At the top of the stairs, I fumbled for the knob, and the door swung open, unleashing a flood of daylight into the cellar. I stepped into the kitchen, stowed my lighter in my purse, and shut the door behind me.

It was one of those old farm kitchens. A behemoth of a range—cast iron—squatted next to a tub sink and a long wooden table, gouged and stained by generations of spills, burns, use, and misuse. A hand-cranked washing machine, complete with washboard, had outlived its utility and was marooned next to a water pump. The floor, as foretold by the gaps leaking light into the basement below, consisted of wide boards, hammered in place once upon a time and now warping atop their joists. One day, an unsuspecting intruder was sure to crash through the failing floor. Tiptoeing out of the kitchen, I chose the more stable planks as if playing hopscotch and emerged into a short hallway, then the dining room. There I stopped in front of the fireplace and caught a glimpse of myself in the cracked mirror atop the sideboard on the opposite wall of the room. A smudge of soot or oil streaked across my face like war paint, undoubtedly applied by my own filthy hand after my crawl on the floor of the cellar. My hair resembled a bird's nest after a nasty windstorm. Nothing to be done about it for the moment.

I dragged a finger over the mantelpiece as I made my way to the parlor beyond. There was another fireplace and a single ladder-back chair in the middle of the room. An overturned crate, doing duty as an end table, was home to a stack of yellowed newspapers.

If I hadn't already come so far, I surely would have given up the fruitless search. This place sure felt abandoned to me. The thought comforted me, and I drew a breath of relief. Whoever might have opened my glove compartment the night before couldn't have been hiding in the caretaker's house. But since my face, hair, and nylons were all a mess, I figured I might as well take a look upstairs.

The steps were covered with painter's cloths, perhaps to protect the boards, though, in truth, that seemed a pointless exercise to me. On the second floor, I found five bedrooms and a couple of baths. There were some old books piled into a corner and covered in dust. And another newspaper strewn on the floor not far away. Nothing but what you'd expect in an abandoned farmhouse.

I bent over and retrieved the newspaper, more from a resigned sense of duty than curiosity. It was the *New Holland Republic*—my paper—probably one of the last poor Lucky Chuck had read, I thought. Then I glanced at the headline on the front page and felt a true shiver over my shoulders, and I knew it wasn't a spider from the cellar. The banner read, "Twin Cosmonauts Return to Earth."

CHAPTER SEVENTEEN

Mining some hitherto unknown vein of courage—or perhaps recklessness—I managed to produce my Leica, plug in a flash-bulb, and shoot a single frame of the newspaper with the chair and some of the room in the background. Then I heard a creak through a wall. I couldn't say which one. Clutching my camera in one hand and my purse and the newspaper in the other, I made for the staircase and kicked something small and hard that scuttled across the floor. It came to rest against a wall, and I scooped it up. It was a small handgun that I hadn't noticed before. It must have been hidden under the newspaper.

I flew down the stairs and straight for the exit. I yanked furiously at the front door, but it didn't budge. Then I remembered it was padlocked from the outside. Glancing over my shoulder to the staircase, I held my breath and looked and listened for what seemed an eternity, though it was probably no more than five seconds. No one was following me. Not yet, at least. But I had no intention of waiting for an update. There, not five feet from the door on each side, a large window beckoned. I bolted for the one on the right. In a trice I unlocked it and threw open the sash. After one last panicked look behind me, I dived through the window and tumbled onto the porch outside where my belongings scattered across the boards. I pushed myself back to my feet, gathered my purse, the newspaper, and handgun, and then I was sprinting for all I was worth toward the highway. My car was parked at the entrance, but I sensed the highway would provide my best chance at safety. It was nearing five in the afternoon, and there would be plenty of traffic on the road. I didn't dare head straight back to my car; that would have involved crossing several hundred yards of the farm out of sight of any passing motorists on Route 67. And I wanted to be seen by somebody. Anybody at all who wasn't already lurking inside the Tempesta caretaker's house.

Ten minutes later, I'd made my way along the highway back to my car. Surveying the area from the shoulder of the road, I felt certain the way was clear. No one had followed me, and no one was lying in wait for me. With key at the ready, I made a dash for my car. In a flash, I was inside, doors locked, engine roaring, and tires spinning in reverse. I wheeled the Dodge around, shifted into drive, and floored it.

♫

Slipping into a hot bath, I willed myself to calm down. In the safety of my own apartment, I felt confident that I'd escaped Tempesta unfollowed. I wasn't so sure I'd gone unnoticed, however. Was the creaking noise that had spooked me merely the sounds of an old house settling on itself? Or had someone else been there, watching me, listening? One thing was certain: someone had indeed been inside the house within the past twenty-four hours. I snatched the newspaper from the stool next to the tub and read the date again: Wednesday, August 15, 1962. I tossed it aside. My thoughts leapt to the .25-caliber Colt pistol I'd grabbed on my way out of the house, and I submerged myself in the soapy water, trying to disappear. Holding my breath under the surface, I wondered if taking the gun was an act of utmost foolishness or a wise decision in the spur of the moment. I knew one thing: I needed to stash it in a safe place until I could hand it over to Sheriff Pryor.

Clean and dressed again, I checked the locks on my kitchen door. A year and a half earlier, I'd had bars installed on the window panel along with a new deadbolt and three surface locks. My investigation into the disappearance of a fifteen-year-old girl inspired a spate of break-ins. I lived on the second floor of a duplex, and the only way into the apartment was through the kitchen door at the top of the stairs. The locks were secure, of course, but I worried that a determined intruder could get in despite the best efforts of the Segal deadbolt and an old wood-panel door. An ax or a healthy kick could destroy the door in a matter of seconds. And, short of a drop to the street below, there was no escape except through the kitchen door.

Why was I worrying about my security? I was sure no one had followed me home. But that provided little consolation in light of the open glove compartment I'd found the night before. If someone had indeed searched my car, he would have found the address of my employer, the *New Holland Republic*, on the automobile registration. That was dangerous enough, but my press pass had been there as well. With my full name. And I was in the phone book, which meant the mysterious squatter knew where to find me.

"What's eating you?" asked Fadge, joining me in my usual booth in the back of his shop.

I'd been sitting alone, toying with the crossword puzzle, which wasn't cooperating. Since it was the dinner hour, the store was quiet. Fadge sold a lot of ice cream in August, but during the week, most of his business came in after seven. He had a few minutes to chat with me.

"I'm fine," I said.

"Any progress?"

I shrugged without committing to an answer. I wanted to tell him about the newspaper from the farmhouse, but not if we were going to be interrupted any minute by a customer.

"How'd you do today?" I asked instead.

"Not bad."

"What's that mean? You lost a hundred? Two hundred?"

"A hundred and fifty. But I was close in a couple of races. I'm feeling encouraged for tomorrow."

I held my tongue, but my face surely betrayed what I thought of his prospects.

"I've been meaning to ask you," he said, ignoring my silent reproach. "You're coming with me Saturday, right?"

"What's Saturday?"

He gaped at me as if I'd just asked what color Washington's white horse was. "The big day. The Travers Stakes is Saturday."

"Oh, right. Sure. I'll go. But I have some work afterward, so I'll have to drive myself."

"What work do you have on a Saturday night?"

I lied. Or stretched the truth a bit. I told him I was covering the charity gala at the casino for the paper. Though there had never been any discussion between us, I suspected Fadge might not appreciate my parading some new beau in front of him.

"That's okay," he said. "I've got to get back here for the Saturday night crowd."

A customer came in for cigarettes, so Fadge went to ring him up. When he returned he said he'd forgotten to congratulate me on my big story. The news that the sheriff suspected Johnny Dornan was the man killed in the fire was the talk of the racecourse after the *Republic* came out earlier that afternoon.

"Did you know that your boss sent a truckload of papers to the track? Sold every one of them."

I was flattered. Tickled, really. And impressed by Charlie's brain wave. Artie Short had been fretting over slipping circulation for the past two years. Maybe this would attract a few more readers in Saratoga County. And it wouldn't hurt my reputation either. But in light of my two scares at Tempesta, I reconsidered my satisfaction.

"They were quoting you on the radio, too. WGY and WTRY. And—get this, El—Channel Six, WRGB. Television."

"They mentioned my name?"

"No, but they quoted the paper as the source."

That was as much as I could hope for. You don't go into small-town newspaper reporting to become famous, after all. I smiled and thanked Fadge. But then I remembered the pistol that I'd found in the caretaker's house. It was weighing down my purse at that very moment.

"Can I ask a huge favor of you?" I asked. He nodded. "Will you lock this in your post office safe until tomorrow?"

He stared bug-eyed at the Colt pistol I'd just removed from my purse. Then he gaped at me and back again to the gun. "Where did you get that?"

"Tempesta. The caretaker's house. Will you keep it safe for me? And this too." I produced a paper bag that contained the newspaper I'd swiped.

Fadge agreed and locked up both items, even though we both knew he was breaking several federal statutes in the process. I slipped into the phone booth and dialed the Saratoga sheriff's office. The deputy who answered stonewalled me, insisting Pryor was unreachable. I left a message for him to call me back right away, giving both the number at Fiorello's and my apartment across the street.

Back at my table, I took up my crossword again to battle my jittery nerves. Then the bell above the front door jingled. Another customer. I heard a man's voice order a cup of coffee, then ask where he could find the john. Fadge never liked the idea of customers invading his sanctum sanctorum, especially ones who ordered only coffee. Nevertheless, I heard him dispense instructions, and a figure brushed past my booth on its way to the back room. A minute later I became aware of a presence hovering above me. I glanced up from my puzzle and gave a start. A most unsettling smile greeted me.

"There she is," said the man. "I been looking for you."

It was Jimmy Burgh.

He took the seat opposite me without a by-your-leave. I watched him, wondering what he wanted with me, since I hadn't printed his name anywhere in my articles, respecting his wishes to the letter. And I worried about his sudden appearance so close on the heels of my adventure in the caretaker's house. Could Jimmy Burgh have been the one skulking around Tempesta Farm? I glanced to the counter to find my three-hundred-pound bodyguard. Where the hell was he?

"Don't worry your curly little head, miss . . . Eleonora, isn't it?" said Burgh, aiming for friendly, I could only assume, but landing squarely on menacing instead.

"I prefer Ellie."

"As you wish. And please call me Jimmy. All my friends do."

"How may I help you . . . Jimmy?"

"I want to ask you a couple of questions. I seen your story in the newspaper today. You weren't lying about being a reporter, were you? I thought you might've been exaggerating."

I shrugged, unsure of what to say to that.

"Anyway, two things," he said, lowering his voice and dispensing with the off-putting grin. "First, how'd you come to know that Viv McLaglen was the lady killed in the barn?"

"I never wrote that she was the lady in the barn," I said.

"Not in so many words. But you made it clear it's likely."

"Yes, I did. I believe it was her. Now I'm trying to prove it."

"What makes you think it was Viv?"

"It sounds as if you know her."

"We'll get to the part where you ask the questions in a minute. I've got something for you. But for now, why do you think it was her?"

"I called every motel and boarding house in Saratoga County until I found one where a lady had disappeared last Friday night without settling her bill."

Burgh's bushy black eyebrows inched up his lined forehead. "Pretty smart of you. And, boy, was I surprised to read that Viv and Johnny Dornan were keeping company, even if it was ex post facto."

I believed he meant "posthumously" because what he'd actually said didn't make any sense.

"Anything else that points to Viv as the lady?" he asked.

"Not much was left of her. Just the smallest scrap of a fox stole, a little red hair, and an earring."

Burgh cocked his head and clicked his tongue, as if to say "tough luck." There was no real sorrow in his reaction, only vague fatalism.

"The second thing is, what can you tell me about Micheline? Any news on her?"

"Not yet. I spoke to her roommates, but they don't seem to know anything. They're worried. And a little secretive about their business."

"I know you talked to Joyce. She don't know nothing," he said in a low voice. "That other one, though, Brenda. I don't like her. Looks like a lady wrestler. And she don't like me none neither."

"Are you worried about Miche?" I asked.

"Sure. She's a good kid who does well for herself. And me, too. Naturally I'd like to know that she's okay."

"Have you tried Lou Fleischman?"

"He claims he never saw her after supper on Friday."

Jimmy Burgh was behaving himself, and I felt in no way threatened by his presence. But still I wondered where Fadge had gotten to. Then I heard a giggle coming from the direction of the counter. I leaned out of the booth to see him holding down a stool with his considerable carcass as he flirted with none other than Joyce Stevens. Jimmy flashed his gold tooth at me in another of his off-putting smiles. She'd come with him, of course. Despite myself, I felt a twinge of anger. It wasn't Fadge's attentions to the pretty young thing that I resented; it was hers toward him. I fumed to think that she was leading him on. Not that he couldn't take care of himself, but I wouldn't have wanted to see some of his hard-earned winnings go into her purse for an hour of contracted passion.

"Your friend seems to like Joyce," said Jimmy. "If he wants, I can arrange something for him."

"Please, don't."

"Suit yourself. But your big friend over there looks game to me."

"He doesn't know what he wants," I said.

"I think he does. He knows real well what he wants, and her name's Joyce."

I let him have the final word on Fadge's wants and desires then changed the subject. "Now that I've answered your questions, may I ask you one or two?"

"Fire away."

"Why the interest in Vivian McLaglen?"

"I knew her back when. About eight, nine years ago. She did some work for me from time to time."

"And did she ever land in county jail for the work she did for you?"

"Might have."

"I see. And my second question is, why do you care?"

"I don't," he said with his sinister smile. "At least not too much. She wasn't the nicest girl I ever met. Plenty pretty back then, but surly-like and greedy. Wasn't going to win any Miss Congenitalia contests. Too bad for her, but life goes on."

I thought Jimmy should return his grade-school diploma—if ever he'd managed to cheat his way to one—with apologies for the offense given to his school.

"The first time we met, you said Johnny Dornan probably deserved what he got. What made you say that? Did you know Johnny?"

"Not to say hello. But an associate of mine came to me about ten days ago with some dirt on him. It seems Johnny didn't do all his business aboveboard. He was involved in some shady stuff."

"Go on."

"This guy tells me Johnny got himself into some big trouble about ten years ago. He was an apprentice rider down south. Some track in Kentucky or Maryland. The guy wouldn't tell me. He was worried people might figure out who talked."

"Doesn't sound all that helpful yet," I said.

"Patience, Ellie. You're a smart girl, but you don't take any joy from conversation. Relax and let me tell the story."

If Jimmy Burgh was willing to share some useful information with me, I was willing to indulge him his snail's pace. After all, I knew precious little about the jockey beyond the inadequate descriptions Lou Fleischman and Carl Boehringer had provided. With those meager details, along with the contention by Fadge's horse clocker that Johnny Dornan was "shifty," I had next to nothing. Yet someone had felt compelled to shoot him between the eyes and incinerate him alongside an over-the-hill floozy in a foaling barn in the dead of night.

"In fact, I came here tonight with Joyce to give you a tip," continued Jimmy. "You see, this friend of mine by the name of Bruce, he told me that Johnny Dornan was riding under an assumed name. If the NYRA knew who he really was, he couldn't get his boots shined anywhere within a hundred miles of a racetrack. And, for the sum of two hundred bucks, he gave me Johnny's real name."

"Bruce, you say?" I asked. "Not Eddie or Phil or Solly?"

"Bruce. What's wrong with a name like Bruce?"

I let it go. But I could see where this was going. "So you thought you might approach Johnny with the information Bruce sold you and offer to keep it to yourself in exchange for a favor."

"A favor or two," he said with his gold-toothed grin. "Johnny was consorting with gamblers, you see. And once a jockey crosses that line, it's hard to get back to the other side again."

"Clever of you," I said.

"As things turned out, no. Johnny went and got himself killed before I even had the chance to speak to him. And now I'm out two hundred bucks. I can't exactly ask a favor from a dead man."

"That's tough."

"I'm a big boy. Some bets pay off; others don't."

"So why tell me this? Why would you share this name with me?"

"I thought maybe I could recoup my losses."

I certainly didn't have that kind of money to throw away on a tip. And I was sure that paying for information amounted to crossing into murky ethical territory.

"Jimmy, I don't have two hundred dollars," I said.

"I figured as much. But maybe you could scare up fifty bucks. To soften the sting of my loss."

"I'm sorry, but I can't give you fifty dollars or even five. There's the question of journalistic principles."

"Suit yourself," he said again. "Me, I don't have the luxury of principles."

Then, placing both hands on the table, he slid himself out of the booth and rose to take his leave.

"Jimmy, wait," I said. He stopped and glared at me. "I want to ask you something."

"Shoot."

"Is Micheline worth fifty dollars to you?" I was appealing to his personal decency if not his business sense.

His face hardened. Gone was the creepy gold-toothed grin, replaced by an even more menacing glare. He retook his seat in the booth opposite me.

"Sure she is."

"Then please tell me Johnny Dornan's real name, and I'll track down his past, who killed him, and . . . what happened to Micheline."

Jimmy stared me down for a long moment. "You've got nerve, I'll say that."

Sensing a crack in his resolve, I decided to push my luck. I asked him for another favor. "Do you know anyone named Robinson?"

Johnny Dornan started his riding career under the name John Sprague. It came as a surprise to Jimmy Burgh that Johnny was Canadian, and he'd never heard of anyone named Robinson. At least none who came to mind.

I spent an hour nursing a drink and chatting with the Bell Canada operator from my apartment. Using a 1956 Rand McNally road atlas to navigate around Manitoba, I checked off city after city, wondering how many pages my telephone bill would add up to the next month. I figured a jockey would most likely come from a rural area, and so I avoided Winnipeg for the first thirty minutes. Then the operator, who by that point was all in on the sleuthing exercise, suggested we look at the capital and, bingo, we landed on a John Sprague Sr. at an address near the Assiniboine River, a stone's throw from an oval marked "Polo Park" on my map. I slapped my forehead. It was a racetrack.

CHAPTER EIGHTEEN

It was nearly midnight but, with the time difference, an hour earlier in Manitoba. Awfully late to be phoning, but, shameless, I decided to brazen it out. And good thing I didn't wait till morning; the disoriented man who picked up the receiver on the ninth ring probably agreed to answer my questions only because he'd taken the trouble to climb out of bed, tie on a robe, and shuffle to the kitchen to answer.

"Who did you say you were?" he asked, voice heavy and full of sleep. I was sure he was in the habit of retiring—and rising—with the sun.

"Actually, I didn't say. My name is Eleonora Stone."

"I don't know any Stones except Edgar Stonecipher in Selkirk. Are you one of the Selkirk Stoneciphers?"

"I'm not a Stonecipher at all. I'm just a Stone, plain and simple."

He fussed down the line from a thousand miles away and confessed he didn't understand what I wanted.

"I apologize, Mr. Sprague," I said. "I'm a reporter from the *New Holland Republic*. We're a newspaper in New Holland, New York."

"You're Dutch?" he asked.

"No, I . . . I'm calling to ask you about Johnny Sprague. Is he your son?"

"Who are you again?" he asked, impatience testing his civility. I sensed he was ready to hang up the phone.

"Mr. Sprague, I have news for you," I said, thinking that might stay his hand. "And I'd appreciate it if you'd answer a few questions for me."

He seemed to weigh my request. And even without saying a word, he made it clear that this was not a conversation he wanted to have.

"We don't speak of him around here. Not anymore."

His voice betrayed his pedigree. This was a hardscrabble, plain-talking, working man. His bitterness bled through, like a growing bruise.

"Oh," I said, then waited a healthy ten seconds before he spoke again.

"I haven't seen him in nine years. Nor spoken to him. Not since he left for Maryland."

"What can you tell me about that?"

He didn't answer right away. He stalled, squirrelly, as if searching for an escape. Or maybe he wanted to find the right words to tell a complete stranger—one who'd admitted to being a newspaper reporter and who might well take liberties with a story about his son—that his boy had disappointed him.

"About Maryland? Nothing to tell."

"I see. What about Mr. Robinson?"

"Who? I don't know any Mr. Robinson."

I lay back on my sofa, receiver to my ear, and held the five-and-a-half-by-eight photo of Johnny Dornan at arm's length, stretching it toward the painted tin ceiling. Gazing up at it, trying to extract his secrets from the smiling eyes, I said nothing, though a sigh of contentment escaped my lips as I put my stockinged feet up. My new shoes—a pair of stacked heel pumps I'd found at the Paris Shop on Main Street—were stylish but tight. I thought I'd drop them off at Giuffre's Shoe Repair in the morning to have them stretched a bit. John Sprague called me back from my reverie. I tossed the photograph onto the end table and turned my attention to the matter at hand.

"I don't understand why he didn't stay here in Winnipeg," he said. His voice oozed regret and reproach. "We've got Polo Park a few blocks from our house. A fine track. He was an apprentice, training there. He could've had a full career right here close to home."

"I can't argue with that." I examined my nails from my reclined position. Definitely time for a manicure. Of course, I wasn't happy with the job Doreen from Francine's Beauty Parlor had done the last time, so naturally I wondered whether I should try New Wave Beauty or the old standby, Mr. Paul's Salon. Mr. Paul was a sweet old fellow whose hands never once grazed your bosom, even when he was brushing you off after a styling. His tastes were said to run to handsome Spanish boys.

"But he wouldn't listen to me or his mother, no," said Mr. Sprague at length. "Even Mr. Spears—Robert James Spears, no less—wanted him to stay and ride in Canada."

"I'm sorry, but I don't know who Robert James Spears is."

Sprague nearly choked. Then he huffed that Spears was the father of Thoroughbred racing in western Canada. "He built Polo Park," he said. "And Whittier and Chinook, too, in Alberta."

"And he couldn't convince your son to stay?"

"He's no son of mine." His tone was the sharpest since we'd been speaking. The pump was primed, and he went off like a hand grenade. "Johnny disgraced himself. Brought shame to his family and his country. And to the sport of kings. His blessed mother, rest her soul, died of a broken heart. That boy is no good, and he's dead to me."

I swung my feet to the floor and sat up straight on the sofa. How should I break it to him that his son was indeed dead? And not only to him, But to me. To the world. To everybody.

"Mr. Sprague, I have some news about your son. I'm afraid it's not a happy ending."

After an understandably lengthy pause to collect his thoughts and emotions, he cleared his throat and asked if I meant that Johnny was dead. I answered yes.

"I blame it all on that tramp. That woman who turned his head."

"A woman? Who was that?"

"The one who lured him to Maryland with all kinds of crazy ideas in his head."

"Do you remember her name?"

"Vivian," he said, almost spitting his disgust. "Vivian Coleman was her name."

❧

After my scare at Tempesta that afternoon and the curious timing of Jimmy Burgh's visit at Fiorello's, I was feeling jumpy. Every noise—the creaks, thumps, and footfalls—from downstairs or from the street below sent me to the kitchen to investigate. Even with the sturdy new storm door that Mrs. Giannetti had installed a year and a half earlier after my fleeing aggressor somersaulted down the stairs, straight through the glass, and onto the sidewalk, I worried that someone would try to gain entry.

At half past midnight, I truly fretted for my safety. New Holland was a small town, after all. If someone wanted to find you, someone could. I checked the kitchen door again, found it securely bolted, then poured myself a couple of ounces of courage. I set my drink down on the end table in the parlor and selected an LP to play—softly so as not to disturb Mrs. Giannetti downstairs—and eased myself back into the sofa cushions. The first strains of Schubert's incidental music to *Rosamunde* washed over me, relaxing me as if by an incantation. Then, just as I was putting thoughts of marauders out of my head, the door buzzer sounded, startling me enough to send half of my drink down my blouse and into my lap.

I glanced at my watch: 12:44 a.m. Who could be calling at that hour? I doubted it was Fadge. I'd watched him from my bedroom window closing up the store at least forty-five minutes earlier. And then I'd heard his Nash Ambassador backfire twice, sounding like two reports from a howitzer, before he roared away down Lincoln Avenue. I dashed to the kitchen and armed myself with the longest knife in the drawer. If someone intended to do me harm, he was going to pay dearly for the privilege. The door buzzed again.

This was silly, I told myself. Whoever was downstairs was still on the wrong side of a locked storm door. And what self-respecting marauder rings the bell? Congratulating myself on my pluck, I drew back the bolts, and, barefoot, I slipped out onto the landing, my thumping heart and rapid breathing contradicting my delusions of bravery. From my vantage point at the top of the stairs, I couldn't quite see the whole door at the bottom, which only heightened my unease. I descended slowly, taking each step with care and dipping my head to the side in attempts to make out who was calling at a quarter to one. A pair of men's trousers rose into view. Then a jacket, checked, and an open collar. It was Freddie.

I bounded down the last few steps to let him in. He made a feeble attempt to appear sheepish, but my arms around his neck and my lips on his rather obviated the need for apologies. I wasn't sure if it was entirely out of attraction that I was overjoyed to see him. There was also the question of my fears of an unwelcome midnight intruder interrupting my sleep with a pillow over my face.

I didn't unload my worries on Freddie. At least not right away. A while later, as we caught our breath and pretended such exertions were normal for people of our short acquaintance, I told him about my visit to Tempesta that afternoon.

"That's spooky," he said, settling back into the pillow. He reached for his cigarette case on the bedside table, popped it open, and held it out to me.

I shook my head. "Spooky doesn't quite describe it."

"And you're sure it was yesterday's paper in the caretaker's house?"

"Do you recall two Russian cosmonauts orbiting the earth at the same time before this week?"

"I see your point. So someone was in that house this week. Maybe he was up to nothing more nefarious than catching up on the news."

"Did I mention there was a pistol on the floor?"

"A pistol? Where is it now? What did you do with it?"

"It's in a safe place," I said, knowing I couldn't tell him. Not that Freddie would have turned Fadge in to the postal police, but he didn't need to know the exact location.

"What about the newspaper?" he asked. "What are you going to do with that?"

"Hand it over to the sheriff."

"What for?"

"Fingerprints, for one. Newspaper ink is wonderfully messy. Or maybe whoever was reading it wrote something inside."

"Of course if you hadn't taken the gun and the paper, whoever's hiding in that house wouldn't have known you'd been there."

"He knew already," I said. Freddie seemed confused. "I visited the farm two nights ago and left my car unlocked as I snooped around. When I got back, the glove compartment was open. Someone rooted through my car."

"If I were you, I'd get rid of that newspaper as soon as possible. Give it to the sheriff. I'll do it for you if you want."

I rose from bed and crossed into the parlor where I grabbed the bottle on the end table. Back under the sheets, I poured a drink for each of us. Freddie stubbed out his cigarette, wrapped his arms around my waist, and pulled me roughly against him, effectively putting an end to our conversation.

FRIDAY, AUGUST 17, 1962

In the morning—a couple of hours later, actually—I told Freddie more over a pot of coffee.

"Did you know that Johnny Dornan is an assumed name? Changed it nine years ago. He was born John Sprague Jr. in Winnipeg, Manitoba."

"That's news," said Freddie, and he took a sip of black coffee. "Why did he change it?"

"Some kind of gambling scandal. I spoke to his father last night on the phone."

"And he didn't know the full story?"

"Maybe. But he wasn't telling. Claims he hasn't heard from or spoken to Johnny in nine years."

"Gamblers might explain how he ended up in that barn."

"Say, Freddie. You're something of a horseman. Did you ever hear of Johnny Sprague down in Maryland about nine or ten years ago?"

"No."

"What about the racetracks? You must know them. Where might a nobody from Manitoba have ended up riding down there?"

Freddie took a bite of the charred wheat toast I'd prepared especially for him and reflected on my question. I hadn't burned it on purpose, of course. Cooking, alas, was not my long suit.

"Not sure," he said.

"Didn't you say you used to haunt those tracks? Isn't there one where gamblers might have been fixing races?"

Freddie chewed his toast like a trouper, too polite to complain about the blackened bread he was crunching between his teeth.

"In Maryland, Pimlico is out, of course," he said. "That's where the Preakness is run. Not some backwater. Clean. Cheating's pretty rare. And I'd rule out Keeneland, too. Nice place."

"What about in Kentucky?"

"Not Churchill Downs, for sure. Can you imagine your Johnny what's-his-name riding in the Kentucky Derby?"

"Maybe not. Anywhere else?"

Freddie gave it some thought, then said there were a couple of tracks he and his friends used to frequent several years ago. The Maryland Fair Racing Circuit. Not exactly the major leagues, but there were betting and fun times.

"I remember Hagerstown and Marlboro," he said. "Marlboro's small enough, I suppose. And Hagerstown is about as glamorous as it sounds. And Timonium, too. Out of the way, but there's some decent racing at those tracks."

"But you don't remember any betting scandals anywhere in the region?"

He shook his head.

"How about a man named Robinson? Johnny Dornan wrote that he was meeting someone named Robinson on Friday at midnight."

He shook his head. "I know a couple of people named Robinson, but I don't see how they could have been in contact with your jockey. Kent Robinson was a schoolmate at Woodberry Forest. Went on to divinity school. And Junior Robinson worked for my grandmother in Charlottesville. Nice old fellow. Taught me to tie my shoes. Of course he died fifteen years ago."

"Fat lot of help you are," I said. "I thought you were a track rat."

"Not hardly. I love the sport, but I don't live for it."

"And yet we met at seven in the morning at the training track. You were even armed with binoculars and a stopwatch. I figured you were a bridge jumper."

"You say the funniest things, Ellie Stone. Sometimes you sound like a gangster's moll. But, no, I'm careful with my betting. Some fellows can't sit out even one race. They simply have to be in the game, whether they're confident of their strategy or not. It takes patience and discipline to win at this."

I told him I had a dear friend who also thought he could beat the system. "But he's a plunger. He told me he once dropped two hundred dollars on a single race."

"There are more like him than you might think. Two hundred bucks is too rich for my blood."

I would have thought the opposite, at least in terms of his blue blood. It was clear that Frederick Carsten Whitcomb III came from money. I'd had tea with his mother, after all, and she threw off a healthy odor of greenbacks. And old ones at that. Still, even if one was swimming in the stuff, profligacy and lack of self-control struck me as wrong. Throwing away money in such a cavalier manner, when so many others were truly in need, was bad manners if nothing else. So Freddie's responsible habits, despite his wealth and privilege, were to his credit.

"I've got to run," he said, dabbing his lips with a napkin. "How about I take you to the Travers tomorrow and squire you around like a Southern belle?"

"I'm afraid I already have a date for the race."

"Your friend the plunger?"

"The very one."

"Does he have a box in the clubhouse?"

"No, but there's a bench near the paddock where he sets up shop."

"Fine. I'll pick you up here tomorrow at seven for the gala. That means you'll have to leave after the Travers if you're going to make it back here in time. It's the sixth race, so the horses will probably be in the gate a little before five."

"I have a better idea. It's a lot of driving to rush back and forth to Saratoga. And there's no way my friend will ever miss the last three races. I was thinking of taking a room at a motel in Saratoga."

He grinned at me. "Sounds naughty when you say it."

"The Friar Tuck Motel on Route Fifty. Seven thirty. Be on time and I might invite you back later for a nightcap."

Yes, I considered myself a "modern girl." And, as in the case of the horse that ran off, I saw no value in locking the barn door now. And though I spent little time analyzing my own behavior in this regard, I knew that I was happy with the freedom I granted myself. Freddie made me laugh. He was smart, athletic, and attractive. I owed explanations to no one. I smiled just thinking of that. Then the specter of my landlady, Mrs. Giannetti, invaded my thoughts and wrecked whatever self-satisfaction I was feeling. As I accompanied Freddie down the stairs to the street, I prayed she wouldn't be watching through her chintz curtains to catch me at my most shameless once again. Hallelujah, the coast was clear. Freddie gave me a peck on the cheek and tweaked my nose as if I were a child. Then he slipped out the storm door, turned right, and strode down the sidewalk about fifty yards. He'd had the good sense to park his roadster a respectable distance from my apartment. What a gentleman.

"Late night, dear?" came a voice to my left on the front porch. Damn it.

"Good morning, Mrs. Giannetti," I said and turned to trudge back up the stairs to sew a scarlet A onto my blouse.

CHAPTER NINETEEN

"Have you seen the *Saratogian* this morning?" asked Norma Geary over my shoulder.

She placed it on my desk and folded her arms across her chest, as if to dare me to read the front page. I gathered up the newspaper and snapped it open. There in the upper-right-hand corner of the front page stretched the headline, "Tempesta Barn Victim Is Jockey Johnny Dornan: Sheriff Pryor." The byline was Scotty Freed.

"Isn't he a track writer over at the *Saratogian*?" I asked Norma. She nodded. "And now he's writing front-page copy? He must be the sheriff's man at the paper."

"At least you beat him to the punch."

"Yes, but this means the sheriff is willing to share information with Freed. It won't be long before he's a step ahead of me."

"So what's your plan?"

"This," I said, tearing a page out of my trusty Underwood typewriter along with a sheet of carbon paper and the copy underneath it.

Norma took it from me and, sitting on the corner of my desk, read out loud.

"'Was Johnny Dornan in the Pocket of Downstate Gamblers?'"

Jimmy Burgh had agreed to go on the record for certain details, including that he'd been told by anonymous sources that Johnny Dornan was working under an assumed name. Then, quoting John Sprague Sr., I jumped to my late-night telephone conversation with the victim's father. The details of that call provided the most stunning revelations of my investigation to date. He had, after all, corroborated the ubiquitous rumors of Johnny's involvement with gamblers by establishing the connection between his son and the woman suspected of having died alongside him. To wit, Vivian Coleman/McLaglen.

And I'd written a second story on the missing Micheline Charbonneau. I handed it to Norma, who read it in a trice. Without actually naming Micheline as a girl for hire, I gave the facts. She'd accompanied Johnny Dornan to dinner after the races on Friday evening and hadn't been seen since about 10:00 p.m. at Mrs. Russell's Boarding House in Ballston Spa. I was sure the cantankerous landlady would be furious about the publicity, but you can't always change names to protect the innocent. Or the wretched, for that matter. I quoted Micheline's friends Joyce and Brenda as saying she'd gone to Montreal, but I left Jimmy Burgh's name out of it altogether.

Norma glanced at her wristwatch. A couple of minutes past ten. "I think we can still get these into this afternoon's paper if we hurry."

"Yes," I said, picking up the phone and asking the switchboard for Charlie Reese's line. "But Charlie's going to have to go to the mat for me on this. Artie Short will swallow his cigar at the cost of redoing the front page."

∂⟩

Charlie said Artie was out of town, and he approved the stories immediately. He sent my copy down to the typesetter via Norm Belcher, who glowered at me when Charlie wasn't looking. Earlier that morning, I'd thumbtacked eight-by-tens of his *sweet little derrière* throughout the office. I'd heard several bouts of raucous laughter coming from the coffee urn and the watercooler before the lummox was put wise and ripped them all down. My pal Bobby Thompson from the photo lab—no relation to the Giant great, and his name was spelled differently to boot—had kindly provided me with four sets of prints, and I planned on exhibiting them in the weeks to come.

"That's some fine work, Ellie," said Charlie once Norm had picked up his charm and dragged it out of the room.

"You won't catch any flak from Artie Short for redoing the front page at the last minute?"

"I can handle him. He's always harping on about losing circulation to Schenectady. I'll remind him that Saratoga is a rival, too."

I'd be lying if I didn't admit to feeling flattered. But then Charlie burst my bubble the next moment when he mentioned my society piece on the Saratoga fundraiser.

"I liked it so much I want you to do more of that kind of thing. The social angle is popular with our female readers. Gives them something to aspire to."

"Charlie," I whined. "I just handed you a major scoop on the Tempesta murders, and you want to send me back to covering tea and cucumber sandwiches?"

He looked stunned. A little hurt, even. "I'm sorry, Ellie. I only meant you'd done a fine job."

I caught Fadge as he stepped out of the store. The guilty expression on his face told me half of what I needed to know. The keys in his hand told the other half.

"Please say you're not locking the door," I said.

"It's just for a couple of hours."

"Fadge, you've got a problem."

"No. Zeke is the solution to my problem. He's tied up today till three, but starting tomorrow, I'm all set."

"That's not what I meant. You've got to take care of your business."

"It's a couple of hours, El. Zeke will be here by three fifteen. He's a good kid. Doing a great job. I should've hired him years ago."

"He's fourteen."

"Gotta run."

"Wait," I called after him. "I need to get that thing I gave you out of the safe and turn it over to the sheriff."

"No time. I'm late as it is."

I sighed. "I'm coming with you. I've got some business at the track."

"How's the Johnny Dornan story going?" asked Fadge as he sped along Route 67.

"His real name is John Sprague. It appears he was riding down in Maryland or Kentucky about nine or ten years ago."

"Johnny Sprague?" he asked. "That sounds familiar. But he would've been pretty young back then, wouldn't he?"

I shrugged. "Eighteen. Maybe nineteen."

"Then I doubt he was riding at Pimlico or Keeneland. Certainly not Churchill Downs. Too inexperienced. Must've been one of the smaller courses."

"Hagerstown maybe?"

Fadge threw a surprised look in my direction. "Sounds about right. How do you know about an out-of-the-way track like Hagerstown?"

"A girl has her secrets."

⁂

When we arrived around one thirty, Fadge made a beeline to the racecourse. I wandered across Union Avenue to the Oklahoma training track, looking for Mike the jockey. As promised, I had some nice shots of him and Purgatorio to deliver. A stableboy at the horse barns told me the place was closed. But he assured me that Mike would get the photos.

"Is this where the Harlequin horses are stabled?" I asked.

"Over there," he said, pointing down the row of barns.

After a few minutes of searching and a couple of inquiries of various grooms and stableboys, I found a magnificent stallion biding his time quietly in a shed. Someone had scrawled "Purgatorio" in white chalk across the bottom half of the Dutch door. My favorite Thoroughbred was alone, with an empty stall on either side of his, presumably to isolate him from the other horses. He stood still, facing the wall in the back.

"Tory," I called to him through the door. His long ears swiveled, and he turned his head to see me. "Come here, boy."

Motes of dust hung in the warm August air, swimming slowly, as if alive, out of the shadows into the light that streamed through the gap between two planks in the wall. The thick smell of horse leather, sweat, hay, and manure overwhelmed me, but not in an unpleasant way. The place smelled like a barn, of course. All was quiet except for a smithy hammering on some iron at the far end of the stables. I fancied he was fitting the shoes for a horse that would run for glory across the street someday soon. Purgatorio regarded me for a moment, his big black eyes clear and sober, and then he sauntered over and pushed his head through the Dutch door.

I held out my palm, offering him a handful of Cheerios I'd brought along especially for him. He dipped his head and picked my hand clean with his long lips in a gentle, almost dainty fashion. Once he'd finished, he looked up at me, then back at my hand, as if searching for more. I obliged him with two more fistfuls of the cereal, but then I was tapped out.

"I'm afraid that's all there is," I said and rubbed his muzzle.

He seemed to like that. I stood there for several minutes chatting with him. He mostly listened, blinking, head still, level with my cheek and mere inches away. He breathed slow and deep. At length, I thumped him firmly on the neck as I'd seen Mike do a few days before, and told him I had to leave. He watched me go, his head and long neck protruding from the Dutch door.

CHAPTER TWENTY

I spotted Freddie Whitcomb sipping a tall drink and chatting with four other swells—three well-heeled young men and a pretty young blonde woman—in a clubhouse box above the winner's circle. He was glib, suave to the point of caricature, what with his bright smile, strong white teeth, and tanned face. The life of the party to anyone watching. As was I. The blonde was decked out in a flowery print sundress, with a rather silly white hat draped over the wooden rail separating her from the next box of blue bloods. The hat remained in place, despite the energetic batting of its owner's eyelashes. I fancied Freddie's hair was waving under the influence of the breeze, which was aimed in his direction.

When the race began, all five turned to watch, cheering gaily as the horses streaked down the backstretch. They clutched rolled-up programs in their mitts and exchanged smiles of delight as the leaders rounded the turn for home. Then all five rose as one, jumping and exhorting their charges for the final push. The field thundered past them, hooves pounding the dirt, colors flashing by in a blur, until one reached the wire ahead of the rest. The crowd of sixteen thousand, including the five in the box I was fixated on, exhaled as one with the conclusion of the contest. I didn't notice which horse had won. I only saw the blonde woman throw her arms around Freddie's neck in celebration of what must have been a victory for her.

I stood there green-eyed, pathetic, wondering if Freddie had visited Blondie in her room—the way he had twice climbed my stairs in the dead of night—for celebrations of another kind. I felt deflated. Small and out-classed, as the *Racing Form* might describe a Thoroughbred that *also ran* and never challenged. And despite my best efforts to explain away the intimacy and familiarity I'd just witnessed, I failed. Yes, Freddie was taking me to a gala the following evening. But what would he be up to that Friday night?

Why did I care? I barely knew Freddie. What did I expect was going to happen between us? Was he going to sweep me off my feet? Carry me back to Old Virginny? I was only interested in a little diversion, not a

major commitment. So why should I begrudge him his friends? For all I
knew, the blonde woman was his cousin. And I wasn't forgetting that I was
attending the races with a friend as well. True, whenever anywhere near a
racetrack, Fadge paid as much attention to me as he might to a fly perched
on a streetlamp across the street. But that was beside the point.

I wandered over to the Jim Dandy Bar, where the bartender, having
recognized me from previous visits, thought himself clever and served up
a gin and tonic before I could order it. I smiled weakly and apologized.

"No thank you," I said. "I'd really rather have a Scotch."

"Troubles with the ponies?" he asked.

"Something like that."

⁂

"Good day at the races?" I asked Fadge when I finally tracked him down at
the concession stand after the eighth race. He was stuffing a hot dog with
the works into his mouth.

"That depends on how you define good," he said.

"I see. That means you lost, but you were ever so close to winning."

"I'm up six fifty," he said with all the smugness he could muster. "That's
six *hundred* and fifty dollars, El."

I felt conflicted. On the one hand, I wanted him to develop some
sense of responsibility toward his business. And for that, he'd probably
have to learn the hard way. By losing. But at the same time, I was secretly
thrilled that he'd won so much. Despite my better instincts, I was questioning whether Fadge had the right idea after all. He'd already banked
three thousand in one day, and now more than six hundred another. Sure,
he'd lost several hundred here and there, but he was sitting on an impres-
sive pile of winnings for the August meet.

"That's it," I said. "You're buying me dinner tonight. And not a hot
dog with piccalilli or relish. And you need to give Zeke a couple of bucks
as a thank-you."

"I see you don't mind my gambling when I win."

"That's right. But I'll be there to pick you up when it all goes south.
Remember that."

He turned white. "Jesus, don't say that. You'll jinx me. Take it back and
spit on the ground."

"I'll do no such thing."

But after a five-minute harangue on superstition and Lady Luck, my three-hundred-something-pound bodyguard and best chum had me recanting my statement and expectorating on the dirt, mere steps from the refreshment stand and a crowd of people enjoying their snacks. I only hoped none of Freddie's friends had witnessed my performance.

As we passed through the gate on our way to Fadge's car, which he'd parked directly across Union Avenue on the most expensive lawn in Saratoga, he grabbed a copy of the *New Holland Republic* that someone had discarded on a bench. He stopped to show me the front page, which was dominated by my two stories, the one linking Johnny Dornan, né Sprague, to downstate gamblers, and the other describing the plight of the missing Micheline Charbonneau.

"You're getting good at this," said Fadge. "But are you sure you want to be writing about organized crime and gambling? You'll start attracting the wrong kind of attention."

"Thanks for the reminder. But I didn't name any names."

"All the same, be careful, will you? These sound like a rough crowd. That Jimmy Burgh, for one."

"Who do you think told me Johnny's real name?"

He folded the secondhand newspaper, tucked it under his arm, and we set off for his car. Once inside he remembered something.

"By the way, I spoke to a couple of my clockers and asked them if they knew anything about Johnny Sprague."

"And?"

"They definitely remembered something about a scandal eight or ten years ago. Didn't realize that Dornan was Sprague, though." He threw the car into gear and inched toward the makeshift parking lot's exit, following a long line of cars. "Anyway, it seems Johnny Sprague tried to throw a race with a couple of other jockeys down in Maryland. My guys thought it might have been at Laurel Park or Hagerstown."

"That narrows it down somewhat."

"And I asked them if they'd ever heard of anyone named Robinson. No luck."

"That helps," I said. "I can ask Norma to start looking into those race-tracks. Of course there's a two-year period to cover, and it was a long time ago. Still, this gives her a fighting chance. Thanks."

"A mere bagatelle," he said with characteristic magnanimity.

Fadge's promise of dinner didn't exactly pan out. In truth, he hadn't promised anything; I'd demanded. But Friday nights at Fiorello's were busy ones, especially in summer when the weather was hot. Not only did the locals turn out in droves for ice cream, but the high school kids descended upon Lincoln Avenue, which was the place to meet and greet. They hung out on street corners, making noise and creating mischief. From time to time, the residents would grow tired of the inconvenience and call the police to keep the teenagers moving. But however the authorities harassed them and chased them into the ball fields a few blocks away, the kids still piled into the booths and filled the counter at Fadge's place from eight to eleven every Friday and Saturday night. He complained that they hardly bought anything. Cherry Cokes, egg creams, or the occasional song on the jukebox. But by dint of their sheer numbers, the teen population of New Holland accounted for a significant slice of Fadge's business.

So instead of tying on the feedbag in a fancy Saratoga eatery, Fadge tied on a fudge-spattered apron at the store and, along with poor Zeke, who was pressed into a double shift of soda-jerking duty, held off the marauding hordes of teenagers that night. I waited at my place across the street for him to finish. Another in a series of late-night pizzas would have to suffice for my special dinner.

I phoned Norma Geary at home, regretting the interruption of her evening. She was a widow with a retarded son named Toby and had her hands full without much help. Her aged mother did what she could, pitching in afternoons when Toby returned from school. But mostly Norma was on her own.

"Are you busy?" I asked straightaway.

She insisted she wasn't. Toby was fast asleep at 8:30 p.m. I filled her in on the new information Fadge had provided. Johnny Dornan/Sprague had been involved in some kind of betting scandal eight or ten years earlier at one of two tracks in Maryland. I gave her the names, and she said she'd start digging first thing in the morning.

"Tomorrow's Saturday, Norma. This can wait till Monday morning."

"It's all right, Miss Stone. Toby can come sit with me at the paper. I don't mind taking him along when the place is empty. There's no one for him to disturb on a Saturday."

I felt like a wretch, knowing that I would be enjoying myself at the racetrack the following afternoon, while Norma toiled away and made excuses for her poor child. I tried to convince myself that the story required me to visit the track, but I knew I was getting the better end of the deal.

At eleven thirty, Fadge buzzed, and I skipped down the stairs to join him. I waited till he'd stuffed himself into the driver's seat from the passenger's side door before I climbed in.

"Scafitti's or Tedesco's?" he asked.

I was about to say Tedesco's, since we'd been to Scafitti's two nights before. But before I could cast my vote, a voice from the backseat called out, "Scafitti's."

I reeled around, half expecting to find my erstwhile car snatcher, Joey Figlio, sitting there with a knife in his hand. But it wasn't crazy Joey, at all. It was Zeke, Fadge's newest employee. And next to him in the seat slouched Bill, the dishwasher, Fadge's oldest.

"Tedesco's," said Bill.

I said hello to the two, then turned back around to face front. "What happens if it's a tie vote?" I asked.

"I'm driving," said Fadge. "I decide."

And he chose Scafitti's. This time, though, we had the pleasure of two new companions. Bill wasn't a big talker, but when he said something, it was usually memorable. Somewhere in his forties, with a crew cut and thick glasses, he was an idiot savant. A whiz at math, he particularly enjoyed adding up the prices of groceries in his head and calculating the current balance of his passbook account, which on that particular night was $37,496. And thirty-two cents. Bill, you see, was the older son of the late Thomas Goossens, whose Goossens Broom Company had once been a successful manufacturer on the city's South Side. Bill and his younger brother, Stephen, had inherited whopping sums when their father died. Stephen had long since moved away, while Bill lived with his elderly mother on Wilson Avenue, a few blocks away from the store.

"Hey, Bill," said Fadge, throwing a wink at me. "Why don't you tell Ellie what you had for supper before work?"

Bill nudged his glasses farther up his nose with his right forefinger then recited the menu. "Three kielbasa, stuffed cabbage, baked beans, and four ears of corn."

"That's it?" asked Fadge.

Bill thought it over a moment then added, "Peas. And three beers."

"Nothing else?"

A grin spread over his lips. "Two Slim Jims."

I poked Fadge in the ribs for making fun of poor Bill, who chose that moment to unleash a rumbling belch that confirmed, at least approximately so, the composition of his supper. Bill, for all his money and mathematical talents, suffered from some form of mental retardation. People could tell he was a little off on sight, but he managed quite well living with his mother. He rarely spent a penny of his own money for goods, always having the correct combination of coupons or Green Stamps to exchange for dented canned goods or old cigars and cigarettes with his daytime employer, Lou Martello, of Louie's Market on the East End.

After gulping some fresh air from my window, I turned my attention to the second passenger in the backseat, Jeff "Zeke" Zeitner. He was a nice brown-haired fourteen-year-old kid, always hanging around the store asking Fadge for a job. It appeared that his performance of the past couple of days had earned him a permanent spot in the rotation. And that privilege included the occasional late-night pizza excursion.

"Isn't it a bit late for you to be out, Zeke?" I asked. "Don't your parents mind?"

"No, they trust Fadge."

"Then that's their first mistake. How are you enjoying jerking sodas?"

He flashed a brilliant smile at me. "It's great. I get to wait on all the pretty girls, and they have to pay attention to me."

"So you should be willing to work for free," said Fadge.

"How much is he paying you?" I asked Zeke.

"Plenty. Fifty cents an hour."

Again I poked Fadge in the ribs.

"Hey, cut it out, El. That hurts."

"How can you pay him fifty cents?" I hissed. "Minimum wage is a dollar fifteen."

"First of all, don't go trying to unionize my workers. Second, it's not even legal for him to be working for me in the first place. He's only fourteen. And, third, he can eat all the ice cream he wants, plus I take him out for pizza after work on the weekends."

"Yeah," said Zeke from the backseat. "You gotta admit, Ellie, it's a pretty good deal."

It was fun getting to know Zeke and Bill a little better, even if the topics of discussion never surpassed a ninth-grade level. At one point between the hors d'oeuvres and finger bowls, Bill jumped out of his seat and began dancing a kind of jig in rhythm to the song playing on the jukebox. We asked him what the heck he was doing, and he responded through his teeth, "Leg cramp." Zeke spent an inordinate amount of time chatting with me, asking questions about my favorite singers, my boyfriends, and other such nonsense. He was cute, but the cow eyes set off alarms in my head. I'd had my fill of teenage boys falling in love with me. Fadge enjoyed the role of ringmaster of his own little circus, and, all told, it was a nice time. But I looked forward to Saturday evening's gala fundraiser at the casino and a chance for some adult conversation. Fadge, of course, insisted on picking up the tab.

It was past twelve thirty as we sped up Market Hill. Fadge would drop off Zeke first, then Bill, then me. He turned onto Howard Street from Arnold Avenue.

"Hey, Fadge," said Zeke from the backseat. "That car back there has been following us since we left Scafitti's."

We turned as one to look through the window. All except Fadge, who squinted into the rearview mirror. In the dark, it was impossible to distinguish any identifying characteristics of the car except that there were two headlamps shining at us.

"Are you sure?" I asked.

"Yeah. I've been watching it for a while now."

"Let's try this," said Fadge, turning sharply onto Victor Street.

We drove on for thirty seconds, nearly reaching the next corner, when the car swung into view some fifty yards behind us.

"No one lives on this little street," said Fadge. "Whoever that is must be following us."

"Maybe it's a cop," I said.

"No, I saw it," said Zeke. "Just a regular car. A sedan of some kind. I couldn't tell the model because it's pretty old."

Fadge turned again, this time right onto Grant Avenue. He eased his speed, glancing into the rearview mirror every couple of seconds, until the car appeared again, now barely thirty yards behind us. Fadge made two more right turns, daring the car to follow. Having made a complete circle, we were back on Victor Street, but this time with no shadow. The driver must have figured out that Fadge was onto him. Or her, I suppose. Anything was possible. When we reached the corner of Grant this time, Fadge turned left and floored it. For all its dents and dings, his Nash Ambassador could still fly when he took the whip to it. Five minutes later we pulled up to Zeke's house on McClellan Avenue. Fadge cut the engine and doused the lights. Everything was still at 12:45 a.m.

"That was close," said Zeke. "Really cool the way you lost him, Fadge."

"Could it have been some kids having a little fun?" I asked. "Trying to scare us?"

Fadge frowned. "Yeah, you're probably right."

"They followed us to Scafitti's, too," announced Bill. In the commotion, I'd nearly forgotten he was there.

"What do you mean they followed us to Scafitti's?" demanded Fadge.

Bill laughed in his characteristic manic way, though I saw nothing funny about the situation. "Followed us from the store all the way to East Main Street," he said, still chuckling.

"Why the hell didn't you say anything?"

But Bill didn't answer. He never answered when Fadge yelled at him. Whether he'd broken a sundae dish in the dishwater or done a poor job of washing a rack of Coke glasses, Bill rarely argued back. He pouted, eyes fixed straight ahead for several seconds. Then he'd open some new topic of conversation to deflect attention. That night he didn't change the subject. Instead he said, "DUT 5639."

"What?"

"DUT 5639. The license number of the car that followed us."

CHAPTER TWENTY-ONE

After Fadge dropped off Zeke and Bill, he drove me back to my place. Casing the block from the front seat, we decided all was clear. It was one, and I confessed to Fadge that I was feeling more than a little frightened. I dreaded the idea of another break-in.

"I didn't want to say anything in front of Bill and Zeke," I began, "but I don't think that car was full of joyriding teenagers trying to scare us."

"Me neither," said Fadge. "I think it's someone you cheesed off. Maybe one of those gamblers you wrote about."

"I told you I didn't mention any names at all."

"But you did shine a light on them. Maybe gave the police ideas about who might be responsible for Dornan's murder. You gotta be careful, El."

"Horse. Gone. Barn door. Too late."

"Come on," he said. "I'll walk you up to your place and make sure no one's lurking in the shadows."

꩜

We sat in my parlor for an hour, listening to some jazz, and considered the situation over a couple of drinks.

"Let's say you're right and it was gamblers," I said. "Maybe they were trying to send me a message. Trying to scare me a little. Maybe they won't come back."

"Let's hope not."

"We've got the license number. We can ask Benny Arnold at Motor Vehicles to trace it."

"Yeah, but not before Monday. What do we do in the meantime?"

"Maybe Frank Olney can check with the state police for me."

We sat quietly for a few minutes more, sipping our drinks and listening to the Oscar Peterson Trio. It was one of Fadge's records, a live LP from the Newport Jazz Festival, which he'd lent me a month or so before. I'd hoped it might soothe my anxiety, but in truth it did not.

"You don't suppose it was an admirer of yours," said Fadge.

"An admirer?"

"Yeah. Maybe someone whose heart you broke."

"I don't break hearts," I said. "And I can't think of anyone who might be obsessed by my charms to the point of tailing me around town after midnight."

Fadge chuckled.

"This isn't funny, chum."

"I know, I know. But I was thinking of Zeke. He's got a big crush on you, you know."

"Oh, God."

"I told him I'd see what I could do. You know, feel you out. See if you were interested."

"Again. Not funny. Remember that kid from the reform school, Frankie Ralston? He wanted to marry me. I don't need another teenager in love."

Fadge apologized for real, and we sank back into silent contemplation of Oscar Peterson. But I had a thought. One that I couldn't share with Fadge. It may have been wishful thinking, but I wondered if, by chance, Freddie hadn't dropped by for another late-night visit just as I climbed into Fadge's car. What if he'd been seized by jealousy and followed us down to East Main Street and Scafitti's Pizzeria? And then perhaps waited outside until we'd finished and followed us home? I laughed at myself, though not so Fadge could see. What nonsense. For one thing, Freddie drove a little roadster, not a nondescript old jalopy. I was sure the thought was motivated by my seeing him with his friends earlier that day at the track. The twinge of jealousy stung a lot less if I pictured Freddie guilty of the same weakness.

Finally, a little before two, I told Fadge to go home and get some rest. He made a lewd suggestion that he'd rest perfectly fine in my comfy bed, but I pushed him out the door with an admonition to drive carefully and watch for cars in the rearview mirror.

"Be at the store tomorrow at noon," he said at the kitchen door. "And don't be late. Traffic and parking are going to be hell tomorrow. Travers Day."

SATURDAY, AUGUST 18, 1962

I phoned Frank Olney at 8:00 a.m. Home on a Saturday morning for a change, he was nevertheless up, dressed, and ready to jump into the saddle if crime called. It did, in the form of me and my spooky encounter with DUT 5639.

"Can you get a trace on the owner by any chance?" I asked.

He paused before answering, and I fancied I could hear him scribbling the number into a pad of paper. "I'll see what I can do," he said finally. "Might take a day or two. But maybe someone can get me this before Monday."

"Thanks, Frank. I owe you."

"Say, Ellie, I saw your piece in the paper yesterday. You're not messing around with gamblers and criminals again, are you?"

"Don't worry. I can take care of myself."

Norma Geary was waiting for me when I arrived at 8:30 a.m., and a familiar pang of guilt needled me. I craned my neck to see beyond her. There, halfway across the newsroom, her son, Toby, was sitting at her desk, rocking from the waist, staring in the direction of the far wall but without any focus that I could determine. It was heartbreaking to think of the poor child and his uncomplaining mother. Norma surely noticed my distress, which only made things worse. Now, to add to her burdens, she was embarrassed.

"I'm going to say hello," I said, flashing her the brightest smile I could manage.

Toby didn't remember me, but he smiled all the same when I produced a small brown bag of Cheerios that I had packed that morning for Purgatorio, in case I made it over to the stables later in the day. I was aware that I was guilty of dehumanizing Toby, equating him with a dumb animal, albeit with the best intentions, but his eyes lit up at the sight of the cereal.

He picked one O from my hand and nibbled on it for a moment. Then he helped himself to three more, and that was all he wanted. He chewed on them, drooled on them, and ended up dropping them onto the floor. I smiled at Norma and told her what a great boy Toby was. She fidgeted and changed the subject.

"I finished off my list of Robinsons last night," she said. "I'm afraid none of them panned out. Unless they were lying to me."

"It was a long shot."

"But on the Johnny Dornan front, I've located newspapers in the Hagerstown and Laurel Park areas. I'm about to telephone now, though they're not major dailies. I'll try Baltimore and Lexington and Washington, as well. But they might not have run anything on Johnny Sprague if all this happened at a small-time racetrack."

"And it's Saturday, so there might not be anyone at home at those small papers."

"I've already got phone numbers of several libraries in the area. Librarians read and have good memories. And they tend to stay put in their jobs for years. I think I'll get something before the day is through."

I'd never thought of quizzing librarians for local race-fixing history, but it made sense. Norma Geary never failed to impress me. I retrieved a five-dollar bill from my purse and told her firmly that she was to buy herself and Toby lunch. When she bucked, I lied and said Artie Short had authorized the expense. That it wasn't my money. In the end, she took it and thanked me with a stiff smile. It wasn't easy to fool her. And she hated being pitied.

*

I spent a couple of hours working on several pieces that had been languishing in my Not Urgent folder. Then I tackled a couple of stories that Charlie Reese had asked me to finish for a colleague whose mother had passed away three days earlier. It wasn't hard stuff. Some city council meetings, a tax assessor story, and a profile of an exchange student from France.

Next, I plotted out the dramatis personae of the Johnny Dornan case. There were the two victims, Johnny and his erstwhile love interest,

Vivian McLaglen. They seemed an unlikely pair to me, but love, like water, seeks its own level. He'd been a wet-behind-the-ears kid from Midwestern Canada. A fine riding prospect, but headstrong and unwilling to follow the rules. According to his father, Johnny had turned his back on a fine future riding in Canada to pursue a redheaded tramp to Maryland. Other reports on Johnny Dornan's character didn't paint a rosy picture, either. Consorting with gamblers, he was variously described as a mean-spirited, unpleasant frequenter of professional girls.

Vivian McLaglen was twice married. Widowed, then remarried to her late husband's younger brother, with whom she'd carried on a not-so-secret love affair. People who'd known her described her as selfish, demanding, conniving, and plain no good. That last characterization had come from the lips of her own father. Testimonials from Jimmy Burgh and her abandoned husband, Tommy McLaglen, did little to rehabilitate her reputation.

Next, assuming—perhaps mistakenly so—that Johnny and not Vivian was the key to the murders, I considered those closest to him: the Harlequin Stables team. There was his minder, Carl Boehringer, and his employer, Lou Fleischman, and even Nick Blakely the jockey. And what about Mike, the morning rider? I wasn't sure how well he'd known Johnny or what reason he might have had to want to do him harm, but hadn't he admitted that he disliked him? A long shot, perhaps, and a nice guy to boot, but who could say? I asked myself if he might not profit from Johnny Dornan's death by inheriting some of his rides. After all, Johnny too had won his big chance and proven himself in part thanks to the injury of another jockey.

Carl Boehringer professed no love lost for Johnny. He'd called him a little prick, arrogant, and a midget. I'd been intrigued by Carl's role in the Harlequin organization from the first moment I'd met him. He appeared to have no part in the racing or training side of the business. He wasn't a veterinarian or an accountant or a lawyer. Both he and Lou Fleischman had declined to explain what his job was until I'd pressed the latter and been told that Carl was "like my right hand." *Like my right hand*, not "He's my right hand." Did that matter? Was I overanalyzing the relationship? Might that right hand carry a pistol to defend his boss? Or perhaps enforce for his boss? That most certainly depended on my opinion of Lou Fleischman.

Lou looked like any *zayde* one might find sagging into a webbed lawn chair at a Catskill Mountains resort. I wondered if he was, in fact, a grandfather; we hadn't touched on his personal life. I knew him to be a man of simple tastes. He didn't keep Shabbos, cheated on his kosher diet, and smoked despite his doctor's and wife's wishes. A man who enjoyed the simple pleasure of a cold Schaefer's beer. He struck me as a nice old man, but I'd sensed a darker side to the gentle soul who'd strolled through Congress Park with me, watching the ducks and enjoying the fountains. And there was the clever way he'd skirted my question about Vivian McLaglen. It was as if he'd been schooled by some shyster on how to avoid perjuring himself under questioning. And then there was the shadow that had crossed his face when I asked him what happened to Thoroughbred horses that didn't earn their keep. I wasn't forgetting either that Lou Fleischman had procured a prostitute for Johnny Dornan the very night he was murdered. No *zayde* I knew did that kind of thing and then dandled his grandson or granddaughter on his knee. But a man who felt the need to keep a shady type such as Carl Boehringer as a right hand might. He'd called Johnny a bad name in Yiddish, too. Had Johnny Dornan done something to provoke Lou to put him out to pasture? I liked Lou, but I hardly knew him. And what I'd seen left me suspicious.

My list grew. The gamblers, thugs, and racketeers. Jimmy Burgh—he of malapropisms and gold tooth—may have sounded like an understudy from *Guys and Dolls*, but I was laboring under no illusions; this was a dangerous man. And though we'd seemed to have reached an entente cordiale, I hadn't forgotten that he'd once threatened me—obliquely—to keep his name out of the newspaper. Furthermore he traded in sex, blackmail, and extortion. He'd told me to my face that he intended to use compromising information to force Johnny Dornan to throw a race or two as a favor. Only Johnny's death had prevented him from following through on his plan.

Jimmy was also the only person I'd met who came close to knowing both victims, and he was the man who'd set up Micheline's appointment with Johnny Dornan on the night he died. Until Micheline resurfaced, who could say for sure if she hadn't met with foul play herself? I imagined any number of scenarios to explain her continued absence, and most of them ended badly for the pretty young girl with the shapely caboose. Maybe she was an unlucky remainder in the Johnny Dornan–Vivian McLaglen equation. A witness? Sitting in the car waiting while Johnny met with Robinson—whoever he was—and then disposed of by the murderer to tie up all loose ends? Eventually she had to turn up, one way or another. Dead or alive.

I hadn't met Bruce, Jimmy's source on Johnny Dornan's past, but he sounded like a prince. Of course he knew the betting scandal would sink Johnny's career. Again. And he'd sold the information to a man who had the means to parlay a two-hundred-dollar investment into a healthy profit. My only question about Bruce was why he hadn't used the dynamite himself? Perhaps he didn't have the stomach or muscle to play rough. Maybe he was content to pocket a small-but-sure bundle and watch the action from the safety of the grandstand. I wanted to talk to this Bruce fellow, ask him where he'd secured the dirt on Johnny, but Jimmy Burgh wasn't about to arrange that meeting.

I added Micheline's name to my list. She might well be a victim, I reasoned, but, for all I knew, she could also have been an accomplice in the double murder. Maybe Jimmy Burgh had cooked up the scheme when his attempts at blackmail failed. At the very least, I couldn't eliminate her as a possible victim or suspect.

Moving on, I entered Joyce and Brenda's names below Micheline's. I doubted Joyce was a murderess. She'd sought me out on her own, driven from Rensselaer to New Holland to tell me she was sick with worry for her friend. Then again, she was one of only a couple of people on my list who'd actually met Johnny Dornan. And I realized at the same time that she was happy to play for pay. But loose morals did not a killer make. I supposed I was proof of that.

Brenda Schuyler, on the other hand, intrigued me. A tough dame, she was levelheaded and fearless, willing to stand her ground with me and even a goon like Jimmy Burgh. But what reason might she have to do Micheline harm? She seemed to want to protect her at all costs. And did she even know Johnny Dornan?

I needed a new page. I added Vivian's husband, Tommy, to the cast of characters. He claimed he hadn't seen her in three years, but in my experience guilty people are not averse to lying to hide their crimes. She had humiliated him and broken his heart, after all. And he certainly had a checkered past with arrests and underworld connections. I couldn't absolve him of any crimes until I knew more.

Which brought me to the end of my catalogue. Only one name remained, and I had no idea how to find that person. Who was Robinson, and why had Johnny Dornan planned to meet him at midnight the previous Friday? Learning about Johnny Dornan had proved hard enough, but this Robinson was a ghost. No trace beyond the scribbled name in a newspaper. Could he have been the squatter at Tempesta? Or was it one of the others I'd catalogued in my list? One thing was certain: whoever had been skulking around the abandoned farm knew who I was and where to find me.

CHAPTER TWENTY-TWO

I got to the store at 11:30 a.m., armed with a small overnight bag containing a change of clothes, some makeup, and toiletries for my evening transformation. Fadge and I were driving separately, but I'd promised to meet him before to synchronize watches.

Zeke was there, all smiles in a brilliant white apron, happy to be in the lineup. Uncle Sal, too, was standing by, though rather less enthused at the prospect of a long afternoon shift. I suspected Zeke would be doing most of the work.

"Where's Ron?" I asked.

"In the back room," said Zeke. "Getting dressed."

And on cue, the big fella emerged from the rear of the store wearing a pair of white linen trousers, a red-and-white-striped jacket, and—if you please—a scarlet cravat.

"What are you all duded up for?" I asked. "The Oxford-Cambridge Boat Race?"

He gaped at me open-mouthed. When he finally found speech, he said he was dressed for Travers Day. "That's too informal," he said, referring to my outfit. "Go put on something flowery, summery, will you? You're going to the clubhouse, not a pool hall."

Mildly insulted by his insinuation about my dress, I nevertheless resisted the urge to ask him which way to the bandstand. Instead I ran across the street and pulled off my work clothes and searched my closet for something appropriate for the social set. Several competing factors prevented a simple choice. For one, some of my dresses were at the cleaners. For another, much of my wardrobe was several years out of date, at least for the crowd we would encounter in the clubhouse at Saratoga. And some of my nicer things were better suited for fall or winter. On top of that, I was expected to live up to Fadge's sartorial splendor and not embarrass him. What about him embarrassing me?

I'd already packed my evening gown for the gala fundraiser, a green fitted bodice and flowing chiffon skirt that I'd only worn once—for a New Year's Eve date—and not for very long at that. But now I needed a daytime outfit. Rifling through the clothes on the rod, sliding the hangers back and forth and losing hope by the second, I remembered a shirred white skirt with bluebells. It was three years old, but it might do for a day at the races. That satisfied Fadge's requirement for flowery. Now for something *summery*. I found a sleeveless pale-blue blouse that matched the skirt nicely, but there was a large red-wine stain at the waist, the enduring memory of an eager date who'd attempted to fold me in a passionate embrace just as I raised a glass of Burgundy to my lips. The wine ended up in my lap. He, alas, did not. Paint me old fashioned, but I believed the dinner table was an inappropriate setting for amorous exertions. I dug a wide white belt out of the closet, and it covered the offending stain with barely an inch to spare. A pair of white gloves completed my ensemble, and I was ready to match Fadge thread for thread.

Twenty minutes later, we were racing down Route 67 single file in our respective cars. Fadge led the way, driving quite fast, occasionally cutting across the double-yellow line to straighten out the gentle curves of the road and shorten his journey by a couple of feet. Even as a driver, he was lazy and careless.

Traffic was snarled and aggressive in Saratoga, but we managed to find parking on the most expensive lawn in town. We nabbed the last two spots at ten dollars apiece. I nearly wept at the price as I parked my car. But Fadge, big shot that he was, didn't blink. Once he'd pulled the brake, though, he realized there was no room for him to dismount from the passenger side due to the tight quarters. I rolled my eyes and climbed back into my car to switch spaces with him. Still, it was a tight squeeze for him to get out, and by the time he had, he was sweating buckets in his striped coat.

"That wasn't so bad," he said without irony, and we made our way across Union Avenue to the racecourse.

After Fadge had placed his wagers and stuffed a stack of betting slips the size of a deck of cards into his jacket pockets, we took our seats in a clubhouse box, located about halfway down the homestretch.

"How did you swing this?" I asked.

"I had a pretty good day Monday. And yesterday, too," he said, peering at the starting gate through a pair of binoculars. "Three and a half grand buys a lot of box seats, even on Travers Day."

"Why is there no one else in this box with us? How much did you spend on this?"

He told me not to worry about it.

"You bought the entire box just for us," I said to accuse.

The subtle blink and pursing of his lips confirmed my suspicions. I despaired for his profligacy. He'd better keep winning, I thought, or he was going to end up in the poorhouse.

He didn't win the first race. A horse named Brass did and paid $4.30 to win. And Fadge didn't win the second race either. In fact, he was on a losing streak that stretched to the fourth race. He didn't seem concerned. I remembered Freddie telling me that betting on the horses required patience and discipline, two qualities not normally associated with Ron "Fadge" Fiorello.

Fadge was absorbed in his *Racing Form*, making the final tweaks to his fifth-race betting strategy, so I scanned the crowd, taking in the ladies' dresses and hats. Everyone looked happy and rich. No one in the clubhouse was risking the rent payment on the next race. These folks had plenty of money. For them, the horses were more a social function than a gaming one. Next door in the grandstand, the dress code was more relaxed, but not the atmosphere. The bets may have been lower on the other side of the railing, but the stakes were so much higher. Too many of those people needed to win. Losing was a luxury reserved for the rich.

Back in the clubhouse, my eyes came to rest on the pretty blonde I'd seen with Freddie the day before. She was about twenty yards away, but I could see that she'd done some sunbathing since. Her tanned cheeks and arms gave her a glow of beauty and health that I envied. Especially when I spied Freddie sidestepping into the box bearing two tall drinks—gin and tonics, if I was any judge of liquor. And I was, even at twenty paces. Freddie handed one drink to the girl then took the seat next to her. They clinked their glasses, turned to face the track below, and sipped their refreshments.

Not far away, a familiar greasy head of hair and scalp was bowed over one of those mimeographed tip sheets that the handicappers sell at the front gate. It was George Walsh. A goo of perspiration trickled from his temples, oozing over his flushed cheeks and down his neck before disappearing into his yellowed collar. Bound up in his tight ensemble of white shirt, loud plaid jacket, and crumpled straw boater's hat, he was sweating like a horse. He mopped his forehead with a wrinkled handkerchief. I could see all this, even from a distance, thanks to my camera and the long lens I'd retrieved from my purse for the express purpose of spying on him. Georgie Porgie was with his wife and father-in-law—my publisher—Artie Short. I watched as George tried to wedge his way into their conversation with a shoehorn. But they were having none of it, repelling each assault as if swatting a pesky mosquito.

"I'm going for a walk," I said to Fadge.

"The fifth race is next. Don't be late for the sixth," he warned. "That's the Travers."

I didn't want a drink. Certainly not a G and T, so I strolled along the horse path and over to the paddock. The entrants for the fifth race were already on their way to the track, but the start was still ten minutes away. I had a half hour more before the sixth, so I figured there was time for a quick visit to my favorite horse across the street.

I hurried down the long lane to Purgatorio's stable, digging in my purse for the bag of Cheerios as I went. He was in the back of the stall again, still facing the wall as I'd found him the day before. I clicked my tongue twice, and he actually whipped his head around to see who was there. Upon recognizing me, he scampered across the stall to join me at the Dutch door.

"Hello, handsome," I said, patting him on the muzzle.

He dipped his great head and greeted me with a gentle nicker. I produced the Cheerios, and he made short work of the snack, practically swallowing the paper bag along with the cereal. I praised him and continued petting his nose and cheek. He seemed to like that almost as much as the Cheerios. We stood there for five minutes, discussing the pleasant weather, the odious neighboring horses, and his recent workouts. I asked if he'd like something different to eat next time I visited. He stared at me with his right eye and blinked.

A voice startled me from behind. "Don't bring him any food." It was Carl Boehringer, hands on his hips, cigarette between his lips. "He's on a strict diet. A handful of Cheerios is okay, but nothing more."

"I didn't think anyone was listening," I said, surely blushing at my silly conversation with a horse.

"Did he give you a good tip?"

"I'm afraid the conversation was mostly one-sided."

Carl joined me at the Dutch door and reached out to pat Purgatorio's neck. The horse eyed him as if he knew him. He remained calm, almost indifferent to Carl, but he didn't shy away. After a moment, Tory turned back to me and resumed his companionable stance, head next to mine, putting me between him and Carl. Then he uttered a deep sigh.

"He likes you," said Carl.

"I've been visiting him lately. And not for tips."

"Maybe Lou will sell him to you."

I must have looked terrified because he told me to take it easy. "I'm only kidding. He's not for sale." He reflected for another short moment. "Not yet, at least."

"So Lou intends to get rid of him?"

"You know how it is in racing. These four-legged beauties eat a lot of hay. They cost a small fortune to stable."

I stroked the horse's long muzzle and fretted in silence over his future.

"He's getting fitted for a hood tomorrow," said Carl. "The trainer thinks that might help."

"Tell Lou not to sell him without contacting me first."

He chuckled.

"What's so funny?" I asked.

"A little girl wants to buy him too."

"Little girl?"

"Ruby. Just a ten-year-old kid. Daughter of the farmer who sells hay to Harlequin Stables. Guy by the name of Pete Brouwer. He can't afford him," he said, referring to the horse. "And neither can you. He may not sell for what Lou paid for him, but he's worth a couple of grand at least."

I gazed into Purgatorio's big right eye again. He nickered once more, almost a whisper this time. Standing there, immobile, head thrust through the Dutch door, he looked like some kind of equine statue.

"You remember last week you were wondering about Johnny?" asked Carl. I nodded. "Well, I heard something interesting about him the other day."

"Yes?"

"I told you there was rumors about gamblers some time ago."

"And?"

"And it looks like there was something to those rumors. Turns out he was mixed up in a fixed race at Hagerstown down in Maryland."

"How can you be sure?" I asked.

"The guy who told me knows."

"Was his name Bruce by any chance?"

Carl nearly swallowed his cigarette whole. "Yeah," he stammered. "As a matter of fact, it was. Bruce Robertson."

Robertson? That nearly rang a bell. Pretty close to Robinson, but not quite. Could Johnny Dornan have written the name down wrong in his newspaper? I realized that Carl was one of the few people I hadn't asked about Robinson. I remedied that oversight immediately.

"No. I don't know anyone by that name," he said. "But how do you know Bruce?"

"Work sometimes takes me to the other side of the tracks."

"You should be careful. You don't want to mess with guys like him."

I hadn't, in fact, messed with Bruce Robertson. I'd never even clapped eyes on him. I'd only heard his name from Jimmy Burgh.

"What else did he tell you?" I asked.

"That Johnny was named as the jockey who threw a race. He was riding the favorite, but managed to finish third behind a couple of dogs."

"Did Bruce happen to mention any other names involved in the fix?"

"A guy name Hodges. Mack Hodges. A small-time owner. Used to own trotters. Never had a flat runner that could finish in the money. Unless he cheated, according to Bruce."

"Where's this Mack Hodges today?"

"I don't know. Probably still down in Maryland running fifteen-year-old nags at county fair races."

Just what I needed. Another mysterious name I couldn't pin on anyone.

"Anyone else?"

"Not that he mentioned."

"And what happened to Johnny Dornan?"

"Johnny Sprague, you mean. His name was mud, so he changed it. He was banned from Maryland racing, and he disappeared."

"Until last year when Lou found him at Aqueduct?"

"Not exactly," said Carl with a wicked grin. He took one last puff of his cigarette. I was sure he wasn't supposed to be smoking near the horse barns. He stubbed it out thoroughly against the stable wall. "Our Johnny boy had to find other work after he got the heave-ho. He tramped up and down the Eastern Seaboard searching for riding work, but none of the big tracks would let him through the gate. The county fair circuit is a short season and doesn't pay much. He landed with a breeder in Florida for a while, exercising horses, mucking out stalls. That kind of thing."

"Sounds like good honest toil. Not very lucrative, though."

"And then the breeder got wind of Hagerstown, and Johnny was out on his duff again. That was seven years ago."

"So what happened next? What did Johnny Dornan do for six years before sneaking his way into Aqueduct last year?"

Carl glanced to his left and his right as if to make sure no one was listening. He leaned in and said in a gleeful half whisper, "He changed his name to Dornan. Couldn't find any work as Johnny Sprague. And he finally landed a job as a rodeo clown for six years." A snorting laugh escaped his nose. Then a second and a third. He stood up straight and laughed properly. "The arrogant little bastard was a rodeo clown," he repeated, as if I hadn't heard or understood the first time.

"Why would Bruce tell you all this?"

"Information has value only so long as someone wants to keep it under wraps. Johnny's dead, so what good is it to Bruce now?"

I reached Fadge's box in the clubhouse as the horses were being loaded into the starting gate for the Travers Stakes.

"You're all out of breath," he said. "Was that you I saw running last in the fifth race?"

"If I lost, you must have bet on me."

He grinned. It was one of those cat-that-ate-the-canary smiles.

"What aren't you telling me?" I asked. "How did you do in the last race?"

Now the smile disappeared, replaced by what I could only describe as a guilty expression.

"You lost, didn't you? A lot."

"Actually, I won." He paused. "A lot. BF's Favorite. He was a long shot. Paid thirty-one bucks to win. I had him five times."

"Then why were you looking like you'd sold the family cow for a handful of beans?"

He squirmed in his seat, and I pressed him some more. Finally he came clean.

"It's just that I never seem to win when you're with me."

I laughed. "So I'm a jinx?"

"I wouldn't say that."

"Do you want me to leave?" I asked. "You know, to change your luck?"

"Come on, El. I'm sure you're not a jinx. It's a coincidence."

I pouted for a minute or two, and then Fadge said he'd treat me to that dinner he'd been promising.

"I can't tonight," I reminded him. "I'm covering the fundraiser at the casino."

"Then tomorrow."

"Am I going to have the pleasure of Bill and Zeke's company this time?"

He promised it would just be the two of us. And a nice place, too. I gave in.

"You can't stay mad at me," he said.

"Don't bet on it. You'll lose."

"Where were you anyway?"

"Visiting a friend in the stables."

"That horse across the street again?"

I nodded, then asked if he'd ever heard of an owner named Mack Hodges. He hadn't.

"So who do you like in this race?"

His eyes narrowed, a sure sign that he was focused and serious. The only other times I'd seen that look in his eyes were when he was discussing what he wanted to eat. "I've been doing my homework on this race since the meet began. It's going to be Ridan or Jaipur, I'm sure. Everyone knows that, of course. Those two are the class of the race. Even with the extra weight they're carrying."

"More weight than the others?" I asked. "That hardly seems fair."

He showed me the program and explained that it was intended to make the race more competitive. "See, Jaipur and Ridan are carrying a hundred and twenty-six pounds each."

"Plus the jockey," I added, feeling smart.

He gaped at me with his hyper-thyroid eyes. "No. That includes the jockey."

I wanted to ask how much the jockeys weighed, but decided to keep my mouth shut and listen instead.

"The other horses here are all carrying less. One fourteen, one fourteen, one twenty, and so on."

"So which one did you bet on?"

"I'm sitting this one out," he said.

"Wait a minute. Is this because I'm a jinx and you don't want to lose?"

"Come on, El."

"But you've been handicapping this race for three weeks."

"I can't come up with an approach that would win me anything. Look at the odds," he said, indicating the tote board in the infield below. "Jaipur is three to two, and Ridan is five to two. Even if I bet a hundred on one of them, the payoff isn't worth the risk. And place and show would only pay pennies."

"You're sure no other horse will win?"

He shook his head. "I don't see it. So I'm going to sit back and enjoy it."

"I feel like betting on this one," I said. "It's the biggest race of the season, after all. I want to participate."

"There's no time to go place a bet now. They're loading the last two horses into the starting gate."

"Then bet with me. I'll take that Jaipur horse. You take the other one."

"All right. Two dollars to win?"

"Deal."

We shook hands and turned our attention to the track. The bell rang.

CHAPTER
TWENTY-THREE

Seven horses bolted out of the gate as one, but after a few strides, two broke clear of the pack.

"What number is Jaipur?" I asked, standing on my tiptoes to see.

"Three. And mine is number two. That's them in the lead."

"My horse is wearing a hood," I said, remembering what Carl Boehringer had told me about Purgatorio. Maybe that was a good sign.

The field rumbled past the clubhouse and the winner's circle, with Fadge's Ridan a half-length ahead of my Jaipur. The others were easily three or four lengths farther back. I jumped up and down to see better as the pack rounded the first turn.

"Our horses are still in front," I said. "It looks as if they're even."

"Ridan's about a neck ahead."

The track announcer called the order over the loudspeaker. Ridan and Jaipur maintained their lead over the rest of the field, and were head and head with each other at the half mile. Nothing changed on the backstretch. Now I could see the pitched battle for first straight on. I grabbed Fadge's arm and squeezed a mite too enthusiastically. He wrestled free and said to take it easy.

"Sorry. This is exciting. I got carried away."

Ridan and Jaipur streaked down the backstretch at a furious clip, holding a strong lead over the rest of the field. They seemed to move as one, and if not for the asynchronous bobbing of their heads, I would have thought there was only one horse leading the way.

Approaching the home turn, Jaipur nosed ahead of Ridan, and the field inched closer to the two leaders. At the top of the homestretch, the entire crowd rose to its feet and roared, and I felt the collective temperature, emotions, and energy swell. The two leaders ran neck and neck, holding off the pack as they coursed toward the wire. Ridan pushed ahead again, with a horse named Military Plume charging hard in third for the final quarter mile. But as the field stormed past our position, Jaipur found some new speed. I doubted he had enough ground left to catch Ridan before the finish. At the sixteenth pole, Ridan maintained his lead by a head. Jaipur rallied one last time, and the two horses were even, the lead changing with each stride and alternating lunge of the head. I froze. Everything went quiet. I was moved by the beauty and courage of the two champions, dueling side by side for more than a mile already, and never more than a neck separating them. I clutched my race program, crumpling it in my white-gloved hands, and beat it against Fadge's arm. Then the crowd's roar returned, surging into a deafening din in my ear as the two favorites neared the wire. Ridan and Jaipur, having led from the very start, thundered across the finish line together, leaving clumps of flying earth and the rest of the field in their wake. I couldn't say which had crossed first. Neither could anyone else.

"Photo finish," said Fadge. "We'll have to wait a minute to find out who won."

The spectators milled about, buzzing and smiling and chatting in edgy anticipation of the verdict. I spotted Freddie in his box, staring a hole into the tote board in the infield. His blonde friend was nowhere in sight. I turned back to Fadge, whose gaze was fixed on the tote board as well.

"What are you looking at?" I asked.

"Waiting for the stewards' decision," he said.

"Why are you so worried about the outcome? You didn't even place a bet. Just two dollars with me."

"Yeah, that's what I told you. I've got a bundle riding on Ridan for the win."

"You dirty liar," I said just as the entire clubhouse erupted into a chorus of competing cheers and groans. Fadge was among the groaners.

He dropped a packet of betting slips to the floor, turned on his heel, and opened the *Racing Form*.

"What happened?" I asked.

"Jaipur," he said and nothing more.

He was already immersed in the study of the next race. If he was upset at having lost out by less than a nose, I couldn't see it in his expression. Maybe this was a job for him, after all. No room for emotion or could-have-beens.

Since I had no intention of betting again—I had won the only two wagers I'd placed to date, after all—I wasn't interested in the *Racing Form*. I chanced a quick peek over at Freddie's box instead. He and his friends were backslapping and smiling, which I took as a sign that they had bet on Jaipur or were still high from the excitement of the race. Even I had to admit it had been a thrilling duel.

Not far off, Jaipur was being led by a groom to the winner's circle. He knew he'd won; you could see it in his gait. His hood had been removed, and he looked like a proper Thoroughbred again, not some kind of war-horse in protective armor. A magnificent stallion, he danced lightly, his dark bay coat shimmering in the late-afternoon sun as he savored his victory march back to the judge's stand. His jockey was still perched in the saddle. Fadge told me later that his name was Bill Shoemaker, who'd already won two Kentucky Derbies and three Belmont Stakes, including the one two months before aboard the very same Jaipur. Lips stretched into a broad grin full of teeth, Shoemaker sat atop the thousand-pound champion and waved to the cheering throng. Once in the winner's circle, he reached down to shake hands with some important-looking men, and then he slid off Jaipur's back and set about unfastening the saddle. The groom helped pile the entire kit into Shoemaker's arms, and the jockey stepped through a gate for the post-race weigh-in. A minute or so later, the crowd roared again. I asked Fadge why, and he indicated the tote board in the infield. He said the result was now official.

"Good," I said. "Now pay up. You owe me two bucks."

He reached into his pocket and pulled out a wad of bills that would choke . . . well, a horse. After peeling off the two most crumpled notes he could find, he handed them over. I complained about the condition of the ones, and he told me I was lucky he didn't have two hundred pennies handy. And with that, he returned to his paper.

By the time I left the track for the Friar Tuck Motel, Fadge was still up $130 for the day. Not too bad, considering he'd taken a bath on the sixth race, having lost eighty on Ridan. I thanked him for the wonderful afternoon, straightened his cravat, and told him I'd see him sometime the next day. He was fully absorbed in his *Racing Form* and barely noticed.

My favorite motel clerk, Margaret, showed me to my room, a serviceable if dingy affair with air-conditioning, where I showered and dressed carefully. I knew everyone was going to look fabulous, particularly Freddie's blonde friend, and I didn't want to let down the team. I sat before the mirror, applying more makeup than I normally wore, and, with twenty minutes to spare, slipped into my green gown and sat before the air conditioner to cool off.

I used the free time to phone Norma Geary. She was still at the paper, digging into Johnny Dornan's checkered past. I shared the information Carl Boehringer had provided.

"Forget about the other place," I said. "Narrow your search to stories involving a track called Hagerstown in Maryland. Johnny Dornan was implicated in some kind of race fixing there. Probably nine years ago."

"That's a help," she said over the line. "Everything's closed now. I'll try in the morning, but tomorrow's Sunday. I might have more luck Monday."

"At least we know which haystack to search."

As fate would have it, Freddie was fifteen minutes late. I was quite collected—cold actually—and dry by the time he knocked at the door.

"Oh, no. Is the gala this evening?" he asked as he stood there easy and sophisticated in a black dinner jacket and tie. Not a wrinkle in sight. "I thought we were going bowling. Now I've got to change."

"Come on. Let's go."

"We've got time. No one arrives early for these things. And I've brought a little bottle of something."

He produced a pint of whiskey from under his jacket.

"Great," I said. "But didn't you bring anything for yourself?"

The Canfield Casino was built in 1870. The three-story, red-brick Italianate building was humming with activity when we arrived at a quarter past eight. To protect my unruly hair from a windswept disaster, I'd insisted Freddie raise the roof of his convertible. It was muggy enough as it was; I didn't need a tornado to redo my hair. A long line of sleek cars waited to disgorge passengers at the casino entrance. I watched through the window of Freddie's roadster as bejeweled women in gowns, escorted across the lawn, up the stairs, and into the casino by husbands in black tie, floated as if on air. They greeted old friends and social rivals, exchanging hugs and kisses with equal doses of genuine affection or falsity, indistinguishable one from the other to the casual observer. Once he'd parked his car behind the east wing of the casino, Freddie offered me his arm, and we joined the swells inside the gaming room on the first floor. He was set upon by all and sundry, men and women, eager to shake his hand or kiss him on the cheek. Freddie suffered the attention gladly; I could see that he enjoyed the role of cock of the walk. And yet he never failed to interrupt the niceties in order to introduce the smallish girl on his arm to his friends. True, the wiseacre told them my name was Eleonora, but it was a gentlemanly gesture on his part. Still, I felt his impertinence deserved a sharp pinch of his side after the third introduction.

We worked our way through the throng into the bar, where Freddie managed to tackle a waiter holding a tray of champagne flutes aloft. He salvaged two for our consumption. I felt transported on the bubbles and on an intoxicating rush of self-satisfaction prompted by my companion's attentions. Not normally one to have my head turned by the trappings of wealth, I felt, nevertheless, beguiled and enchanted by the elegance of the occasion. I told myself to get a grip. I was not Cinderella, and Freddie was not Prince Charming. This was a fun evening of make-believe with people who had more money than they knew how to spend. Have a good time, I muttered under my breath, and then get over it.

I found myself face-to-face with Georgina Whitcomb. She was resplendent in a peach organza gown and an effulgent smile.

"I wasn't expecting to see you here this evening, Ellie. And with my naughty little boy. Why didn't either of you two say anything?"

"Would it help if I said I was here for the newspaper?" I asked.

"Not a bit. But you look lovely, my dear," she said, taking my free hand in hers and squeezing it affectionately. "What a lovely gown. Come. I want to introduce you to some friends."

I threw a backward glance at Freddie as I was led away—like a horse. He smiled at me and waved good-bye. Then he took a sip of his champagne and turned to greet another friend.

Given her role as chairwoman of the charity drive, Georgina Whitcomb was the hostess of the evening. She spoke to everyone in the room, devoting care and attention to each, surely making them all feel special in her estimation. And she presented me to every last person she addressed. I was the brilliant young newspaper reporter from nearby New Holland. Her guests indulged her the hyperbolic introduction and smiled politely.

"Have you met Helen Stansbury?" she asked as we sidled up to Freddie's blonde racing companion. "Helen, dear, this is Eleonora Stone. Ellie to her friends."

Her hair pulled back in a tight chignon, Helen was stunning in a gold lamé gown and a diamond choker that could have covered the gala's fundraising goal by itself. If it was real, that is. I couldn't tell, of course, but I assumed others in the room could. Which meant it had to be genuine. And worth a king's ransom.

"Hello," she said, baring a row of straight white teeth behind her full, red lips. "What lovely hair you have."

I had a doubt. Was she mocking me with false praise? While it was true some people thought my hair remarkable for its volume and curls, I usually found myself wishing it would behave, especially in the humid summer months. I smiled, nevertheless, and complimented her on her lustrous blonde tresses. She nodded as if she'd heard that a thousand times.

"Ellie is here as Freddie's guest," said Georgina.

A small gasp of recognition escaped Helen's throat. "So you're the Ellie he's been telling me about. He certainly wasn't exaggerating your beauty."

Now I knew she was pulling my leg. Beauty was certainly an overstatement, as my trip to Los Angeles had confirmed the previous February. I was told more times than I cared to recall that I was pretty, but not "Hollywood pretty."

"I must say hello to some old friends," said Helen, signaling her departure. "Let's chat later. I want to hear all about you."

She shimmered off like a vision to join some attractive young people not far off. When she reached them, she made a quarter turn and glanced back at me. Her guard was down for a brief moment, and I saw the scrutiny in her eyes. She was assessing me as women sometimes do. A simple sizing up of the new girl. Or perhaps her intentions were more personal. I wondered if she considered me a rival to be chased off.

Whatever her feelings toward me might have been, I felt a twinge of disquiet that Freddie had discussed me with her in the first place. I weighed the possibilities. Should I be flattered? Or were Freddie and Helen simply pals in the habit of sharing laughs over the latest notches on his bedpost?

"Ellie, dear. You're miles away." Georgina took my arm and waded into another wave of well-heeled guests.

Every few minutes, I would lift my head and hazard a glance around the gaming room, searching in vain for a sighting of my escort amid the throng. Georgina was keeping me busy. Despite my strong memory, I struggled to absorb the sheer number of faces and names, which, I assumed, I was expected to remember.

"And here are some neighbors of yours," she said. "This is Judge Harrison Shaw and his wife, Audrey. And this is my friend Miss Eleonora Stone."

I would have swallowed my gum, had I been chewing any. Judge Shaw was the last person I wanted to see that evening. Even less so now that he'd been sprung on me without warning.

"We are acquainted with Miss Stone," he said in his cold baritone.

"How nice to see you again, Judge Shaw."

"Miss Stone—Ellie—and I chatted at the Gideon Putnam a few days ago," volunteered Audrey Shaw. "She was very curious about Tempesta Farm and my first visit to New Holland all those years ago."

The judge regarded her in what seemed to me a reproachful manner, as if he wished she'd informed him of our meeting before that moment in the gaming room. Perhaps he, too, would have preferred to steel himself before having to exchange social niceties with the likes of me.

"Then I shall leave you three old friends to talk," said Georgina. "I see I'm needed by the event planner."

And with that she flitted off to deal with some emergency or other, leaving me in the awkward company of the Shaws.

"I'm surprised to see you here," said the judge.

"The paper wants a piece about the fundraiser."

"And she's turned the head of Freddie Whitcomb," said Audrey Shaw to her husband. "Our Miss Stone is climbing the social ladder."

I felt a sudden stiffening of my spine. "No, really. I quite know my place. I'm writing a profile on Mrs. Whitcomb, and her son generously lowered his standards to squire me around for a couple of hours. This is a charity event, after all."

Audrey Shaw, I had come to know, was a damaged soul. Even after our—mostly congenial—visit a few days before, I labored under no illusions about her stability. She might smile one moment, then slap your face the next. And, of course, she associated me with her daughter's murder. Why should I expect her to act like a decent person with me now?

Judge Shaw frowned. "No one is suggesting you're not good enough, Miss Stone."

After an awkward silence, which included a glare aimed at his wife, who kept smiling as if she hadn't just insulted me, he asked me how I was keeping.

"Fine, thank you," I said.

"I've been following your career with interest," he continued. "You're doing fine work at the paper. One of these days, Artie Short will promote you."

I doubted that, but I kept my mouth shut. Another excruciatingly long pause interrupted our banter. Finally, I could bear it no longer, and, despite the social nature of the event, I brought up business, if only to break the silence.

"I'm sorry to discuss this at such a happy event," I began. "But I was hoping I might ask you two or three questions about Tempesta Farm."

He pursed his lips, then told me that it was bad manners to engage in work at a charity event.

"Nevertheless, it will only take a few moments, I promise."

He huffed a sigh of annoyance and agreed. "Audrey, why don't you go say hello to some friends while Miss Stone and I take care of *business*?" He pronounced the last word with ill-concealed disdain.

Pointing to the nearby staircase, he invited me to lead the way up to the second floor where we could speak in private. The red carpet muffled our steps as we trod down the long hallway—past the gold-flocked wallpaper, mahogany-and-glass cases, and dark paintings of noble horses—to a small gaming room. Judge Shaw tried the knob, which obeyed on command and fell open with a groan. Inside, a worn Oriental carpet anchored the center of the room, along with a settee and two stuffed chairs for the comfort of its visitors. Alongside some portraits of long-deceased gray men in whiskers, a stately grandfather clock—its hands frozen at ten twenty—stood against the wall, opposite a glass trophy case. The judge offered me a seat on one of the chairs. He settled into the other. A large antique globe provided a geopolitical buffer of sorts between us.

"I'd like to get this over with as quickly as possible," he said.

I studied him carefully. His face was drawn, thinner than I'd remembered. His hair now showed more salt than pepper, and a bit of scalp as well. The two years since his daughter's murder must have been hard on him.

"Did you know Johnny Dornan or Vivian McLaglen?" I asked, coming right to the point.

"You're direct, if nothing else. No, I had never heard of the jockey, and I certainly didn't know that woman. Why would you ask me that?"

"Because they died on your property."

He frowned and shook his head.

"What about a man named Robinson?"

"Robinson? There's a Robinson in my office in Albany. He's a junior clerk. Is he involved in this?"

"Probably not. Johnny Dornan had a meeting Friday at midnight with someone named Robinson. Maybe Robinson and the initial *S*. I've been asking everyone."

"I'm afraid I can't help you. As I said, I didn't know either of the victims."

"What about a man named Mack Hodges? Races horses down in Maryland."

He shook his head.

"Isn't your wife from Baltimore?" I asked. "Do you think she might know him?"

"Only if he was around twenty-five years ago. Audrey has lived in New Holland since we were married. And she was never much of a racing fan."

I moved on. "Who is the legal owner of Tempesta Farm?"

"The farm is owned by the Sanford Shaw Trust. My two brothers and I are the administrators."

"Is there any value to the property now?"

"Just the land. The buildings are worthless. That's why when vandals burn them down every few years, no one pays much attention." He stared at me for a long moment, then added, "Except you."

He explained that the Saratoga Sheriff had told him how the bodies had come to be discovered in the barn.

"So, if not for you, Miss Stone, those two people might never have been found at all. They would have lain there for God knows how many years. Maybe forever."

I didn't know how to respond to that. Was he grateful or put out that I'd unearthed the bodies? It was probably something of a headache for him and his lawyers, but that had nothing to do with me. I didn't kill Johnny Dornan and Vivian McLaglen. I only found them.

"Can you tell me when the farm was last occupied? Who lived there and for how long?"

"Chuck Lenoir was our last caretaker. He passed away late last year. He'd worked for my father for many years, and we kept him on after he suffered an accident. A horse kick to the head. There was really no need for a caretaker once we closed the farm after the war, but my father wanted to make sure Chuck was taken care of."

"So there was nobody else living on the farm during the past fifteen years? Just Lucky Chuck?"

The judge couldn't quite suppress a smile. "You've done your homework on Mr. Lenoir, yet you didn't tell me. I'd forgotten how efficient you are. You've always got a surprise for anyone who underestimates you."

"Did he live alone on the farm? Or was he married? Any children?"

"He never married, and I'm certain he lived alone. In his younger days, he was a stableboy on the farm. I believe he worked mucking the barns and stalls. No one ever considered him for a job such as caretaker; he wasn't smart enough. But when everything was closed down, my father felt he could handle watching the grass grow, so he put him in the caretaker's house."

"Are you aware of any problems with trespassers and squatters on the farm?"

He shifted in his seat and crossed his right leg over the left. "These are odd questions, even from you. Are you suggesting someone has been living on the farm?"

"I wouldn't say *living* on the farm. But there may be someone hiding there from time to time. Inside the caretaker's house."

He treated me to a long probing stare, then asked if I'd been inside the house myself. I lied and said I hadn't. I wasn't sure how he'd take such news.

"But I visited the farm late Wednesday night. I wanted to see the burned barn again."

"Then what makes you suspect someone has been staying there?"

"That night, when I returned to my car, I found the glove compartment open. It had been closed when I'd left it."

He dismissed my concerns, arguing that I must have been mistaken. Or maybe the latch was loose. He was sure. So was I. I knew someone had searched my car. And that same person had been reading Wednesday's edition of the *New Holland Republic* inside the caretaker's house as late as Thursday afternoon.

"Is there anything else, Miss Stone? I really should be getting back."

Now it was my turn to make him uncomfortable with a stubborn, intrusive stare. He reacted much the way I had. He squirmed, at least inside, then asked what I wanted to know.

"How do you think the fire got started?"

"The fire? I have no idea. Whoever killed those two people, I suppose. Why ask me?"

"Not the fire last Saturday," I said. "The one in thirty-seven."

His eyes grew wide, and he swallowed hard. "Thirty-seven? You mean the one that burned down the Racing Barn?"

"And killed twelve of your finest Thoroughbreds."

"Why would you ask me about that? It was a tragedy beyond words."

"I'm trying to understand everything about these murders. But, I confess, the fire of thirty-seven interests me for the horses that died. Do you believe, as some people maintained, that an employee started that fire?"

"There was plenty of suspicion to go around. Some said a groom lit the fire, but I couldn't believe it. Even if an employee had been disappointed with his position or salary, he wouldn't have killed those horses. Everyone associated with the farm loved the animals. I'm sure of that."

"It's a sad story."

"I trust you're not suggesting these two people found on the property had anything to do with the fire so long ago."

"Of course not."

"Then why bring it up?"

"I don't like loose ends or remainders. I was curious."

"That's all fine and good, Miss Stone. But the tragic fire at Tempesta is really none of your business."

"Funny," I said. "The fire that killed twelve horses is the one you call tragic."

That ruffled him. "Of course it's tragic that those two people died, but the horses were in our care. They had no choice. We as a family bear the ultimate responsibility for their deaths. I can tell you that it turned me for good against breeding. My father, too. He couldn't stomach the idea of raising more horses after that."

"Was it Lucky Chuck Lenoir who started the fire?" I asked, flustering him yet again. "By accident, of course."

"Why do you think that?"

"Maybe because your father felt guilty about the accident that left Chuck impaired, both physically and mentally. And because Chuck was devastated by the fire that he caused."

"One minute I'm convinced you're a bright young woman of remarkable talents, and the next you disappoint me with your irritating manner and wild suppositions. I am returning to the party downstairs."

With that he stood and let himself out. It wasn't lost on me that he hadn't denied Chuck's responsibility for the fire. From all I had heard about the tragedy, from Audrey Shaw, Fadge, Sheriff Pryor, and Frank Olney, I'd formed the opinion that Lucky Chuck Lenoir was a poor soul who'd served his lord as a loyal vassal would. His devotion was rewarded with the permission to live in the caretaker's house for fifteen years after the farm had been shuttered and—as Judge Shaw had so aptly put it—to watch the grass grow. There was no reason to pursue the matter, of course. By all indications, the fire of '37—the one that had nearly torpedoed Harrison and Audrey's engagement—was a terrible accident, perhaps caused by a man with reduced mental capacities. Lucky Chuck was now one of the ghosts of Tempesta. I wouldn't mention him again.

But there had been one more question I'd been itching to put to the judge. Perhaps I should have asked it before chasing him away with talk of Lucky Chuck Lenoir. It was a personal question for the judge himself. I wanted to know how he had been coping since the murder of his only child, the tragic—twelve Thoroughbreds tragic—and beautiful and talented Jordan Shaw. I knew I wouldn't mention that to him either.

✿

"Where have you been?" asked Freddie. "I've been looking high and low for you."

"I had some work to take care of."

"Work? Here? Come on. They're about to herd us inside for dinner, and I want another drink before that."

Armed with a couple of whiskeys, we entered the ballroom where dozens of tables had been laid with white linen, fine china, silver, and crystal. Guests were finding their places as waiters scurried hither and thither, pouring water and wine and slipping chairs under the backsides of the wealthy patrons. I took a moment to admire the octagonal stained glass windows adorning the magnificent vaulted ceiling. There must have been more than a hundred. I couldn't see what scenes were depicted on the glass, due to the darkness outside.

Some of Freddie's friends were standing off to the side, near one of the alcoves that segmented the walls of the ballroom at regular intervals. They were the same people I'd seen that afternoon in his clubhouse box, with a couple of new faces as well. Helen was at the center of the gathering, surrounded by the men. All smiles, they were hanging on the words of a tall strawberry-blond fellow, who was telling a joke. Freddie and I arrived as he delivered the punchline.

"So the tire salesman says, he says, 'It's our latest model, Mr. Cohen. It's called the Firestein Nylon Supreme. Not only does it stop on a dime, it picks it up, too.'"

I stiffened a bit but managed to refrain from throwing my fresh drink on him, ice cubes and all. As Jewish jokes went, this was not the worst. Still, I developed an instant dislike for the man. I felt a twinge of shame, as well, for not saying something straight off. It would have been uncomfortable for everyone, of course. For Freddie most of all. But I hated myself for holding my tongue. And for not announcing to all present that I was a Jewess. With the exception of Helen, the others chuckled at the joke. It wasn't funny enough to deserve a belly laugh. I glanced at Freddie to gauge his reaction. There didn't seem to be any. He was just smiling gently at his friends. Then he cleared his throat and introduced me.

The one who'd told the joke was named Ned. Tall and gangling and a strutting ass. Then there was Todd, a little man with a round face and receding hairline. And Mark, a stocky man with jet-black hair and a Thomas Dewey mustache. The introductions complete, their conversation turned to talk of the Spa City.

"It's gone downhill, for sure," said Mark. "I remember coming here with my parents before the war. There were so many hotels and so much glamour back then."

"And there was an active social scene," added Todd. "Lots of parties and beautiful Victorians rented for the entire month by the out-of-towners."

"So many of those homes have fallen into disrepair," said Helen. "Such a shame."

"I don't know if I'll come back next year," added Todd.

"Are you kidding?" asked Freddie. "After that race we witnessed today? You're not coming back? I can tell you I'll be here next August. That was the greatest duel I've ever seen."

"I'll grant you that," said Todd. "But at a certain point, you have to weigh the excellence of the horseflesh against the general decay that's starting to creep in. If they're not careful, this place will end up like one of those backwater tracks in Maryland. Remember Timonium, Fred? And Hagerstown?"

"Barely," said Freddie.

Todd laughed. "You used to haunt those places. Till you learned your lesson."

"Next year is the centennial of the Saratoga racecourse," said Helen. "My mother's on the planning committee. She's been in touch with the governor and lots of muckety-mucks, including Senator Javits. Everyone is working hard to make the anniversary special and restore some of the former grandeur to the town."

"Who cares about all that?" said Ned. "I've got another joke for you."

"Not right now, Ned," interrupted Freddie. Helen seconded his motion.

"Why not? It's a good one. And I promise it's clean."

Helen, who was standing beside the oaf, leaned over, turned her head to hide her mouth, and whispered something in his ear. He gulped and turned a shade whiter than he already was. Then his eyes darted to me and back to Helen.

"Really? She's Jewish?"

Helen shook her head in dismay and rubbed the bridge of her nose. How had she known I was Jewish? I actually found myself wondering if I looked particularly Semitic. Or had Freddie said something?

"I didn't mean anything by it," Ned offered by way of an inadequate apology to me. "I heard it the other day and thought it was funny. You know. A joke. Not to be taken seriously."

"Bad taste," said Freddie. "Why would you say that?"

"Because I didn't know she was Jewish."

I appreciated Freddie's indignation, but wondered where it had been a few moments earlier when Ned told his joke. Was his pique sincere or a tardy reaction to discovering that I was actually a Jew? I couldn't be sure. Had Freddie even known I was Jewish? And if he hadn't, did he care now?

"Let's find our table," he said, taking my elbow.

My cheeks burned, surely bright crimson, as he led me away. Why was I letting him drag me off in defeat? I knew his friends' tongues would be wagging as soon as I was out of earshot, and I wished I'd stood my ground instead of turning tail at Freddie's urging.

"Don't worry, Ellie. I'll change our table," he said as we crossed the ballroom. "You won't have to sit near Ned."

"You'll do no such thing," I said. "I want to sit with your friends. And right next to good old Ned."

Freddie stopped mid-stride and faced me. "You're not going to make a scene, are you?"

"I'm not the one who told the Jewish joke back there. And I have no intention of making a scene in front of you, your friends, or your mother."

Dinner was awkward, at least at first. I certainly didn't enjoy breaking bread with Ned Eckleston, as I found out his full name was, but I was determined to take the high road. I wanted to give a good accounting of myself. And I'd be damned if I was going to run from a man who'd made a stale joke at the expense of my tribe. Ned, it turned out, spent much of the dinner finding excuses to flit from table to table, visit the restroom, or fetch himself a drink from the bar back in the gaming room. And I felt triumphant.

With dessert, the speeches began. Georgina Whitcomb delivered another inspiring address on the importance of literacy and education for all races and creeds. A couple of library board members and the mayor of Saratoga also spoke about the noble mission of lending a hand to the less fortunate in our community—particularly the disadvantaged races—to better their social condition through education.

When the live auction came around, I confess that I felt like a pauper.

Dinners, books, gift certificates, and passes to the winner's circle were sold to the highest bidders, who forked over outrageously generous amounts for relatively pedestrian offerings. The exercise was humbling for me but heartening, as well. Some extremely rich people were doing good with their unneeded cash.

The evening ended with a plea for all those in attendance to dig as deeply as they could and donate something to the cause. I ponied up twenty-five dollars and still felt like a cheapskate.

We repaired to the bar in the gaming room and enjoyed a couple of drinks while the crowd thinned. Freddie said he didn't want to compete with the traffic, and I was happy to soak up a little more of the atmosphere of the old casino along with some champagne. I didn't even mind being left alone with Helen and Todd—Ned had decamped—while Freddie disappeared to hobnob as was his fashion.

I asked Helen what Freddie had told her about me. She said not to worry; he'd only given my name, rank, and serial number.

"He said you were a newspaper reporter. How glamorous."

"Not really. The news is months or years of PTA meetings, punctuated by the occasional murder. My biggest scoop last year was the ten-year-old spelling bee champion."

Todd wanted to know about the murders, and I tried to dissuade him. Proud though I was of my accomplishments, I was uncomfortable holding forth. He and Helen seemed genuinely interested, though, so I obliged them. I left out the fact that one of my biggest triumphs at the paper had been the investigation of the murder of Judge Harrison Shaw's daughter, Jordan. I focused instead on my recent success in Los Angeles, where I'd been dispatched to profile a local boy who was set to star in one of those beach pictures. His Hollywood ending never materialized, alas, but I managed to bring home a bigger story. With Todd and Helen keeping me busy with their salacious questions about the seedy underbelly of Tinseltown, I didn't even notice that Freddie had been AWOL for twenty minutes. When he finally returned, he looked all in and suggested it was time to call it a night.

"It's only eleven thirty," said Helen. "Since when did you become such a wet blanket? At least leave us Ellie. She's been entertaining us with stories of debauchery and murder in Hollywood."

I was feeling fine after the inauspicious start to the evening. Gone were the memory of my difficult interview with Judge Shaw and the unpleasant-ness of Ned's joke. Helen and Todd had turned out to be quite nice, and I wished Freddie hadn't pulled me away so soon. But he was my escort, after all, and I didn't want to walk back to the Friar Tuck in my evening gown.

"Did you have a nice time?" I asked him as we sped down Route 50, convertible top down. I didn't care if my hair ended up in knots now.

"Of course," he said in a most unconvincing fashion.

I didn't press the issue. I'd enjoyed myself and wasn't about to beg him to cheer up. In my experience, moody men stayed that way if you indulged them. He drove on in silence for about a mile, and then he asked what Helen had said to me.

"She said you told her all about me. Name, rank, and serial number."

"Nothing else? Nothing about my mother?"

"No. What would she tell me about your mother?"

He didn't say a word for the longest time. Something was bothering him.

"What would Helen tell me about your mother?" I asked again.

"It's . . . I have to work on her, that's all."

"Work on her?"

"I want you to come down to Virginia to visit after the meet ends. Maybe in October or November. Thanksgiving would be nice."

"Sounds serious," I said. "So why do you need to work on her?"

His jaw flexed. He stared straight down the road.

"Freddie?"

"She told me not to see you again."

I managed to squeeze a "why" out of my dry throat. Freddie twitched. He tried to put me off and avoid answering my question. When I finally broke him down, I saw his lip curl as he formed his words.

"She said she doesn't want me marrying a Jew."

CHAPTER
TWENTY-FOUR

Freddie begged me to stay with him at the motel. He promised he could convince his mother to accept me. And if she didn't, he didn't care. I told him through my tears that I didn't want to marry him. I barely knew him. He understood, insisted those were his mother's words, not his. He held me tight and comforted me, but I couldn't do it. I bore him no ill will. He was a wonderful young man, one who'd lit a spark in me that I hadn't felt in a long time. More than that, he'd captured my interest in a way that no man had ever quite done. He was witty and fun, attentive and urbane. And there was something elusive, too, that attracted me to him. I couldn't explain why I liked him so. But neither could I stay with him that night. I didn't care about the falsity his mother had shown me, her phony affection and insincere charity toward other races, other than how it pertained to her character. She was a horrid person, I knew now. A hateful wretch. And I had little interest in quoting Shylock to her across the Thanksgiving dinner table. I'd resisted that urge earlier when Ned told his joke. Nor did I want to feel sorry for myself now. Yet I did. And I felt fury. I was angry. I was powerless. God, I wasn't in love with Frederick Carsten Whitcomb III, but I wanted the option to be.

❧

It was past one when I threw my small bag into the trunk of my car. I hadn't even bothered to change out of my gown. I only wanted to get home and climb into my own bed with a glass of whiskey. Alone. I allowed myself a couple of tears as I raced along Route 67 toward New Holland. Not tears for Freddie, but for myself. Caused by the awful woman who'd hugged me, called me dear, then told her son I had horns and stripes. And that was the end of it. As I dried my cheeks with the back of my hand, I put to rest all sorrow and self-pity. Georgina Whitcomb—and her bigotry—disappeared into the swirling darkness behind me.

⌀

I passed Tempesta Farm and spotted far ahead, atop a hill about a half mile off, six or seven cherry tops spinning. As I came nearer, I slowed to see what was going on and caught sight of Frank Olney's large profile in the flashing lights. Sheriff Pryor was there as well with a couple of his deputies. I pulled over to the shoulder thirty yards past the county cruisers and made my way back to the scene in my heels and long green gown.

"Is that you, Ellie?" asked Stan Pulaski, who was directing what little traffic there was at one thirty in the morning on a deserted Route 67. "Wow. You look beautiful."

What a sweetheart Stan was. His eyes glazed over, and, after my disappointing evening, I almost threw my arms around his neck for a tight hug. I resisted the urge.

"What's going on?" I asked instead.

"Someone reported a car behind the trees down there. And there's a body inside."

The news set my heart pounding. "It's not a young woman, is it?"

Stan nodded.

"Don't tell me it's a black Chrysler."

"It is. How did you know that?"

"I can tell you the license number, too," I said. My memory was pretty strong when engaged in a search. "B-Y-W-sixty-six."

⌀

Frank Olney made time to speak with me once the ambulance had carted away the body. He was kind enough to refrain from commenting on my attire. Pryor stood at his side, none too pleased to see me there, and without the good manners Frank had shown. He said Halloween wasn't for another two months. I asked him if he was planning on masquerading as a sheriff for trick or treat. That stung, especially when Frank Olney laughed. After my little funny, Pryor said I was neither needed nor welcome at the crime scene and told me to leave.

"You see that signpost over there?" Frank asked him as dry as a bone. Pryor and I both turned our heads. "It says you're in Montgomery County, Henry. I'll speak to whoever the hell I please."

Pryor shuffled a bit, and, clearly cowed by his large colleague from the neighboring jurisdiction, he changed his tune. "Sure, Frank. I was only trying to help."

"Was that Micheline Charbonneau in the car?" I asked.

Frank nodded. "Looks like it. There's a passbook in her purse. And a bill from Niagara Mohawk in her name."

"So what happened?"

"The fellow who owns this land discovered the car parked behind a grove of trees down there." He pointed to the southeast. "Car doors locked with a dead lady at the wheel."

"Has Fred Peruso been out here to examine the body?"

"He's over there. Writing up his preliminary report. You can talk to him when he's through."

I noticed Pryor watching closely as Frank and I talked. Whether he was curious, surprised, or simply cheesed off, I couldn't say. But our familiarity and spirit of cooperation must have confused him. In fact, a change seemed to come over him, as if he wanted to be part of our little coterie. The moments passed, and his interest grew. He even started to smile and pretend to share in our trust.

"The ignition was still on," said Frank. "Not running, though. And the tank was empty."

"So the car ran until all the gas was gone?"

He nodded. "Appears so. Probably a day or more, depending on how full it was."

"Carbon monoxide poisoning?"

"Not quite. Her neck was snapped. Someone placed her in the driver's seat. Maybe to make it look like she was driving. But as far as we can tell, she didn't even have a license."

"How long has she been there?"

Frank motioned in the direction of the county coroner.

"Fred will have a better idea than anything I might estimate. Still, I'd say it's been a while. Skin doesn't turn that color overnight. Not a pretty sight."

"Maybe a week?" I asked.

"She was pretty ripe," said the sheriff. "If I was a betting man, I'd say she died the same night as the other two on Tempesta Farm."

"And barely a half mile away."

Pryor finally found speech and broke in. "I'd say it was the same murderer. Ditched the body and the car here after he killed the others and set the barn on fire."

"So we're after the same guy?" I asked.

"*We* already found him," he said. "I picked him up this afternoon at the racetrack. A guy by the name of Robertson."

"Bruce Robertson?"

"That's right. Do you know him?"

"No. But I heard he was a gambler shopping around information on Johnny Dornan's past. Some kind of betting scandal in Maryland nine years ago."

"Exactly. This seems pretty straightforward to me," he said. "Gamblers and jockeys. It's a bad combination. I think Robertson tried to blackmail Dornan to throw a race or two. Maybe Dornan didn't want to cooperate."

"How does Micheline Charbonneau fit in?" I asked.

"She was with Dornan the night he died, right? A witness to the murders on the farm. She had to go, too."

"Sounds logical," said Frank. "But why is she here and they're back there over the county line? Why not burn her with the others?"

Pryor didn't have an answer for that. But he explained it away. "There doesn't have to be a reason."

"I offered you information several days ago," I said, shifting gears. "You weren't interested in the man Johnny Dornan was meeting at midnight last Friday. Robinson."

"No, I wasn't. And I've got my man. Robertson."

"There was also the tip on the identity of the female victim in the barn. I tried to tell you, but you only listened when Sheriff Olney shared the name."

"There's no use holding a grudge, miss," he said. "Tell you what. How about I slip you some details? You know, stuff that will do nicely in your newspaper stories."

"I thought you saved your best tips for Scotty Freed at the *Saratogian*."

"Look, I have a job to do, and so do you. And so does Scotty. But I'm telling you I'm willing to share information with you now."

I had an idea. It would make for a fine feather in my cap if he agreed. And I had a tantalizing quid to offer in exchange for his quo. I put it to him.

"If you let me talk to Bruce Robertson in the jailhouse, I'll give you a piece of information that no one else besides me knows."

He studied me for a long moment. Frank Olney was keeping quiet during our back-and-forth. I would have given him my information for nothing, of course, but what I had to offer was on the Saratoga side of the county line. At length, Pryor came to a decision.

"All right, Miss Stone. You got a deal. Tomorrow at ten a.m. I'll let you interview Bruce Robertson. That is if he's on board with it." He paused. "And his lawyer."

Usually I like to receive cash on the barrelhead for my tips, but in this case, I agreed to deliver my goods in advance of my payment. Frank Olney would be my insurance if Pryor tried to weasel out of his promise. So I told him. I told them both that someone was haunting the caretaker's house on Tempesta Farm.

"What proof do you have of that?" asked Pryor.

"I visited the house on Thursday afternoon. And I found a newspaper on the second floor."

"And?"

"It was Wednesday's edition of the *Republic*."

"Anything else you've been withholding?"

I cleared my throat. "There's also a pistol. A small-caliber Colt."

Pryor shook his head. "You should have told me right away. There might have been fingerprints."

"I phoned your office Thursday afternoon and left an urgent message. You didn't return my call."

"Well, I'm sure whoever left that stuff there has had plenty of time to get rid of it by now."

"Time, yes. Stuff, no," I said. "I have both the newspaper and the gun in a safe place."

"How did you manage that?" asked Frank. "That house has been boarded up since Chuck Lenoir died."

"The storm cellar door was unlocked."

"That might be construed as trespassing," said Pryor.

"Are you going to arrest her?" asked Frank. "She's giving you a gift, here. Is that how you thank her?"

Pryor removed his hat and wiped his forehead with the back of his hand. He nodded at length and said we had a deal. I would be given access to Bruce Robertson in the morning, and he would investigate the caretaker's house right away.

"May I come with you?" I asked.

"Dressed like that?"

✦

I prevailed upon the sheriff to wait until I'd had a chance to speak to Fred Peruso, the Montgomery County coroner, before driving all of six hundred yards to Tempesta Farm. I'd known Fred for several years, but he became one of my favorite guys during the Jordan Shaw murder case. Since then, the cigar- and pipe-smoking doctor and I were old chums. He agreed to call me Ellie as long as I called him Fred. For a sixty-year-old man, he was in good shape and remarkably vain. His head of closely cropped white hair gave him the look of a fallen angel. Or a defrocked priest.

"Junior prom?" he asked when he spotted me.

"No. Skydiving," I said.

He smirked and asked what I was doing on a lonely road at 2:00 a.m. in an evening gown.

"Looking for a handsome doctor to tell me about Micheline Charbonneau."

"I'm your man. But we haven't formally identified the body yet."

"Can you tell me more or less how long she's been dead? I won't quote you on it until you're sure."

He produced his pipe and a pouch of tobacco from his vest pocket. He packed the bowl and lit up.

"Come take a walk with me," he said, and we set off toward a tree stump not far away.

Once we were out of earshot of the lawmen he asked if I really wanted to hear this. "Not all corpses are going to be as beautiful and as well preserved as Marilyn Monroe."

"Are you forgetting Darleen Hicks?" I replied. "If I could stomach that, I can take what you have to say now."

He puffed on his pipe. "Fair enough. The body has already putrefied.

Smells worse than anything you can imagine. Made even worse because it was shut inside a locked car. And the skin was black and blistering."

"So how long?"

"And the maggots were having a feast and lots of them in the pupa stage," he continued, ignoring my question. "The body is bloating, and excreting fluids from all the orifices and ruptures in the skin. No one's going to want to buy that used car, I can tell you that."

I felt green. "Okay, so what does all that tell you about how long she's been dead?"

"Best guess is at least a week. Maybe seven or eight days. No flies yet. A lot depends on the temperature and moisture. But she's been in that car more than five days and fewer than ten. Unless she was refrigerated before being dumped here."

"Cause of death?"

"Neck appears to be broken. An x-ray will confirm that in an instant."

"Any other possible causes?"

"When the decomposition of a body is so far along, it's not easy to determine from a cursory physical examination. The skin's so black you can't see bruises or lacerations. Even stab wounds or bullet holes are hard to distinguish from the natural ruptures in the skin caused by the decomposition and the buildup of gases. Of course I'll know a lot more after I finish the postmortem tomorrow morning."

"I'll stop by to get the verdict, if that's all right."

"Eight a.m. at City Hospital. I've got a tee time at ten. Don't be late."

"Some of us want to get to bed before the sun comes up," said Pryor when I told him I was ready. "Tell you the truth, I don't know why I'm letting you come along. This is police business."

"I'm a witness," I reminded him. "Plus, I know where to look inside the house. It'll save time, and you'll be able to get to bed before the sun comes up."

"Cool your jets. You can come along. Let's go."

I led the sheriff and two of his deputies—Bell and Sinclair—to the window I'd tumbled through while making good my escape Thursday afternoon. It was shut now, and I must have turned white.

"Did you close it?" Pryor asked.

"No. I just ran for my life."

He motioned to one of the deputies to try the window. It took a couple of tugs, but it opened. Whoever had shut it hadn't locked it again. Pryor thought it had fallen shut by itself.

"The sash cord is probably rotted through," he said.

Convinced that my second tour of the Tempesta caretaker's house would be less terrifying, given my armed escort, I learned nevertheless that the expected outcome isn't always the true one. My protectors inspired little confidence, particularly when Pryor asked me to lead the way.

"After you."

"I'm not going in there first," I huffed in a low voice. "It's someone else's turn. Send one of your boys in there with a flashlight."

"All right, we're going to search the place in two teams," said Pryor to his deputies once we had all climbed through the window. He coughed, frowned, and clarified. "Bell and Sinclair, you two check out the upstairs. Miss Stone and I will—" Another cough. "We'll take the rooms down here."

"I think we should abort the mission," I said in full voice.

They all gawked at me as if I'd just yelled fire in a crowded theater.

"Fire," I said calmly. "This place is on fire."

CHAPTER TWENTY-FIVE

The caretaker's house was indeed burning, and fast. Deputies Bell and Sinclair led the charge through the window, leaving me and the sheriff to fight over who would exit last. To his credit, Pryor ceded me the right of way, even if his chivalry was accompanied by a sharp shove of my rear end to grease the skids, as it were. Outside again, we raced from the building, me in heels and long evening gown, sparkling, too, I imagined, thanks to my jewelry. From our position thirty yards clear of the house, we watched the flames shoot through the slats of the third-floor shutters. Then, the fire slipped through the frame and crept up the face of the house, licking the eaves beneath the mansard roof. Inevitably, inexorably, they chewed through the rafters and, with a hissing rumble, escaped the attic and leapt into the night. Now with a whooshing supply of air feeding the fire from within—bottom to top, thanks in part to the window we'd left open—the old timbers didn't stand a chance. The blaze swelled like a dragon's roar.

"Shouldn't we call the fire department?" asked Deputy Bell at length.

Pryor threw him a glare that screamed "idiot" loud and clear. A few minutes later, the building crumbled and collapsed upon itself. We retreated another ten yards for protection from the flying sparks and billowing heat. The fight was over. A knockout.

I turned to Sheriff Pryor. "Can I still interview Bruce Robertson in the morning?"

It was nearly 4:00 a.m. by the time the fire trucks left and Pryor took me back to where I'd parked my car. The Montgomery County deputies were still at it, securing the crime scene. A wrecker was emerging from behind the trees with Vivian McLaglen's car in tow. Frank Olney asked what the big fire was all about. He'd seen the clouds light up as the house burned. I gave him the short version and said good night.

Whoever had torched the caretaker's house must have slipped away while we were watching the place burn. Pryor ordered a search of the property, but he didn't have the manpower to cover eight hundred acres. The property was dark, with hills and overgrowth and outbuildings enough for a shadow to melt into the night without anyone the wiser.

This was, of course, arson, most certainly set to prevent the law from finding evidence that someone had been hiding there since the murders a week before. Or perhaps the intention was to kill all of us. Pryor agreed, but he would have to follow procedure and ask the fire department to establish the cause of the blaze. I had no such formalities to observe, so I mapped out my plans for later that morning as I drove home along the lonely stretch of Route 67.

I pulled up to the curb outside my place on Lincoln Avenue and checked my watch—4:22. Lugging my suitcase up the stairs might well wake Mrs. Giannetti, if she weren't already peering out the window to catch me sneaking in with another in a series of disreputable escorts. I decided to leave the bag in the car and crept up the stairs. The phone was ringing when I let myself in. I hadn't even had time to remove my heels, which were caked with mud from the firemen's hoses and dirt of the farm.

"It's Jimmy Burgh," came the voice down the line.

"Why are you calling at this hour?"

"I'm across the street in the phone booth. I gotta talk to you."

I didn't like the idea at all. In fact, it gave me chills to think of him lurking downstairs waiting for me.

"Jimmy, it's late. I have to be up early tomorrow. Today, as a matter of fact."

"Then you won't need your beauty sleep. Look, I'm no danger to you. I just want to ask you something. I won't stay long."

I don't know what whim or caprice shanghaied my better judgment, but I heard myself saying yes and then letting the ruffian into my home at four thirty in the morning. I cautioned him to keep quiet, lest my landlady catch me with him. Not that my reputation would have suffered much in her eyes at that point, but I thought Jimmy Burgh represented a new low in my own mind, even if his visit was business instead of pleasure.

"Can I offer you something?" I asked, once we were seated at my kitchen table.

"I wouldn't say no. You got something strong?"

I fetched a fresh bottle of White Label from the hutch in my parlor and poured us each a couple of fingers. After the night I'd had, from my crushing humiliation at the hands of Freddie Whitcomb's mother to the discovery of Micheline's body and the fire at Tempesta, I too wanted something strong.

"You look real nice, by the way," said Jimmy, raising his tumbler to me. "What are you all dressed up for?"

"An evening in high society." My tone dripped with irony.

"You got soot all over your face, though. Not bad, but I figured it ain't supposed to be part of your getup."

I brushed my cheek in a lazy attempt to wipe away the black but gave up just as quickly. I didn't really care. On the bright side, however, something in Jimmy's demeanor told me straight off that I had nothing to fear from him that night.

"I heard they found a body out on Route Sixty-Seven," he began. "A woman in a car."

"Yes, I was there. I'm afraid it's Micheline."

Jimmy frowned, his bushy black eyebrows knitting themselves together in gathering anger. Or was it sorrow? His jaw tightened, lips curled, and his eyes burned. He drained his glass, and I poured him another.

"They're sure it's Miche?" he asked.

"The sheriff found identification in her purse."

"Who the hell would do that?"

I shook my head. "I don't know."

"I heard they picked up Bruce Robertson."

"The Saratoga sheriff thinks he's got his man. He's going to let me talk to him at ten o'clock this morning. Do you think Bruce Robertson could have killed Johnny Dornan? And Vivian McLaglen and Micheline Charbonneau?"

Jimmy stared at me, his blue eyes shot red and tired. He blinked. "He's capable of it, I suppose. But I've never known him to be a killer."

"Tell me something, Jimmy. What is it about Micheline that's hitting you so hard?"

He nudged his glass an inch to the left, then back to the right. "She was a good kid. I hate to see this happen."

"Anything else?"

"What do you want me to say? That I blame myself?"

"Do you?"

"I don't think all fancy about things the way you do. Bad stuff happens sometimes. Even to nice kids like Miche."

"Then you're in the clear, Jimmy."

He fixed me with a hard stare. I wondered if I'd pushed him too far. "Yeah, I blame myself," he said at length. "Maybe I'm going soft, but I wish I'd a never sent her out with that Johnny Dornan. And I want to get the guy who did this to her. I want that so bad. So I guess even I've started thinking all fancy now, because I feel I gotta do something to avenge her. To win back some of my own self-respect or I don't know how I'll live with myself."

"What do you want to do, Jimmy?"

"I want to strangle the son of a bitch with my bare hands. I want to crush his windpipe with my thumbs and squeeze so hard his eyes pop out of their sockets."

I recoiled in my seat. The violence of his words swelled as his face grew redder. But he wasn't finished. "I want to choke the life out of him and kick him in the head about fifty times when I'm done. Till he's a goddamn bloody mess. I want him to take back the guilt I got burning in my chest since Miche disappeared. And then, when I'm all out of breath from kicking his head off his shoulders, then—just for poetical justice—I'm gonna set him on fire and watch the bastard burn to a crisp, black piece of shit."

Jimmy poured his drink down his gullet and grabbed the bottle standing between us on the table, startling me with the speed and wrath of his action. He sloshed more Scotch into his glass and swallowed it straight-away. Then he slouched in his chair, breathing hard and staring at nothing in particular. His fury cooled over time. I didn't dare say a word.

"You're going to find him for me," he said. "And I'm going to kill him."

Whereas I hadn't feared him earlier, I was now frozen in place, sure he'd strangle me, just for practice, if I said the wrong thing. But as the minutes passed, I realized he was thinking. Planning, perhaps. Then he finally spoke. Squinting as if trying to recall some distant memory, he asked me if I'd said I was going to speak to Bruce Robertson later that day.

"At ten," I answered in a rough voice. I cleared my throat and repeated yes.

"Ask him about Mack Hodges," he said. "And Ledoux. Dan Ledoux."

"I've heard of them. What do they have to do with all this?"

He shrugged at me. "I don't know exactly. But they were right in the middle of the shenanigans nine years ago at Hagerstown. This whole thing goes back to Johnny Dornan throwing that race. And Bruce Robertson knows what happened."

"Do you know where I might find this Mack Hodges? Is he still in Maryland somewhere?"

"Yeah. Not far from Pimlico. Six feet under."

CHAPTER TWENTY-SIX

SUNDAY, AUGUST 19, 1962

Eight a.m. sharp. I commandeered the last stale piece of Danish, which, I was sure, had been left out the day before. Or maybe Friday. Still, I was feeling hollow and needed to get something inside me. Seated at the long table in the doctors' lounge, sipping cold coffee and puffing on a stale cigarette, I scratched out the beginnings of a story on the thrown race at Hagerstown nine years earlier. It was mostly notes to myself, reminders to research this and that. Too many holes—dates, horses, accomplices—but it helped organize my thoughts. Then Fred Peruso burst through the door, cigar fuming between his teeth, trailing a swirling cloud of blue smoke.

"Eleonora," he said to tease me.

"Federico," I answered in kind, stubbing out my cigarette in the aluminum ashtray. "So what's the verdict?"

"Broken neck. Dead before the car was abandoned."

"And can you confirm it's Micheline Charbonneau?"

"You'll have to ask Frank. He's on his way down here now."

"Estimated time of death?"

"Impossible to fix it exactly. But like I said last night, it's been at least a week."

Fred and I went over the condition of the body, height and weight, and details of the injury to her neck. I took notes for my story, which I would review with Charlie Reese and deliver to the typesetter before 10:00 p.m.

About fifteen minutes later, the big sheriff sauntered in, turned a chair around backward, and took a seat.

He greeted Fred then nodded to me. "Ellie, I see you've turned back into Cinderella."

I smiled. "What about you? Get any sleep?"

He shook his head. "No, but I just got off the horn with Schenectady police. I had a hunch maybe Micheline was arrested once or twice. They confirmed she got picked up a year and a half ago for shoplifting at Breslaw's on State Street. I'm driving over there in a few minutes. We got one decent print off the body and hope to match it to the ones they have in their files."

I wrote down the information. "Can I call you later today for the results?"

"I should know one way or the other within two hours."

"Anything in the car you can tell me about?"

"Besides the awful smell? Registered to Vivian Coleman like we expected."

"Good morning, Ellie," said Henry Pryor.

So we'd moved on to first names? That was fine with me. I liked to cultivate friendly relations with law enforcement. Till now, the Saratoga sheriff had been standoffish at best, so I was sure I could turn the warming trend to my advantage.

"You're looking chipper today, Henry," I answered, flashing my brightest smile for good measure.

In truth, he was drooping and wearing the same wrinkled suit of clothes he'd had on the night before. The chitchat concluded, he told me his men were still searching the farm for evidence of the arsonist. So far no luck.

I explained that the pistol and newspaper were safe but unavailable until later in the day. He didn't appear concerned, saying that he'd send a deputy to pick them up as soon as he could.

"Tell you the truth, I don't think your squatter is involved in this. Why would he stick around the farm, for one thing? Too dangerous."

"Perhaps. But shouldn't you look into it?"

"Of course. We'll get to your gun, Ellie. Don't worry."

"What about Bruce Robertson?" I asked. "May I see him now?"

"He wasn't too keen on it at first, but then he got to thinking he'd like to get his side of the story out there. And when I told him you were a pretty young thing, he was all for it."

"Not sure how I feel about that."

"Don't worry. You'll be safe. He's barely as tall as you. And as skinny as a rail."

"His lawyer doesn't object?"

"He fired him yesterday. Supposed to get a new one. But he signed a paper waiving his right to have his lawyer present for this chat. Says he's innocent and has nothing to hide. Not too bright, but there you go. Shall we?" He feigned a bow to invite me to go first.

Bruce Robertson was a weaselly little man of about forty. At first glance, one would be hard-pressed to believe he was capable of any crime more violent than stealing candy from a baby. But his steel-gray eyes told another story. There was a hard coldness in his persistent stare. More than just a creep picturing me naked in his mind, he gave the impression that nothing mattered to him beyond his own wants. He didn't smile. Didn't engage on any human level I could discern. He watched. I was uncomfortable, frightened even. Even with the sheriff at my side and a roomful of armed deputies on the other side of the door. And I wanted a shower. I wondered how Jimmy Burgh could have said this reptile was incapable of murder.

Pryor took a seat off to the side of the table while I faced the prisoner directly, not three feet away. The sheriff reached for the phone on the wall and told whoever answered at the other end that we were ready, please send in Mrs. Blaine. A few moments later, there was a knock at the door, and a deputy pushed his way inside. He held the door for a middle-aged woman in a dark dress. Her hair was short and styled with marcel waving held down by bobby pins. She wheeled in a small portable desk bearing a stenograph, and the deputy fetched a chair for her. Within seconds, she was smoothing the fabric of her dress over her thighs and past her knees. She adjusted her eyeglasses, placed her hands on the keyboard, and nodded to the sheriff.

Pryor began. "As you agreed in writing, Mr. Robertson, Miss Stone is here to interview you for a story for her newspaper. She's going to ask you some questions. I'm present to make sure everything is on the up and up. That's why I've asked for a stenographer. I don't want you claiming later on that I tricked you. Are you still in agreement?"

Bruce Robertson nodded. Mrs. Blaine waited.

"You've got to actually say the words," the sheriff informed him. "Are you still in agreement?"

"Sure," said the prisoner, and the stenographer tapped silently to record his statement.

"I'll get right to the point, Mr. Robertson," I said. "Did you kill Johnny Dornan or Vivian McLaglen or Micheline Charbonneau?"

"You're a pretty little thing," he said in a soft, hoarse voice that emanated from somewhere in the back of his throat. Mrs. Blaine finished her typing a beat or two after Robertson had shut his trap.

I shook a tremor off my shoulders and forged ahead, ignoring his comment. "Did you kill Johnny Dornan or Vivian McLaglen or Micheline Charbonneau? Or do you know who did?"

His gaze ranged from my face, over my bust, and back again. He cocked his head as if admiring a mystical vision. "Your hair is unusual. Don't see many girls with such curls. And I don't mean like grandma's over there." He threw his head in the direction of the stenographer.

"Johnny Dornan and Vivian McLaglen," I prompted.

"You ain't some kind of mix, are you?"

I said nothing.

"Is your daddy a coon? Maybe your momma?"

"That's enough of that," said the sheriff. "Answer her questions. This isn't some kind of entertainment for you."

"Tell me about Johnny Dornan," I repeated.

Using the coarsest language imaginable, he proceeded to explain that he wasn't necessarily against congress between the races, at least not a white man with a Negro woman. That was understandable from both ends of the equation, he said. But he drew the line at Colored men spoiling white women.

"That ain't right."

"Okay," said Pryor. "Get up. You're going back to your cell."

I pushed myself out of my chair and stood to leave. "Thank you for your time, Mr. Robertson," I announced. "Look for my article in the paper tomorrow."

"Wait a minute," he called after me as I reached the door. "Where you off to so fast? We were having a nice conversation."

"Me? I have a date with my black lover. Good-bye."

Mrs. Blaine choked, and her fingers fell suspiciously silent. She looked to the sheriff as if to ask "Should I record that?" He shook his head.

"Wait! What?" asked Robertson.

"If you have nothing to tell me about Johnny Dornan, Vivian McLaglen, or Micheline Charbonneau, I'm leaving, and you can go back to your cell, as Sheriff Pryor says."

"You can't go like that. I know stuff."

I turned the doorknob. "I'm not interested in hearing what you know about fornicating with Colored women."

Mrs. Blaine gasped.

"No, I mean stuff about Johnny Dornan. You have no idea what I know."

I yanked open the door. "I'm sure it will all come out in your trial. Not in my newspaper."

"Johnny Dornan threw a race nine years ago in Maryland," he blurted out. Mrs. Blaine resumed her typing.

I paused in the threshold and peered back at him. "Can you tell me about that?"

"Sure. Come back in and sit down. I'll tell you. They're not gonna pin this on me."

Bruce Robertson behaved after that. In fact, I suspected that his bravado and profanity was all an act, one that he'd practiced for years to compensate for his unimpressive physical stature. In his business, he surely ran up against tough guys every day. A paperweight like him needed to project confidence and ooze malice or he'd be flattened by some other Caspar Milquetoast of a gangster. And I thought Jimmy Burgh deserved more credit than I'd originally given him. I, too, was doubtful that Bruce Robertson had it in him to kill a man.

"Tell me about the race," I said.

"It was a small track. Nothing like Pimlico. Or Saratoga. A dirt oval with a crappy grandstand. Horses maybe a step or two faster than an army mule. But they had pari-mutuel betting, so folks didn't care if the horses weren't Ridan or Jaipur, ready for the Kentucky Derby. They still came out thinking they could handicap the nags and win."

"Not a big-time racecourse," I said. "I get it. Now, about Johnny Dornan."

"Whatever happened to painting a picture?" he asked. "Geez, some folks don't appreciate a raconteur."

"Johnny Dornan."

"Okay, okay. So, Johnny was a morning rider back then. Went by the name Johnny Sprague. Only about twenty or twenty-one. He had promise, to be sure. But he was a kid. Rough around the edges, but not afraid to push his mounts and take chances. He arrived from somewhere in Canada one fine day in the company of a lady. Well, lady might be giving her too much credit."

"Vivian McLaglen?"

"That's her. Only she was going by Coleman at that time. Hiding from her past, I think, because she wasn't some daisy-fresh maiden, if you'll pardon my language."

"I've heard that kind of thing happens. What's next?"

"So Vivian Coleman brought the green kid down from north of the border and introduced him to her boyfriend, a fellow named Dan Ledoux."

"She was playing with both Johnny and Dan Ledoux?"

"She was the town bicycle. Everyone had a ride." That prompted yet another snort from Mrs. Blaine. Robertson continued unfazed. "But Johnny was a project of hers. Ledoux worked for a guy named Mack Hodges, a local crook trying his hand at horse racing. The two of them baked up this idea to throw a race, but they needed a patsy."

"Enter young Johnny Sprague."

"Bingo. And Vivian Coleman was the bait to lure him."

"So how did it work? The fix, I mean?"

Bruce Robertson was in his glory now. A born storyteller, he reveled in the spotlight and enjoyed the sound of his own voice. Even his cold eyes had warmed as he unfurled his tale like a mainsail.

"The horseflesh wasn't exactly the best in the country, but there were some decent runners. Someone's gotta win, after all. Unfortunately for Mack Hodges, none of his horses were gonna do better than the occasional show. Not much money in that. So he got the idea that, with a little help—on the perfect day—maybe his best horse could eke out a win over a big favorite. The purse, plus some heavy betting, would make for a handsome payday."

"But how was he going to beat the favorite?" I asked.

"That's where Johnny came in."

"He rode the favorite?"

"Exactly."

I reflected on that bit of information for a moment. Something didn't make sense. How could Mack Hodges control who would be riding the competition? And an apprentice rider at that.

"Wait," I said, holding up a hand. "If Vivian McLaglen lured Johnny Sprague to Maryland for her boyfriend, Dan Ledoux, and this Mack Hodges, how did he end up riding someone else's horse?"

"That's what I don't know. I got my sources, but they didn't know everything. Or they weren't telling."

"Who was your source on this information?"

"I'm not telling you that."

"Was it Ledoux?" asked the sheriff, breaking his silence.

Bruce frowned. "I can't reveal my sources. But if it was Dan, I sure as hell wouldn't tell you."

"Without a source, you look more and more guilty," said Pryor.

"I can't help that. If I told I'd be risking my own neck when I get out of here."

The sheriff laughed. "That's a good one. What makes you think you're ever getting out?"

"I swear I didn't kill them people," he shouted. "I had no reason. Why would I do it?"

"I heard you were selling the information on Johnny Dornan to other gamblers," I said.

Robertson scoffed. "Why would I sell the dirt on Johnny? I just told it to you for free."

"Only because you can't sell it now that Johnny Dornan's dead. You can't blackmail a dead man."

"Doesn't matter. I'm not admitting to selling no information. And I still didn't kill no one."

I shifted gears and tried to rile him. "You met Johnny Dornan at midnight the night he disappeared, didn't you?"

"What? No. I didn't meet him then or any other time."

"He had an appointment with someone named Robertson."

"Must've been some other Robertson."

"Maybe someone named Robinson?" I asked.

"Robinson who? Crusoe?"

I was getting nowhere fast. Bruce Robertson was sticking to his story, which seemed reasonable to me anyway. He didn't know crucial bits of the tale of Johnny Dornan's race-fixing scandal nine years earlier. And without the complete picture, I was hardly better off.

"Where were you the night of Friday, August tenth?" I asked.

He smirked. "I already told the sheriff. I was in the company of a lady."

Pryor snorted a laugh.

"Okay, not exactly a lady," said Bruce. "But she had all the right parts; I can tell you that 'cause I inspected 'em all myself." He paused to look me in the eye. "Three times."

Mrs. Blaine took a moment—and her fingers off the keys—to wipe her brow with a handkerchief before transcribing the last statement.

"Yeah, you're a real ladies' man, Bruce," said the sheriff to mock. "But we still haven't located this make-believe hooker of yours. And until we do, your alibi is nothing more than a fairy tale."

I jumped in again and asked the prisoner where I could find Dan Ledoux. He shrugged and said he didn't know.

"He usually shows up at the track during the meet, but I ain't seen him this year."

"What's he look like?"

"I don't know. I'm not in the habit of ogling men."

"Tall? Short? Medium? Dark? Fair? Old? Young? Surely you can tell me the color of his hair."

"He's got brown eyes, I think. Black hair. Maybe he's forty, like me. And about my size, too."

"If he's anything like you, he must be a prize," said the sheriff with a chuckle.

Robertson scowled at him. I thought Pryor's comment was unnecessary. For all his odious qualities—and he had them in spades—Bruce Robertson couldn't really do much to improve on the irregular parts God had given him to work with.

"I do okay, thanks, Sheriff," he said bitterly, but I could tell he didn't believe it himself. "And why shouldn't I get girls? Johnny Dornan did just fine with the ladies, and he was no taller than me."

I'd squeezed about all I was going to get out of Bruce Robertson, but I had one last question. I steered the conversation back to the mystery of the thrown race and asked about Mack Hodges.

"What can you tell me about him?"

"Not much. Except he's dead."

"When did he die?"

"Last January or February, I think. Died in his sleep."

"Old age? Heart attack?"

"His house burned down with him in it."

CHAPTER
TWENTY-SEVEN

Frank Olney confirmed positively the identity of the body in the car. It was twenty-four-year-old Micheline Bernadette Charbonneau of Terrebonne, Quebec, a suburb of Montreal. I felt a pang of regret as he pronounced the name, even if I'd already known it was she. The finality of an official identification smothers the last gasp of hope. Of course if it hadn't been Micheline in the driver's seat of Vivian McLaglen's Chrysler, it would have been some other poor girl, murdered for some unknown reason. Why shouldn't I have mourned her as well? Perhaps I should have simply been happy that an anonymous girl had survived the cruelty of the world for another day. I found no comfort in my rationalizations.

I sat at my kitchen table until the sun went down, typing out my story for Monday afternoon's edition of the *Republic*. My photographs of the scene, shot the night before in my evening gown on the side of Route 67, would provide dramatic evidence of the tragedy. I hadn't yet seen the developed film, but I recalled having captured fine images of Sheriff Frank Olney looking resolute and in charge of the scene, the wrecker pulling Vivian McLaglen's ghostly black Chrysler out of the field and back onto the highway, and the ambulance—rear doors closed and windows dark— that carted away the body. I presented the news in straightforward fashion. The body of a woman linked to the double murder on Tempesta Farm a week before had been discovered in an advanced state of decomposition on the Montgomery side of the county line. The sheriff's office had confirmed the identity of the woman, and the coroner had determined that the cause of death was a severed spinal cord between the third and fourth cervical vertebrae. The car had been registered to one of the victims of the Tempesta murders, Vivian McLaglen, née Coleman.

I wrote a second article on the chief suspect in the murders, Bruce Robertson. Basing my story on the interview he'd so graciously granted, I painted the picture of a career petty criminal and gambler, who denied all involvement in the killings. I even detailed the alibi he'd offered to the Saratoga County sheriff and district attorney, to wit that he'd been breaking commandments with a prostitute on the night in question. In deference to the sensibilities of the *Republic*'s readers, I omitted the number of times he'd claimed her as an alibi.

Then I slipped another piece of carbon paper between two fresh sheets of paper and rolled them all into my portable typewriter. My third story dealt with the fire that had claimed the Tempesta caretaker's house. I hoped my photos of the blaze would turn out well.

I struggled to justify including my observation that someone had been squatting inside the house before it was razed, because I was the only witness. Yes, I had the one frame of Wednesday's *Republic* in the second-floor room as evidence, but, if I was honest with myself, I had to admit that it was hardly indisputable. It might have been taken anywhere. In the end, I wrote the article without mentioning it and resolved to ask my editor for guidance.

I phoned Charlie Reese at home and of course got his wife on the line. After a cold, lingering silence, she passed the receiver to her husband and we reviewed my three stories. He gave me some notes, and I made the changes.

"I'd really like to find this Dan Ledoux," I said. "Somehow I think he's right in the middle of this whole thing. He was Vivian McLaglen's lover, for one. Second, he helped his boss, Mack Hodges, fix the race nine years ago. And last, he was in on the scheme to lure Johnny Dornan into the plot."

"Any idea where he is?"

"Not yet."

I asked him about including the squatter in my story, and he thought it better to leave it out. At least for now.

"Not enough supporting evidence," he said. "We don't want your piece to sound like a ghost story."

I agreed. Then he congratulated me and asked if I needed any other help.

"Maybe you could answer your phone once in a while. Your wife really hates me."

Feeling drained and exhausted from lack of sleep, driving all over creation to interview coroners, sheriffs, and self-described thrice-a-night fornicating murder suspects, I dropped off my film and stories at the paper around nine thirty. Seeking succor and perhaps a dirty joke—anything to make me laugh—I dropped by Fiorello's at ten. The place was quiet late on a Sunday night, even if it was August. Fadge was studying his *Racing Form* as *Candid Camera* blared from the television behind the counter. I asked him for a Coke, and he mumbled for me to get it myself.

"If this is any indication of the attention I can expect, I'm never going to marry you," I said.

"Yeah, sure. Help yourself."

"Are you going to the track tomorrow?" I asked once I'd settled in next to him on a stool at the counter.

"Of course. This coming Saturday's the last day of racing. Only six days left in the meet, and I'm only up twenty-one hundred bucks. I've got to make this last week pay."

I felt green but said nothing.

From the television, Allen Funt was prattling on with a toothy smile about some prank he was preparing to spring, and Fadge interrupted to ask if I could do him a favor the next afternoon. He was expecting Mr. DeGroff, the television repairman, to fix his Sylvania HaloLight television at his place on Philips Street.

"That thing's a relic. When are you going to get a new set?" I asked.

"There's nothing wrong with it. Why would I buy a new one?"

"If there's nothing wrong with it, why do I have to meet the repairman at your house tomorrow?"

"I'll take you out for pizza, and we can eat it in the car at the drive-in at Vail Mills. They're showing that new movie *Paradisio* next week."

"No thanks. I'm not going to some nudie movie with you at a drive-in."

Just then Bill emerged from the back room, his hands and forearms dripping dishwater. Despite the wet, he was pinching the stub of a green cigar between his right thumb and forefinger. Fadge yelled at him to watch the soap. Someone might slip on it.

"I was wondering if cheapskate Ellie was treating us to pizza tonight," said Bill with a grin.

I objected to his characterization of me as a cheapskate, but had to admit that Fadge did most of the paying when we went out.

"Yes, pizza on me," I said, figuring our usual music appreciation night would have to wait another week. Ten minutes later we were off to Tedesco's.

Our late supper was fun. We left all talk of dead jockeys and jezebels at the door. We ate too much and drank a little too much, too. Jimmy Tedesco wanted to close up the place, but as long as we were spending, he was willing to indulge us. Fadge played the jukebox—Buddy Holly—and Bill stuffed his face with pizza, washed down with beer. We teased him about his mother, whose fondness for Polish food turned the conversation to scatology, which was Fadge's long suit. Bill didn't say much. Probably didn't understand. But apropos of nothing, he informed us of the price of sweet corn. Ten ears for twenty-nine cents.

We laughed and exchanged stories with Jimmy Tedesco until 2:00 a.m., when Bill fell asleep in his chair and started snoring. Reluctantly, Fadge said it was time to go.

"I've got to be sharp tomorrow," he said, suddenly serious and responsible when it came to the horses.

I rolled my eyes and paid the bill.

MONDAY, AUGUST 20, 1962

Norma and I phoned newspapers, libraries, and even the racecourse at Hagerstown, searching for some kind of record of the fateful day Johnny Dornan threw a race nine years earlier. They tried to help us—at least the newspaper and library did—but without a date, name of a horse, or some other information to narrow the search, they said they'd do their best but could promise nothing. The operator who answered the phone at the racetrack sounded defensive and, after much pressure, told us that someone would call us back later. We weren't holding our breath, especially with expensive long-distance rates in the mix.

Charlie Reese stopped by my desk at ten and informed me, long face and all, that he wanted to see me in Artie Short's office. The publisher was there, glowering behind his desk like a displeased monarch, and to his right sat the court jester, George Walsh.

"Miss Stone," said Artie without preamble or good morning. "I want you to share all information and background research you've got on these Tempesta murders with George here."

I stared at him but said nothing.

"Did you hear me, Miss Stone?"

"I did, and . . ."

"She heard you, Artie," broke in Charlie, throwing me a frightened glance meant to still my tongue. "We'll work with George, of course, but you should know that Ellie has done a wonderful job on this story under the most difficult circumstances."

Artie chuckled. "Difficult circumstances? Like attending a black-tie gala fundraiser dinner Saturday night? Or betting on the horses every day at the track?"

"Yes, Mr. Short," I said. "I bet on one race and won thirty cents. How much did you and George lose Saturday at the Travers Stakes?"

His eyes grew and face flushed crimson, presumably in reaction to my effrontery. Or maybe, possibly—hopefully—he was actually suffering an apoplectic fit. Either way, I would have paid for a front-row seat to witness the spectacle had I not provoked it myself.

"How dare you speak to me that way?" he blubbered. "Remember I own this paper, Stone, and you work for me."

"Take it easy, Artie," said Charlie. "She was only joking. She's a regular clown, our Miss Stone. Isn't that right, Ellie?"

I smiled brightly. Then I crossed the Rubicon. "Yes, that's right. Clowns work at the circus, after all."

Charlie whisked me out of Short's office, quite red in the face himself, and, dragging me by the arm, scolded me in the most forceful tone he'd ever used with me. But I have a temper, too. Girls are raised to behave. Grow up to be a lady, keep your knees together and your mouth shut. Look pretty, by all means, dear, but fetch me another cup of coffee. And, while you're at it, Georgie Porgie, here, is going to take credit for all your hard work.

I stopped in my tracks and wrenched my arm from Charlie's grip. He wheeled around only to receive my gale-force fury face-first.

"I am not sharing anything with George," I said. "Except maybe a swift kick in the seat of the pants."

Charlie's attitude changed. Sometimes when people realize the leash has broken and the mastiff is free, they take a different tack. He tried to calm me, encourage me to lower my voice and listen to reason.

"Take a breath, Ellie," he said. "I can fix this. But if you don't work with George, Artie will fire you today."

"And who'll finish the story? Georgie Porgie? He doesn't even know who the sheriff of Saratoga County is. And what about Bruce Robertson? You think he has any idea who that is? Or Dan Ledoux? Mack Hodges? Where did Johnny Dornan come from? What's his real name? Who was Vivian McLaglen's first husband? He doesn't know any of it, and I don't have time to teach him just so he can steal the credit when he finally reads the ending in some competitor's newspaper. Does Artie Short know that the *Gazette*, the *Times-Union*, *Knickerbocker News*, and the *Saratogian* are all hot on this story?"

"Please, Ellie, calm down. I'll talk to Artie and put things right."

"Tell him this, Charlie. If he fires me, I'm driving straight over to the *Gazette* offices and offering my services to them. For free if necessary."

Charlie's red face had turned white. He gently urged me into his office where he closed the door and offered me a seat. I felt eerily calm. The catharsis had done me good. The ball was in Charlie's—and Artie Short's—court now, and no matter what they hit back at me, I was resigned to accept the consequences for my outburst. It's a liberating sensation to know that you've finally told a dancing bear where to get off.

Charlie's phone rang.

"Reese," he barked into the receiver.

I could hear the metallic, strangulated yammering coming through the earpiece, and I knew it was Artie Short, chewing out Charlie and demanding my head. I watched with alarm as the color returned to my editor's face, rising out of his neck and filling his cheeks like red mercury climbing a thermometer.

"Listen to me, Artie," he said. "Fire Ellie Stone, and you fire me too. I'm the editor of this paper, and I'll make the assignments according to my best judgment."

I gasped. Charlie listened some more, then asked Artie if he really thought he could run a newspaper without him. After a couple of more exchanges, the pitch of the whistling tea spout sank to safe levels, and Charlie showed signs of returning calm.

"All right, then," he said and replaced the receiver in its cradle with the care of a mother putting a babe down for a nap.

"My God, Charlie," I said with a gulp. "What did you do?"

"I saved your job," he answered in a hoarse voice. Then he wiped his dry mouth and sat down. "Artie says you stay on the story. For now."

"What do you mean *for now?*"

"He's trying to save face."

"And you were really willing to lose your job over me?"

He pursed his lips around a cigarette, which he lit with a trembling hand. "Of course not. One just needs to know when and where to pick one's battles."

"I'm going to find this Dan Ledoux," I said, standing to leave. "And when I do, Artie Short better not try to give the credit to his son-in-law."

"So you think he's the one behind all this? This Ledoux fellow?"

"I think that when I find him, this case will be solved."

CHAPTER
TWENTY-EIGHT

The afternoon edition of the *New Holland Republic* featured my three stories—two on the front page—along with photos of the Micheline Charbonneau murder scene and the caretaker's house fire. Sheriff Frank Olney looked fierce in a grainy picture I'd snapped roadside, and the blazing building came out better than I had hoped. Dramatic, with leaping flames and broken windows visible, the photo made me appear to be a better photographer than I was. Still, my double scoop thrilled me, even more so when I noticed that George Walsh's only piece in the paper that day was another in his series of "Walsh's Witticisms," which consisted of groaning jokes and riddles that a fourth grader could solve. The caricature of George that accompanied the byline of this embarrassing column was priceless. I'd made a habit of cutting it out of the paper each time it appeared and drawing different mustaches and beards on the cartoon figure of George. Sometimes I'd add a balloon caption with a "witlesscism" befitting the newspaperman who thought double agent Kim Philby was a woman.

"Let's see," I said aloud as I considered the caricature in my usual booth at Fiorello's. "Maybe some muttonchop sideburns today for Georgie Porgie."

I drew them on, extra bushy, then shaded the lenses of his thick spectacles to make him look like some kind of pervert on the prowl. But the pièce de résistance was the pigtails I drew sprouting out of the side of his head, just below his bald pate, replete with tiny polka-dot bows. And I blacked out three of his teeth to give him some of that Dogpatch charm. I decided to frame it and display it proudly on my desk the next morning.

"Who are you talking to, Ellie?" called Zeke from the soda fountain. He was filling in for Fadge who was at the track yet again.

"Myself. Mind your own business."

The phone rang, and Zeke answered it. I noticed how easily he fit inside the booth compared to Fadge, who needed a running start and some 3-in-One oil to squeeze through the folding doors.

"Fiorello's," he said into the receiver. "No, he's not here right now. Can I take a message?"

Zeke listened, then scratched a message onto the pad of paper hanging inside the booth. I went back to admiring my picture of Georgie Porgie.

Jim DeGroff showed up on time and set about inspecting Fadge's ancient Sylvania HaloLight. I heard some grunting and swearing under his breath before he finally came to me in the parlor to say he'd have to take it into the shop.

"I gotta order some tubes," he said. "Why doesn't he just spring for a new set?"

"I'm afraid he collects things, Mr. DeGroff. I've tried to convince him."

"Tell him I've got some new Zeniths down at the shop. I'll give him a nice deal on one." Risking a hernia and a tumbling header down the stairs, Mr. DeGroff hauled the heavy set down to his truck on Philips Street below. I took a minute to sweep up the dust he'd disturbed moving the television, then grabbed Fadge's keys, stepped out onto the landing, and locked the door. I paused.

I opened up again and let myself back inside. After tossing the keys onto the coffee table in the parlor, I made my way through the kitchen and out onto the back porch. Fadge lived on the second floor of a modest duplex on the west side of town, not far from Tedesco's. I occasionally spent the odd evening swilling drinks and listening to jazz records with him in his apartment. That afternoon, I stood on his porch staring at a dozen or so listing piles of newspapers at least seven feet high each, wondering where to begin.

It was just about four thirty, long before the sun would set, but the back of his house was dark. I punched the light switch. Nothing. I knew Fadge had paid the Niagara Mohawk bill, since the television had lit up, if not dispatched its duties, a few minutes earlier for Mr. DeGroff. So the problem clearly was

Fadge's sloth. He hadn't replaced a burned-out bulb. I rummaged under his kitchen sink, then in a cupboard in the pantry before finally finding a fresh bulb to screw into the socket. Once light had been restored, I climbed up on a chair and pulled a paper from the top of the oldest-looking pile. Time and weather had taken a toll on the newsprint. It was from 1956. Fadge seemed to have no system for organizing his archive of the *Racing Form*. I cursed him as I pulled copy after copy from the stacks of papers, searching for something from 1953. Finally, about three and a half feet from the bottom of one of the middle piles, I located an edition from 1954. Farther down, I hit pay dirt, so to speak, when I found a January 1953 *Racing Form*. Ten minutes and three pounds of perspiration later, I unearthed April 1953. Then May and March. August and December were in the stack on the end, and February, June, July, October, and November were shuffled together as if by a giant card dealer. September had slipped down the back and was hidden behind the most recent editions Fadge had hoarded.

Each month of papers measured approximately six to eight inches high. I lugged them inside, stacking them neatly on and around Fadge's cluttered kitchen table. Then I fetched the bottle of White Label I knew he kept for my consumption, poured myself a modest one, and sat down at the table to examine the pile of newspapers.

There was no evidence of Hagerstown Race Track in the *Racing Form*. At least not for the first twenty minutes I was searching. I'd started with January, until I realized that Maryland was probably too cold for racing at that time of year. I soldiered on, until I finally found a section dedicated to the small track in the middle of October. I slowed my pace now, scanning each race result for any clue to point to Johnny Dornan or even Mack Hodges. And, as a matter of fact, I came across Hodges's name a couple of times, my heart skipping a beat, but nothing came of those sightings.

I took a sip of my whiskey and, realizing it was nothing but watery slush, ditched it in the sink and fetched some more stale ice from the freezer. Then I poured with great largesse a second drink for myself and retook my seat at the table. I flipped through several more editions of the paper, sure I was tilting at windmills. There were plenty of races, some involving horses owned by Mack Hodges, but no Johnny. And then there it was. I spilled my drink on the *Racing Form*.

On October 1, 1953, Johnny Sprague finished third out of eight in a six-furlong stakes race at Hagerstown Race Track. I studied the chart. Thanks to

Fadge, I knew how to read the summary and understand which horse had led at several points in the race. Johnny's horse had jumped out to the lead at the start, holding onto the first position through the quarter pole. That was when he dropped to second. Then fourth, then sixth. The recap said he'd been boxed in at the rail before finally managing to rally and finish third.

I scanned the summary, as I looked for anything that might help solve the mystery of who killed Johnny Dornan. Of course that was a fool's errand. This was a simple chart showing the horses, their jockeys, owners, and the order of finish. It wasn't going to unmask a killer or provide any epiphanies for me. But then it did. The name of Johnny's horse. It fairly leapt off the page. My God, how could I have been so blind to the evidence right under my nose all that time? On October 1, 1953, in the third race at Hagerstown Race Track, Johnny Sprague had been aboard a horse named Robinson's Friday. I slapped my forehead. Bruce Robertson had been on target, albeit inadvertently, when I'd asked him if he knew anyone named Robinson. He'd answered smartly, and surely unawares, "Crusoe."

Hagerstown Race Charts

Copyright 1953 by Quadrangle Publications Inc.

Thursday, October 1, 1953

91 THIRD RACE--SIX FURLONGS   Purse $900   Three-year-olds and upward. Allowance. Values $1,145, $410, $200, $120 MUTUEL POOL $25,147

Starters	Wt.	PP.	St.	1/4	1/2	3/4	St.	Fin.	Jockeys	Owners	Odds
Bomber Jacket	114	2	5	2^1	2^1	1^1	1^2	1^1	T. Shames	M. Hodges	18.25
Doctor Hilbert	116	4	3	3^h	1^2	2^3	2^2	2^h	L. Rader-Day	D. Mayer	3.05
Robinson's Friday	126	5	1	1^h	6^1	5^1	4^1	3^2	J. Sprague	L. Fleischman	1.85
Dave the Wave	114	7	6	6^1	3^3	3^1	3^2	4^1	A. Eskens	J. Maxick	6.35
Bennie My Boy	126	6	4	5^h	5^3	4^2	5^2	5^3	R. Yocum	J. Bonar	22.70
Prince Chaz	118	1	7	7^2	7^5	6^5	6^4	6^2	L. Sweazy	R. Rotstein	5.75
William the Conq.	114	8	2	4^2	4^1	7^6	7^7	7^6	L. Kincheloe	J. Cooke	7.65
Giuseppe Zee	120	4	8	8	8	8	8	8	S. Spann	J. Kurtz	12.25

$2 Mutuel Prices:

2-Bomber Jacket	$36.50	$16.25	$11.50
4-Doctor Hilbert		$3.00	$2.60
5-Robinson's Friday			$2.10

IN GATE—2:03. OFF AT 2:03 EASTERN DAYLIGHT TIME. Start good. Held on to win.
BOMBER JACKET held off DOCTOR HILBERT and driving ROBINSON'S FRIDAY to win. Favorite ROBINSON'S FRIDAY boxed in at quarter pole. Rallied gamely but came up short.

But the revelations of the October 2, 1953, *Racing Form* didn't end with the horse Johnny Sprague had ridden. There were two other names in the race that I recognized. First, the owner of the winning horse, Bomber Jacket, was listed as M. Hodges. This was the infamous race, all right, I told myself. But the name that sent my skin to crawling was the owner of Robinson's Friday, Johnny's horse. I blinked and had to read it twice. It was L. Fleischman.

CHAPTER
TWENTY-NINE

I sat there in the low light of Fadge's kitchen, trying to piece together the significance of what I'd just discovered. I'd been all wrong about Johnny Dornan's midnight appointment on the night he died. Now I realized that he wasn't meeting anyone named Robinson on Friday. He'd scribbled Robinson's Friday, the horse he'd ridden into exile, but why? I pictured the torn piece of newspaper Fadge had swiped from Johnny's room. It was possible that the apostrophe hadn't come through on the ink transfer, or that, in his haste or ignorance, Johnny hadn't included it at all. But I was sure now that it was the name of his horse, not some mysterious, unknown person.

Was Johnny simply musing over his past transgression when he wrote the note? I doubted that. He'd taken the trouble to write "midnight" next to the name Robinson's Friday, which told me he was meeting someone who either knew about the thrown race or had actually been involved in the fix. Whoever it was murdered him and Vivian McLaglen that night. I wondered if someone was killing off the conspirators one by one. After all, Mack Hodges had died in January or February in a similar fashion, burned to death. As best I could tell, only two possible conspirators remained alive: the elusive Dan Ledoux and the grandfatherly Lou Fleischman. I had no idea where to find the former, but I knew Lou would be at Grossman's Victoria Hotel. And I figured he was either the killer or he was in great danger. I bounded down the front stairs, the October 2, 1953, *Racing Form* in hand, leapt into my car, and sped off toward Saratoga.

"He's not here," said the elderly woman who answered the door of room 312. It was a little after seven. "Who are you, and what do you want with Lou?"

"My name is Eleonora Stone. I'm a friend—an acquaintance of your husband's. I'm a newspaper reporter."

She eyed me guardedly, distrustful of my motives or perhaps even my intentions. She appeared to be sixty-five, a little stooped in her posture, dressed in a dark skirt and untucked blouse. A crooked brunette wig was perched atop her head. My knock on the door must have caught her by surprise.

Her ashen face betrayed a premonition of bad news. "What is it? Is Lou in trouble?"

"I don't know, Mrs. Fleischman. I need to find him right away."

"He said he was meeting someone at the track. The training track."

I didn't stick around to exchange pleasantries or reassure Rose Fleischman that everything would turn out all right. I certainly didn't know that. What was I thinking, driving over to the Oklahoma training track as the sun was sinking into the August gloaming?

I was relieved to see Lou Fleischman's drooping figure was neither alone nor in danger. He was reviewing some kind of chart with three men near the entrance. I recognized two of them. Carl Boehringer stood a few feet away from the conference, which included Mike, the morning rider who'd been training Purgatorio the week before. The third man, short and slender with graying temples and horn-rimmed glasses, was doing all the talking, citing horses' names, distances, and times. I pegged him for the trainer, Hal Brown.

I kept a respectful distance, loath to interrupt their business, but Mike saw me first. Then Lou, noticing the jockey had glanced up, followed suit and spied me not ten feet away.

"Hello, Ellie," he said. I may have been imagining things, but I fancied he was put out by my sudden appearance. "I'm almost finished here."

I assured him I was in no hurry and he should take his time.

"Why don't you go visit your friend Purgatorio?" he suggested. "I'll join you in a few minutes."

I wandered off in the direction of the stables, where I located my favorite thousand pounds of horseflesh, facing the back wall of his stall as was his habit. I clicked my tongue, and he wheeled around and approached—not quite at a gallop—but as quickly as a horse could manage in such tight quarters. He blustered and bobbed his head at me, then presented it gently against my cheek before resting his chin on my shoulder. I stroked his muzzle and greeted him by name. Then I pulled back and retrieved a carrot from my purse. I'd packed it that morning in anticipation of giving him a treat. He took it whole from my hand and crunched it seven or eight times before sending the orange mash down the hatch.

I reached into my purse again, this time for my camera. But Tory thought I was digging out another treat, and surely couldn't understand why I hadn't any Cheerios or apples in my bag. He submitted to my attentions all the same, posing and showing off with the humility of a peacock on parade. I shot an entire roll of Kodachrome in the falling light, adjusting the aperture and shutter speed to compensate. When I'd finished I complimented him on his beauty. Then Carl Boehringer appeared.

"Oh, miss," he called.

"Ellie," I prompted.

"Lou says you should meet him in his car. It's the green Buick Eight in the parking lot. Past the barn over there." He pointed the way.

I confess the summons alarmed me. Why shouldn't we meet in the open as he had with everyone else? I rubbed Purgatorio's nose and stalled.

"Are you joining us?" I asked.

He shook his head.

I glanced toward the parking lot with some trepidation, still patting the horse.

"Will you tell me the truth, Carl?" I asked. He said he would if he could. "What's really going to happen to Purgatorio?"

He shrugged. "He's never going to win a race, I can tell you that much."

"Then will Lou sell him off? To be slaughtered for meat?"

"Lou wouldn't do that. He's got a soft heart."

I was relieved.

"But there's no telling what the guy who buys him off Lou will do. That horse of yours costs a lot of money to buy and to feed. The next owner might not be as sentimental as Lou."

I thanked him for his honesty. As I set off down the path toward my rendezvous with Lou, Purgatorio nipped at my shoulder and tore a tiny bit of fabric from my sleeve. He swallowed it before I could even say ouch. Then he withdrew into his stall.

CHAPTER THIRTY

The old Buick Eight sat at the far end of the lot, parked amid some high grass. It was a little after eight, and the sun had set a few minutes before. There was one other car in the area—and it was mine—at least thirty yards away. All the windows of the Buick were down, and cigarette smoke was oozing from the driver's side.

"Lou? Is that you?" I called.

"Come, Ellie," he answered, and I climbed into the front passenger seat.

The heavy door took some pulling to close, but when it did a loud, metallic bang was the result. The bench seat was worn, the fabric fraying where I sat, and I wondered why Lou didn't drive a nicer car. But I wasn't there to ask him about his set of wheels,

"Why the intrigue, Lou?"

"Intrigue? What do you mean?"

"The car? Making me come to you?"

He drew a puff from the last half inch of his cigarette, then dropped it out his window. "Are you crazy? My hips are killing me. My left foot, too. Do you know how hard it is to stand all day when you got rheumatism and gout?"

"Does smoking help?" I asked.

He waved me off. "Can't hurt. So what did you want to see me about?"

"Hagerstown," I said, diving right in.

He looked trapped.

"October first, nineteen fifty-three."

He regarded me for a long moment with something akin to terror in his eyes. He was sizing me up, wondering what or how much I knew. What should he say? Deny everything? Brush it off, play it down, or act dumb? He decided to feel me out.

"Hagerstown?" he asked at length.

"Were you there that day? Or was the advance planning all that was required of you?"

"Tell me what you know, Ellie."

"I know that you were the owner of Robinson's Friday, the horse Johnny Sprague rode that day."

He nodded, eyes still betraying hesitation, still unsure of where our conversation was headed and what it spelled for him.

"You can imagine what's going through my head," I continued.

"Actually, I can't. I have no idea what you want from me."

"The truth."

"And what will you do with the truth?"

Now *I* studied *him* with unsure eyes. We were getting down to brass tacks. "You know what I'll do. I'll put it in my news story."

"That's not what I wanted to hear," he said with a sigh. "Ellie, you've got to realize that Robinson's Friday was a long time ago. Even the poor horse is dead. Died two years ago, fat and happy after a peaceful retirement as a stud."

"And he's not the only one. They're all dead. Everyone except you and Dan Ledoux."

Lou shifted in his seat, the grimace on his face the result of his rheumatism or perhaps our conversation. "You're not suggesting I killed Johnny, that Vivian woman, and poor Micheline, are you?"

"I'm asking you about that day in October fifty-three. Who planned the fix?"

"Ellie, it's ancient history. Times were different back then. I was struggling to make a living. Today things are better. I've had some success, traded some good horses. I've won my share of races that pay enough to make a good life for me and my family."

"Fair enough, Lou. But I still want to know who approached whom. Was it Mack Hodges who proposed the fix?"

He chewed on that question for a moment, possibly reasoning that since Hodges was dead, where was the harm in placing the blame at his feet? Or maybe Hodges had indeed devised the plan. Whichever way, Lou Fleischman confirmed that Hodges had suggested the idea that would make some money for all concerned.

"Robinson's Friday was the heavy favorite. He was the best horse I had back then. Pretty good up to seven furlongs. Couldn't last in the longer distances."

"So Hodges asked you to throw the race in favor of one of his horses?"

Lou nodded. "The idea was that we would all bet on his horse, Bomber Jacket. And we'd put a jockey on Robinson's Friday who could get himself boxed in along the rail. By the time he broke out it would be too late, but he'd finish in the money to make it appear legit. Place or show."

"But not win."

"No," he said softly. "Anything but win was the deal."

"And you all cleaned up with nobody the wiser."

"Not exactly. There was a gonif who used to hang around the stables for tips. A right little *meeskite* named Bruce Robertson. He found out from someone—Dan Ledoux, maybe—and he must have blabbed to someone else. Next thing we knew, everyone seemed to be suspecting our scheme. Mack and I had to pay off a couple of shady types to quash the story. We avoided an investigation by the state racing commission by a whisker. After that I decided never to race again in Maryland, in case someone remembered Bomber Jacket and his unlikely win."

I let his words fade into the August night. We sat quietly for a long moment before I asked him if he'd had anything to do with the murders.

"Nothing," he said.

"Then who do you think did? Dan Ledoux?"

"Maybe. Another unreliable little man. Him and his red hair. And an anti-Semite, to boot."

"Were any of the victims Jewish?" I asked.

"No, but he's a Jew-hating bastard all the same."

Despite the situation, ignoring that I might at that very moment have been sitting trapped in a ten-year-old Buick Eight with a killer, I thought of Georgina Whitcomb. She, too, was an anti-Semite. But hers was a civilized hatred. No brawler she. No cussing, no ugly slurs to describe the Hebrew race and our greed, hooked noses, and depravity. She smiled and opened her arms wide, seemingly to welcome, but, in fact, the gesture was a trap, not an embrace. I felt disgust for her, much as, I was sure, Lou Fleischman did for Dan Ledoux.

"I have another question," I said. "How did you end up hiring Johnny again a year ago?"

Lou shrugged. "Why not? He was a damn good rider. What happened in Maryland was a distant memory, and we hardly knew each other. We spoke only once back then, and that was to review the strategy for the race. I told him, all things being equal, Robinson's Friday liked to save ground and hug the rail. So we agreed Johnny would get himself boxed in if possible. That would make everything believable. If not, he was to run wide and make sure he lost."

"And he did his duty."

"Performed exactly as instructed. I knew then he was a good rider."

"So you sidled up to him at Aqueduct and said how'd you like to ride for me again?"

Lou pulled out his package of cigarettes and popped one into his mouth. He lit it from a book of matches.

"Not exactly. Johnny found me and asked for a job. I wasn't for it at first, but he was persistent. And he hinted that he had nothing to lose. Maybe he'd let slip to the wrong people what happened at Hagerstown."

"He blackmailed you?"

"It wasn't so obvious as that. He said he paid a worse price than anyone else. He was the one who got banned, and I was doing good now. So I said okay and gave him a chance. It worked out for both of us."

"Then what did you think when you heard he was dead?"

"I felt bad for him, even if he was an unlikeable sort personally. He was talented. The kid was putting his life back together, and then this happened. He made a mistake of youth."

I wondered how Lou would explain away his own error. He certainly couldn't blame it on youth.

"Are you going to print my name in the paper?" he asked, puffing billows of smoke into the close air of the car. "About the fixing?"

I thought about it. How could I possibly leave him out? The murders all traced back to the thrown race in '53. To ignore it would amount to a breach of ethics. Or would it? I wondered if I could expose the plot to fix the outcome without mentioning Lou by name. Perhaps just give the horse's name? I was confused and wasn't sure what I would do.

"I'm sure the statute of limitations has expired," I said, though, in fact, I had no idea.

"It's not jail that I'm afraid of, Ellie. It's banishment. I'll be kicked out of racing in all fifty states and Canada, too."

"Lou, your job is to race horses, isn't it? And my job is to report the news, as truthfully and accurately as I can."

"Maybe this once you could blur the line? Look the other way? It was so long ago, after all."

"If I blurred the line, I'd be guilty of the same sin as you."

He nodded and drew a sigh. His hand, holding the burning cigarette between his fingers, rested on his knee. The ash, which had grown long as we spoke, succumbed to gravity and dropped onto his trousers then to the floor.

As I climbed down from the rusting old Buick, I told Lou that I'd try to protect his name and reputation, but I could make no promises. I stood in the high grass and watched as he started the engine and backed away. Then he drove off, his tires kicking up dust from the unpaved lot as he went.

CHAPTER THIRTY-ONE

I waited in the dim light of a booth at Gloria's Dancing and Cocktail Lounge on Jay Street in downtown Schenectady. The taxi dancers had disappeared years before, of course, surely retired and relaxing in an old folks' home somewhere. But there was an orchestra of sorts—Sid Barker and the Chromatics—consisting of an upright piano, a bass fiddle, an electric guitar, a trombone, and a snare drum. They played a mite too loud and out of rhythm, as if they were used to performing at burlesque shows where patrons didn't come in for the music. And when my watery Scotch arrived on the tray of a shuffling old waitress, the Chromatics, in fact, broke into a limping rendition of "Night Train."

I glanced at my watch—10:05 p.m.—wondering what was holding up my appointment. Then I saw him wading through the congested bar, scanning the crowd, presumably searching for me. I waved until he spotted me.

"Sorry I'm late," said Jimmy Burgh, taking the seat opposite me on the Naugahyde bench. "I had to see a fella about something that'll interest you."

"What's that?"

He reached into the breast pocket of his jacket and retrieved an envelope. Inside was a photograph.

"I know a guy at the *Gazette*. Takes pictures for the sports pages. He dug up this gem for me."

To see it better, I held it close to the red-glass chimney of the candle lamp on the table. In the low light, it looked like a photo of the winner's circle. I could read the caption on the picture: "No. 6 Clean Hands, Wednesday, August 8, 1962. Saratoga Race Course. Race 9." There was a horse in the middle, of course—the aforementioned Clean Hands—a group of well-heeled folks beaming at the camera, and some bystanders in the background.

A cigarette lighter appeared next to the photo, and a thumb spun the flint wheel, producing a spark then a flame.

"You'll need more light to see," said Jimmy. "There, in the back, to the right of the lady in the big hat. See him?"

"This guy?" I asked, indicating the man in question with my left index fingernail.

"That's the one."

"He looks like a strangler of small children."

"He does have a certain Medusa twinkle in his eye."

Surely he'd meant to say Medea, though from which dark recess of his education he'd plucked that reference was beyond my ken; I wasn't about to correct him.

"Who is it?" I asked.

Jimmy flicked the lid of his lighter closed, dousing the flame, and withdrew his hand. "That's Dan Ledoux."

I gave a lot of thought to Dan Ledoux as I drove west on a darkened Route 5, heading for New Holland. His eyes had been fixed somewhere near the horse or the owner; it was impossible to say for sure in the small photo, but the general impression he threw off was both unsettling and unforgettable. I recalled an old physiognomy chart I'd seen in a history book in college. It purported to show the physical facial characteristics of criminals. There were pronounced brows, narrow eyes, small crania, and the like, each supposedly a marker for villainy, depravity, and immorality in humans. I had thought at the time how wrongheaded such theories were, and I knew that some had used similarly offensive illustrations to depict Semitic features to promote their racist agendas. Grotesque exaggerations of fat lips, hooked noses, and swarthy complexions. All that was missing was the horns. But the book I'd studied at Barnard came back to me as I stared down the lonely road as "Breakin' up Is Hard to Do" crackled on the radio. I had to admit that Dan Ledoux's physiognomy struck me as the very model of a modern major murderer. His close-set eyes, seemingly without lids, like a snake's; the crooked, broken nose; and the twisted smile that surely concealed a set of vulpine teeth made me grateful I was speeding along at sixty miles an hour in a locked car, far from wherever he might have been at that moment.

Jimmy Burgh had assured me that he was hot on the trail of the elusive Dan Ledoux. The two men roamed the same mean streets, after all, one in Schenectady and Albany, the other in Baltimore and points south.

"I can't promise you he won't be dead when I'm finished with him," he'd told me in the booth at Gloria's a half hour before.

"Do you really want to tell a reporter that?" I asked.

He smiled, baring his gold tooth. "We have an understanding. I know you won't quote me."

It might well have been the suggestion of Dan Ledoux's evil, from Lou Fleischman and Jimmy Burgh, but I had swallowed the bait. And, while I felt no desire to confirm my worst assumptions—at least not without a gorilla like Fadge or a grizzly bear like Frank Olney at my side for protection—I knew that I would have to meet him face-to-face at some point. For now, however, I was content that the chilling eyes staring out of the photo figured nowhere in my immediate future.

Neil Sedaka chanted in my ear, seemingly urging me to calm-a down; at least that was what it sounded like to me in my agitated state. I pushed the gas pedal a touch closer to the floor, coaxing more speed out of my Dodge in hopes of reaching home sooner and pouring myself a friendly drink behind a locked door.

I found a note shoved into the mail slot of the storm door downstairs from my place. It was from Fadge.

Stop by the store when you get in. I've got some news for you.

I glanced across the street and saw Fadge clearly through the plate-glass window. He was seated on a stool, mouth open, leaning on a broom and staring at the television behind the counter. I was tired and wanting that drink, so I resolved to phone him instead. I trudged up the stairs and let myself inside.

"Hey, I'm home," I said into the phone as I poured myself a drink in the kitchen. The bottle of Dewar's Jimmy Burgh and I had cracked open the other night was still sitting on the kitchen table.

"I'm closing up in a bit," said Fadge. "I'll stop by."

I dragged myself into the parlor and shuffled through my records, finally deciding on Glenn Gould playing Bach partitas and fugues. Like a ticking clock, Bach's metronomic precision somehow always eased my mind into a mood that fostered clear thinking. I kicked off my heels, collapsed onto the couch, and closed my eyes to listen. For several minutes, I thought of nothing beyond the music. Then I sipped my drink. The sting of whiskey acted like a tonic on my weary body. I put my stockinged feet up on the coffee table and savored my late-evening reward.

The partita number 6 in E minor played. Wedged into the cushions of the sofa, I wondered what was so important that Fadge felt compelled to leave a note inside my door. Probably wanted to brag about winning another bundle at the track. I shrugged and took another gulp of Scotch, figuring I'd find out soon enough. Then I noticed the breeze. Had I left a window open that morning?

I pushed myself up off the sofa, crossed to my bedroom, and switched on the light. The curtain in the west window, the one that faced Mr. Brunner's house next door, was fluttering gently in the night air. I took a step toward it, intending to close it, but I stopped in my tracks. There was broken glass on the floor.

Turning to hightail it back to the kitchen where I intended to barrel down the stairs, I ran headlong into a man.

I gasped, breath gone in one terrifying instant, and he raised his left forefinger to his lips, a sign for me to keep quiet. Disbelief, horror, fear, all wrapped up in one cruel surprise. I stumbled backward into the bedroom doorjamb, and the strange man stepped forward, displaying a long knife vertically for my benefit. He pressed me to the frame with his body, holding the blade lengthwise against my cheek. Crossing my eyes, I tried to focus on the gleaming edge of the weapon, but it was too close. I closed my eyes tight and held my breath as he drew his face to mine. He smelled like an ape—old, sour perspiration permeated his clothes. And there was a strong odor of campfire about him. Nose nearly touching mine, he whispered to me.

"Make one sound and I'll slit your throat."

Then I felt him back off, slowly. I opened my eyes and saw him holding the knife cocked at the ready in case I tried anything foolish. I remained flat against the doorjamb, trembling and afraid to move, even to exhale. My gaze was firmly fixed on the long knife in his right hand. One of my carving knives. He must have been in my apartment long enough to go through the kitchen and arm himself.

My intruder stood still, three feet away, giving me room to breathe but not enough to risk an escape. Now, for the first time, I studied his face. Then the entire man. Dressed in soiled, rumpled trousers, shirt, and a tweed cap, he looked to be about five feet eight or nine. A patchy light-brown beard grew on his cheeks and chin. He gave the impression of a desperate man who was slowly starving. The face was familiar, but I couldn't place him. Something was different and throwing me off. Then, like a forgotten name, it suddenly came to me, and I dismissed the thought just as quickly. Impossible. He stared back at me, blinked, and I looked harder. My first hunch had been right. He was too tall, of course, but it had to be him. I glanced down at his heavy boots. Heels at least two inches high, and the cap on his head added another two inches of height. The man glaring at me—the one holding a knife to me in my parlor as Glenn Gould played Bach on the hi-fi—was probably closer to five-four or five-five. I gazed at his face again. Those fair eyes against tanned skin. Yes, it was him. There, beneath a beard I never would have expected, stood Johnny Dornan, wild, menacing, and very much alive.

CHAPTER THIRTY-TWO

"You're supposed to be dead," I stammered at my most inane.

"Don't play dumb," he said in a low voice. "You knew I wasn't dead."

I shook my head. Should I deny his accusation? I doubted it would have helped me out of my current predicament, since I was now painfully aware of the knowledge he'd clearly wanted to keep hidden.

He motioned toward the kitchen behind him and ordered me to go sit at the table. I stepped past him, and he helped me along with a little shove. Once in the kitchen, he pulled out one of the aluminum chairs, scraping it along the floor, and indicated that was where I was to sit. I complied, and he eased himself into a seat opposite me. We stared at each other for a long moment. The bottle of Dewar's stood tall between us on the table.

"You want a drink, do you?" he asked. "Well, you're not getting one."

"You reek," I said. "Do you know that?"

He watched me with hard eyes. "I haven't had a bath in over a week. No running water in that house on Tempesta Farm. And now no house on Tempesta Farm, thanks to you."

"What do you want?" I asked.

"You've got two things that belong to me. I've come to get them."

"I don't know what you mean."

"No games. I know you took the newspaper and my pistol. Where are they?"

"How did you get in here?" I asked, avoiding his question and trying to buy some time.

"Through the window. I'm a good climber. Now where's my stuff?"

"You have no right breaking in here."

I realized that was a weak argument to use against a triple or perhaps quadruple murderer, depending on whether I counted Mack Hodges or not, but I was desperate to stall him until Fadge showed up as promised.

"So call the cops," he said. "And besides, I'm only returning the favor."

275

"That wasn't your house I broke into."

"I want that gun now."

I gulped. "It's not here."

He slapped his left hand down hard on the table, startling me. "Did you turn it over to the police?"

How to answer that? If he knew that the gun and newspaper were lost to him, there was no reason to continue with threats. No reason to keep me alive. He'd slit my throat and flee into the night, still deceased as far as anyone else knew.

"No. The Saratoga sheriff thinks he has his man."

"Bruce Robertson?" asked Johnny.

"I tried to hand it over, but he wasn't interested."

"So where is it?"

"Not here."

"Okay," he said, pushing back his chair and rising to his feet. "Let's go get it."

"It's in a safe deposit box at the bank," I lied.

He stood there, staring me down for a long moment. "Show me the key."

I asked for permission to fetch my purse. He nodded. Two years earlier, following my father's death, I'd taken out a box at the First State Bank of New Holland to store some stock certificates and family jewelry. Johnny Dornan would have no way of knowing there were no Colt pistol and the previous Wednesday's edition of the *New Holland Republic* inside the safe deposit box. At least not until the morning. And then, only if I was still alive and able to appear in person to retrieve them.

He followed me to the parlor, his boots thumping across the kitchen floor, as he held the knife inches from my back. I reached into my bag and fished out my key chain. Johnny snatched it away and herded me back into the kitchen.

"Sit down," he said as he examined the keys. I did as I was told. "Which one is it?"

"The long one. Brass."

He turned the key over a couple of times, surely wondering how he was going to get in and out of a bank in the middle of the night. Or in the morning, for that matter.

"Do you have something to eat?" he asked at length. "Bologna or cheese or something?"

"In the icebox."

He opened the door and rummaged through the contents, pulling out some cold cuts, mustard, pickles, and one of the two quarts of beer left over from my last music appreciation evening with Fadge.

"Bread?"

"In there," I said, indicating the breadbox next to the toaster on the counter. Arms full, he hooked an open bag of potato chips with his pinky finger and hauled his shopping spree back to the kitchen table where he dumped it without ceremony. He slapped together a sandwich with one hand while the other held the knife. Then he fell on the food, tearing into the sandwich, eating the chips out of the bag, and washing it all down straight from the bottle of beer.

Once he'd had his fill, he glared at me. "Who did you tell about me?"

"No one. I thought you were dead."

"Don't lie to me. Who did you think you were chasing down on the farm? You knew, and you must have told someone. Your boss, maybe? Or that big guy you were with?"

Fearing my denials would only antagonize him, I said nothing at first. He reached for the bottle of beer again, all the while holding the knife tight.

"You've seen the papers," I said finally. "If I'd known you were alive, I would have printed it. I was trying to track down someone else. Someone who I'm just starting to understand has been dead for ten days."

"And who's that?"

"Dan Ledoux."

"You're too smart for your own good."

"I really thought you were dead. And so did everyone else. You did a great job covering your tracks. If you hadn't barged in here tonight, no one would've ever suspected a thing."

Perhaps I should have kept that last bit to myself. After all, I was still the only person who knew he was still alive. And I didn't want to remind him of that easily remediable situation. But he wanted his gun and newspaper. That was the only card I had to play. I decided to keep him talking.

"What happened nine years ago? Why did you go along with the plan to fix the race?"

Johnny drew a breath and closed his eyes for a short moment, as if the memory caused him physical pain. When he opened them again, I saw the red. His face flushed as if he might be holding that breath he'd just taken. It wasn't the healthy red that comes from exercise or brisk weather, but from intense pressure, like a blood vessel about to burst. In fact, his temples seemed to throb under my scrutiny. Then a big, rolling drop of a tear escaped his right eye.

"It was for her," he said, barely managing more than a croak from his throat.

"Vivian?"

He nodded as he pinched both his lips and eyes in an effort to stem the tears. "She asked me to do it, and I said yes."

"Why?" I asked, wondering if I could make a grab for the knife while he struggled to compose himself.

"I was in love with her, what do you think? She could've asked me for anything, and I would've done it."

"Whose idea was it to throw the race?"

"Mack was the guy behind it all. I found out later that he made twenty thousand on that race. Twenty thousand. And what did I get? Blackballed from racing. My career ruined."

"Did Mack approach Lou Fleischman to have you ride Robinson's Friday?"

Johnny wiped the back of his hand across his nose. "Yeah. Ledoux set me up as a morning rider for Mack. It was part of the plan. Bring in some young rube who would do as he was told. That was me."

"And Vivian was with Ledoux? Even while she pretended to be in love with you?"

"Who wasn't she with? Mack, Ledoux, me, the blacksmith, the track announcer . . ."

I chalked up the last two to sarcasm on Johnny's part but, in truth, wasn't entirely sure. At any rate, I didn't want to break his momentum with stray questions about Vivian's catalogue of lovers, so I encouraged him to tell me how he'd fallen for her.

Johnny's voice was low and measured and rough. Careful. "I saw her for the first time at Polo Park in Winnipeg. She was standing there in her light dress, looking like a million dollars. God, those legs. She was so damn beautiful."

"And she spoke to you?"

"She turned on the charm. A couple of megawatts' worth. Smiled at me, batted her eyelashes, wet her lips just so. I thought she really liked me.

Maybe she was one of those crazy fans, I figured. The girls who'll do anything to get close to a jockey."

"Are there such girls?" I asked, then realized it might have come out all wrong. He didn't seem to notice. "So she seduced you?" I continued. "But it was all a lie?"

"Yeah, and I was such a sap I fell for it. She told me we'd go to Maryland and get married. I could be a jockey at Pimlico and Churchill Downs and Saratoga and Belmont." He paused to laugh bitterly and take a swig of beer. "Get married? She was already married. Twice. And she had a boyfriend and was sleeping with his boss to boot."

"And you."

"Yeah. Me too. She liked small guys, you know. Jockeys. Some kind of weird thing with her. Ledoux was a shrimp, too. No bigger than me."

"It doesn't make any difference now," I said. "But I really thought you were the dead man in the fire."

He looked deflated. "You're right. It doesn't matter. Not anymore."

"How did you find me?" I asked.

"You should've locked your car that night at the farm."

"So you figured out I worked for the *Republic*?"

"Yeah. I started following your stories in the paper. Then when I realized you managed to get inside the caretaker's house, I was sure you knew it wasn't me who died in the fire."

"And that was you who followed us to the pizzeria that night?"

"Your friend caught on. Kept driving in circles and slowing down until I had to give up."

I didn't tell him that Bill Goossens had memorized his license plate number, and that reminded me that Fadge was supposed to call Benny Arnold at the DMV. Was that the important information he wanted to tell me? Where the hell was he anyway?

"And you didn't feel any guilt about cheating?" I asked, returning to the nine-year-old race-fixing scandal. "You must have realized it could end your career or land you in jail if you got caught."

"All I could see was her eyes. And the rest of her. She got under my skin. I wanted her. So when she laid it all out and promised me it was a lead-pipe cinch, I said sure. I told myself it would just be that one time. Lou was on board, too. How could we get caught? And I figured I wasn't hurting anyone."

"What about the bettors?"

He shrugged indifference. "So what if a couple of guys lost a few bucks? No big deal, right? And I did it for love, not money. I got nothing more than my rider's fee and the promise of more rides." He frowned. "And that never happened."

If Johnny was expecting absolution from me, he'd mistaken me for a priest. And he showed little remorse besides.

"I should've expected it," he mused with regret. "Someone was bound to recognize me. But I thought I could plead coincidence, say I wasn't Johnny Sprague, and point to my new driver's license as proof. But then I ran into Bruce Robertson. I never thought he'd show up at Aqueduct a year ago last spring. He always worked the South. And he knew me too well to be fooled."

"So he approached you to blackmail you?"

"He said he'd keep quiet in exchange for a favor now and then."

"And did you agree?"

"I didn't even have the chance. He turned around and sold the information that I was riding again to Mack Hodges. Out of the blue, Mack turned up and asked me if I'd be interested in saving my career from ruin."

"Then Mack had the good manners to die in a fire," I said.

"Shouldn't have been smoking in bed."

"Didn't that solve your problem?"

"It's like one of those monsters from Greek stories. You cut off one head and another sprouts up."

"The hydra."

"That's right," he said, reflecting with a glossy look in his eyes. "Nine heads. Nine years. Nine races on a race card. My unlucky number."

"And after Mack went up in smoke, it was Vivian and Ledoux's turn to squeeze you?"

He nodded and sipped the beer. "That started here in Saratoga, at the beginning of the meet. I got a message from Viv. She wanted to see me again. To make things right."

"Did you believe her?"

"Maybe I was in love with her once, but I'm not stupid. I knew she was the same lying tramp as before. But I also figured her and Ledoux were the only people left who were part of the fix. So, if they were out of the picture . . ."

"Aren't you forgetting Lou Fleischman? He was there at Hagerstown, too."

"Lou's no risk to me. He's a businessman, and I'm good for business. He never double-crossed me, and I never did anything but make money for him."

I wanted to know exactly how deep into the mud Lou had waded. "Does he know you're alive?"

Johnny shook his head but said nothing. His mood soured. The beer must've tasted bitter on his tongue because he made a face as he took a sip. He stood and began to pace the room, his heavy boots clopping across the floor like a plow horse. He put my question to one side for the moment. Apparently he preferred to defend his actions first.

"Do you have any idea what my life was like after Mack and Ledoux started the rumors that I threw that race?"

I nearly corrected him by pointing out that he had indeed thrown that race, but thought better of it in light of his agitated state and the long knife in his hand.

"They blackened my name throughout racing. Even without any proof, the racing commission banned me for life. It took about two minutes for every other state to do the same."

"How did you get by?" Keep him talking, I thought.

"I mucked out stables, worked as a farmhand, gave riding lessons to little girls. And when things got real bad, I stole. Armed robbery, burglary, even blackmail."

"And you never got caught? Never went to jail?"

He stopped his pacing. "I'm too smart to get caught. And no one's catching me this time either. I'm going to clean up this mess and get out. Go back to Manitoba and start over."

"Why haven't you left already? Why stick around?"

"I had to take care of Bruce Robertson once and for all. Then you stuck your nose into it, and I knew I couldn't leave until I was sure of what you had on me."

I gulped. He knew now exactly what I had on him. Everything.

He resumed his pacing. And I considered my options. As things stood, I had no weapons, no defense, and little hope of finding any at my kitchen table. The only thing within arm's length was the bottle of Dewar's. What was I going to do with that? Drink him under the table?

"They took everything from me," he continued. "I did what they wanted, and still they ruined me. I had to work as a goddamn rodeo clown! Because of them. Because of her."

His voice boomed through the house, practically rattling the windows. He paced faster now, waving the knife in the air as if cutting a path for himself. Where was Fadge?

The telephone rang. Johnny stopped and looked to me. Did he think I knew who was on the other end of the line?

"Don't answer it," he said. "It's a little late for people to be telephoning."

I sat on my hands, and we waited ten rings before whoever was calling gave up. But fifteen seconds later the phone rang again. And again we waited nearly a minute for the caller to hang up.

Johnny seemed annoyed by the interruption, and clearly he blamed me. The calls stopped after the second try, and he returned to his pacing, this time less frantically.

"So Vivian contacted you," I said. "Then what?"

"I was on the road to getting my life and career back. I had a good meet going this year. Fourth most wins among the jockeys at Saratoga. I was making money again, and Lou was happy."

"What did Vivian offer you?"

He stopped in his heavy boots again and gazed off into space. "She said she loved me. That it wasn't her fault what happened. I told her to get lost. Then Ledoux came into the picture. He showed up at the boarding house where I was staying in Ballston Spa and made me a proposition. Acted like it was just business. Like him and his whore hadn't ruined my life and trampled my heart."

"What was the proposition?"

"I was supposed to throw a race for them, only this time Lou wouldn't be in on the fix."

"So you decided to get them out of the way once and for all?"

"No. I had to plan things first. Like where to do it, when, and how to make sure no one suspected me. I let them think I was considering it."

"What was in it for you this time?"

"Ten thousand dollars. At least that's what I asked for. They said they could get me five, and we set up the Friday midnight meeting."

"Why Tempesta?" I asked.

He chuckled. "That was their idea. They thought it was safe. And it turned out to be the perfect spot for me to hide out afterward."

"You didn't think it was a little risky? Staying so close to the place where the bodies were found?"

"To tell you the truth, I didn't think anyone would ever find anything. I figured someone would come and snoop around, see a burned-down old barn, and move on. You ruined that for me."

I doubted an apology would satisfy him at that point.

"But after the first couple of days, the sheriff left the place alone anyway," he said. "I stashed my car a couple of miles away and moved into the caretaker's house."

This was news to me. I was under the impression that Johnny had no car. But I figured this wasn't the moment to interrupt and ask him.

As he recounted the details of his revenge, he relaxed. He must have been at peace with his decision to murder the people who'd ruined his career. And his own voice must have distracted him because he didn't hear the footsteps on the stairs. I'd become quite expert at detecting visitors climbing up to my landing, even when they were trying to be quiet, as was the case now. Johnny was still unawares, but my pulse quickened. I had no doubts that Fadge could dispatch the diminutive jockey without breaking a sweat, but I worried about Johnny's knife. How could I warn my friend in time?

If Johnny had missed the noise coming up the stairs, the knock at the kitchen door attracted his attention straightaway. He reeled around and assumed a defensive posture, his weapon poised to strike at whoever came through the door. I didn't move. Neither did Johnny. He stood there, his breath short and tense, ready to attack. There was another knock, and then Mrs. Giannetti's falsetto voice called through the door.

"Are you in there, Eleonora?" she asked.

Johnny turned to me. He repeated the gesture ordering me to maintain silence. I mouthed the word "landlady," and he turned back to watch the door. Mrs. Giannetti knocked a third time. There was nothing for almost a minute until we heard a faint rustling noise from the landing. Johnny's stance slackened somewhat, as if he thought the worst had passed and Mrs. Giannetti had given up. Then we heard the key in the door.

CHAPTER
THIRTY-THREE

What happened next took all of three seconds. Mrs. Giannetti opened the door, Johnny took a step toward her, and I bashed him on the back of the head with the bottle of Dewar's. He fell to the floor, dropped the knife, and I threw myself on top of him. We struggled for control of the knife as Mrs. Giannetti screamed bloody murder. Actually. She was already halfway down the stairs, shrieking, "Murder! Murder! Murder!"

Johnny was stunned and sluggish, but still conscious. And strong. We weighed about the same, were the same height more or less, but he was a trained athlete, after all. The only advantage I had over him was his dazed state, the result of the blow from my trusty bottle of Dewar's, which lay intact and unharmed on the floor next to our wrestling bodies. Still, I managed to push the knife away, through the open door onto the landing. Johnny grabbed my right arm and twisted, turning the tables on me as his wits returned. Like a wrestler, he wriggled out from his position beneath me and, though woozy, took control. Not quite up to punching or throttling me, he squeezed me in a suffocating bear hug. Now I could see him shaking the cobwebs from his head, swearing a blue streak as he did, and I bit him. Hard. On the shoulder. Then he flipped off of me and stood. I reached for the bottle of Scotch, managed to wrap my fingers around the neck, and swung it at him, clipping his nose. He staggered backward, holding his wounded shoulder and broken nose, all the while treating me to a catalogue of unflattering names. Then he turned and darted down the stairs.

I heard a grunt, a rustling, and some swearing; then Fadge appeared in the doorway, holding Johnny Dornan aloft by the collar. Johnny kicked and flailed in vain, scratching and swinging at the big guy. In return, the jockey got a thorough shaking for his trouble.

Fadge dragged him like a rag doll into my parlor and threw him onto the sofa. Then, as I live and breathe, he sat on him, thus putting an end to the struggle. Johnny wasn't about to move the mountain of a man who outweighed him by more than two hundred pounds.

I phoned the city police and then Frank Olney at his home number. Then I called an ambulance. If Johnny didn't need a doctor for his injuries, I was sure Mrs. Giannetti would for the stroke she must have suffered. Last, I dialed Charlie Reese's number and, of course, got his wife on the line. She read me the riot act until Charlie wrenched the phone out of her hands.

"Where the hell have you been?" I demanded of Fadge when I hung up.

"I was watching the late show at the store when I heard Mrs. Giannetti screaming."

I glared at him, huffing for breath.

"Hey, would you mind getting me a beer from the fridge?" he asked. "I'm a little dry after my exertions."

I complied gladly, ignoring Johnny's muffled cries from beneath Fadge's rear end.

When the police arrived, they relieved Fadge of his duties and took the suspect down to a squad car in the street. At first they refused to accept my explanation that it was Johnny Dornan whom my large friend in the parlor had squashed to within an inch of his life.

"Johnny Dornan's dead," insisted Sergeant Philbin, an officer I'd had the displeasure of meeting on a previous occasion a year and a half earlier. He'd kicked out one of my brake lights and given me a ticket for it.

Frank Olney showed up and shoved the cop aside. "I spoke to Chief Finn on the phone ten minutes ago," he told Philbin. "This is connected to the Charbonneau murder out on Route Sixty-Seven. I'm taking over here."

Philbin tucked his chin into his collar and let Frank assume control, standing off to the side and listening, but asking no more questions.

I told Frank I could use a drink, and he ordered Deputy Halvey to pour me some whiskey from the bottle rolling around on the kitchen floor.

"Not that one," I said. "It's evidence. That's the bottle I used to bash his head in. There's a fresh one in the hutch in the parlor."

I explained the events of the past hour to the sheriff, who was as surprised as I'd been that Johnny Dornan was alive. He complimented me, nevertheless, on my fine work.

"What do you mean, fine work?" I asked. "I thought Dan Ledoux was the murderer. I was sure Johnny Dornan was dead."

"Look," said Frank. "You painted him into a corner. Made him think you were onto him. That's why he showed up here."

I wasn't convinced.

"Each case is different," he continued. "Some are obvious. The husband. The lover. The gangster. Others take more time to figure out. Some you never do. And every now and then, you get a little lucky. And this time, you made your own luck."

I felt like a fraud.

With all the commotion of police and deputies tramping around my apartment, along with Mrs. Giannetti's panic and my own nerves, I accepted Fadge's generous offer to put me up for the night at his place. He had a spare room that used to belong to his late brother, Robert. It was now filled from floor to ceiling with records. Robert, who'd contracted polio as a small boy, had been a collector. He'd died of some kind of congenital heart disease before his eighteenth birthday. Fadge often played his older brother's music, which was mostly jazz and big band, with some classical mixed in.

But that night, I was too agitated to listen to music. I just wanted to calm down and spend some time with my pal and a quiet drink. We sat in his parlor, talking about my close call until four.

"What did you want to tell me that was so important?" I asked.

"Remember that car that followed us Friday night? Benny Arnold from the DMV got me the name and address of the owner."

"Let me guess. John Dornan."

"Close. John Sprague, of Yonkers, New York."

"I wished you'd written it in the note you shoved through my door. I never would have gone upstairs."

Fadge refilled our drinks.

"What I don't get is why he killed that Canadian girl," he said, handing me my glass.

"We may never know. Mrs. Giannetti showed up before I could ask him. Who knows if he'll talk to the police?"

"He'll probably make a deal to avoid the chair."

I sipped my drink. "My God, I could have killed him with that bottle."

"Yeah, but it didn't even break. You owe your life to your drinking habit."

That provoked a soft chuckle from me. "And to Mrs. Giannetti. I don't know what would have happened to me if she hadn't heard Johnny stomping around the kitchen in those boots of his. She's warned me so many times to have my guests remove their shoes. But she actually had the nerve to open the door with her key. What if I'd been standing there in the nude?"

Fadge's eyes glazed over for a moment, seemingly conjuring a mental image. Then he took a sip of beer and noted that Mrs. Giannetti was a nosy old broad. "And if it makes you feel any better, you can take off your clothes and stand in my kitchen in the nude anytime. I won't judge you."

EPILOGUE

Freddie Whitcomb contacted me several times after my Saturday night humiliation at the gala fundraiser. In fact, we had a coffee together on the terrace of the Gideon Putnam Hotel the day before he was to leave for Virginia. If I'm honest with myself, I'll admit that I agreed to meet there in the hopes that his mother might stumble upon us. I even entertained the idea of letting him have his way with me in his room, on the off chance Georgina might catch us in flagrante. But, in the end, I liked Freddie too much to toy with him that way. I preferred to think of myself as a generous soul when it came to forgiving the shortcomings of others, but I knew that I granted few second chances. Especially to men who'd had their wicked will of me. But maybe someday, I thought as I watched him sip his tea on that late-August afternoon. That made me smile.

"So when will I see you again?" he asked as I climbed into my car in front of the hotel.

"How about Friday afternoon?"

"Sure," he said, positively beaming at me. "I can delay my departure. Where are we going?"

"To services at the Congregation of Israel in New Holland," I said, thinking of Issur Jacobs and his invitation.

Freddie turned white. Whiter than a ghost. Whiter than a WASP. I patted his hand and said I was only kidding. Then I caught a glimpse of him in my rearview mirror as I drove off. He looked perplexed. And miserable, poor thing. I certainly wished him no pain, even if our affair had ended up hurting me more than he would ever know. I wondered how I would react if I ran into him the following August at the racecourse.

$\gg$

I dragged Fadge along on a mission to Saratoga a few days after the August meet ended. As he zoomed along Route 67, past Tempesta Farm, I asked him how he'd fared for the month.

"What do you mean?" he asked.

"How much did you win?"

He frowned. "You're looking at this all wrong, El. Like I told you, it's not about the short term. I'm in this for the long haul."

"You're not going to sit there and tell me that you lost."

"Not much. About seven hundred."

"Seven hundred? You were up three grand on one day."

"I had a run of bad luck the last week. Don't make a big deal out of it."

I lectured him for a few miles, even though he'd warned me several times to spare him all judgment.

He shook his head finally. "You don't get it. Robbie was born unlucky," he said, referring to his brother. "I'm not wasting my chance."

And I let it go. For whatever reason, Fadge loved the chase. He wanted to be in the game, and not just for pennies. He was after the big payoff. And I truly believed it wasn't for the money alone. It was the lifestyle. The sense of purpose. And maybe even for his brother. The pursuit of winning was at least as much of a pull as the money on the other end of the ticket. And even when he lost, as he did that August, he enjoyed himself more than at any other time of the year. Despite my concerns for his financial well-being, I envied him his passion.

As we entered the Spa City, I remarked that the glamour seemed to have faded with the exodus of the out-of-towners after the last race. He had to agree.

"This place isn't so different from New Holland once August ends," he said. "A little smaller, maybe. And some nice history. But it's only the race-track that sets it apart these days."

"Still, it's a world away from New Holland. Might as well be Paris."

He nodded.

"Turn here," I said, and Fadge took a right. "That's the place up ahead. Robinson's High Life Tavern."

He threw me one of his perplexed looks. "This is the Colored section of town," he said. "Are you sure you're not lost?"

"I owe someone dance lessons at Arthur Murray's."

Horace Robinson was behind the bar when we entered. The patrons regarded us with mild curiosity, but soon enough returned to their own business. To my surprise, Fadge and Horace knew each other. Quite well, in fact. Horace, it turned out, was one of Fadge's regular clockers at the track. One of the guys who shared information and tips for a modest fee or the occasional drink.

"You know this lady, Ronnie?" asked the proprietor, indicating me.

"She's in love with me. I've been trying to let her down easy."

I poked him in the ribs. Hard.

"Why did you tell me you didn't know anyone named Robinson?" I asked Fadge.

"I didn't know, I swear. I only know Horace by his first name."

Horace confirmed Fadge's version of events, then turned his attention to me. "And you. I've been waiting on you to deliver me my dance lessons certificate."

"Here it is," I said, holding out an envelope. "I can't wait to see your moves."

"Young lady," he said with a twinkle in his eye, "I do my dancing between the sheets."

I surely blushed.

When I wrote the final story on the Johnny Dornan case, I did something I wasn't too proud of. I left Lou Fleischman's name out of the race-fixing scandal. I tried to convince myself that I had no corroborating witnesses to Johnny's claim that Lou had been in on the scheme. But, in fact, Lou himself had confirmed his involvement. So why did I give him a break?

"I don't know how to thank you," said Lou as we sat on the porch in front of Grossman's Victoria Hotel. He was smoking a forbidden cigarette, and I was enjoying a gin and tonic.

"You're not going to thank me," I said. "That would imply a quid pro quo. I did what I did for my own journalistic reasons. Not for you."

He gaped at me, clearly unsure of what to make of my gesture.

"Tell me, though," I continued. "I really took an interest in that horse of yours, Purgatorio. What's going to become of him?"

A great relief settled over the old man's face, if a heaving sigh and a mushy grin meant what they used to.

"You know," he began, "I was thinking of selling him to a little girl. Her father owns a nice little farm not too far from here. I sometimes stable my horses there during the meet."

"Is that Ruby Brouwer?"

Lou nearly swallowed his cigarette. "How do you know her name?"

I smiled. "Come now, Lou. We're past asking that question, aren't we?"

He attempted a chuckle, but seemed fairly spooked all the same.

"But how could she possibly afford to pay you what he's worth?" I asked.

"Look. The poor horse is never going to pan out on the racetrack. And that little girl is so cute with her pigtails. I was thinking of selling the horse at a great loss to me personally. A couple of thousand dollars, give or take."

The expression on my face told him all he needed to know. He began negotiating with himself then and there as I sat silent.

"Maybe five hundred. Or better yet . . . two fifty."

I sipped my drink. "How about a hundred?"

The figure surely pained Lou, but he got over it. I had him.

"A hundred dollars," he said with a shrug. "Why not?"

I jutted out my chin and feigned deep thought. "And you know, Yom Kippur is coming up soon. You should do something as atonement for your past sins. Why not donate a hundred dollars to the Friends of the Library Society literacy campaign?"

⁂

Johnny Dornan pleaded guilty to the three Tempesta murders. When asked why he'd shot Ledoux but strangled Vivian, he said one of them had to die quickly so he wouldn't be outnumbered. That was Ledoux. And he'd wanted to murder Vivian with his bare hands because it was more personal that way. He never admitted to having killed Mack Hodges, perhaps to avoid the hassle of a second trial in Maryland. When asked to explain why he'd murdered Micheline, he shrugged, according to Frank Olney, and said that had been his one mistake. Improvised. A spur-of-the-moment decision. If only she hadn't stuck around to chat after the sex. But she had. And when their conversation turned personal and Johnny asked if he could see her again, she shot him down in flames.

He lost his cool. She'd only been pretending to like him. Faking her affection for him for the money Lou Fleischman had paid her. He'd known that she was a professional girl, of course, but she'd been so convincing that he was reminded of Vivian McLaglen's perfidy. An hour before meeting his old lover and Dan Ledoux at Tempesta, he beat Micheline senseless and snapped her neck, all because she'd spurned his invitation to see him again. And because she hadn't left. The little whore didn't think he was good enough for her.

With Micheline dead, Johnny had an extra body to dispose of and no time to do so before Vivian and Ledoux showed up to drive him to their rendezvous at Tempesta Farm. He stashed her under his bed at Mrs. Russell's place for the time being. He couldn't leave her there, of course, so after the double murder, he drove Vivian's black Chrysler back to Ballston Spa, climbed the external stairs to his room, and carried Micheline's body back down to the car shortly before sunrise. Then he waited till after dark Saturday night when he coolly ditched the Chrysler amid the trees where it sat for more than a week before someone discovered it.

I asked Frank about Johnny's car. "I thought he didn't have one."

"He said he kept a car down in Yonkers. From his days at Aqueduct. He took a bus down on Sunday and was back in the Saratoga area Monday morning," he said. "That's when he set up housekeeping in the caretaker's place on Tempesta Farm. He figured no one would look there again after the initial search."

Johnny waived all appeals, despite his lawyer's entreaties, and sat on death row until executions were declared unconstitutional ten years later. His life, the one that had shown such promise when he was a young apprentice rider at Polo Park on the banks of the Assiniboine River, took as dark a turn as any tragic hero's, thanks to a terrible error of youth. I wondered what he might have become had he never met Vivian McLaglen, had she never seduced him and pointed him down the path to ruin. Might he have found success as a rider? Or was his wickedness predestined? Stamped into his future as clearly as his fair eyes and short stature? For years after Johnny's murders and confession, I asked myself if he'd crossed the moral line because of Vivian McLaglen. Or had he been standing on the wrong side of it his whole life, waiting for his moment to act?

AUTHOR'S NOTE

For reasons made necessary by the plot of this book, I took the liberty of fiddling with history and created a couple of fictional races—the ninth race on August 10, 1962, at Saratoga, when a fictional Wham's Dram ruined Fadge's parlay, and a race from October 1, 1953, at Hagerstown, Maryland. Apart from those two concessions to plotting, "all things are as they were then, except you are there," including the thrilling duel between Jaipur and Ridan in the 1962 Travers Stakes at Saratoga.

ACKNOWLEDGMENTS

Thanks to Seth Merrow for generously sharing his expertise on horse racing and handicapping; to Anthony Duchessi, for advice on the Saratoga Race Course and arson (yes, arson); to my editor, Dan Mayer, who saw something in a plucky "girl reporter" named Ellie Stone and decided to give her a chance; to Jeffrey Curry, for his sharp eyes and blue pencil; and to my agent, William Reiss of John Hawkins & Associates, who's been at my side from the very first Ellie Stone mystery. As always, I'm grateful to my beta readers Lynne Raimondo, Dr. Hilbert, and Dr. Kunda. Also, to my sisters and brothers Jennifer, Mary, Joseph, and David Ziskin, who lent support, encouragement, and invaluable feedback on the manuscript. Last and most of all, to Lakshmi for everything.

ABOUT THE AUTHOR

James W. Ziskin, Jim to his friends, worked in New York as a photo-news producer and writer, and then as director of NYU's Casa Italiana. He spent fifteen years in the Hollywood postproduction industry, running large international operations in the subtitling/localization and visual effects fields. His international experience includes two years working and studying in France, extensive time in Italy, and more than three years in India. He speaks Italian and French. Jim can be reached through his website www.jameswziskin.com or on Twitter @jameswziskin.